JES

BRIDE

OF THE SUN

AN ICARUS
RETELLING

BRIDE OF THE SUN
LOVE OF LEGENDS
JES DREW

BOO'S BOOKS PUBLISHING

Copyright © 2024 by Jes Drew

Printed in the United States of America

First Printing, 2024

ISBN: 9798865097389

Boo's Books Publishing https://agencyofbooksandspies.blogspot.com/

Cover design and title page by Getpremades

Logo and couple illustration by Maddy Moore

Single character illustrations by Paige Coffer

Chapter heading and scene break images by Holly Dunn Design

Author Photograph by Amy S.

Poetry resourced from the Public Domain

Edited by Katy Mauerman

Formatted by Atticus

In memory of Uncle George
1949-2023
His favorite verse was Hezekiah 3:17 and his favorite person was
Aunt Diane.

Also dedicated the One Who will put my family back together one
day.

CONTENTS

GLOSSARY OF TERMS

Mortal Terms:

Chiton: A gender-neutral full-body garment fastened at the shoulders

Daktylos: A unit of measurement similar to an English inch

Epaulia: The day after the wedding ceremony when the bride is brought into her new husband's home

Gamos: The day of the wedding ceremony where vows are exchanged

Morosoph: "Learned fool" an insult

Nymphokomos: A female attendant to the bride who helps her dress and adorn herself for the wedding

Peplos: A full-body draping garment worn by women

Perizoma: A type of loincloth worn by both men and women

Proualia: The time of preparation before a wedding, usually the day before, where the bride honors the customary rites

Stróphion: A cloth worn by women around their chest like a brazier

Primordial Terms:

Ancient Laws: The laws written by the Creator on the souls of all after the Great Corruption released Chaos and her brothers upon the realms. Only mortals may rule in the mortal realm, only fae in the fae realm, and only primordials of their own bloodline may rule in their respective domains.

Kiss: The name of the ritual in which a primordial gives a part of their essence to a consenting mortal so that they can survive in their domain and potentially live as long as they do, with a share of their abilities.

Awoken: The name of a mortal who has taken the Kiss of a primordial.

Ascendant: The name of a mortal who has slain a primordial and taken a share of their power

PREFACE

Thanks to stars, incomparable ones,

   that blaze in the depths of the skies,

   all my destroyed eyes

   see, are the memories of suns.

   I look, in vain, for beginning and end

   of the heavens, slow revolve:

   Under an unknown eye of fire, I ascend

   feeling my wings dissolve.

   And, scorched by desire for the beautiful,

   I will not know the bliss,

   of giving my name to that abyss,

that knows my tomb and funeral.
     —Charles Baudelaire (*Lament of Icarus* abridged)

PROLOGUE

Apollo

Primordials are not meant to feel pain. Yet that is what I feel each time I close my eyes and see her face. Not that her visage is monstrously hideous and causes physical remorse to all who gaze upon it. Quite the opposite, in fact. Hers is a beauty so delicate it makes me ache to see it, though everything in my vision is muted by shades of golds and blues.

Therein lies the confusion, for until I dreamed of her, I could not have told you what discomfort felt like. Nor did I understand to what heights a soul could soar.

For one who flies the sun to its place every day, it came as quite a surprise to realize I've only ever glided and never truly *flown*.

"Who are you?" I whisper as the woman dances past me, swirling her hips and throwing out her hands. There is a brightness in her brown eyes that somehow makes the sun seem paler in comparison. They gleam against a still darker complexion, more radiant for the contrast.

The fair dancer doesn't answer my question. She never does. No one in my visions ever interacts with me as I see them now, only how I will interact with them in the future. But then, I've never *wanted* them to. Not until this strange maiden danced into them and remained for three hundred and sixty-four days. I've only had three repeat visions before her, and they were all omens of great tragedies.

A flash of brown curls distracts me from thoughts of the Trojan War that has not even occurred yet. The girl may never live to see it. Or she may be born long after. It is hard to tell time in my visions, apart from the steady pattern of sunrise and sunset.

"I wish I knew your name," I say even though I know no answer will come. Mayhap the Creator will take mercy on me and send some clue in tomorrow's vision.

The woman giggles in response, as she always does at this point in the vision. She swirls faster, her long blue *peplos* flaring at her ankles, the loose material moving with her as gracefully as a gentle breeze.

"Very well," I say, stepping toward her. "I will accept a dance as substitution for your name."

Holding out one hand, I pretend to hold her outstretched limb. My other hand moves just over her waist. Then we move in perfect synchronization, as if I truly were here, dancing with her. I have had a year to memorize her movements and learn to dance beside her.

"Someday," I tell her, though she cannot hear despite how closely she sways beside me. "Someday, we shall dance like this, but you will hear me, and I will feel *you.*"

Even though the words are mine, they feel like a promise from a higher power. This girl, whoever she is, and in whatever eon of time, is mine. I merely have to wait until she illuminates my path with her smile.

Chapter One

Icarus

F lying is just like dancing, only even more freeing. And on our tiny island, under the thumb of King Minos, freedom is precious and rare.

It is certainly an experience worth a little risk.

However, my father does not agree, so I have to be silent as a feather as I climb out of bed. Thankfully, since Papa was appointed Master Architect, we were given our own tower, which offers not only our work room for private projects but also *two* bedrooms adjacent to our living quarters. It was certainly a blessing to us both for him to be promoted as I was approaching my troublesome years.

Those years have long since passed, but I am still thankful for the privacy as I slide out of bed and silently dress. In the wee hours of the night, I cannot tell what colors I put on. I only know that it is one of my loose *peplos* Papa has imported from Athens, since I prefer the looser style that allows more movement, comfort, and modesty than the Cretan garments. It also reminds me of far more innocent days when I was a very young girl playing by a river in the forest before entering the darkness of the Minoan court.

I secure both sleeves, using the brooches that I redesigned as a child to hold up my garments even if they were made entirely of bronze. There was no particular reason for that, only that I wanted to see if I could. Papa had me test it on bronze breastplate, so I know it worked.

Thankfully, my linen is much quieter than bronze would be, keeping my steps silent. I tie my sandals together with a rope and hang around them my neck so that my steps remain quiet. Well, as quiet as possible when wearing the complicated key ring and the magnet I need in order to get back into my tower.

I climb carefully onto my window ledge. We are in the highest chamber on this tower, so the breeze feels especially wicked from up here. It carries the chill and wildness of the ocean below.

Thankfully, I have a pulley system set up, and I step onto the wooden plank dangling from one rope. Then I pull at the rope that in turn tugs my plank upward.

The system takes me to the top of the tower, and I climb onto it, moving to the cured leather canvas I have tightly bolted into the floor. I undo its ropes and reach underneath it. My fingers brush over soft, downy feathers.

Smiling, I tug out my most prized possession, the invention I take more pride in than anything else Papa and I have worked on. Two wings are bound, almost pure white. One of these days, I'll be able to replace the seagull feathers with swan and it will be perfectly beautiful. But I'll wait until I've worked out the hiccups in this design first.

Though even then, I cannot help but secure a few laurel leaves among the feathers for good luck. A reminder of the child I used to be, playing amongst the laurels growing by my beloved river, when every moment felt like flying.

I untie the rope binding the wings compactly together, and they snap out, making a span longer than I am tall. They are held together by a carefully structured plywood skeleton that connects to elbow bands, shoulder bands, and harnesses over both my chest and my waist. These I slide on as quietly as I can despite the awkwardness of the assemblage and the way my hands are shaking with eagerness to fly. I take the time to tighten the straps, though, notching the belts at my waist and elbows. It would do no good to slip out of my wings, after all.

"Icarus!"

If my wings were not already heavy weights secured to my shoulders, I'd drop them.

Sighing, I move toward the other side of the rounded tower, my wings not quite long enough to drag on the floor.

I peer over the side to see my father frowning up at me. In the moonlight, it's hard to make out what I know to be there, the pure white curls on both his head and his chin despite his relative youth and his mighty frame. However, I can still sense his frown.

"Yes, Papa?" I call innocently.

"What have I told you about going out into the dark?"

I shudder at the mantra echoed over the past fortnight. Do not be outside the castle walls after sunset. The city is no longer safe. People are vanishing in the dark of night . . .

Blaming the shiver on the chill rather than dread, I call, "I won't be going into the city, Papa. And no one can touch me in the sky."

He grunts, not sounding convinced. "Your wings, though impressive, are not suited for long-distance flight."

"That's why I need to keep testing them. To discover the flaws so I can correct them." And then maybe 'llI have a chance at escaping the confines of Crete and see the world beyond what King Minos says it must be.

"You remind me too much of myself at your age." Papa sighs heavily.

"And did you let anything ever get between you and your scientific pursuits?"

He shakes his head wearily. "If only I did not promise to let you select your own bridegroom. I could have married you off, and he could be the one to worry over you every moment of the day and night."

I smile sadly, remembering the two promises Papa gave me. First, that I could choose whom I wed, a promise given to me as a young girl who'd just discovered man's evil and was terrified of being sold to one. And the other, an assurance made in the same breath that Papa would always protect me, no matter what. "I know the parameters."

"Repeat them."

"No one is to see my wings." Papa says Minos has enough of his designs and mustn't taint mine.

And once he has mentioned that the wings will be our only chance of escape since he doubts Minos will ever let him go of his own volition. I've frequently asked for clarification on that, but Papa hasn't uttered another word about it, or much else that pertains to his work for Minos.

"And remember their limitations. Do not fly too close to the water or too close to the sun."

"Which hasn't even risen yet," I point out, stepping onto the edge of the tower. "I know the rules. I'll be safe."

With that assurance, I jump off the ledge.

I let the fall continue unobstructed, letting the breeze carry me a little further away from the tower before I spread out my wings by stretching out my arms.

Not only are they connected to me via my straps but also with handholds that I can grab and release at will farther down both sides of the wings. I clutch these and use them to direct the wings upward.

Catching the updraft from the ocean, I let it carry me upward before settling into the glide. Since our tower is built into the castle wall on the edge of the island rather than facing the town, I do not have to fear any obstruction if I stay on this path.

I close my eyes and feel the wind coasting around me, nothing to stop me from going where I desire. I am free.

Yesterday, I practiced maneuvering with these wings. Today, it's time to test speed. Of course, it depends on how hard and how long I can flap my arms, yet how deftly I can capture the breeze. So mayhap it isn't my wings I'm testing, but myself.

I flap harder, rising higher in the sky. And then I see a distant gleam on the horizon. The sun is rising.

That will make an excellent baseline, using the sunrise to measure how far I can go.

Smiling at the sun, I straighten my back, letting the breeze help me keep my legs directly behind me lest they become cumbersome. "It's a race, then."

Chapter Two

Apollo

F lying is my sacred duty and was once my greatest joy. That joy has diminished somewhat as my designated flight takes me over the same— albeit global— path every morning and evening.

My new joy is my nightly vision. But I still enjoy flying. So do my swans.

Clicking my tongue, I pet my lead swan, a lovely lady called Kyknos. She is nearly large enough for me to ride on just her. However, she needs the help of her two sisters in order to pull my golden chariot.

I pet each of them, smiling as they nuzzle their downy heads against my palms. Then I go to stand in my golden chariot and grasp the reins. It's almost time.

There is a glimmer of light in the distance, just enough to reveal the signs of movement. My sister is almost here.

Finally, her five golden-horned deer come into sight, pulling her silver chariot, which is more streamlined than mine. She created it for speed while I made a larger girth to better bear the greater weight of the sun.

Artemis skillfully lands her chariot next to mine on the ledge of our part of Mount Olympus. The moon gleams from where it's harnessed to her chariot.

"Good morning," I call.

"I prefer evening, but I suppose this morning may be good yet." Artemis' flicks back her long, silver-blonde hair that somehow gleams from the moon behind her, though the sky is dark between our rides.

"Mornings would be better if you didn't decide to hate them so."

"They are so brash and inconsiderate, though. Kind of like someone I know." Artemis gives me a pointed look with her eerily black eyes before grinning.

Shaking my head at her good-naturedly, I check the tether binding the brilliant sun to my chariot. "Tell me, any news carried to you on the evening breeze?"

"Not much happens at night in the mortal realm." Artemis removes the bridles from her deer, which all bolt the moment they are free. She'll catch them all again before she puts the moon back in its place. "There was some word from a fellow Primordial."

"The Guardian of Mortals?"

Artemis shakes her head. "No, Atum has recently been reborn and is coming into his duties again. Which is unfortunate because Hades is bolder in his absence."

"What has the Guardian of the Dead done?"

"Declared a short-lived war and taken a mortal bride as a peace offering."

"How . . . odd." Both that Hades, a first-generation Primordial and Firstborn of the Firstborn, took a bride after all these eons, and the idea of marriage itself. Matrimony is an otherworldly concept to me, even though I'm a second-generation Primordial. Though Father, of course, had our Awoken mother by his side until death took them both. But with the responsibilities of my domain to fill my days and eons, negating a need to produce an heir, it just doesn't seem like something that concerns *me*.

At least, not until I solve the mystery of the maid in my visions. I notice Artemis does not ask me for the visions last night. My foresight was once a of great amusement to us, and we'd seek the heroes of my visions to observe their lives as a break from the monotony of ours. Since all I've dreamed of late is the dancing maiden, though, Artemis has become bored with my dreams. Not me, though.

"I pity Hades' bride," Artemis whispers. "If she had escaped to me, I would have made her one of my huntresses and protected her. She could have earned my Kiss and immortality without sacrificing her body." She shakes her head sadly.

"She definitely would have no desire to sacrifice her body after taking your Kiss," I say. No one is sure if Primordials were meant to take spouses and create offspring since the Creator gave no command concerning it like He gave the mortals.

But it has obviously been proven possible. And the Primordial gift of granting a Kiss to chosen mortals to give them a share in our immortality seems to encourage it, making mortal lovers more than momentary heartbreaks. Strangely enough, though, Artemis' Kiss grants celibacy along with immortality. It is for the best she has only granted it to women who flee to her for protection rather than any prospective suitors.

"The poor woman," Artemis says again. "Even with Hades' Kiss, I doubt she will survive long in the Underworld. It was not meant for the living."

A haunting tune hums in my psyche at the thought of the poor woman's fate. My soul longs to play it on my lyre the moment I attend to the sun. I shall put words to it and make a ballad in her honor, so she will not be forgotten in the mortal plane even if she has been banished from it.

The Firmament, though, is not hostile to mortal brides. Our mother survived until Father's death, after all. If I ever found the woman in my vision . . .

I shake my head and return to my reins. I ought to stop thinking of her, to focus solely on my duty. But I cannot shake the feeling that the visions are a promise from the Creator to me after eons of faithful service and to carry me through eons to come.

Especially since Father has proven that death can, in fact, come to our kind in specific circumstances. A death that takes us beyond the Underworld, for we have searched for Father there. He is past the Veil now, and all that remains are his memories and the domain he was given to rule over by the Creator. It has since been divided between Artemis and me, though not completely.

The weather— once Father's faithful servant— obeys neither of us.

Artemis snorts, drawing my attention back to her as she shakes her head. "As a Firstborn, he should realize that mortal women were not meant to help him in his duties over his domain and remain content with what the Creator gave him."

"Speaking of the duties we were given, I believe it is time for me to attend to mine. And then later, mayhap we can plan our next hunt?" Apart from flight, playing my lyre, and discovering the healing properties of plants, the hunt gives me the most joy. As long as I do not become so lost in it that I neglect my duties. The few times that that has happened, my powers became severely limited until I returned to them with vigor.

Artemis salutes me. "Until evening then, my brother."

"Until then." With a swat of my reins, my swans take flight, drawing my chariot after them.

The first rush of wind against my face is always the best part of the flight. Feeling the air flowing over me makes me feel free in a way I can't explain.

Other Primordials like Hades may mutter about the Creator limiting us when He assigned our domains, but I never feel that when I fly. I'm exactly where I'm supposed to be, doing what I'm meant to do, and in that, there is joy. Mayhap not as much as in the beginning, but it is present, nonetheless.

My swans know well their way through the Firmament. I close my eyes to enjoy more of the sensation of flight on a tactile level as I brace myself for the view. It never grows old, no matter how many days, weeks, years, and even centuries I fly this path.

I open my eyes again and make sure my swans are still on course. Then I slowly look over the ledge of my chariot, taking in the view of the crystal blue ocean below. That is governed by another Poseidon, but I am certainly allowed to look. Next comes a great landmass—Dionysus' territory.

Now comes my favorite part of the journey, where land and water intermingle naturally. The view is breathtaking here. One island in particular has captured my attention. Artemis tells me that unlike other mortal cities, this one goes completely still at night. She believes they act on instinct, hiding from something hunting them, but she has yet to find the alleged monster on her own hunts.

The Firmament fills my psyche with a sense of contentment expressing its pleasure to have the sun at the right time. I smile, pleased with myself even though it's a simple enough task.

The breeze makes the simple task pleasurable as it draws its fingers through my golden curls. It also tugs on my loose white *chiton* and the golden mantle Mother gifted me as an indicator of my position. Though it is the golden signet ring on my finger from Father, that is the true symbol of my authority.

My swans squawk, and I turn my focus back to them. Their attention seems to be on another bird.

I squint, tightening my reins so the swans don't get any ideas as I look down.

The white wings soaring maybe one hundred cubits below me belong to the largest bird I have ever seen. Also, the boldest bird, for other than my special swans, I have never seen a bird fly this high.

The familiar itch that crawls through me whenever Artemis challenges me to an archery contest returns tenfold. The thrill of the hunt. Because that bird . . .

I *must* have that bird.

On days when I have more visions to sort through than music to compose, I take the sun through its full journey. But I've learned enough to not have to complete the journey each time. I have come far enough with enough speed for it to continue its path without me.

Releasing the tether, I let the sun go sailing over me. Then I grip the reins of my swans and tilt them to chase after the majestic bird below. My fingers itch to reach for the bow and quiver of arrows I always keep in this chariot at my feet, lying beside my lyre. But I want this bird alive.

I'm not sure if it senses my pursuit or not, but it suddenly dives, outpacing me by almost dropping out of the sky. The land rises, though the bird is moving directly toward the ocean.

I pull my reins up last-minute to keep the swans from diving straight into the ocean. Then I hold them steady as they flap in place, and I watch the bird crash into the salt water.

Instead of continuing its dive for a fish, it surfaces. And then its wings fall backward.

Hovering several cubits in the air, I expect to see a beak and webbed feet. I am wholly unprepared for the sodden woman climbing half on top of the wings, choking on salt water.

What in the three realms is this?

Laughter intermixes with her coughs now and she smooths soaked strands of flattened hair back from her face.

Her face, which boasts shining brown eyes that I have seen every night in my visions for a year.

"*You,*" I whisper.

Her brown eyes shine as she slides off the wings, shaking her head to herself. "I suppose it's back to the drawing board." Then she clutches one wing and begins to awkwardly swim toward the beach some ten cubits away.

I cannot tear my gaze away from her. The thrill of the chase continues to run through me even as a new tune winds through my psyche, and I know. The hunt is not over.

I *must* have that woman.

Chapter Three

Icarus

Papa will not be happy with the state of my wings, but I cannot help being a little thrilled. They took me up higher than ever before, so I know we're on the right track. Now if I could only find a way for them to be more durable for longer flights . . .

At least, I made it halfway to the Spire on the tiny island I can only just see from the distance. It serves as a watchtower against the mainland, but it has since become my goal to prove my wings' durability.

I wade to the sand and drag my waterlogged wings with me, feathers fluttering off after the moisture dissolved a considerable amount of glue. Then, clutching my soggy *peplos* halfway up my legs with one hand and gripping the awkward wings in the other, I climb onto the beach. Thankfully, this enclosed portion of it is reserved for the household of King Minos, and no one else cares to utilize it this early in the morning.

However, the knowledge of the many mornings in the past when I have been left undisturbed here does not prevent the way my skin prickles. The hairs on the back of my neck stand on end more from the eerie silence than the chill breeze. I glance around, searching for the source of this sensation of being watched.

A seagull flaps away, but nothing else stirs. There does not appear to be any life on this beach but the sea animals and me.

Still, I lower my skirt a little more, hoping I don't trip over it, and waddle a little faster. I wish these wings weren't so cumbersome.

The castle wall edges the beach where the stone cliffs don't make a natural barrier, blocking it off from the rest of the island. The only way on or off this strip of sand is by the sea or through the thick wooden door in the stone wall that leads into the castle courtyard.

Well, there is one other access point, a cave hidden in the cliffs that leads to a complicated network of natural and manmade tunnels beneath the island. As a child, I explored them with the Prince and Princess, but to my knowledge, no one else uses them except the crypts closer to the village. Still, the thought of someone coming upon my sacred place when I least expect it sends prickles across my skin.

I hurry toward that door, my ears craning for the sound of pursuit over the splashing waves seagull squawks. Then the door swings open without my assistance.

I stumble back to avoid it hitting my wings. Then I peer over the feathers as a young woman steps through. Her auburn hair is neatly pulled back to flow evenly down her back between hoops of gold except for strategic strands of curls, unlike the wild waves flying all over my face.

Setting my wings down, I rush forward. "Ariadne!"

My closest friend lights up to see me and welcomes my embrace with open arms. Though I am older than she is by a couple months, my head only just reaches her shoulder. The hug would be awkward, except we are so well-practiced at it.

"Icarus! When you weren't in the workshop, I suspected you would be out here somewhere." Ariadne pulls back and gives me a knowing smirk. "Should I assure your father that you were tutoring me all morning like you were supposed to? Your free day isn't until tomorrow, after all." Ariadne rolls her eyes with excess drama.

I glance at my rather worse-for-wear wings that are missing at least fifty percent of the feathers. "That won't be necessary. Besides, I'm not *that* late for your lessons."

Ariadne gives a pointed glance at the sky, and the sun that is now fully risen and well on its way to noontime heights.

"Oh. I suppose my swim took longer than I expected." I flash Ariadne a contrite smile.

"It's perfectly all right with me. I'm not the one who wants to spend all the livelong day cooped up inside over books and scrolls when there's an island to explore. No to mention the sun is out *here*." Ariadne boldly steps forward, her brown skin lighter than mine and contrasted against her purple *peplos*. Her father commissioned it for her when she begged him to let her match my wardrobe when we were much younger.

Concern flashes through me as I remember the alarm that I felt just moments ago. "Wait!"

Ariadne pauses mid swirl and turns back to me. "What is it?"

"I felt . . . *watched* earlier."

She glances around the secluded and obviously vacant beach with pursed lips before raising an eyebrow at me.

"Honestly, I felt watched while I was flying, too." I bashfully shrug. "Mayhap someone spotted me during my flight."

"Whomever it is must have been very confused." Ariadne giggles at the thought. "One rarely looks out their window to see a woman soaring by!"

"Yeah . . ." Her words make sense, but I still feel so unnerved. Mayhap because Papa forbade me to let anyone know of my wings apart from Ariadne. He says it's bad enough for Minos to have his inventions, let alone mine.

Not to mention the near treasonous plots that are hinged on these wings.

Ariadne narrows her eyes at me and steps forward. "Wait, were you worried whoever saw you fancied you or something?"

"Fancied me?" I roll my eyes. "I pity any fool man takes a fancy for me."

"Whatever for?" Ariadne smacks my arm, apparently suspecting me of a self-disparaging remark. "You are quite lovely and terribly clever. Any man would be blessed by the gods to have you as his bride."

I snort. "That is not the part I doubt. Or even the part about Papa giving his blessing. He would never like to lose me, but he would also let me leave for a man I loved. But he's not the one who a man would legally need to go to for my hand in marriage."

Ariadne sighs. "Ah, yes— my father."

Leaning my walls against the wall, I lean with them. "Since I live in his castle, King Minos thinks he owns me."

"He thinks he owns everyone, Icarus." Ariadne rolls her eyes before twirling again dramatically.

Watching her dance makes me itch to join her. But we're already late for the scholarly part of our lessons before we can practice the one athletic feat Minos permitted us to learn.

"Well, he doesn't." I stare off at the sky. Once my wings are durable enough and my arms strong, Papa and I will both fly from this island. I'll return when Minos finally gives his power over to his son, who is twice the man Minos could ever be. That might not happen in my lifetime, so I'll have to find another way to see Ariadne again . . .

Suddenly, there is a great whooshing above us, like a magnificent bird just took flight.

I hurry out from underneath the alcove of natural stones abutting the man-made stone wall. I expect to see some great feathers fluttering down for my use, but there is nothing.

Goosebumps freckle my arms, and I rub them absently. "And anyway, it doesn't matter. Because in a perfect world, even if a prospective suitor got past your father and earned the blessing of my father, he would never win *me*."

Ariadne stops spinning and studies me. "Obviously, no man is worthy of you."

I almost mention that her brother might just be but hold my tongue to keep her from throwing herself into the ocean. Every other woman already wants Orion. Ariadne simply could not handle it if I admitted I was among their numbers again. Especially since it was so long that I couldn't even glance at a man with romantic desire.

"It's not that," I whisper, walking past her to look out at the horizon, that beautiful blend of freedom where the sky and ocean meet. "It's not even that I do not care to fall in love. I just want to be free more."

"Free?" Ariadne sighs. "What even *is* freedom?"

"It's the breeze on my face, blowing my hair back." My eyes slide shut as I remember the glory. "It's the sound of the waves crashing below. And it's the knowledge that for at least a few glorious moments, no one can control me or even *touch* me."

When I open my eyes, Ariadne is studying me. "That sounds . . . like the opposite of being a Princess."

"It's not an experience meant for an architect's daughter, either."

"Mayhap we should both run away to swear fealty to Artemis and become her huntresses."

I smile at the thought. It was a dream from my childhood, but I've long outgrown it. And Ariadne could never make herself leave her beloved Crete and the Minoans she adores so much.

With a sigh, I turn back toward the castle. "But sometimes, there's a chance to steal a few moments from destiny." I snatch up the wings that give me that possibility. "And when they present themselves, you just have to take them."

CHAPTER FOUR

Apollo

"**K**ing Minos thinks he owns me."

The bitter words of the woman from my vision— who became flesh in the witness of sky and sea— wash over me. And fill me with *rage*.

Who is this mere mortal of a King who thinks he can possess the woman my visions promise to *me*?

"He thinks he owns everyone."

As much as I wish I could stay perched on these stones and listen to the lyrical voice of the feathered maid, I know I cannot. Nor can I give into the temptation to continue to take on animal forms to follow her about her daily schedule just to be near her.

I have my duties to see to come sunset. But first, I have other business to attend to.

Icarus. Her name is Icarus.

Spreading the wings of the bird form I have assumed, I take flight. It is time I pay this King Minos a little visit.

I am admittedly no expert in mortal customs and habits. However, I know enough of them that if I want to speak to the one who has made himself mightiest of all, I can find him in the largest building.

Soaring past windows, I search for a sign of anything other than servants scurrying by to complete their tasks.

The palace is a set of square-shaped chambers grouped together in rectangles around open courtyards. Several of these square chambers climb high to the heavens.

Despite the bustling courtyards, there is no sign of a King. So, I circle the largest courtyard in the center of the expansive building. There is a great balcony coming out of it and looking over the city below. As I fly closer to investigate, two men step out onto it.

The men both appear to be in the prime of their mortal existence. One is thin, all lines and angles, and doesn't appear to have ever picked up a weapon in his life. By the silhouettes of two more men standing inside the building at the entrance to the balcony holding spears, it does not look like he's ever needed to.

I turn from the thin man with tight brown curls on his head and in his beard. He wears a purple cloak that partially covers his chest and a leather kilt that drags a little over his sandals.

Then I turn instead to the man beside him. His hair and beard are less curled and completely white, a contrast against his darker skin color. His hair makes him seem significantly older than the man beside him. But the muscles in his arms and legs, revealed by his sleeveless *chiton* that brushes his knees, show that some youth yet remains in him.

"The gods truly smiled upon me," says the thin, brown-haired man as he strides to the edge of the balcony. "I truly do not know what I would have done without you, Daedalus."

The white-haired man— Daedalus— claps his hands in front of him and comes to a stop a cubit behind the other man. "I live to serve, my King."

King. I have finally found him.

I soar into the air, above the clouds, toward the ledge where my chariot is waiting for me. The moment I land, I resume the near-mortal form I was born with. My skin is bronze and my hair gold, as though I have been kissed by the sun in every way.

But I can become more terrifying if necessary.

My skin radiates sunlight, obscuring my mortal features and making me appear like the Primordial of the skies that I am.

This should put the fear of me into him.

I step into my chariot, and we take flight. There is no time to delay if I want to meet this King while I am at my best advantage— in the sky.

I circle overhead and see the same two figures on the balcony. Smiling, I begin my descent, until I'm hovering just next to the balcony.

Both men see me at the same time and step backward in shock.

Then the so-called King drops onto his knees before me. "Behold, a god has come from on high! What do you require from your servant?"

Daedalus realizes his King is kneeling and slowly follows suit. There is no humility or fear in his expression, only careful cunning.

Not unlike the King, who looks ready to trade his own soul for a good bargain.

This shall be quite simple after all. "I am Apollo, appointed Guardian of the Sun!"

The King leans toward me, prepared to press his temple against the floor. But then his guards rush onto the balcony, spears out.

The King jerks back upright and waves them down. "Can you not see he Is a god?! Those will be no good here." He turns back to me. "Forgive me of my men's sins. I will offer you a sacrifice."

I watch them stand down, glancing between their prostrate King and me before bending their own knees.

"They have not sinned," I answer, my swans flapping their wings rapidly to keep us in place. "But I will accept your offer of a sacrifice, and I will name it— name *her*."

Daedalus glances up at me, worry in his gaze.

"The maid Icarus."

"You cannot have her." Daedalus jumps to his feet.

The guards jump to their feet likewise and charge forward.

My skin flames hotter at the mortal defiance. "You *will* give me Icarus as my bride as I have demanded, or there will be consequences!"

"No!" Daedalus cries, moving toward me. But the guards grab him and restrain them, apparently not charging me after all.

"Name the consequences, great Apollo, that we may take heed," the King says, still on his knees but sitting upright now. There is a strange gleam in his eyes. "And the boons."

I honestly hadn't thought this far ahead. I just assumed that the reverence the mortals seemed to hold for my position would have this Icarus handed over to me without another word. But now that he offers the terms of a bargain . . .

It feels as though shackles are being placed over my very soul. A Primordial is virtually immortal. There are but a few exceptions to our eternal reigns. One is to break a bargain. While we did not lose our ability to lie outright like the Fae did following the Great Corruption, we cannot break a bargain in any way. We are bound by our words.

And we cannot turn down a bargain once offered. I may push back and forth on it until it is something suitable for my goals. But I cannot turn him down completely. It is a shackle put on us by the Creator to keep us from becoming too proud as the firstborn of His creation, I suppose.

The King smirks up at me, his posture the only humble thing about him. "Great god of the sun?"

"If you do not grant me Icarus as my bride, I will fly the sun too close to your kingdom and set fire to it for your defiance." That threat is lethal, and not just to them. While it will not kill me to neglect or misuse the responsibilities of the domain the Creator granted me, it will weaken me. After all, if I cannot fulfill my responsibilities, why should I also experience the power that comes with them?

"A serious threat indeed." The King bows his head to touch the balcony before glancing up at me again. "And is there no reward likewise?"

"Is the sun rising and setting not enough for you?!" Centuries of repeating the same task every day, and this is the thanks I receive? What an ungrateful mortal!

"I have enjoyed that with all gratitude from my infancy until now." The King cocks his head to the side. "And for some of that, it was while enjoying Icarus. Now I shall not enjoy her and still have only what I began with?"

My blood twists with the bargain yet in the air. I will know no rest until this bargain is brokered between us— and then until I honor it. "What would you ask for the bride-price?"

Daedalus twitches but says nothing.

And King Minos stands. "I ask for but a token of your great power that I may forever remember this momentous day, when a god visited his humble servant." He half-bows again before straightening.

"You would take a . . . token?"

"I know that gods can grant a share of their power and immortality to favored mortals with a Kiss. I ask for less than that. Rather than permitting me to harness your power— lowly savage that I am— I ask that you press a mere glimmer of yourself to remind me of this great day."

Thank the Firmament that he does not wish for my Kiss, which would bind his soul to mine and give him near immortality. That is something I would like to give to Icarus alone. "And what kind of token do you request?"

"A few strands of your golden hair, great one." Minos bows lower.

My hair is imbued with power, but in a very limited quantity. It is an acceptable gift I have given to mortals before, my closest acolytes in fact, to make them my oracles. "Very well. I shall not set your kingdom ablaze and I shall grant you a few strands of my hair. In return, you will give me the hand of Icarus in marriage on the Summer Solstice, when you are in the habit of sacrificing to me."

Daedalus wavers, but then straightens.

And Minos smiles. "It is a bargain, great Apollo."

"See that it is done," I answer.

Minos nods.

For a moment, we just study each other, I'm not sure what else to do then, so I just whip my reins and burst upward, soaring out of sight as fast as I can.

But already, I'm plotting my return. Why did I state the Summer Solstice? That's too far away to wait for another glimpse of Icarus.

Mayhap I'll have another vision of her tonight to tide me over for the four three sunrises.

Smiling, I fly toward the horizon, feeling lighter than the air around me as the song filling my soul seems to take me higher than ever before.

Chapter Five

Icarus

"**P**rincess. Little morsel."

I stiffen, my hand grasping the door I didn't get behind quickly enough.

Ariadne turns to the offender. "Vassilis. I do not believe there is anything a Supreme Commander needs to concern himself with in this wing."

"Princess, you wound me."

Vassilis' voice feels like frigid water swallowing my skin, threatening to drown me with fear. I was not prepared to see him today. If I hadn't been late, Ariadne and I would be safely inside the library, studying.

"As the Supreme Commander, it is certainly my business to check on the two fairest maids in the land and ensure their safety."

I cannot stand keeping my back to him any longer. As horrifying as the sight of the man who has tormented me from childhood is, not knowing how close he is to me is worse.

When I turn, the sight of him sends the familiar jolt of fear and disgust through me. Nearly a decade my elder, Vassilis likes to pretend he was a child with us and that that gives him some kind of right to our attention.

Though, that might just be women in general that he thinks he has ownership over. Another one of his delusions is that his long, dark hair is attractive, or that it is appealing that he struts about in only a cape and a loincloth.

I should speak— add my order for his banishment to Ariadne's as I have done before. But I was prepared for those times.

My wordlessness seems to bother Vassilis, though, so mayhap it is best I kept my silence.

He barely bows in Ariadne's direction. "I will not take any more of your time." His gaze slithers toward me. "Little Morsel."

With a swish of his cape, he turns away. But not before one of his long, bony fingers brushes over my hip.

I want to scream, but I hold my peace. Then, the moment he has turned the corner, I push open the door and rush inside.

Ariadne slams the door behind us. "Orion should slay the monsters here rather than on the mainland."

She and I both know she means more than whatever it is that snatches people from the streets by night.

Papa barges into the library so suddenly, I knock over two of the larger tomes on unnatural beasts.

Ariadne looks up from the largest of all three tomes. "Oh, good noon, Master Architect. Have you heard tell of the manticore? Apparently, it's something else for Orion to kill."

I roll my eyes at her. "We were supposed to be studying current trading treaties with the mainland, but *someone* wants to make sure her brother isn't in too great of danger."

"Too great of an *adventure*," Ariadne counters. "And I am far from done researching manticores."

"But you really need to know—"

Ariadne lifts her nose into the air. "My mind is made up, and none can change it."

When Papa doesn't say anything, I turn to find him in the doorway. If I didn't know any better, I would say he was trembling.

I jump to my feet. "Papa!"

Not sparing a glance at Ariadne, Papa charges toward me. His dark eyes are wide and more earnest than I've ever seen them. He reaches one hand toward me, the slightest tremble in his reach.

Fear laces through me to see him in such a state. Papa is feared by many, but he rarely experiences fright himself. "What is it?"

"We need to discuss your project in my workshop." Papa grasps my hand, and the tremble is gone, leaving only firmness in his grip.

I try to search his gaze for some hint of what is to come.

However, he looks away, turning instead to Ariadne. "If you'll pardon us, Princess."

Ariadne smiles, but I see the flash of worry in her gaze. "Of course." Still, her eager fingers move to the maps of the tunnels beneath Crete that she has been obsessing over as a potential location the missing persons are taken to.

A moment later, Papa is tugging me out of the room and up the tower until we're safely locked in our quarters.

"What is it?" I ask as Papa releases me and scours the room, like he expects a spy crouched under the table or behind a stack of wood.

"You flew too close to the sun." His voice comes out sterner than I was anticipating.

My stomach sinks. "I'm sorry, Papa. I'll repair the wings. You know I will. And I landed safely—"

"No, you don't understand. You flew too close to the sun, and the Sun saw you!"

"No, I don't understand." I purse my lips. "What are you saying? You know I flew at dawn."

Papa moves to his workbench and sweeps the items littering it for his current project onto the floor. "A being like a man, yet so much more, flew down to King Minos today." His entire body trembles as he tries and fails to thread the needle we use on the feathers.

I move closer to him and hold out my hands to take the needle. "I don't understand. Are you saying you saw a god? You say the pantheon doesn't exist. I thought we were pursuing the secrets of the Unknown God, science itself—"

He gives me the needle and hardy thread before pushing his hands through his hair. "What they call a god, I call a Primordial. He came like the stories say they do, demanding a sacrifice from mortals in return for blessings. In this case, it was for Crete not to be set ablaze by the sun."

I'm becoming more and more nervous about Papa being so agitated when I've never seen him in this state before. "And you believe he had the power to do so?"

"I have no reason to doubt it. One does not have to be a true god to have power."

I force the thread through the eye of the needle. "And what did he demand in return for not stealing our source of light?"

"You."

Papa's voice is suddenly so cool, I almost don't notice when I accidentally prick myself with the needle. "*Me*?"

He nods solemnly, not looking away or even blinking, as though I'll be snatched away in a mere blink. "Apollo himself came down from the heavens, and he demanded you for his sacrificial bride."

The Summer Solstice. I have until then to be free. Four days starting now. Which means we need to work quickly if we're to repair my wings. No, more than that— Papa's wings need to be made ready, too.

Yet, knowing I have precious little time to fight for my freedom, I'm still staring at the same untouched, unsorted pile of feathers as when I sat here Olympus knows how long ago.

Papa is lighting the torches in our tower. We'll be working long after the sun goes down.

The sun.

Horror grips me anew, and dots play at my vision as though I've just completed some strenuous task. And not sat here, useless as time slipped away faster than my freedom.

Suddenly, Papa is kneeling in front of me, taking my hands in his, making realize how frigid I've become.

"King Minos can't do this," I whisper. Mayhap if I can make Papa believe, make myself believe, the rest of the world will comply as well. "Marriages are only legal between two free citizens. I am hardly free, apparently." Of course, the most celebrated marriages are those made in the state's best interest, for procreation and treaties.

Mine will certainly be in Crete's best interest, though certainly not mine.

My entire body is trembling as my mind desperately tries to find reason and logic and anything to save me from this nightmare. "I can't wed in the summer. Hera, the so-called goddess of marriage, has decreed that they be held in winter to honor her." Do I care one whit about Hera's blessings and mortal tradition? Right now, I do if it can somehow spare me.

Papa stops rubbing warmth into me and grips me firmly instead. "Icarus, listen to me." His warm, dark eyes finding mine. I can see the earnestness in his gaze. "I won't let this happen to you. You are my daughter, not Minos'. You don't owe him or Apollo anything. And I won't make you pay them anything, least of all yourself. Not when I vowed to you to let you choose your own bridegroom."

"Of course, we don't owe Apollo anything," I murmur. "We're practically atheists as it is."

Papa smiles. "That's my girl. We serve only the Unknown God of order and science who is above the cruelties of the Primordials." He pats my hands, then releases me and stands. "We'll have to work in secret and in swiftness. Minos was never going to willingly part with me, and now he certainly won't let you go free."

"Because all of Crete is at stake." No longer is just my body cold, but also my very soul.

"Crete is not our concern." Papa lights the final torch before returning to his desk.

I stand. "But Ariadne!"

"*You* are my only concern, Icarus." He takes up his needle to sew together the down feathers.

He doesn't have enough over there to cover one wing. I need to sort our stock.

Kneeling back down, I draw the pile of feathers we kept on hand closer to me. There still isn't enough after the damage I caused to my wings, let alone with all the extra we will need to test longer distances. But there is enough to cover us for tonight. If I can only make myself sort.

"King Minos will find another solution to save his skin," Papa says. "That is his nature. Not even a Primordial could slay him before he was ready to perish."

I laugh dryly, blowing a couple of feathers to the corner. I gather them and slowly sort, waiting for my mind to catch up with my task.

It's not just shock and fear muddling my thoughts. There's something else distracting my focus. Something that should be directing me more clearly.

Rage.

I grit my teeth as I remember Vassilis' unwelcome touch because I was a female who crossed his path. King Minos' dark leer because of the power that makes him untouchable. And now Apollo wants to own my very being and control my future merely because I wanted to feel the wind in my hair and the freedom in my soul.

Why couldn't it have been *Artemis* who made note of me? At least then I would receive a portion of what I desired and give nothing up. Not like Apollo, who has chosen my liberty and maidenhood as his next offerings.

The rage erupts from my psyche.

"No!" I cry.

Papa glances my way, and I take a moment to realize he was muttering something about the Primordials' wrath upon Crete for crimes I am innocent of.

But the rage is already pouring out of me in words, and I cannot curb it even for a question. "I will not surrender. I will not submit."

He places a hand on my shoulder. "Remember what I always tell you. If you surrender to the Unknown God, you need not surrender to any other."

I nod through the angry tears welling in my eyes. "No man will control me, and certainly none will own me!"

"Not while there is yet wind to fly us both away from here," Papa agrees. "And certainly not while I have breath in my lungs."

"Nor in mine." Lifting my chin, I grab a handful of feathers. Then I begin to sort.

CHAPTER SIX

Apollo

I wipe my palms against the cool cloth of my *chiton* as I do my best not to pace on the cliff our home is perched upon while I await my sister. There is no banishing the grin on my face, though. Even the somehow calming thrill of fulfilling my duties to the Firmament cannot overcome the excitement I feel for my imminent future.

"Well, now, how was *your* day?"

At Artemis' voice, I spin around to face her.

The light from the moon parked behind her casts a graceful glow over her. Her hair shines and her features seem softer. But there is still a sharpness to her gaze and the half-twist of her lips.

I hurry to her, grasping her hands from where she crossed them, and pulling them apart. "I saw my vision today, Artemis!"

She blinks. "Which one?"

"The dancing woman! The one I see every night."

Artemis shrugs. "You see visions most nights. What makes this one so special?"

"Because I don't normally see the same one over again."

"Did you see her again, then?" Artemis glances toward the stables, looking bored enough to consider helping her huntresses harness the deer to her chariot.

"I did! But this time I saw her in the realm of the mortals rather than my mind."

Artemis raises an eyebrow. "We have, on many an occasion, watched the heroes from your visions from afar. Was this one more entertaining than the others?"

"No, you're not understanding." I huff, trying to order my thoughts enough to speak with enough eloquence to make her understand an event I've never had to communicate before. "I'm going to *wed* her."

Snatching her hands out of mine, Artemis stumbles backward in a rare show of gracelessness. "You're *what?!*"

I grin. "I've been having visions of the same woman for nearly a year now. Then this morning she was flying below my chariot."

"She was *what*?!"

"Her name is Icarus. She is a ward of King Minos of Crete. I bargained with him for her hand."

Artemis' gaze snaps to mine, all color gone from her skin. "How could you willingly bargain with a mortal? You know, if we cannot honor our end, we perish for the trespass. It is part of our very nature because of the vow our father made by the River Styx."

She is being far less joyous of this than I was expecting. Though, I suppose if Artemis were the one telling me she was making another man more important than me, I would be jealous, too. "Not to worry, my dear sister. I will honor it and turn my wrath aside as long as they grant me my bride on the Summer Solstice."

"*Grant* you your bride?" Artemis drops onto a boulder, as though she can suddenly not find the strength to stand. "Oh, dear Firmament. Did your bride-to-be have no say in this new course of her future?"

I frown. "She is a ward of King Minos, so he was whom I had to make arrangements with. That is how mortals conduct this kind of business."

"I am well aware." Artemis massages her temple, her silver hair falling around her like a curtain. "Half of my huntresses come to me to escape the decisions of their fate made by others. The other half to hide from lecherous males who didn't even do them the honor marrying the women before preying upon them."

"I would never hurt her!" I resist the urge to flinch under Artemis' accusations. "I will be a good husband."

She just shakes her head. "I cannot even take her into my hunting party if she flees to me, or else you'll have to honor your part of the bargain."

"Flying the sun toward them . . ." My voice is low. But Artemis still hears it even as the once joyous tune in my head comes to a crashing crescendo of a halt.

Artemis bounds to her feet. "You bargained that you would defy your sole responsibility? Our father received one task from the Creator— to keep order in the Firmament. Father assigned you only *one* part of that to oversee. If you cannot honor the Creator's orders with the gifts that He's given you to complete them, He will strip them away."

I stare at her, letting her think aloud for me as she spells out the consequences that I did not think of in my excitement over laying eyes on my vision.

"And willful disobedience at that magnitude . . ." Artemis sits again, looking like she's playing the role of Atlas with the world on her shoulders. "You would surely be stripped of your Primordial power forever."

"But if I don't honor it . . ."

"You will perish, you fool. You learned fool. You *morosoph*." Artemis rubs a hand down her face. "Which leaves your marriage as the only viable option. For you. That poor girl, though . . ." She turns away from me, like she cannot even bear to look at me. "Why did you do this? Our kind does not need to reproduce when we can potentially live forever."

"Maybe it's not about living forever," I whisper, "but living fuller?"

She looks at me in confusion before narrowing her eyes. "I knew all males were brutes. But I thought *you* were the exception."

I reach forward, grasping Artemis' shoulder. "What can I do to correct this for her?"

Artemis shrugs my touch away. "I'm not sure there is a way to correct this. But I have my own duty to fulfill." She moves toward her waiting silver chariot.

Lunging forward, I slide between it and her. Artemis still has time before she must bring moonrise.

"Now you would get between me and my responsibility to the Creator?" She turns away from me again.

My stomach sinks. Artemis hasn't been this furious with me since before Father passed into the Veil. "*Please*, Artemis. I see now that I made a legendary mess of this. But I saw her in my visions for nigh a year. I know in my soul I'm meant to love her."

"Then you must make her desire to love you in return."

I startle to see Artemis' silver gaze trained on me after she'd banished it from me. "And how do I do that?"

"Woo her."

"Woo her." I nod slowly as Artemis rounds me.

"But not as yourself." She slides gracefully into her chariot.

I stand frozen behind her. "What in the Three Realms are you talking about?"

"We are as gods to the mortals. Having one such as us coming down even to show the gentlest affections is just almost as terrifying as one demanding a bride. Especially when they are one and the same. At that point, is barely more than a pretense of gentility the poor girl must play along with."

"I-I don't want to terrify her. I won't touch her if she doesn't want me to. I just . . ." Want to be near her. Forever. And that is something a mortal cannot grant a Primordial. Not since the Creator shortened the mortal lifespan after their part in the Great Corruption.

But a Primordial can undo that with a Kiss. She can become my Awoken bride and rule the sky by day with me for all eternity. As long as neither of us succumbs to the rare exceptions of death even immortals cannot fully flee from.

"We were born with mortal forms inherited from our Awoken mother," Artemis says. "And the ability to shift our shapes however we please as our Primordial inheritance from our father. Use these gifts to make you seem like any other mortal on equal standing with this bride-to-be of yours. Let it be her choice whether she accepts your company, with no coercion at all."

"And then I woo her?" I ask to prove that I've been paying attention. I can be taught.

Artemis takes hold of her reins and glances over her shoulder at me. "Yes. Woo her. Make her see that a life with you might not be a sentence in Tartarus after all."

"I can do that." I nod. "Yes, I can certainly do that. I will win her heart before I take her hand." I've seen mortals go about their lives morning and evening for eons. Surely, I can put together normal behavior from that. Except . . . which of those behaviors were part of wooing? "Artemis, how do I win a woman's heart, exactly?"

"Take care what form you craft for her," Artemis offers, tossing her hair over her shoulder like streaming silver. "Women prefer something pretty to look at."

With that, she whips her reins and soars into the dusk.

"Something pretty to look at . . . What do mortal women find pretty?" Raking a hand through my hair, I glance toward my swans. I chuckle dryly. "I'm doomed, aren't I?"

Chapter Seven

Icarus

Papa insists that I not leave the tower until the first strains of sunlight find us. Not when so many vanish by night.

But the sun no longer makes me feel safe.

I shiver because there is still not enough dawn to grant warmth. But still enough to make me feel as though I'm being watched.

Dawn was once my time of solace. Now I know it has been forever violated.

Soon I will be, too. Unless I can find enough feathers.

Shivering for dread now, I plod across the sand. The breeze plays the Doric-cut *peplos* that falls to my ankles. Not that it prevents men from leering at me.

Or gods, either.

"There's no time for self-pity," I mutter to myself as I check a nest hidden behind several stones. I pluck out the loose feathers to place in my basket, but I'm careful not to touch any eggs.

I move toward the next easiest to reach nest I discovered during my many feather-gathering trips. Though, I will probably need to climb the cliffs to reach others I've seen if I'm to gather all the necessary feathers. The last time I did so, I fell and sprained my wrist. After that, I determined that as desperate as I was to fly, falling without the hope of any friction of my wings to slow my descent was not worth it.

My freedom is worth the cost, though.

But is it worth Crete?

The gentle lapping of the crystal blue waves is my only response.

With a sigh, I gather three more feathers. "Why, oh why, did I have to fly so close to the sun?"

Shaking my head, I climb around the embedded stones and move closer to the shoreline. It's easier to travel here as the sand becomes stonier the more I travel southward.

"This is penalty for my hubris," I mutter, casting my gaze toward the ocean. After all, how dare I, a woman, think I can be safe and happy with no husband in this cruel world? It is not as though Papa will live forever to protect me while I soared toward dreams that would be ridiculous even among men. "A penalty delivered by the gods themselves—"

In the distance, I see something among the waves. It's too large to be a bird swimming. Not the right color, either. But it doesn't look like driftwood either. No, it almost looks like—

I drop my basket. Then I glance down at it to make sure none of my feathers fluttered out before draping my *peplos* over it. I was not anticipating going for a swim when I selected an ankle-length skirt.

Wearing only the *stróphion* binding my chest and the *perizoma* wrapped tightly around my hips, I plunge into the ocean.

The man is bobbing around where I landed yesterday. The trip had been an exhausting one, but I needed only to take myself and my wings to shore. Now I must go to him and return.

"I've not been flying today," I remind myself as I make of broad as strokes as possible toward him. "I have more strength this morn than yesterday."

Stroke. Kick. Don't think. Swim.

I reach the struggling form— a full-grown man. I'm relieved to see that he's conscious, even if he's barely staying afloat.

"Stop fighting!" I yell over his splashing.

He turns to me, and I'm struck to the core by the warm, vibrant blue hue of his eyes. It is as though the sky itself swims within his gaze. The man seems startled by my appearance, because he stills.

Then he immediately goes under.

I dive after him, clutch him by the front of his *chiton,* and tug upward. Thankfully, he doesn't fight me and rises to the surface.

"I didn't mean to stop fighting so abruptly," I gasp as he locks his arms around me like a vise. His touch on my bare skin and desperate gestures threaten to drag us both into the depths. "Be calm, but not completely still."

The man listens to my directions, gazing at me like his life depends on it. I suppose it does.

I remove his hand from my naked waist. "Now lay back. Gently."

Sheer confusion blooms across his face, but he complies.

Treading the water, I help guide him into position until he's securely floating on his back.

"There, that's it," I say, sliding my hand under his shoulder. "Now that you're floating, just move with me. I will guide you to shore."

He doesn't speak, and I move onto my stomach. Then I swim froward the best I can between my kicking and one arm. The man carefully kicks as well, and then we're both steadily moving toward the shore.

The ocean shallows, and then we're both stumbling to shore. We collapse side by side, me on my stomach.

I take several moments to let my body relax. Gritty sand bites into my bare skin, and my soaked hair hangs in tangles around me. But I'm alive, even if my body is trembling from the exertion.

Turning, I find the man I rescued lying on his back. He is turned toward me, though, his gaze sweeping over me, taking in my form while I wear only my undergarments.

"Hey!" I cry, stumbling upright.

"What?" His gaze returns to my face, his expression strangely innocent, as though he wasn't just leering at me a moment ago.

"I didn't rescue you so you could gawk at me!" I stumble away from him, humiliation coursing through me. I drop to my knees next to my basket and tug my *peplos* over my head. I clings to my damp skin.

Most of Crete celebrates the human body and has no shame showcasing it. But I have simply never been comfortable with that. Especially while living in the palace with Vassilis.

"Please forgive me," calls the stranger I rescued. His voice is hoarse, and I wonder how much ocean water he inadvertently swallowed before I came upon him. Then I hear his footsteps drawing near.

I whirl around, wishing I had more than a basket of feathers to defend myself with.

The man freezes where he stands, looking almost as terrified of me as I am of him. "I'm not familiar with your culture, and I did not mean to offend."

He stares at me, his deep blue eyes imploring me for forgiveness. Though he stands a head and shoulders taller than I do, with twice my girth, he appears so vulnerable. Mayhap it's the damp, dark hair sticking to his firm jaw, much shorter than my tangles. Or it could be the way water is dripping down his remarkably chiseled yet forlorn face. His *chiton* is torn off one shoulder, hinting at an impressive musculature and bronzed skin.

I snap my gaze back up to meet his, mentally scolding myself for gawking at him so soon after snapping at him for doing the same. This man, whomever he is, is almost as beautiful as Orion.

And yet he looks so lost as he takes another cautious step toward me, his sandals leaving deep imprints in the sand. "Thank you for rescuing me, kind stranger."

His soft tone banishes some of the coiling stress on my shoulders. "Of course. What is your name, stranger?"

"Yes, I'm . . ." He hesitates for a moment, looking confused, and I fear he's gotten too much sun. Then he nods to himself. "Phoebus."

I give him a tentative smile. "I am called Icarus. What led you to your peril? You are certainly no Minoan."

"No, that I am not." He chuckles. "I come from much farther north."

I peer beyond him, as though I might see the northern mainland from here. "Was there a shipwreck? Should I rally help to search for survivors?"

"No need. I came alone."

Startled, I turn back to Phoebus. "*Alone?*"

He rubs the back of his neck bashfully before glancing back out at the waves. "Yes." Phoebus turns to me. "I do not know what I would have done if you had not fished me from the sea."

"Thankfully, I'm a strong swimmer."

"I should reward you in some way." He steps closer. "Tell me, what do you like?"

His words sound lecherous, but his tone is kind and his expression innocently open.

Pursing my lips, I glance down at his person. His *chiton* was obviously made of fine material but is barely more than rags now. "You don't have any type of currency, do you?"

"Is that what you want?" His expression lights up with almost childlike glee. "Whichever currency you wish, in whatever amount—"

"No, not for me, but Crete is mercenary. And do you have somewhere to stay tonight?"

"Anywhere you want."

I blink. Minoan is not his first language, because there is a barrier between us fully understanding each other. "You absolutely cannot be outside at night. Sojourners especially have a bad habit of vanishing in the dark."

Phoebus says nothing as he gazes at me.

Suddenly very self-conscious, I pluck at my washed-out *chiton*. Then I glance back at him. "And you're barely wearing rags."

"Would you rather I wear nothing?" He reaches for the remaining sleeve of his *chiton*, his expression still one of complete innocence.

I hold out my hand. "No! I mean, I believe my father has some old garments he doesn't wear anymore. I'll fetch one of those for you, and then we can sort out your next steps." I nod to myself. Yes, that is what I ought to do. What anyone ought to do in this case if they do for one so close to death?

Especially one that appears to have had some sort of affluence in a past life. Mayhap if I see him safely back to his homeland, he can make a place for my father and me there.

More confident now that I have a plan to focus on rather than this stranger's arresting gaze, I pluck up my basket of feathers. "We'll have to be careful because the guards are rarely my allies. So just follow me, Phoebus."

He smiles. "Anywhere."

Chapter Eight

Apollo

I carus is the bravest, most beautiful mortal who ever lived. And if there is one thing I've discovered this morning, it's that being mortal is quite difficult.

I can only hope and pray that Artemis never learns how long I toiled over what form to assume. And after all that, I just reverted to the form I was born with from my Awoken mother before I assumed the full range of my power when Father passed into the Veil.

Though, I've made a few adjustments, just in case someone saw through the glow I wore around myself when I came down as a demanding Primordial. I made my hair dark brown rather than sunshine gold curls to better assimilate with the people here and softened my sharper facial features.

When I saw Icarus come to the beach I was circling over, I stepped off my chariot. The plan was to swim to her and make introductions. Possibly sweep her off her feet.

Instead, I learned that while I know how to swim perfectly well the one time I took the form of a dolphin, my mortal body did not know what it was doing.

So, my dear, sweet Icarus swept *me* off *my* feet. Or, rather, set me back on them. The melody has returned to my psyche, and I'm itching to lose myself to it as I always do whenever the Muses gift me a tune.

But I long to lose myself to Icarus still more.

I can't stop grinning at her as she leads me into the castle that she calls home. Icarus peers around each hallway before telling me it's safe to follow her. I'm not sure why she feels the need for secrecy, but I am content to simply follow her.

And now that I've thoroughly convinced her that I'm a fragile mortal just like herself, she is certain to fall for me long before the Summer Solstice. With how fleeting mortality is, three days is surely more than enough time for her to choose me of her own volition.

We ascend a spiraling staircase. Just as we reach the top, she holds out her hand for me to halt again.

I do, waiting as she vanishes around the corner; the loss of her presence is as dramatic as a cloud passing over the sun.

To think, I thought seeing her was the climax of my life. But to actually speak with her, not to mention feel her touch . . .

The experience is like when I first take flight. The breeze lightly blows over me, gently teasing me, before completely taking my breath away with the thrill of flying.

"Orion!" Icarus calls suddenly with her sweet voice. "What are you doing here?"

"I was looking for Ariadne. She said there was something we needed to discuss before Father ships me off on my next quest. And I've just received word that he will send me sooner rather than later. Manticores being deadly and all that."

"Oh, today is her free day. She's probably investigating the latest disappearance."

The name "Orion" sounds familiar. I think I had a vision about him once. Artemis and I went out to watch his first kill, if I recall correctly.

This Orion is sighs deeply. "That should be my responsibility, not hers. I do not know why Father is so concerned with me slaying monsters in other's kingdoms when there appears to be one lurking in ours. I should go see what assistance I can offer her while I can, though. I won't even be here to see you off on the Summer Solstice. Not that there should be any need for such a thing . . ."

His voice gets louder, as well as the sound of footsteps. I wonder if I should duck down the stairs. But I did not see anywhere to conceal myself easily. I'm not even sure why I would have to.

Icarus comes back into sight, along with a mortal man who must be Orion. He is the same man as before, but he has grown in height and girth. He looks more the part of a mighty warrior now, with dark hair falling to his broad shoulders. Far too much of him is bare, since besides his sandals, he wears only a short kilt loincloth with rich embroidery and a triangular cut— also, Icarus' gaze, which hasn't left him since he came into view.

"I am so sorry my father is offering you as a sacrifice," Orion tells her, looking far too intently into the eyes of a woman promised to another. "If the desolation of Crete was not the consequence, I would not let this happen."

Oh, please— like *he* could oppose me, mere mortal that he is.

Orion sees me a moment after I've scrutinized him. He raises one thick eyebrow and glances between Icarus and me. "And who's this?"

"Hmm?" Icarus asks as if in a dream before jolting and turning to me. "Oh, this is Phoebus."

Oh, so the *guards* we need to hide from, but this Orion is safe? No, thank you; I'd prefer an entire army over him. But I'll happily demolish him as easily as I would that army . . .

"Phoebus . . ." Orion draws out curiously, as though he has a right to utter my name, even if it isn't my actual title.

"My lover!" Icarus blurts.

Both Orion's eyebrows ascend now.

I just grin and join them in the hallway. Then I slide one arm possessively around Icarus and draw her tightly against my side. Her warmth permeates me with greater sensations than even the sun when it rides behind me. "Yes. I am her lover."

Just for good measure, I press my lips to the top of her head as I have seen many mortals do before when departing from their lovers as I set the sun. Unsurprisingly, Icarus smells like the ocean. But there are also the underlying scents of iris and parchment.

"Then I hope you enjoy what time you have left together."

Startled, I turn back to Orion.

Rather than mirroring the raging jealousy I feel in my soul, his expression is solemn, a pitying gleam in his eyes.

"I wish my father had found another way to appease the sun god," Orion whispers. "My condolences."

Then, with one last nod toward us, he turns and descends the spiraling stairs.

The moment he vanishes from sight, I turn to Icarus. "Who was that?"

"Orion, heir apparent of Crete." Icarus glances at my hand on her shoulder, as if noticing it for the first time. She gently nudges it away and then steps out of my grip.

As much as I despise this prince, I want him to return so I can have an excuse to touch Icarus again. "So, nobody important, then?"

"It depends on whom you ask." She moves down the narrow hallway and places her hand on a door. Then she turns back. "How long do you intend to remain in Crete?"

"Just until I get some business sorted out."

"Then you should probably address him as Prince Orion in the future. He and I grew up together, but you *are* a stranger."

"I'm not a stranger," I mumble. "I'm Phoebus— your lover, re-member?"

Icarus ignores me and pushes open the door.

A moment later, she's ushering me into a circular room that must be larger than it appears. It bears more workbenches and shelves of tools and supplies than should be possible. There are two more doorways leading from this room.

Icarus hurries to the room on the right and takes a brass band off her sleeve. She inserts various mechanisms into different slots on the doorpost before swiping a rock to the side. Several moments later, she pushes that door open and gestures for me to follow her.

I do and find myself standing in another cylinder room crammed with unfinished projects. There is also a bed and a wardrobe mixed with the workshop furniture and planks of wood stacked at random. The wings Icarus wore when I first laid eyes on her are spread out across two tables. A second pair of wings, untouched by the elements, are folded into themselves and mounted on the wall.

There are three glassless windows in the stone wall, placed at equal distances from each other. Canvasses rolled on top of them are ready to be released to cover the windows if necessary.

I move toward the center window and peer out at a bustling courtyard. Mortals hurry back and forth performing the same tasks I've always seen them complete, though with little understanding why.

"Here."

Icarus' words draw me back to the reality of her, which I somehow lost sight of.

I turn to Icarus and find her holding a clean cream-colored chiton out to me.

"My father never wears this," Icarus says. "And whatever business you came here to carry out would be better done if you did not look like I dragged you from the sea."

"Yes, very wise." I grasp the remaining sleeve of what once was the finest *chiton* I owned, a gift from one of Artemis' huntresses.

Before I can finish sliding it off my shoulder, though, Icarus grasps my hand, stalling me.

I turn to her expectantly. Her soft hand rests on my skin, her breath is warm on my chest, and her face is so close to mine.

There is little I understand about the mortal mating rituals I have witnessed in passing. But they all seem to climax with a meeting of lips. I suppose it is because we were formed by the same Creator. For a Primordial and a mortal, the great climax is when the Primordial grants a Kiss to the mortal, making them immortal. But that is more complicated than the affections exchanged between mere mortals.

I would certainly like to know more about their version of the tradition.

"What are you doing?" she hisses.

Well, that wasn't the tone I was expecting.

"I was about to ask the same thing."

Icarus releases my sleeve to whirl around toward the man standing in the doorway, intruding on our moment.

Her quick release causes my sleeve to slide the rest of the way down my arm. I have to hurry to catch my *chiton* before it falls away.

The man in the doorway steps forward. I recognize his white hair and wiry form, who stood beside Minos when I forged my bargain with him for Icarus' hand. Daedalus.

"Papa!" Icarus calls, rushing toward the man.

Papa? My gaze snaps to the man who must not recognize me.

He's glowering at us both at the moment. "Icarus, why are you disrobing a man in my room?"

Chapter Nine

Icarus

"I wasn't disrobing him, Papa. I was, er, *preventing* him from undressing."

Papa's glare redirects to Phoebus.

I follow his gaze to find the castaway awkwardly clutching his *chiton* with one hand and holding up the other in greeting. There is a somewhat stricken expression in Phoebus past his warm smile. "I was *dressing*."

Oh, so *now* he learns modesty.

"And Icarus was helping."

I wince. This is what I get for showing hospitality to a lost soul who's obviously suffered from too much sun. The gods must want to make a joke of me before stealing me away.

"Who are you?" Papa demands, and the tone in his voice warns that he's one breath away from swinging one of his more unpleasant inventions at Phoebus' head.

"I am Phoebus." Completely unaware of the imminent danger, he steps around me, approaching the man who would slay him with no remorse. "Your daughter's lov—"

I dive between them. "I fished him out of the sea just this morn!"

Papa turns to me in confusion. "What?"

"I was gathering feathers for—" I stop myself before I can give too much away.

But we all turn to Papa's pair of wings propped in full view.

Papa shuts the door behind him.

I hurry toward him and grasp his arm. "Papa, I just saved his life this morn. There's no need to do anything . . . *drastic*."

He tries unsuccessfully to shake me off. Papa may be strong, but I'm stubborn. "If word gets back to King Minos, you'll be awaiting your nuptials in one of the dungeons I designed for him and have no hope of flying away."

"Flying away?" Phoebus blinks in confusion.

Papa wrenches free from me.

I dive between him and Phoebus. "We also need to think of where we are flying *to*. Phoebus may be desolate just now, but I'm sure he'll happily return our hospitality when he returns home."

This finally halts my father's charge. "Where are you from, boy?"

Phoebus twists his nose at the demeaning title. But he finally displays the first semblance of wisdom by not correcting my father. "Elis. My sister and I have a home there and considerable property we inherited from our father."

"Have you need of an architect or an inventor in Elis?" I ask. "My father is a master in both disciplines, as am I."

"Yes." Phoebus' gaze locks on mine, and there isn't an essence of doubt in his expression.

Staring into his eyes is like soaring in the sky. The shade is the same. "Well, inventing is something I like to do, anyway. Papa can do all things well, though." I clear my throat. "If we shelter you while you conduct your business here in Crete, will you shelter us in return at your residence in Elis? At least until we make other arrangements?"

"You never need to make other arrangements." His tone is softer now but no less sincere. "I truly need your skills, Icarus." He clears his throat and glances at my father. "And yours as well."

Papa narrows his eyes. "How do we know you are who you say you are, *Phoebus?*"

"I have a signet ring." Phoebus finally slides his sleeve back over his shoulder. Then he twists the ring off and holds it toward us.

Papa snatches it before I can, so I lean into him to inspect it likewise. The ring is undoubtedly gold, though Papa still bites it to check. The signet is intricately carved, displaying the sun with an ouroboros wrapped around it.

"This obviously belongs to a wealthy man," Papa finally says. He narrows his gaze once again. "But how do I know that man is *you?*"

I startle at Papa so blatantly accusing a stranger of theft.

But Phoebus takes it all in stride, plucking the ring from Papa and then taking my hand. "I suppose you will not until you come with me to Elis. But as an extension of goodwill . . ." Phoebus slides the ring onto my thumb.

I'm surprised by his gentle yet confident touch as well as the perfect fit of the ring. When I glance up and meet Phoebus' blue gaze, so close to mine, I lose my breath.

"Take this ring as my promise, Icarus," he murmurs. "Keep it safe for me and return it only after I have given you the home I have promised."

My lips part, but I cannot say anything under the intensity of his gaze.

Then Phoebus releases me and turns to my father. "This way, even if I fail, you will have a measure of financial security."

"Thank you," I whisper.

He smiles, revealing perfect white teeth combined with a happiness that threatens to be more brilliant than the sun.

Papa grips my arm. "A word."

I let him lead me into the common room. Mostly because I'm too preoccupied by Phoebus' smile to notice anything happening to my body. Vassilis could be luring me away and I wouldn't notice.

Papa closes the door behind us, locking Phoebus in his bedroom. Then he seems to wilt against it. "What is this about, Icarus?"

"What is what about?"

He gestures behind him.

"I told you— Phoebus was drowning, and I fished him out of the sea."

"Are you sure it wasn't *you* who were drowning?"

I wrinkle my nose. "Yes, I am fairly certain—"

"Of despair." With a sigh, Papa places a hand on my shoulder. "I told you— I will not let them sacrifice you to the sun. You need not abandon your virtue just to prevent Apollo from seizing it."

"Excuse me?!" I recoil. "Papa, how could you even think that?! I was just showing kindness to a stranger. Mayhap one of the other gods would look favorably upon us and grant me shelter from the sun."

Papa purses his lips. "The Unknown God is all the divine assistance that we require."

"He is the one allowing all this to happen. You said He's the most powerful of all the gods, yet here we are, His servants living in fear."

"He is the *only* God. The others are part of His created order, same as the storms and seas, Minos and us."

I cross my arms. "You mean the storms that only become more savage with each tempest? And the King who sold me to the first bidder?"

"The Unknown God created the scientific order that we study, Icarus, and that is how we come to know him. But He gives us all the choices to remain under His moral authority that is part of that created order or else reap the consequences of chaos."

Mayhap *I* should have made the choice to serve Artemis after all. She at least would have sheltered me from the unwanted attention of a male. Or she might have sacrificed me to her brother herself.

I sigh. "Well, I choose to take all the help we can get." I reach for the door.

"Just make sure that this Phoebus is a help and not a hinderance. We have no time for distractions."

"Don't worry— he's *hardly* as distracting as Orion." I push open the door.

And freeze to find Phoebus standing in the center of the room, three planks of wood strewn over his shoulder like they weigh nothing. There is just the faintest sheen of sweat visible on his temple, but he looks much more put-together wearing my father's *chiton*.

Phoebus also freezes when he sees us and glances at his wood planks awkwardly. "I noticed you had a stack started on that wall." He points toward where Papa had been storing his good wood before we lost the energy to finish stacking them. The stack is now almost as tall as I am, and Papa's room looks halfway livable again.

I say nothing, struck mute by the bulge of his strained arm supporting what I know from personal experience to be a great weight.

Then Papa grabs my shoulders and turns me to face him. For a horrifying moment, I think he's going to scold me for being distracted.

Instead, he wraps his arms around me and holds me tightly against him.

I lose myself in the security of his embrace, feeling my body uncoil from its tension.

"No matter what must be done," Papa whispers, "I will not let Apollo take you. No matter what must be sacrificed, it won't be *you.*"

Chapter Ten

Apollo

I stare at the scene before me.

Daedalus holds his daughter so tightly that I doubt the combined power of every Primordial Guardian could tear them apart.

Yet, that's what I'm trying to do, isn't it?

My stomach sinks. Artemis is right; I *am* a fool. One that Icarus seeks to flee from. To *fly* from, if their secrecy around the wings is anything to go by.

I set the planks down more roughly than I intended, and the pair pulls apart before I'd even separate them.

Daedalus' expression hardens as he studies me with a skepticism I well deserve. "You need to understand that I still do not trust you."

"Understood." I rub away the shavings of wood from my hands. Then I suddenly do not know what to do with my beefy mortal hands. Why did I design them so large?

"You are not to leave this tower except in the company of my daughter or me," Daedalus adds.

I hide my hands behind me. No, that seems suspicious. I fold them in front of me instead.

"Papa!" Icarus cries, turning to him. "He has his own business to attend to."

"This is more important," I counter, gesturing to them. "*You* are my business now." I need to convince Icarus I am not to be feared. And that appears to rest a great deal on securing Daedalus' trust. And keeping him in Icarus' life after we are wed.

Why did I fly in pretending she was an orphan, assuming she had no one to leave behind? Marriage would certainly lose most of its appeal if it meant I was to be forever separated from Artemis.

"My lands need an architect and an inventor," I add firmly. "And I'll do whatever you need to make that happen."

Daedalus studies me for a long moment. Finally, he nods. "Icarus, show him the scaffolding we need to set up."

Icarus nods and steps forward. She lightly rests her hand on my arm, sending a jolt through me. If that's just a touch of a hand, how much more awaits us?

"Follow me," she says, her voice sweet enough to play my harp to. I smile. "Anywhere."

Anywhere apparently includes the top of her tower. The pulley system does not look ready to support my weight, so I elect to take the narrow stairs.

I sense Icarus' fretting each narrow step I ascend, which makes me nervous. I won't die even if I fall from this height, but I doubt I can explain away why I'd survive. And I am not sure how I will frame my reintroduction into Icarus' life with a new identity since she probably has reached her limit of strangers she's willing to fish from the sea.

Icarus exhales when I finally step into the flat, semi-walled tower. "The scaffolding is over here."

She moves to where several wooden poles are folded together. "These are already built. I just need help sanding them."

When she kneels beside it, I follow suit, brushing against her side.

Icarus glances at me for a moment but doesn't recoil. She turns back to the poles.

I smile. I *knew* it. She's not impervious to my charm. Soon, she will come to enjoy this hunt as much as I do.

And even if she flies, mayhap she would not be opposed if I caught up to her?

"Just hold it right here." Icarus takes my clumsily large hand and places it on the pole. She curves my fingers around it, her hand so small but not as soft as I first thought. I feel calluses from hard labor.

I do as she says, delighting in the lingering touch before she grasps her side of the pole. "We heave together. Ready?"

With a smile, I nod. When she lifts, I follow suit. It is far lighter than the planks I carried downstairs. The poles are delicately unfolding and settling into their positions. I believe our joint effort had more to do with protecting the integrity of the device than dealing with its weight.

It expands into a rack like Artemis and I hang our prized bows upon in our home on Mount Olympus. But this is obviously built for something larger and more intricate than the offerings of mortals we hunted beside.

"There." Icarus rubs her hands down her *chiton*. "Now for the troublesome part. Carrying the wings back up here."

"I can handle that," I assure, moving back to the stairway. "Can't risk my new Master Inventor straining herself."

"But isn't my father going to be your Master Inventor?"

Pausing, I think back to our exchange. "I thought your father was the architect and you were the inventor? I need both positions filled."

"By Papa, I thought."

Did I completely misread the entire situation? Though, I've never been good at understanding anything the huntresses don't directly say, so mayhap it is just mortals I cannot read. "Didn't you invent the wings?"

"Papa and I did together. But the current design is my model. We've been working together to improve on it, but I've been tinkering with it to bring the wings to new heights, you could say."

I peer over my shoulder to catch her sly smile. "Would your father be offended if I named you my Master Inventor and him only my Master Architect?"

"Oh, no— Papa much prefers architecting to inventing. He only does as much as King Minos expects and helps me with my projects. His true passion is designing empires."

"Good. Then it will be as I said. You will be my Master Inventor."

Icarus beams at me, the excitement in her eyes joining in the glory of her smile. "You differ from most men I know."

"What do you mean?" Panic rises in my chest. I haven't even played at mortality for one full day, and already she suspects me?

"Most men— my papa and Orion being the exceptions— don't think women can be an inventor. I am honored to be the Princess' tutor and companion, but that is as honored of a career as I will ever be allowed."

Turning, I take a step toward her. "No. You were meant for far more than that, Icarus. You were meant to have no limitations but the sky itself."

She tilts her head to one side, her frizzing curls falling over one arm. "What makes you say that? You do not even know me."

I think of all the visions I had of her dancing freely in my arms. Dancing even though she didn't know I was there. "Your spirit burns as brightly as the sun. And the sun is not meant to be limited, but to soar freely through the sky."

Icarus flushes but doesn't look away. "I think you might have gotten too much of that sun while you were lost in the sea, Phoebus."

Taking another step closer, I hesitate before I close the distance.

Then she grants me that bright and beautiful smile of hers. "But I appreciate your brand of insanity."

"I will take that as the highest compliment, coming from your lips."

She throws her head back and laughs, and I feel the same rush of victory as the one time I caught a stag before Artemis.

Our gazes lock, and her laughter blows away with the warm breeze. Something else replaces it, though, with no name. Something that has me reaching toward her, my hand curved to brush her face. If I can just have one touch, I can walk away from her, fulfilled for the moment.

Or mayhap I will never be satisfied again.

"Maybe it is," Icarus whispers, "considering most men only see me as an untouchable beauty to fantasize over or a pawn to gain power in their political games. And my King has sentenced me to be a sacrificial bride." Icarus winces.

I drop my hand. "I'm sorry."

"It's not your fault."

Somehow, I keep my wince at bay. "Let me fetch those wings."

She smiles softly. "Thank you."

Nodding, I turn away. But I don't deserve her gratitude. Certainly not her confidence.

Will I be able to earn her affections?

Chapter Eleven

Icarus

My free days normally fly by, especially when they align with Papa's. But reworking the entire structure of my wingspan should have countered that. Not to mention checking each minute feature for damage and correcting it.

Today, though, working alongside Phoebus, I think I blinked the day away. Every time we brush, which seemed to happen far more than it should have, I am minutely aware of the contact. The scent of the ocean is strong on him. That mixes with the sea breeze and the lightness I shouldn't feel given the circumstances, making me feel as though I'm soaring over the waves already.

"There." Phoebus steps back from the gluing in place a replacement structure the length of my hand and width of my pinky. It is hollow to help with the weight. "I think I finally have it this time."

He's had it the last couple of times, but Phoebus is endearingly cautious about making sure we do everything right. I appreciate that since it will be my life at stake.

"It's perfect." I run my hand over it just to be sure. Then I nod proudly. "You have been the best of students." Certainly better than my beloved, but easily distracted, Ariadne.

"I've had the best of tutors." Phoebus grins.

Smiling, I duck my gaze. Then I pluck up my basket of laurel leaves and begin securing them to the frames.

Phoebus plucks up one and examines it. "What are these for?"

"For luck."

"Luck?"

I'm not sure why I feel suddenly shy when I've been working elbow to elbow with him all morning, but I know the heat on my skin doesn't come from the invasive sun. "It's just something I do."

"Which god's favor do you seek doing this?"

"None. It just reminds me of my girlhood days running wild between laurel trees with no restraints. I relive those days when my wings help me sail above those restraints now."

When I glance up, Phoebus is silently studying me like he can read into my very psyche.

I clear my throat. "So, maybe it's Artemis whom I seek favor from. I often pretended to be one of her huntresses in those days, untamed and free."

"Icarus."

We both turn to see my father trekking up the stairs.

I hurry to him. "Papa! I said I would come downstairs to refill the glue."

It takes me a moment to realize his hands are empty. However, his face is still ruddy from the heat he toiled over to create the waxy glue we've been utilizing today.

Guilt stabs through me. He wouldn't have had to push himself so hard if I had just not flown so close to the sun. My wings wouldn't have been so damaged, nor would I be betrothed.

Papa stares at me blearily. "Minos has summoned me."

"But it's your day off!"

"It is almost sunset, so Minos no longer considers it so."

I grasp Papa's arm. "But you've been working all day with me instead of resting—"

He presses a kiss to the top of my hair. "I prepared some supper while the last batch of glue boiled. I should return with the dawn, if not sooner."

First, Minos gives away my hand to a god, and now he's stealing away what he would consider one of my last evenings with my father. The man is a tyrant. How he sired souls as wonderful as Orion and Ariadne, I'll never know.

"Papa, what is so vital to Minos that he needs you tonight?" I whisper.

His reaction is just like with every previous attempt to broach the subject of how Minos uses Papa's designs. A haunted gleam comes to Papa's eyes just before his face hardens. His gaze becomes an impenetrable fortress with no trace of the truth.

"It doesn't pertain to you, little bird." Papa pats my hand and pulls away. "Go downstairs. I need to have a word with our . . . guest."

Pursing my lips at the bitterness of being shut out of this vital part of Papa's life, I move to the edge of the tower. I configure my pulley to allow me to descend.

Behind me, I hear Papa clearly, despite how low his voice has dropped while he converses with Phoebus. "Do not think that just because I am not present, you can have your way with my daughter."

The rope rushes out of my hand and my step slides down to the base of the stairs without me.

Phoebus' voice is loud and clear. "Of course not, my good man. May Artemis strike down any man who would even think to force themself upon her."

While I turn the handle of my pulley, I glance over my shoulder. Papa's back is to me, and Phoebus is not looking at me. But I can hear the sincerity in his voice even so.

"Since you have mentioned the gods, I think it is only fair to warn you that she is betrothed to Apollo, the keeper of the sun himself."

Phoebus raises an eyebrow. "Oh? Is that so?"

I glance away. I had alluded to my status earlier, but does he think I am a tease to flirt with him when I am betrothed to another? Even though neither my father nor I had any hand in that betrothal or have any intention of seeing it through?

Will he think I put his life at risk? *Did* I put his life at risk? Could Apollo see us atop this tower? Did he somehow sense the way my heart stuttered at Phoebus' innocent touches?

Worse, has he overheard my father and me speaking treachery against him?

Papa is right. I do not have time for distractions, or even further rebellion. Not when I've already put so many lives at risk.

"I am sure," Papa continues, "that if you lay a hand on my daughter, Apollo will seek to pour out his wrath upon you. But you need not fear him."

"I don't?" Phoebus' eyes widen, and he seems more terrified after that assurance than before.

My step finally ascends, and I steady it.

"Apollo will never find you," Papa adds. "Nor will King Minos. Not even your ghost will find your corpse when I am finished with it. Good evening."

Too humiliated to dare another glance at Phoebus, I step into my contraption and lower myself to the living quarters of the tower.

I quickly wash my hands in the basin and take my seat at the small table. It's already set for two, since only two can fit around it. That's all Papa and I have ever needed, though. Still, it is my duty to prepare it for food, not Papa's. I sigh to be failing him as a daughter in small ways and large.

Papa enters, and I give him a perfunctory kiss before he departs. Then Phoebus joins me.

Glad he yet lives despite being alone with my father, I gesture toward his seat.

Once he's settled, and before he can mention the humiliating conversation, I rise to serve him his food. "Tell me more about yourself, Phoebus." Hopefully he doesn't notice that I already ate some of my supper.

Phoebus blinks. "I possess land, a home, and enough power to appoint your father and you to esteemed positions. What else is there to know?"

"A great deal, if you want me to trust you enough to accept that so-called great position." Once I have finished serving him carp and millet, I hide my hands behind my back to twist the signet ring he entrusted me with.

"Like what?" He fidgets with his food.

"Well, you mentioned a sister. We can start there."

Chapter Twelve

Apollo

"**M**y sister?" My eyes widen. "My sister!" I glance out the nearest window. She hasn't hung the moon yet, but as Daedalus mentioned, the sun really ought to set soon. The Firmament beckons me.

"Is she well? You spoke of her with fondness earlier."

Turning, I see that she's creased her brows in concern.

"Oh, yes, she's fine." I spoon my millet, wondering why Icarus hasn't settled in her seat yet. "I just miss her." I stuff half of the seasoned millet into my mouth to either show how fine I am or else prevent her from asking further questions.

"I'm sure you do." Her brows smooth, and she glances at the *kylix* at her vacant place, with its tiny stem and wide brim painted like any other piece of pottery. "It's only been Papa and me for as long as I can remember. I can't imagine being parted from him."

I nearly choke on my bite of carp. Yes, I need to check with Artemis regarding how long she waits to restore her strength between Awakening huntresses.

Swallowing hard, I gesture to the empty couch. "Please, sit. Eat and drink what your father has prepared me and finish telling me about yourself."

Icarus furrows her brows. "That would be rude—"

"To refuse the request of a guest?" I raise both my eyebrows in a challenge.

Icarus purses her lips but settles onto her couch. She picks up her *kylix* and takes a small sip. "My mother perished bringing me into the world."

I choke again and drop my spoon. "I'm so sorry."

"I am sorry for my father." Icarus clears her throat and sets her *kylix* down. "What's your sister's name?"

Before I can give away my sister's goddess title, I remember the name Mother gave her— her regular name and not her true name, her *Ren,* that can summon her from anywhere— before we inherited our father's power and assumed the titles he left for us. I was truly once Phoebus. And she was— "Selene."

"Selene." Icarus smiles. "Such a lovely name."

"Indeed." I glance back outside. There it is. The moon slowly rising.

I throw back my wine since my mortal body craves more sustenance than my choked-down biscuit offered. Swallowing hard, I stand. "I'm actually quite weary."

"Of course." Icarus stands. "My father will not need his cot tonight. You may sleep in his."

I cock my head to one side teasingly. "Not yours?"

"No." She turns away before I can read her face.

Icarus leads me to her father's bedroom for the second time today and opens the door for me. "Let me know if you need anything."

I move to step into the room. The sooner that door is closed, the sooner I can hurry to perform my duties before the penalties for shirking my responsibilities begin.

But I cannot make myself not move back toward her until I can feel her warmth. "You."

Icarus inhales sharply but says nothing.

Smiling, I turn back into the room. Icarus closes the door behind me.

Then I rush to the window and whistle.

My swans swoop down, dragging my chariot behind them. Thank the Creator the huntresses already had them harnessed for me.

Shedding my mortal form and throwing on my golden mantle, I climb out of my window and drop onto it. I grasp my reins and direct us to Mount Olympus, where the sun is waiting for me.

As is Artemis, with her arms crossed and a glare sharper than any of her arrows.

I park hastily. Then I stumble toward the sun's energy.

"You are so ill-prepared to woo a woman," Artemis says. "You can't take a wife if you can't also fulfill your roles!"

"Easy for you to say. You get a whole night off once a month."

Artemis narrows her eyes.

I sigh. "I'm still getting situated." I harness the sun to my chariot. "This was only my first day."

"And how did it go? Besides distracting you from the source of your Primordial powers while playing at mortality?"

I think back to the way she blushed every time we brushed . . . But also, the way she recoiled ever so slightly when I stood too nearby. "Very well. She's halfway in love with me already."

Artemis crosses her arms and raises one silver eyebrow. "So, you don't need any advice whatsoever? No wise words from a woman's perspective? Or even suggestions for the care and keeping of your pre-Awoken mortal? They are such delicate creatures."

The sun energy almost releases from my hands. "I mean, if you have some sage proverbs for me . . ."

"Pursuing a woman is just like hunting a stag." Artemis nods confidently. "Slow and steady until the prey lets you draw close enough to deliver the killing blow. The trick is to not scare her away."

I frown. "I'm not trying to slay her."

"Marriage. Death. They're all the same." Artemis shrugs. "For mortals, both fates are inevitable once they come of age."

"Actually, I was hoping you'd have advice along the lines of what gifts mortal women appreciate."

Artemis shrugs, moving toward the woods. "I'll ask my huntresses."

"Thanks." I sigh as I climb into my chariot.

"Apollo, where's your ring?"

I jerk and then awkwardly turn toward Artemis. "I . . . gifted it."

She crosses her arms, her dark eyes flashing. "To Icarus?"

"It is only a symbol of my power— not a token of it." I clear my throat. "And mortals quite like gold."

Artemis continues to glare at me for a long moment. I expect her to berate me. Instead, she takes several deep breaths to calm herself as she twists her own silver signet ring on her finger. Then, quietly, she says, "Do you know if Icarus knows anything about becoming an Ascendant?"

I'm so taken aback by the question that I just stare at Artemis. "Surely not. So few mortals know about the . . . *alternative* way to achieve immortality."

The primary way is to, of course, accept a Kiss from a Primordial and become Awoken. The process binds the mortal to the Primordial and grants them longevity, power over the respective domain, and sometimes additional gifts.

But Primordials do their best to keep the alternative method a secret. If a mortal somehow slays a Primordial, they will receive the immortality they stole along with a portion of their power. Though, most of it would go to their children, for a Primordial can only perish if they have an heir to sit on their throne, per the promise the Creator gave.

"Why would you think that?" I ask, my normally warm body going ice cold at the thought. Artemis and I have discussed the possibility that our father's demise came by a now Ascendant mortal since we did not inherit all his abilities at his demise. We inherited his domain, but do not have his control over the weather, which rages with no guidance now.

"I don't. I just want you to be cautious." Artemis' normally steely gaze softens. "I cannot lose you too, brother."

"You won't." It's not a promise. We know better than to make bargains and vows with each other. But it's the truth, at least for the moment. "I will woo Icarus as you have instructed me, and I will live."

And I *will*. When I am not rising and setting the sun, I will be with Icarus.

I will be by her side except in between setting and rising the sun, apparently.

Climbing back into Daedelus' room, I stare at his empty cot. If I were one of the original Primordials, the Firstborn of the Firstborn of creation, I would have no need for rest. But even though my mother was Awoken, I inherited some of her mortality. That includes the need to sleep once every few days. It never seemed so inconvenient as it does now that I have only two days left to win Icarus' heart.

Being born of an Awoken mother also means that Artemis and I have to eat mortal food as well as ambrosia. Thankfully, our hunts and the mortals who leave offerings at our altars satisfy those needs.

As for Icarus' needs, mortals need to sleep almost every night, if I recall correctly. So, there isn't much else I can do at this time anyway except hope she dreams of me.

With a sigh, I lay my head on the pillow. Mayhap I will have a vision that will assist me in this monumental task . . .

"Enjoy your new bride, Apollo!"

Flying over all of Crete, I search for the source of the voice. Or at least for my new bride.

"Or maybe Hades will enjoy her instead."

A terrifying scream rips through the air.

The sun is glaring in my eyes, and I cannot see her, cannot see my Icarus. Everything is painted in shades of scarlet and lavender.

But I can hear her terror. The terror of a mortal facing death. And then I hear—

I awaken with a jolt, feeling as though I have just fallen a great distance.

But it wasn't me who fell. Nor was it my body I that heard shatter.

Desperately, I try to recall the voice of the man who taunted me in the vision. But all I can hear is Icarus screaming.

And then shattering.

Throwing off my bed linens, I stand, peering around the room. All is darkness. Of course, it is. The sun doesn't rise until I do. And I cannot rise until I know she hasn't fallen.

Feeling my way through the crowded room, I find the door.

Icarus' door opens just as easily, and I stare into her room. Moonlight shimmers through the window. It illuminates her fragile form curled onto her cot. Her dark hair glistens in the ethereal light, and her eyelashes cast long shadows over her face. The gentle sound of her breath fills the room.

I close the door again and lean against it.

Icarus yet lives. She is still safe and whole.

And I will ensure she remains so, no matter what the visions decree. I don't care if I've never seen the ending of a vision altered in all my eons; this will be the exception. Icarus will not belong to death. She was promised to me *first.*

Chapter Thirteen

Icarus

I awaken to the most delightful aroma in the air.

Rolling out of bed, I stumble to my bedroom door. My gaze drops to the golden signet ring on my finger, and I freeze as I recall it is not Papa who awaits me outside.

Despite the hunger conjured by the aroma, I take my time dressing in one of my finer *peplos,* one nearly the same sky blue as Phoebus' eyes. I go to battle against my curls to place them in a ladylike updo.

Only after a glance at my polished copper mirror to ensure I look presentable do I open the door and peer out at the scene before me.

Phoebus stands at the table that is laden with roasted venison and the plumpest grapes I have ever seen. And that is saying something since I eat from the second fruits as part of the king's household. Only the gods are offered better than us.

My mysterious guest glances up and beams at the sight of me. "Good morn, Icarus."

"Good morn." I move toward him, trying not to betray my thrill to see either his smile or this feast. "I do not recall having any venison in our larder." This is a far cry from my usual breakfast of barley bread when I don't have to prepare a nicer meal for Papa.

"I have my ways of providing." Phoebus moves to pull out my small dining couch for me.

Trying not to smile at his eagerness, I allow him to seat me even though it flies in the face of social convention. "This looks like a feast worthy of the gods."

"I hope it is." Phoebus continues to grin at me as he prepares a platter. That he then sets in front of me.

I raise an eyebrow. This is the service a woman should give to a man and not vice versa. "Did you sleep well?"

"No." A dark shadow seems to drift over his expression before he brightens again. "But it's dawn, and I see your face, so all is well again."

I duck my head and carve my first bite. "You shouldn't say such things to me."

"Why not?"

Holding up my bite, I spin it on my utensil. "Apollo wouldn't like it."

"Do *you* like it, though?"

Startled, I glance up. I'm immediately caught in the warmth of his gaze. The intensity in it seems to summon my very soul.

But that is foolish drivel for those less scientifically trained.

I clear my throat, hoping that I do not betray how flustered I am by the question no one ever seemed to ask me before. "It doesn't matter. Asking for such things is sacrilege. You could incur the wrath of the sun for such words."

"He won't touch you if that isn't what you want. Of that, you can be assured."

Not sure what to say, I stuff the bite into my mouth. It is well-spiced, and my mouth explodes with flavor. But it's not quite enough to distract me from Phoebus' words.

He just smiles at me, not looking away as he helps himself.

Then there is a knocking at the door, breaking the trance between us.

With a longing glance at my half-eaten meal, I stand. Then I go to the door and stare out the peephole Papa designed. When I see the familiar form, I begin the long task of undoing all the locks and bolts from this side.

The moment I've opened the door just slightly, Ariadne is pushing through. She's slight compared to my muscled frame, but her determination makes her a force to behold.

I don't remember that I have something to hide until she's closing the door behind her.

"Orion told me what Father has done," she gasps.

"Sending Orion on another quest before the Summer Solstice feast?" I shake my head dramatically. "He knows we have more women attending than men."

"Father sending Orion away to keep him from helping me discover what evil lurks in the shadows is nothing new." Ariadne grasps my shoulders, her eyes wide. "But for him to send *you* away *forever*? As a *sacrifice*?!" She pulls me into her arms, embracing me so tightly, I'm not sure even Apollo could extract me.

"Hello."

Ariadne suddenly releases me and peers over my shoulder. "Good morn to you as well." She turns back to me, a mischievous smirk slowly spreading across her face despite the unshed tears in her eyes. "And whom might this be?"

I glance behind me to see Phoebus' tall stature looming right behind me.

"I am called Phoebus," he answers. "I'm Icarus' lover."

Slowly, I raise my gaze to the heavens. Mayhap Apollo will just have mercy on me and smite me now.

Ariadne's gaze darts back to me. "Why is this the first time I'm hearing about this?" Her eyes widen. "Does my father know?"

"I don't make a habit of communicating anything with your father that I don't have to."

She shrugs, understanding.

"Also, Phoebus is not my lover."

Despite my words, he wraps his arm around my waist and draws me against him.

Ariadne raises one eyebrow. "I see."

I shrug out of Phoebus' grip and move closer to Ariadne. "He's just a tease. I fished him out of the sea and have been giving him shelter. But we still don't want your father to know."

She snorts. "I imagine Father would be upset should he learn that his maidenly sacrifice be compromised, which would in turn compromise the safety of all Crete . . ."

It takes all my willpower, but I believe I succeed in keeping a wince from showing on my face. I am compromising Crete, but not how she fears. "It's not like that."

"Father will still suspect when he learns, and he'll discover Phoebus eventually. You should have a different story in place to protect him." Suddenly, Ariadne steps forward again and pulls me into another embrace. "I just wish I could protect you, too. Why you were offered as the sacrificial bride rather than me, I know not."

Because I'm the fool who flew too close to the sun. And I'm the coward who cannot even confess to her that I'm going to betray her and— worse in her eyes— Crete.

"There are several youths from the mainland that were invited to the feast in an attempt to establish greater goodwill since everything that has come to pass since the tragedy . . ." Ariadne pulls away and drops her gaze at the memory, but she continues her plan. "We can make Phoebus into one of them. Mayhap he can even discover for us why it was so important for my father to invite so many strangers to our festival."

"I'm not sure that will work. If this is a plot of your father's, he might have had a hand in the invitations." I place a hand on Phoebus' forearm. "We can just say he's my cousin, come for the wedding."

Ariadne wrinkles her nose at the reminder that, one way or another, our time is almost over. "You say that like my father wasn't considering betrothing me to my cousin before . . ." Clearing her throat, Ariadne turns to *my* 'cousin.' "Do you know any Minoan dances?"

Phoebus rewards her with one of his beaming smiles. "Not a one."

"Then I suppose it is up to my tutor and me to make sure you are prepared for whatever our festivities throw at you."

Chapter Fourteen

Apollo

I follow Icarus and her friend down the winding stairs. We pass several guards, but with the Princess in our company, Icarus is less cautious.

Finally, they lead me into an open room with arching windows that allow light to stream in. There isn't any furniture, just wide-open space. Is this going to be the fulfillment of my vision? I know not.

But I will certainly dance with her here.

"It is a shame none of the musicians are practicing this fine morn," Ariadne says as she glances around the empty chamber.

"If I had a lyre, I could play," I offer.

Ariadne waves my words away. "You're here to dance— not serenade us. Icarus gave me plenty of dance lessons in complete silence, anyway." Then she pats my arm. "You stay right there and watch our steps."

With that, she moves toward where Icarus is studying me.

"Do you think we should begin with one of the dances of Dionysus?" Ariadne asks.

Icarus startles and frowns. "No, most certainly not! When have you had time to sneak off to the Temple?"

"Father never lets me near the Caves of the Wind anymore, so where else can I go to be religious?"

"You know the priestesses allegedly use the Ritual to summon Dionysus. And the last thing we need is to have yet another god on our hands."

Ariadne shrugs one shoulder, her expression turning solemn. "I was just having a tease. Come now, let us truly dance." She nudges Icarus with her hip, drawing Icarus' focus away from me.

Icarus nods back. Then both of them turn to me.

The two women clap in synchronization. Then both kick out one ankle, swirling it around before drawing it back. Then they spin, clapping again, before throwing out one arm each above their heads and twirling it. Then it's back at their sides, clapping, as they spin again. Icarus' blue skirt swirls at her ankles, just like in my visions.

Breaking their synchronization for the first time, the ladies throw their outside arms out and move toward them, separating from each other. And I know just what to do from here on.

Stepping toward her, I take Icarus' outstretched hand in mine, placing my other on her waist.

Icarus startles at our sudden proximity, but her feet know the dance, and she continues to spin. I know the steps as well after a year of dancing with her in my dreams. I spin with her, not breaking contact.

Though this is the fulfillment of my vision, it is so much more brilliant than the dream or anything I could ever have anticipated. Instead of imagining her touch, I feel it, her gentle fingers gripping my hand. I grip her warmth rather than nothing. And the scent of spices and flowers engulfs me, making this seem more like a dream than the vision did.

The greatest difference, though, is that she's looking at me, truly looking at me. Her brown eyes are wide, her lips slightly parted as she stares up at me. The shock on her face melts away to confusion and wonder.

Knowing the next step, I begrudgingly release her waist and twirl her away from me before twirling back to her side. I compensate for that moment of separation by pulling her more tightly to myself as we continue to dance as one.

If I thought I could exist forever in that vision, I was a fool. This—*this* is what happy eternities are made of.

"Am I doing it right?" I whisper, my voice husky to my ears.

"Just . . . move with me."

I obey. Over and over, we spin, repeating the movements from the vision, though we far outdistance the length of it. Icarus does not request we halt, though, and I certainly do not wish it.

Her gaze has drifted closed, trusting me to lead the steps as she loses herself to the sensation of this being a dream. But it is so much more than that, for our steps are not truly scripted. We can break free of them and dance to new steps together.

Reluctantly releasing my grip on Icarus' hand, I grasp the other side of her waist. Then, my fingers circling her, I lift her into the air.

Icarus' eyes flutter open, and she grasps both my forearms. Her silent, questioning gaze finds mine. But the alarm quickly fades from it as the breeze of our own making catches her curls and flutters them around her face. She knows as well as I that she was born to fly.

"Phoebus," Icarus murmurs, her eyes bright and her face flushed as she gazes down at me. "I do believe you have deceived me."

I stare up at her and wonder how she could have seen through my ruse so soon.

Icarus places her hands on my forearms that still hold her upright. "You said you did not know how to dance. Yet you seem to be an expert already."

Because of all the practice in my dreams. "I've had the best of tutors."

She quirks her eyebrows, not looking convinced, but her smile is still wide. "And you've been the best of students."

"Wow," Ariadne mutters good-naturally. "I suppose our friendship means nothing."

"Well now, whom do we have here?"

My dance partner jolts, and I set her down. Then, breaking the graceful pattern of movements we created, we turn toward the intruder.

A man is leaning in the doorway. He seems somehow too tall and too thin at the same time. Yet the arrogance on his swarthy face implies he views himself as much mightier than he appears. Long, greasy black hair is partly pulled away from his face and falls halfway down his back.

Unfolding from the doorway, he steps toward us. He wears a purple short *chiton* with sleeves along with his arrogance.

Icarus seems to duck against me for a moment, as if seeking shelter. Then she catches herself and steps away from me.

Ariadne comes to stand beside Icarus, a pained smile on her face. "Supreme Commander Vassilis, what brings us the pleasure of your presence?"

"Ah, my Princess." Vassilis prowls closer, takes Ariadne's hand between his bony fingers, and presses a long kiss to it.

She snatches it away, and I move closer to them.

Vassilis straightens, not a dark strand of hair moving out of place somehow. I do not think he could have stood a moment longer bowing. "Your father has requested the honor of you and the sweet sacrificial lamb to take supper with him this eve. It's a send-off of sorts to the Prince before he begins his voyage on the morrow." Vassilis' gaze flicks to me. "And I will inform him one more seat will need to be set."

"My cousin," Icarus blurts.

Vassilis doesn't seem to hear her as he rakes his gaze up and down her figure.

Anger wells within my gut until shame distinguishes it. Is this why Icarus did not like me gazing at her yesterday? Because she already has to tolerate such disrespect from *morosophs* like this?

"It truly is a shame your beauty caught Apollo's eye, little morsel," Vassilis murmurs, reaching as if to touch Icarus' face. He restrains himself before I can break his hand. "You would have been *almost* a suitable enough bride for me."

With that, he turns and strides away, but a layer of his presence seems to linger in the air.

Ariadne hisses at him as she wipes the back of her hand off on her *peplos*. "He shouldn't have the audacity to speak to me, let alone *touch* me." She shakes her head. "Why Father keeps him nearer than his own son, I'll never understand."

Icarus shakes her head in agreement before glancing back at the doorway and tensing.

I follow her gaze to find her father standing there. He has circles under his eyes so dark I can see them clearly from here. His shoulders are sagging as he stares at Icarus with heartbreak and disappointment in his expression.

Then he turns and walks away.

She wilts.

I turn toward her as she seems to wilt. "Icarus?"

"The swan pond!" she blurts suddenly. "We should visit the swan pond!"

Ariadne turns to her in confusion. "The swan pond? Whatever for?"

"It seems as good a place as any to go over the guest list for the midsummer festival and cover how best to greet the esteemed guests whom your father invited. Not to mention pour over your map of Crete again to see if there's anything we might have missed before."

The Princess nods slowly, still not looking quite convinced.

"And I rather like it there," Icarus adds, her tone taking a melancholy tone. "I'm going to . . . miss it."

Finally, Ariadne's expression softens even as her eyes flash. "I will fetch the invite list and my maps, then, and meet you there."

Icarus smiles and watches her depart. Then she turns to me, her voice dropping to a whisper as she leans closer than she needs to keep her words secret. But I certainly will not point that out. "While we are there, I need swan feathers. All the loose swan feathers you can find."

I nod once, not speaking, I'm not sure I can as the scent of her once again invades my senses. Without my meaning to, my hand comes to rest on the side of her face.

Icarus' eyes flutter shut for a moment, as when we were dancing. But then she takes a large step back. "You should also refrain from touching me. At least where the sun can see us."

Dropping my arm, I stare after her. "So, I should only touch you at night?"

She drops her gaze and walks quickly toward the door.

I know I should catch up to her, since she knows where to find the swan pond than I. But as she passes under a window streaming in the sunlight that she doesn't want to witness our touch, I see the strange dichotomy that she is. There is strength in her gait and determination in her expression. Yet that is still encased in her fragile mortal form. The same mortal form I heard break in my vision.

Did that fall come despite her wings or because of them? Am I helping her prepare the means of her salvation or creating the weapon of her doom?

Icarus was meant to fly, but is she also destined to fall?

Chapter Fifteen

Icarus

The swan pond is in the secret courtyard of the Palace of Knossos. Not that the courtyard is actually a secret of any kind. But since it is sequestered between walled wings sheltering the dance floor, Minos designed for Ariadne and the main shrines, it is rarely visited. So, Ariadne and I used to pretend it was our special place only we knew of. I think we still do, in our heart of hearts.

Of course, Phoebus ducking around hyacinth bushes in his search for feathers challenges that imagining.

Ariadne and I kneel in front of the marble stool set closest to the swan pond, our maps and parchments scattered across it. Graceful white fowl swim lazily through the water. They weave around the eerily lifelike statue of the bull, painted brown with red eyes. That thing always detracted from the charm of this garden, though some of its paint is chipping away, at least.

The swans know us, and do not fear having their cygnets swim near us. However, if Phoebus draws too close, they always scatter.

"There!" Ariadne announces, gesturing to a point on the map by the cliffs where the beach gave way completely to the sea.

I raise an eyebrow, pretending she's been paying even the slightest attention to my discussion of the guests. "There, Prince Theseus of Athens?"

Ariadne waves my words away. "No, no— who cares about him? There, where I think we can finally see what our fathers have been working on."

"Maybe you can discover it during the Summer Solstice?" I gesture to my list of guests. "You know, your father has a penchant for preferring other men's sons to his own children. And rumors say that Theseus is handsome with a very strong profile."

She snorts. "I'd rather not rely on any man if I can help it. Especially since I think these caves hold the answer. We've both glimpsed your father's plans for expanding on the network of tunnels between us."

I place a pebble on my list and lean back. "But I do not know if that is related to the people who keep going missing?"

"It has to be. I just know it. Where else can someone vanish to on this tiny island, except beneath it?" She taps her map again. "It is very suspicious that no one is admitted any longer to the family crypts. But the cave at the beach is not guarded."

Pursing my lips, I glance at her map. We've been in those caves before. It is a labyrinth of natural caverns beneath Crete that eventually were converted to crypts deeper in the island. And it was once our delight to explore them with Orion as our guide. But then, we all grew older and received additional responsibilities that drove the underground network of tunnels far from our mind. Or at least, far from all our minds except Ariadne's.

"Or mayhap those who disappear are taken to the Spire?" I glance toward the tower just visible on the horizon on its own tiny island. It serves as a guard tower, watching the waters for enemy fleets, and as the distant goal for me to soar to. A goal I will not get to accomplish now that my time on Crete has been cut short. Yet another dream ripped out of my clenched fists.

"Maybe . . ." Adriana doesn't look convinced as she turns her focus back to her map.

"You shouldn't have to do this alone. It's not safe."

"My mind is made up, and none can change it."

I sigh. "I wish I had more time to help you solve this mystery."

Her expression softens, and she glances up at me. "Why must my father's wickedness know no bounds?"

"Come now, this can hardly be blamed entirely on your father. A god threatened him. Better men would be cowed into submission." Not *my* father, though.

While King Minos would sacrifice me for his own life, Papa would spare mine even if it meant all of Crete would suffer.

My stomach churns, and I glance away. Ariadne, for one, would never sacrifice her people for her freedom. But I wasn't born a Princess like her. I've only ever been a sojourner here.

And her friend.

"Hey, now, stay back."

We both turn to find Phoebus kneeling precariously at the edge of the pond. The basket I lent him is set to the side, half filled with feathers, more than I even dared to hope for. However, his full attention is on a single feather drifting deeper into the pool. And also on a nearby swan that looks very offended that he is reaching over her.

"It's all right, Phoebus," I call. "You can leave that feather be."

"But you need it." He stretches farther, and the swan arches its neck angrily.

Ariadne turns to watch. "Lady Nymph doesn't seem to agree."

"Lady Nymph is fine. I'm great with animals. Specifically swans." Phoebus grins down at the offended fowl as he reaches just a little farther. His fingers brush over the floating feather.

I glance at the other swans. Those without cygnets swimming around them are circling Phoebus, as if waiting for a command from Lady Nymph. "Phoebus . . ."

He grasps the feather. "There!" Phoebus grins at me proudly despite his precarious angle.

Lady Nymph takes great offense to him yelling in her face. And she expresses her frustration by biting his arm.

Phoebus was clearly not expecting this, because he totters off balance. "You dare bite me—"

He's cut off when he goes toppling into the water.

I jump to my feet even as the other swans swarm him.

Ariadne giggles nervously behind me as I rush toward the pond.

Not quite thinking, I wade into the pond and blindly reach through the flurry of feathers to feel Phoebus' struggling form.

I tug upward, and he moves with me. Then, amidst the flurry of feathers and assault of beaks, we stumble backward. I crash onto the garden path, drawing Phoebus after me.

He knocks the breath out of me before quickly rolling off me. The swans continue to peck at our ankles.

Phoebus, choking from the pond water, sits up before I'm able to, not breathing at all after his weight was on my lungs. Then he pulls me into his arms like I weigh nothing and jogs past Ariadne.

We must make quite the comical sight, with both of us drenched and him holding me like a babe, because she dissolves into more laughter. Ariadne loses the ability to stand and collapses onto the grass by her bench.

The swans, though, have been awakened by the taste of our blood. They lunge up the shoreline after us.

Ariadne stops laughing and glares at them. "Stop. Go back to the pond."

Just like that, they flap right back to where they belong. They swim so gracefully, like they weren't seeking our flesh just a moment ago.

Then Ariadne knocks the rocks aside and gathers all our parchments into one armful before turning to us. She dissolves into giggles again but manages to stand.

With a groan, I lean my head against Phoebus' head before jerking away from the damp material. At least his arms are warm where they engulf me.

Ariadne walks past us, holding my basket of feathers now, along with all the parchments. "Come on. Let's get you two ready for supper with the King."

Chapter Sixteen

Apollo

I did not realize that being mortal was so perilous.

Nor did I realize that Kyknos and her flock are the exception among swans. The rest of them are apparently wretched and wicked.

With a sigh, I use one of the many bone combs lined up on Ariadne's vanity to smooth down my damp hair. I miss the golden curls I could just shake dry. But I did not expect to be submerged so much when I designed this form.

Smoothing down the purple *chiton* made of an even finer quality than the one I borrowed from Daedalus, I step out of Ariadne's bathing room.

She and Icarus are leaning toward each other on a velvet couch, whispering. They immediately cease when they see me.

Ariadne's gaze slides over me and she nods in approval. "You can certainly keep that *chiton*. I'm not sure Orion ever wore that. He prefers to share as much of his beauty as he can with the world."

I clench my teeth at the thought of Orion, but Ariadne just rolls her eyes, apparently sharing in my general annoyance with that man.

Icarus stands, her matching purple *peplos* falling higher than her usual cuts, skimming her shins rather than her ankles. But I suppose she is taller than her friend. Her hair is still damp from her bath, which transpired in the same washbasin I used, though not at the same time. Icarus and Ariadne have confined her damp curls with strings of pearls. Well, almost confined it— several curls are stubbornly escaping.

"You are breathtaking," I whisper.

Ariadne stands and strides quickly across her large, marble-floored room, away from us.

But Icarus doesn't look away from me, her gaze traveling up and down my person. "How are your injuries?"

"My . . . injuries?" Suddenly, I do not recall a single moment before now, as her gaze is locked on mine.

"Yes— have you forgotten them already?" She holds up one hand, closes her fingers, and then mimes that it's a swan. "Peck, peck?"

I can't stop the burst of laughter that escapes. Icarus giggles in return, her eyes glittering.

Then I grasp my forearm that received the worst damage and clutch it like it's an injured warrior for me to return home.

That does the trick, and Icarus is suddenly before me. The scent of spices and irises she filled her bath with engulfs me nearly as strongly as when I entered the bath water after her.

Hopefully Artemis doesn't notice the scent when I see her tonight, or else I'll never hear the end of it. But I don't mind being reminded of Icarus with every breath.

Icarus gently takes my once injured arm and runs her soft fingers up and down my limb. She purses her lips when she can find nothing to devote her ministrations to. "Where are your bites?"

"They weren't so terrible after all," I offer. Especially since I was born with the ability to heal myself and others quickly, though it is not directly tied to my Primordial power and authority. It is *heka*, or mortal magic, I inherited from my mother. Artemis inherited a selective portion of it, too.

My bride-to-be drops my arms and plants her hands on her hips. Her eyes sparkle with amusement. "You're still lucky I was there to pull you out. Both times." She shakes her head.

"I'm always lucky to have you near," I whisper.

Icarus pretends not to have heard me as she presses an accusatory finger against my chest. "You should just avoid bodies of water in the future."

I nod sagely. "I barely survived my bath." My hand comes over hers, sealing her touch against me. "You should have been there."

"Thank the gods you survived."

Leaning forward, I smile at the slightest shiver that runs through her from my breath on her ear. "Next time, I might not be so fortunate. We certainly shouldn't risk it."

She laughs again, a sound sweeter than my latest composition and more valuable to be pursued than the rarest stag. "I'm sure you will survive many baths without me present."

"But I'm not sure I am brave enough!" I move our hands over the left side of my chest so she can feel the steady beat of my heart. "If I'd perished, then I wouldn't have the honor of seeing your smile again."

This earns me a smile, and I bask in its glow.

"Are you two *cousins* done yet?" Ariadne calls suddenly. "My father is wretched enough to deal with when his meal *isn't* postponed."

"Right, yes, we're coming." I don't look away from Icarus as I carry her hand up to my lips. I press a lingering kiss on her knuckles, brushing my golden ring she wears. It belongs on her hand, just like my lips do.

"*Ahem.*"

Icarus snatches her hand away and then hurries toward her friend. When she reaches the doorway, though, she glances back at me over her shoulder. Even from here, there is no denying the heat in her gaze.

I happen to be an expert in heat.

My little mortal bride is already halfway in love with me.

The dining hall is the largest room in the castle that I've seen yet. Rather than curved like the rest of the rooms, this one is long and rectangular, set neatly in the heart of the palace, near the throne room. I had heard that the Palace of Knossos used to just be dedicated to activities dedicated to governing Crete and offering shrines that are not available in the temple. However, Minos decided he deserved to live in the largest building in Crete and made the palace into a home.

The hubris of that man is truly something else.

Therefore, the banquet hall has been more recently furnished as such. A table of the same shape takes up most of the room. It looks as though it can seat at least thirty people, but only a few seats at one end are being occupied.

I follow Icarus and Ariadne toward that end. King Minos sits at the head, looking far more regal and unconcerned than he did when I was threatening him. A powerful stench of frankincense surrounds him like a cloud.

Orion sits to Minos' right, lifting a *kylix* with bulls painted across it to his lips. He holds it toward us when he spots us, a silent toast.

Vassilis sits to the left of his king and does not appear pleased by that, as though Supreme Commander outranks Heir Apparent. He reclines across as much of the couch as he can. Daedalus sits completely upright next to him. Three more wrinkles appear on his brow when he sees us, even as Orion takes a sip of his wine.

Ariadne curtsies toward her father. "Presenting the Bride of the Sun and her cousin, newly arrived for the ceremony."

Orion chokes and spits his wine back into his *kylix*.

No one seems to notice, though, and then Ariadne I are seated by Orion, with me on her other side. Icarus sits across from me, next to her father. She has eyes only for her platter, though, which servants have laden with fruit, vegetables, lentils, and grains. There is no meat on the table.

I suppose I will be visiting one of my altars for offerings later.

King Minos takes a bite dripping in olive oil before sighing heavily. "I'm going to miss this."

Vassilis leans toward his king, his greasy long hair dipping precariously close to his wine. "Miss what, wise King?"

Minos gestures around the table. "All of us eating together like a family. It will never be like this again."

Icarus puts down her spoon and stares at her food rather than eating it.

And Orion sits straighter. "I can delay my hunt of the beasts in our neighboring isle. We have our own trials that I should attend to first, as your heir."

Minos waves his hand at Orion. "No, no, Oenopion has called for aid, so to him you must go. Vassilis can attend to the 'troubles' here."

Vassilis gives Orion a slippery smile. The much larger man merely narrows his eyes in return.

Ariadne does as well. "Let us not forget the other significant change coming upon us."

I glance down at my plate and almost miss the way Vassilis tries to reach around Daedalus to touch Icarus. My hands fist my borrowed *chiton*.

Thankfully, Daedalus chooses that moment to lean back. He bumps into Vassilis' hand, preventing him from reaching Icarus.

My fingers release my garment.

"Yes," King Minos agrees, shoving another bite into his mouth. "Quite tragic, that. But it will be a glorious wedding to behold."

He grips his *kylix* and raises it high. "To Icarus, who will make the loveliest of goddesses!"

Icarus ducks her face even as everyone else lifts their goblets. I wait until she senses my stare enough to glance up. Then I lift my own *kylix*.

"Songs will be woven and tales will be told of your great beauty and splendor," I promise.

She stares at me blankly, and for a moment, I think she forgets all her plans for escape and excitement to come with me.

In that moment, a single tear trails down her heartbroken face.

Chapter Seventeen

Icarus

I feel as though I have perished, and my soul is watching the strange dining scene from above. King Minos obviously feels no compunction about what he's done. Vassilis seems to only regret that I won't be his one day. Papa betrays no emotion. Neither does my corpse.

Phoebus, despite knowing our plot, is gazing at me with heartbreak and horror. Why? Has he decided not to help us, not to shelter us? Will he try to betray us? Even after he seemed so taken by me?

Ariadne is a Princess and displays no emotion, except for flashes of heartbreak when she glances toward the body I once inhabited. And Orion keeps glancing skeptically between Phoebus and me.

Even though I appreciate every opportunity to be with Papa, I despise the rare invitations to King Minos' table. Not only do they always involve the repulsive Vassilis, who never passes on an opportunity to wrap his tongue strangely around his spoon when he catches my gaze. But also, Minos throws away all social convention when he does.

When Phoebus insists I eat with him or Papa requests it, I feel like an equal. But when Minos demands it of Ariadne and me, it feels like he is offering a great favor. One he will someday call in.

Considering my pending nuptials, he already has.

King Minos suddenly sets down his platter, which he'd been licking legumes from. "I just remembered! You will need a gown for your marriage rites."

"I can provide wedding garments for my daughter," Papa murmurs.

Minos waves away his words. "Nonsense. She must look like a goddess! We do not want Apollo turning on us in a rage for bestowing upon him an unworthy sacrifice."

Ariadne stabs her platter with her spoon. "*He* is the one who demanded *her*."

Phoebus turns again to me, and his gaze helps to draw my soul back into my body. "It is *Apollo* who is not worthy of Icarus, not vice versa."

A stillness falls over the room. Papa almost imperceptibly nods in agreement.

Vassilis snorts. "*Icarus*? Worthy?"

King Minos stands, his glare heavy . . . on Vassilis? "I will not tolerate blasphemy at my supper table!"

However, Phoebus takes the words meant for Vassilis for himself. "If you oppose blasphemy, then I would advise not speaking ill of the future Bride of the Sun!"

Dread laces through me. Is this an act, or has Phebus truly turned his back on our plans, *my* freedom?

I slowly stand as well. "I am very weary. I believe I shall retire now." I glare at Phoebus, so he knows I expect him to retire as well.

Waving his hand, Minos settles back into his red velvet dining couch. "Yes, and expect a *nymphokomos* to attend to you come the morn. I'll have the gown I commissioned for Ariadne's wedding resized for you."

Ariadne whirls around to face him. "*My* wedding?"

Orion whirls on King Minos. "Why is this the first I am hearing of it?"

"And I?!" Ariadne cries.

Vassilis grins, revealing wine-stained teeth. "Because you need not worry yourself about the minutia of state. That's *my* duty, hunter."

Minos curls his lips as a servant takes too long refilling his platter. Then, with a sigh, he turns to his two children. "Not to worry, Ariadne. There will be plenty of time to have a new gown made for you before I can find a man willing to pay the appropriate bride-price."

Ariadne narrows her eyes. "That was not what I was concerned about."

"Finding some fool actually willing to wed her is the true worry," Vassilis agrees.

Both Ariadne and Orion turn their withering stares to him.

And I find myself standing behind Orion. The chaos made me forget even the steps that brought me here.

I lay one hand on his bare shoulder, and he turns to me. His expression immediately softens, and he stands.

"I just wanted to wish you well," I whisper. "In case I never . . ." My voice breaks, so I lower it an octave and plunge on. "In case I never see you again."

Orion wraps his muscular arms around me and holds me tightly against his heartbeat. "Don't talk like that, little bird. We'll meet again, if only for you to come down and tell me to stop killing so many beasts in your honor."

I sniffle and clutch him more tightly. Orion is both an integral piece of my childhood and an important peer in my womanhood. He was my guardian on youthful adventures, and my dream when my troublesome years made me realize he was a man.

Once, I would have given anything for him to not look at me like another Ariadne, a sister he needed to protect. Now I would trade all I have for us to all be young and innocent again, like brother and sisters with no forced marriages on the horizon.

"If your new husband harms you," Orion whispers, his voice low and meant for my ears only. "I have hunted the monsters of the night. I can surely kill the god of the sun."

I nod mutely, tears pricking my eyes. If I betray all of Crete, would he still hold me so tenderly and promise to avenge me against my enemies?

A deep growl behind me has us stepping apart. I turn to find Phoebus standing behind me, scowling at Orion.

With a sigh, I tear myself away from the presence of my second dearest friend. At least I do not have to say my farewells to Ariadne just yet. Mayhap when she has to flee Crete when the sun comes too close, Orion can take her hunting with him. She would like that, even if she'd never forgive me for abandoning Crete to Apollo's wrath.

Phoebus places a possessive hand on my shoulder when I step toward him. He tears his glare from Orion to address the wider group. "Do not fear. I shall make sure she gets to bed."

The way he speaks has Papa narrowing his eyes. But he says nothing as Phoebus draws me away.

He does not need me to lead the way back to our tower. I also say nothing as I go through the long, strenuous process of unlocking the door and then locking it again from the other side.

The moment that is done, and I whirl on him. "Are you in or out?"

Phoebus stares at me in confusion. "What do you mean?"

"Our arrangement. I need to know if I can trust you."

"Of course, you can trust me." He frowns. "Why do you suddenly think you can't?"

I narrow my eyes, all his strange comments coming to mind, his unnecessary aggression toward Orion when he was just trying to protect me. "Are you an acolyte of Apollo? Come to ensure that the sacrifice goes through?"

"*What?*" Phoebus steps back.

And I charge after him, jabbing a finger against his chest. I do my best not to remember the last time I did that, and the sweet affection he offered. If he were an acolyte, why would he touch what belongs to his god?

Unless Apollo doesn't truly need a mortal bride and intends to cast me away to his followers when he's finished.

It's my turn to step back, horror welling within me, feeding upon all the unknowns that surround Phoebus. "You just happened to arrive the day after my hand in marriage was demanded."

Phoebus purses his lips. "I apologize that I did not time my ship-wreck better—"

"You act unafraid to challenge Apollo, or King Minos, two things only a fool would do. Unless they are protected by a god—"

"It's because I want you for myself!"

I stumble backward, my back touching the wall. Grasping it for balance, I glance around for something I can use as a weapon. Just in case.

Phoebus frowns. "Why do you look frightened?"

"Maybe because I am afraid of men trying to own me!"

"I don't think I can own you." His voice is small and his expression chagrined. But I know better than to let my guard down now. "I just think I can love you."

I grit my teeth. "You're all the same. You see my beauty like a rare flower growing in the wild. It is too lovely for you to let it be, flourishing where it is. No, you must *do* something with it, make it your own somehow. Whether you seize it for yourself or give it to your son matters not, as long as you had a chance to command the destiny of something so rare and lovely."

Phoebus opens his mouth. Closes it. Glances down at his feet.

And I push away from the wall, feeling stronger with my rage. "Some men will merely trample a flower because they know not what to do with it otherwise, or because they do not want anyone else to see the beauty they glorified in for a moment. Others will build a wall to protect the bloom because if they can't gaze upon the flower any longer, neither can any other. Some want just a petal to gloat with. Others a seed to make future beauties of their own—"

"What do *you* want, Icarus?" Phoebus' voice is barely a whisper, but his earnest gaze amplifies his words.

"Freedom." I lift my chin. "I want to be free of man's control. I want to be free of his touch, of his wandering eye, of his sense of power over me just because he was blessed with greater strength. I want to fly away from it all."

Phoebus' expression doesn't change, but something about him seems to wilt like my metaphorical flower. "So, you do not want love?"

"Maybe on my own terms, completely derived from my own choice. I would rather a life alone than one controlled by a man in the name of the love he offers me but doesn't trust me to return of my own free will."

"And how should a man love you?" Phoebus moves as if to step towards me but seems to think better of it and remains where he stands.

"As a gift, not an expectation." I close my eyes. Draw a deep breath and then release it. "You may help me if you wish, Phoebus. But do not think that your assistance gives you a right to me. I will be owned by no man."

Phoebus raises one eyebrow. "Or god?"

"No god I have not chosen to serve of my own volition." With a sigh, I hug myself as my body trembles from such an outpouring of vehemence. "I know it is foolish for me to dream of freedom when I was born a woman."

"You are not foolish, Icarus."

I turn away. "But I thought I could be the exception, somehow. I was valuable as a scholar, so there was no need to seek another role for the sake of Crete. My father's protection surrounds me, so there was no need for another man to repel the others. But I suppose even he won't be around forever . . ."

"Apollo will be."

Phoebus winces at my scowl.

Then I turn away, walking to one of the windows. I peer out at the open sky and rolling sea. I wish I could fly between them. Wish nobody's lives and livelihoods hung in the balance of my escape.

I wish I were born a man and none of this would have burdened me to begin with.

If worst does come to worst, though, I suppose I could return to my childhood dream of becoming one of Artemis' huntresses. There wouldn't be much time for my scholarly pursuits, but at least I wouldn't have to submit to a man's touch.

"I will help you, Icarus. And I will do it without bargaining with you."

Glancing over my shoulder, I find Phoebus in the same place that I left him, studying me.

"I will give you my help freely. Not in return for your love or even for the help you could offer me as my Master Inventor."

"And why would you do that?" Crossing my arms, I turn to face him fully.

"Because I want your love. Not the promise of it, but the hope. On your own terms, given freely. But in order for that to be even a possibility, *you* must be free." Phoebus purses his lips, looking unsure of what my reaction will be. "This I vow to you, to assist you with the repair of your wings."

Chapter Eighteen

Apollo

D aedalus finds Icarus and me on the roof, securing the feathers on the frame. Some we glue, and others we tie with twine.

He inspects our work over our shoulders. Then he turns to me. "I would like a word with my daughter."

Nodding, I tie off my twine and stand. Then I glance at the sun shining brightly above us. I wonder if they notice it should have begun to set by now. I'm not truly late yet, but I can sense the wrongness of it.

I am only halfway down the stairs when Daedalus says, "I hope you understand how important it is that you do not become distracted."

"Phoebus was just helping me with the wings—"

"In return for dance lessons?"

I freeze in my descent.

"I cannot give away what I'm doing to Ariadne. She knows about my wings already, and she may be my friend, but she's the Princess of Crete first."

"You are clever enough to keep her off your trail without wasting time. We have only one full day left. Then whatever moments we can spare before your *gamos* on the Summer Solstice."

"And I'll have the rest of these feathers in place before I retire. They'll have the night to dry—"

"You need more feathers. I've finished adjusting mine, but we still need to test them both. And I am to be by Minos' side at dawn tomorrow."

Icarus gasps. "Papa, you need to rest!"

"There will be time for that later."

"Not if you don't survive until later. You will need your strength to fly, and don't think I'm leaving without you."

There are more angered whispers, but I descend too far to hear them.

I glance out at the sky that should be a little darker by now, and then hurry inside. I make my way through their tower and down the hall until I come to a window far enough away from their tower for them not to see me.

There is no one around, so I resume my true form and climb onto the window. Then I whistle.

My swans, which are certainly better behaved than the garden swans, fly toward me. I wait until they pass underneath me before jumping into my chariot.

Feeling all the awkwardness of mortality slip away, I soar with my swans into the sky. I will perform my responsibility. Then I will deal with the two mortals whose goals run both counter and aligned to mine.

I can help Icarus be free. But she must be bound to me as my bride, or else I will perish. So, I merely need to give her the freedom to choose me . . . right?

At least Artemis is not scowling at me when I land next to her already tethered chariot.

Since she seems to be momentarily not upset with me, I decide not to mention that I've entered worse than a bargain, but a vow. There is no payout for me, but the penalty for me not keeping my word to help Icarus with her wings would be the same as if I broke a bargain. Only, since it is one-sided, there is no chance of her violating the terms and thus releasing me from the vow.

But I will help her and, hopefully, in doing so, convince Icarus that she does not actually want to flee. That she wants me as much as I desire her before the sacrifice in two days.

Artemis leans back on her chariot. "How did it go? Has the girl confessed her love yet?"

It looks like she's going to be annoyed with me after all. It seems to be the fashion for females in my life. "Actually, we got into our first fight."

"What?"

I shrug awkwardly and kick at a pebble. Let it bear the brunt of my wrath.

It goes soaring into the heavens.

"That is mildly good tidings, then."

My gaze snaps toward Artemis in surprise. "What?"

"It means she trusts you enough to disagree, and is comfortable enough to not keep things, well, *comfortable.*"

"So, this isn't an obstacle?"

"If it doesn't get resolved, it is. But Aster— who came to me as a widow— tells me resolving it can be the best part." Artemis purses her lips in a rare moment of confusion as she plays with her reins. "I suppose if they consent to your demands and agree that you were right, I can see how that might be true."

Then Icarus must be thrilled right now. "Any other excellent pieces of advice from your huntresses?"

Artemis puts down the reins she just plucked up. "Let me think . . . Aster said you should bring her flowers. Tyche just reiterated her loathing against all men, and I had to remind her that you were the exception. After I threatened to smite her for her sacrilege, she added that mortal women like to be serenaded."

"Serenaded?" I straighten. Smile. "I can do that."

"I thought you might like that one. Definitely worth threatening to turn Tyche into a hare."

I purse my lips. "But you can't do that." We Primordials can alter our forms, but we certainly can't transfer that to another.

Artemis lifts a conspiratorial finger to her lips. "Don't tell my huntresses that." Then she grasps her reins again. Just like that, she's off, sailing into the darkening sky with the moon in tow.

I go to my own chariot and extract my golden harp.

Grinning, I let my fingers pluck at the strings, gentle notes spilling into the night air. "Finally. Something I know how to do."

Resting on a cliff overlooking Crete, I pluck at the golden lyre I keep in my chariot, which is parked beside me.

I try and fail to do justice to the melody that has haunted my soul ever since I saw Icarus flying. So instead, I strum the tune I had been weaving in honor of Hades' new bride. But I alter the words to match my circumstances and increase the tempo from its haunting melody to match the joy in my spirit at the thought of seeing Icarus again. I'll finish my ode for the unfortunate mortal Hades has taken for himself once I finish wooing Icarus.

"The dusk deserted us.
The moon sets in the west.

My lover, where are you?
My lover, where are you?"

I feel pricks of color under my eyelids as a vision announces its coming. I let my fingers and tongue continue to play and sing as I lose myself in the coming dream.

"Apollo."

"The Shadows are coming.
The Shades, they are calling.
My lover, where are you?
My lover, where are you?"

I turn from gazing out at the rising moon to find a far lovelier scene before me, painted once again in golds and blues.

Icarus stands on the marble floor of my private quarters on Mount Olympus, overlooking Elis.

But Icarus, for looking so small and fragile in the largeness of my bedroom, somehow fills every corner with her presence. Her scent drifts to me from the open balcony, her flowers combatting the aroma of nature outside.

"Apollo," she whispers again, and my heart thrills to hear her say my real name so sweetly.

"The darkness has bound me.
But the Sun has found me.
My lover, where are you?
My lover, where are you?"

Icarus moves closer, and stray moon beams reflect off her gleaming curls that flow from beneath a laurel wreath and over her shoulders. One of those shoulders is bare, while the other is draped upon by the blue linen of her peplos *that flows down her slim figure, skimming her thighs.*

I straighten and then bow. "My bride."

"I tried to be true, but you were not there.
I tried to be true, but you did not care.
The Sun, as my new lover, I choose.
The Sun, as my new lover, I choose."

Icarus does not respond, just steps ever closer. She seems to give off her own light, a gentle gold mixing with the silver of the moon. There is a determination in her gaze, nearly concealing a heat that can warm me for an eon to come.

"The glowing orb doth drives away my woes.
The warming, golden rays chase off my foes.
The Sun, as my new lover, I choose
The Sun, as my new lover, I choose."

She comes to a halt before me. I want to close the distance between us, but I don't dare frighten her away.

I let her reach out, placing a hand on my chest.

"Apollo," she murmurs, "I'm ready. Don't—" Her strong, sweet voice cracks for just a moment before returning in confidence. "Don't let me fall."

My hand closes over hers. "Never."

"I was fond of his spark.
But his love waned to dark.
My lover, where are you?
My lover, where are you?"

The vision alters, reverting to a new scene. A familiar scene, what little I can see of it in the sun's glare, with reds and purples.

"Enjoy your new bride, Apollo!"

Knowing what comes next, I earnestly soar over Crete, seeking my new bride before, before—

"Or maybe Hades will enjoy her instead."

"I tried to be free, but you were not here.
I began to flee, but you were not near.
The Day's new lover he has chosen.
The Day's new lover he has chosen."

A terrifying scream rips through the air.

Forsaking the sun that is punishing me, I fly blindly toward the source, not caring if I crash into something. If only I can prevent Icarus from her final collision—

"He called her queen and set her on his throne.
He made her queen and set on her his crown.
The Day's new lover I have become.
The Day's new lover I have become."

I must soar a different direction than last I dreamed, for I find myself under the shade of a cloud suddenly. I can make out what is before me.

Icarus is falling, her hair haloing her wide-eyed face. Her skirts wrap around her legs, and her arms are spread out, as if to help her find balance in her plummet. And she wears her wings. Why is she not flapping them?

Because it's only one wing.

Her gaze collides with mine. She opens her mouth. She says—

"As Day's new lover, I am undone."

I falter out of my vision as my fingers play the last note, a cold sweat matting my curls and making my *chiton* stick to me strangely.

A shrill sound pierces through the night, scattering the resonating echoes of my harp. I set it down and glance at my swans. Two of them have their necks craned in concern. Kyknos is bent into herself, already resting.

Then the sound repeats, clearly a scream now. One that slices me to my heart.

I hurry to the edge of the cliff I selected for my practice, and gaze down at the dead streets of Crete. But not entirely dead, because a woman is awake, and she is alarmed. And is that a bustle of activity in that alley?

Glancing back at my swans, I wonder if I should take my chariot down, or else—

"Unhand the Bride of the Sun!"

Without another thought, I trade my lyre for my bow and quiver. Then I morph into a falcon and dive.

CHAPTER NINETEEN

Icarus

"I'll go out tomorrow morning for the rest of the feathers," I tell Papa before jumping onto my pulley and sliding down the tower.

Once inside, I glance around for Phoebus. He's not in the main room.

I move toward Papa's room and push open the door. He isn't there either.

Frowning, I check my room next. Nothing.

"If you can get them glued on by noon, they should be dry enough to test by sunset," Papa calls.

I quickly close my bedroom door and turn to find Papa ambling in from the staircase.

Moving away from the rooms that do not have our guest, I nod. "That won't be a problem. Ariadne will see her brother off, so I won't have to worry about her."

Papa looks down his nose at me. "And will I have to worry about *you* being distracted by a certain guest of ours?"

Considering that guest is wandering outside the safety of our tower even though the sun is setting outside, that won't be an issue any longer. He either is a betrayal or a disappearance.

I wipe my damp palms on my skirt. "Not at all. I had a stern conversation with him before you arrived. He knows what my goals are and has promised to align with them."

Papa grunts. "See that he does, or else he won't like how *I* ensure his compliance."

Pressing my lips together, I force them upward. I consider mentioning there might not be anything left of Phoebus to threaten if he's outside the castle walls. And if he's meeting someone within the walls, *he* might be our own greatest threat.

Either way, we need to locate him— which means he'll be distracting me this evening. At least there isn't anything else for me to do with the wings until dawn. Well, except rest.

Papa seems to sense my thoughts, because he sags wearily against the wall.

I open my mouth to confess Phoebus' absence, and then close it again. *I* can search for him. Papa requires sleep far more than I do.

He reaches his bedroom and stares into it. Then he turns back to me. "I do not want that boy in your room with you. He is not to be trusted in any way." He gestures toward the dining couch. "Force him onto that when you're ready to retire."

"Yes, Papa. I'll send him there when I've finished my tasks."

Papa studies me for a long moment. I don't even wipe my palms on my skirt this time.

Then he nods and shuffles into his room, only partially closing his door behind him.

I exhale before the tension tightens in my chest. I'm not sure which is worse. The thought that I might have let a traitor into my home and my good opinion . . . Or horror that whatever dark shadow lurks in this land has stolen Phoebus' smile away forever.

Leaving the tower, I check the parts of Knossos he's been to first, keeping to the shadows. But I find neither Phoebus nor a single guard.

My skin prickles with unease, and I hurry to Ariadne's room next. Mayhap she took him there to ensure I will be a maidenly sacrifice?

Before I can knock on her door, though, I'm interrupted by a shout on the other side of the wall.

"I do not trust him!" cries a masculine voice. It's not Phoebus speaking, though, but Orion.

Ariadne grunts. "It's good to know you're not a *complete* fool."

"Trust him or not, I must still obey our father if I ever want to sit on the throne. You know as well as I that he'll happily end his own dynasty by giving Vassilis the crown if I give him the slightest reason."

With a sigh, I back away from the door. Neither would hold that conversation if Phoebus were present.

Turning away, I try to sense the surrounding shadows, like they can somehow communicate with me where my wayward guest is. I am growing more and more convinced that he is no longer within the castle walls.

Which means he's in grave danger.

I move toward a window and peer out into the dusk. There isn't a single movement, as though there is no one and nothing on the streets. But we all know that isn't true. Something is making people vanish. And they'll stop Phoebus if I don't find him first.

A shudder courses through me at the thought of going outside after dark. But I am to be the bridal sacrifice to Apollo. What more can this city do to me?

It has been a very long time since I've been outside after dark, and the few times I was, there were festivities filling the streets. I always remained close to Papa— or if he was working, to Orion and Ariadne.

Tonight, there isn't a soul to be seen. Every clay brick home, square and solid by day, is bolted shut at night. Homes built secure against tempests have become fortresses against whatever lurks here at night.

I want to call out for Phoebus, but I cannot bring myself to utter a noise. I keep the shadows, ready to dive into an alley between homes should something come down the main path. Anything that moves boldly in this stillness is to be feared.

My gut clenches with regret beneath my fear. Because I know I need to go back. I will not find Phoebus this night. Either he will return to us in the morn or we will never see him again, and I'll wonder about his fate.

And if he *is* betraying us, it is best to face that fate in my tower with Papa than out here, where I know not what the outcome will be.

I move to return, but then I uproarious laughter suddenly fills the night, sounding like someone who has consumed too much ale.

Lights come into view farther down the path, and I see several dark forms by the torches they carry. More bawdy laughter emanates from them, followed by haphazard shushing.

Carefully, I slide into the alley next to me, pressing into the shadows. I'm not sure if I'm more frightened of this company of never-do-wells, or what they might summon. But the pounding of my heart threatens to be heard over their raucous laughter.

"Just let them pass," I whisper. I'm not sure whom I'm praying to. Certainly not Apollo. Maybe his sister? Artemis is said to be a protector of maidens.

Except those her brother preys upon, evidently.

I hug my stomach. I should pray to the Unknown God, as Papa taught me. But where is that Unknown God now? An unknown *location*, for sure. At least we know the other gods abide on Mount Olympus.

"I'm not sure what you fools think is so funny," mutters a deep voice from the company. They are close enough that I can see the shadows their torches cast on the house across from me. There must be four at least. "If we don't find a sacrifice, it'll be one of *us* offered to the beast."

"Come now, Asios, there's always *some* drunk fool wandering around."

Another man snorts. "That would be you, Pabaaba."

They must be passing by the house I'm pressed against now.

Remaining flat against the house, I slide deeper into the alley.

Then they pass by, and there are indeed four of them. Their torches illuminate where I just was, but I am now safe from casting a shadow.

Until two of the men step into the alley with their torches, apparently not content with its appearance of vacancy.

I watch in despair as the light finds me, and my shadow betrays me as if they couldn't already see me by the cast of their torches.

The foremost man, who looks nearly as tall as a mast in these ominous shadows and just as thin, leers at me. "Well, well, well, it looks as though we've found a sacrifice after all."

Chapter Twenty

Icarus

"I will return to King Minos of my own volition!" I cry. "Just let me pass, and no trouble will befall us."

The thin man snorts. "King Minos has authorized us to do whatever we want concerning our business."

I slide slowly backward, hoping they won't notice my escape. "What is your business?"

The thin man opens his mouth to answer, but the other man in the alleyway, much shorter and bulkier, punches him in the shoulder. "That's *our* business," he hisses, "and our business alone."

"Well, I have my own business. With King Minos himself." I lift my chin high, bracing myself on the wall.

One of the men standing in the mouth of the alley waves his torch at me. "Is she the Princess?"

The ghastly slim man steps closer to me, the heat of his torch flaring in my face. "No."

"Then her business with King Minos does not outrank ours. Take her and let's be done with this."

While the ghastly slim man is turned toward his companion, I push myself off the wall and launch myself deeper into the alley. If I can only make it to the castle, I'll be safe. I doubt they will pursue me there, and if they do, I know it better than any of them—

Hands grasp my waist before I've even rounded the building across from the one that I hid against. I strain against them, but the arms are stronger than I am, and pull me against a body that feels too thin for its strength. The smells of ale and unwashed male choke me.

"Let me go!" I yell, stomping the man's foot and kicking his shin.

He merely turns me toward his comrades, who are surrounding me.

"I warn you," I hiss threateningly, despite the way my entire body is shaking. "When King Minos finds out you touched me—"

The grim-toned man, Asios, sniffs. "He'll know we were fulfilling our responsibility, honoring the god of the Minoans."

He comes close enough for me to kick his shin. Not that it'll do me any good, but he deserves a good bruise. "You fool, I'm already promised to the god of the sun!"

He just sniffs again. "Why honor the imported mainland gods when we have our own far more primal, powerful force?"

"I'll give you primal force." Summoning every ounce of strength I have and mixing it with pure desperation, I act. I swing both my feet against the legs of the man restraining me, just as I throw my arms out against his.

He releases me, and I collapse into the dirt. But I don't have time to feel pain.

Pushing myself to my feet, I careen around the other men and rush out of the alleyway.

Only for a hand to close around my hair and tug me back, nearly yanking my hair out of my scalp.

I scream for blinding pain, then frustration, then fear, and finally, in a desperate call for help to those bordered inside their fortresses.

So many hands are on me, the men all leering and jeering, except the grim Asios, who silently holds only my hair.

"Such a shame we had to find *her*," the narrow man says. "She's too fair to perish so gruesomely."

I swat away his hand, and then another's.

"Only the best for our god."

There is a sudden whooshing behind me, and I wonder if something has fallen. But I can't even turn my head while trapped in Asios' grip.

Until suddenly, it's gone, along with all the hands. I alone stand in this alleyway, with all the men suddenly flattened to the ground. I should flee while I have a chance. But I sense so strongly that we are no longer the only individuals in this alleyway.

Curiosity convinces my trembling limbs to remain in place for a moment longer. Cautiously, I turn to see why my attackers stumbled to the ground. I almost collapse with them.

A being that can only be my unwanted bridegroom stands before us. Light emanates from him as he looks beyond me to the frightened men, his expression hard. "Who wants to die first?"

I take him in, from his golden curls to his bronzed skin. His beauty radiates like the light he generates, making the torches obsolete. I have never seen Apollo before this moment, but I need no one to tell me that this is him. No other could be so gloriously bright or as breathtakingly beautiful and not be the god of the sun.

He needs no crown when his curls are golden. A bright mantle and a white *chiton* drape over his body. They are obviously meant to protect mortal eyes from being overwhelmed by perfection rather than any genuine need for modesty. Coverings are only needed for the imperfect. And on his back, to remove any shadow of a doubt of his identity as Apollo, is a golden bow that seems to stretch as long as I do.

My knees threaten to give out, and I nearly collapse. Pride saves me from falling on my face, but I still stumble forward, my hands grasping my wayward joints to keep them from betraying me further.

Apollo's gaze moves from searing into the men who attacked me to land on my face. His expression immediately softens. His entire visage becomes more youthful with some of his wrath turned away. "Icarus, are you hurt?"

His voice sounds like music itself, and hearing him utter my name sends me jolting backward. Instead of landing on my knees before him like I almost did, I hit my tailbone hard.

My beautiful bridegroom holds his hand toward me. "Come to me, Icarus."

I stare up at his hand, so many thoughts whirling through my addled mind. Why was I fleeing this being? Why did he pursue me to begin with? How is he here now?

And how do I both want to touch him more than anything in this world, yet long to flee from him to the ends of the earth?

"Icarus." He is so large and untouchably regal. He is almost unbearably beautiful. Yet, he says my name with the tenderness of a caress.

His tone is why I reach toward him, the tips of my fingers sliding over his hand. The warmth of his skin sends a powerful jolt through me, and I would think I'd been smote if it wasn't so pleasant. And I wasn't still breathing.

Instead, I think I've been smitten— a far worse fate.

Then Apollo's hand closes over mine, and I think I stop breathing. He tugs me up as though I weigh nothing. Compared to him, I really must be nothing.

In one graceful move, I am tucked against Apollo's side. From this angle, with me relative to him, he no longer seems like a giant. He is merely a tall and broad man.

But he's not. He's the god— or at least godlike being— forcing me into marriage with him. The monster I must escape, not be melded into, so that there is no separation between us where I am tucked into his side. I cannot even pull if my trembling body allowed me to, with his right arm wrapped around my waist, his hand splayed over my stomach.

At this moment, he is both my support and my captor.

"Icarus," Apollo says, drawing my gaze up his broad chest barely covered by his raiment, past the curve of his shoulder, over the slope of his neck, and above the point of his jaw—

My gaze locks with his, and I am not sure I will ever regain my breath. My soul will merely part ways my body and fly up to the heavens, which are found in the infinite blueness of his eyes.

Yet, that is not the first time I have seen that color in a pair of eyes

"Look away," Apollo whispers. "You need not witness my wrath."

The men I had forgotten about until now cry out, some cursing and others begging for their lives. I do not hear Asios' voice at all.

"Wait, what?" I tear my gaze away from Apollo's intoxicating eyes to the men lying prostrate before us. There are only three in their number now.

"These vermin dared to lay their foul hands on the future goddess of the sun." Apollo takes the bow from over his shoulder and draws an arrow from a golden quiver, all without releasing me.

The thin man looks very much like a worm the way he writhes in penitence, his face on the ground. "We were just vermin carrying out the word of our King."

"Your King promised this woman to me." Using the hand of the arm wrapped around me, Apollo notches his arrow. "You should have been more careful to obey his *every* command."

The menace in Apollo's tone jolts through my mind, and I finally register the carnage about to occur here.

Not quite knowing what I'm doing, I place a hand on Apollo's firm forearm. "Please don't."

His gaze flicks back to mine, confusion written across his expression. It is such a human trait that I'm almost as startled by that as the return of his beautiful eyes in my line of sight. "You want mercy for these learned fools, these *morosophs?*"

"Y-yes?" I glance at them, and no longer see the men who were holding me hostage, trying to take me where I didn't want to go and touching me when I gave no permission. I just see fellow mortals as terrified as I was mere moments ago— by their hand.

Apollo doesn't spare them a glance as he scrutinizes me. Then he turns and frowns toward where my wayward hand still rests on his forearm.

I quickly pull away and see splatters of blood marring his skin. For a moment, I stare in confusion, because I am certain that I did not see blood there before to mar his perfection.

My bridegroom sets his bow down and then takes hold of my wrist. He flips my hand over so that it's palm up. His glowing skin reveals the way my own skin there is torn to shreds, blood dripping from my fingers and palm in multiple places.

It takes several moments more of staring to finally register the pain. I hiss in surprise. This must have been the consequences of my escape attempt.

Apollo's perfect face twists into rage. The innocence of youth seems to melt before his wrath, leaving only cruel beauty.

Suddenly, Apollo twists me around and pulls me close, my right side against him now. I stare over his shoulder at the darkness of the deeper alleyway.

His arm holding me in place moves like it's drawing something back. Then there is a release of pressure, a whizzing in the air, a *plunk*, and cries of horror.

"What are you doing?!" I strain to pull away, but his grip on me tightens. Not enough to prevent the release of another arrow. "Stop it! They are sons of Crete!"

"They are sons of Tartarus now."

I try to turn my head, but Apollo reaches up and gently turns my away again. Then he reaches for the last arrow in his quiver. Frantically, I tug one hand free and snatch it away from him.

Undeterred, he reaches for another arrow that appears in the quiver by some great magic. It whizzes through the air, and then the screams are silenced.

"What have you done?!" I cry, wrenching away.

He releases me, and I nearly topple backward. But Apollo reaches down and wraps his arms before I can collide with the ground again.

"I avenged you, my dear." Apollo swoops me up completely, one arm behind my legs and the other wrapped behind my shoulders. "And now I shall heal you."

Chapter Twenty-One

Apollo

I carus squirms in my grip, and I do my best to keep her angled away from the carnage of my wrath. My wrath still burns that they dared touch her. That they dared draw her blood and screams.

"Where are you taking me?!" she yells, and there are tears mixing with the rage in her voice. "It's not the Summer Solstice yet!"

"I'm not taking you as my bride," I assure, doing my best to gentle my voice for her. "*Yet*. But I need to heal you." I am certain I already said that, but I have learned that mortals are not very good listeners.

Adjusting her in my arms, I lift her enough so she can see I'm carrying her toward the stone temple. It's on a small mount at the edge of the village opposite the far more sprawling palace. In contrast to the careful clay construction of Knossos, the temple looks more like a cave perched on the cliff, made by nature rather than man.

My words do not seem to calm Icarus' fears, because she twists in my arms more violently. She leaves bloody handprints everywhere she touches.

"I'm not going to hurt you." I pull her higher against my chest and try to nestle her against me as I keep walking so I can look her in my eyes. She seems to calm whenever I truly look at her. Does she recognize Phoebus' eyes? It is the part of me I can't alter, even when I've slightly morphed the other features I share with my mortal form.

Just as I hoped, Icarus ceases wriggling against me, stilling enough for me to not fear for her doing something foolhardy. I climb the stairs hewn out of the hill for the temple. For a moment, she just stares at me. Then she turns away, and I keep ascending.

Icarus doesn't speak, which alarms me as much as her writhing did. I glance down at her as I leave the last step.

There are silent tears sliding down her face, glimmering in my glow.

My heart wrenches at the sight, and I hurry between the stone archway of the temple. No priests or priestesses are around, and all the devout believers must be abed. There is only Icarus and me.

I hurry toward a stone slab that isn't laden with food like the altars designed for burnt offerings. Gently, I lay Icarus out on it.

She quickly sits up and turns away from me. Then Icarus swings her legs over the side as if to jump off.

Lurching, I grasp her shoulders and draw her back.

Icarus tries to tug away from me. "Stop touching me!"

I pull back. "I'll only touch you to heal you, sunshine. Your hand—"

Her gaze takes in just how stained I am by her blood. Icarus sways at the sight of it and then begins to fall backward.

Reaching again, I clutch her arms before she can hit her head on the altar or the ground. Then, holding her steady there, I take her injured hand and turn it palm-up. I trace my finger lightly over her raw skin.

She hisses and tries to pull away, but I think it's more reflex than absolute disgust with me.

"I can heal you," I say. "It's a gift of mine. Except for injuries that lead to death, which can only be healed by a Kiss, I can restore you to full health. If you let me."

Icarus purses her lips, but she doesn't pull away. "'Kiss'?"

"That is how I will gift you a share of my immortality by entwining our fates and souls."

She tries to pull her wrist free.

I sigh. "After we are wed; not now. In order to make you Awoken, a Kiss must be freely given and freely received."

"Oh, really?" Icarus wrist goes limp in my hold, and she snorts. "That will be a first for you, I'm sure." Then her gaze falls onto the ring I gave her as Phoebus. Her eyes widen, and then she turns to the temple entrance.

I follow her gaze but find nothing. When I turn back, my ring is off her hand. Is she trying to conceal me . . . from myself?

Clearing my throat, I direct my attention back to Icarus' raw hand. "It will be my first Kiss." I hold it firm with the hand wrapped around her waist as I use my other to circle it, letting my connection to the sun generate a healing warmth.

My sister has made many Awoken huntresses, but as of yet, I simply have not felt the need to make even my oracles Awoken. They are happy with their mortal lives, even though I'll miss them when time steals them away.

A strangled laugh comes from Icarus' lips, distracting me from my work. There is a dark glint to her gaze, like the rays of sun piercing through thunderous clouds still storming. "I meant you giving me a choice. But I am also trying to understand how you could exist for eons and never have kissed before. No wonder you're so desperate."

I quickly turn my gaze back to her hand and resume my work. I see signs of her flesh knitting back together. "A Primordial Kiss differs from what you mortals call 'kissing'. I have certainly pressed my lips to flesh in the mortal habit."

Icarus chokes on more laughter, and if it weren't for my grip on her, I think she'd tumble off the altar. "I am *very* convinced."

"You don't believe me?" I demand, my indignation mixing with relief to hear her laughter again. Even if it's not as mirthful as it ought to be, and exists at my expense.

Now is certainly the wrong time to point out that my prior kisses were gifted to her sweet knuckles.

"I might understand your methods of marriage now," Icarus adds.

I glance down at her hand that is almost completely whole now and then back up to her. "You do?" Understanding is the first step to acceptance, is it not?

"You obviously were unable to woo a woman with your own wiles, so why not demand a sacrificial wife?"

Not sure if I've ever been so insulted in my life, I barely resist pulling away from her.

But Icarus' dark laughter filling the temple is somehow the sweetest offering ever made here despite its bitterness.

When I glance down at her hand, it is now completely healed. So, keeping one arm around her waist, I use my now free hand to draw her palm up to my lips. Then I press one of those kisses she thinks I've never shared onto her skin.

Startled, Icarus halts mid-laugh. She turns her confused gaze to me.

Maintaining eye contact, I gift her another kiss and then another, walking my lips down her palm.

Icarus stares at me in utter bewilderment. I don't think she's even breathing. I have to kiss her pulse on her wrist to ensure she's still with me and not with Hades.

Finally, she closes her gaping mouth, purses her lips downward, and then yanks her hand away from me. She rubs it on the front of her dress, as if to cleanse herself of my touch. Then Icarus glances down at my handiwork for a moment before turning her glare to me. "I'm not your property you can do with whatever you please."

"I didn't say you were."

"You didn't have to." She yanks my arm from around her waist and slides off the altar on the opposite side of me. It becomes a stone wall between us as she grips it and glares at me. "You demanded me for your sacrifice. Toted me around like property. Touched me like— like you had a right to!" Icarus throws her hands into the air.

"I am sorry. I will be gentler in the future. And you needn't fear." I grip the stone altar between us. "Even after we are wed, I will not force my *repulsive* touch upon you. You will receive only the caresses you desire and demand. Your life will still be yours to direct."

She stills for a moment, confusion seeming to strike her mute. Then something dark passes over Icarus' expression. "You say that now, but only moments ago you didn't listen to me. You . . ." Her voice breaks. "You slaughtered those men in my name."

I gesture to her, blood still staining my tunic. "They paid in their blood for what they tried to take from you, my sunshine."

"I didn't want that." She closes her eyes and folds into the rock, suddenly seeming so small when she had been so tall and defiant a moment ago. "I don't want to hear their screams when I sleep at night."

"Soon, I'll be with you by night. I'll protect you from those dreams."

Icarus jumps backward, her eyes open and glaring at me again. "You *are* my nightmare!"

I step back, startled by her audacity. Then I want to step toward her, to remind her of our dance, the swans, the workshop, and all the moments we already shared. But she doesn't know it was me. When she does know, will they soften her view of me— or will I taint those memories, too?

"And you say that your Kiss can only be granted if I accept it?"
"Yes."

Icarus stretches herself to her full height, which still seems so small when I am in Primordial form. "Then I shall never take it. Never become 'Awoken.' What happens then?"

I stare at her in horror. "You . . . remain completely mortal. There will be places I can go that you cannot follow. And someday, someday—"

"I'll go to the one place *you* cannot follow?" Icarus crosses her arms and leans back, a dark smile stretching her lips. "The Underworld will be my escape? In that case, even Tartarus will feel like relief."

Unable to speak, I just stare at her, my mind trying to sort her words in a way that might make them not so painful.

"Because I don't belong to you!" Icarus yells so loudly, I wouldn't be surprised if half of Crete awakens. She stands at the edge of the temple, looking ready to flee under the arch. "I'm not yours to touch or to protect. I'm certainly not yours to kill for." She points angrily at me. "And I am not yours simply because you have decided it to be so."

With that, Icarus turns and flees into the night.

The night was never my domain.

CHAPTER TWENTY-TWO

Icarus

I 'm surprised Apollo doesn't follow me to either smite me or else escort me back to the castle before he can whisk me away forever. But I suppose he considers me safe enough to wander where I please.

After all, if I scream, he'll just kill everyone in the vicinity.

I've only just reached the base of the hill the Caves of the Wind is on when I cannot bear it any longer. The many horrific layers of tonight crash down on me like so many ocean waves.

My knees give out beneath me, and I crash onto the grass. I press the palm of my newly healed hand— with its ghost pain and strange tingling— against my mouth to muffle the wail that wants to pour out of my soul.

If there was some part of my soul that hoped Apollo would have mercy on Crete when I was not presented to him, there is now an arrow through it. Even if the god of the sun is supposed to be more generous to humans than so many other members of the pantheon, he's still a god. To them, we are nothing but playthings and pawns.

Can I truly leave Ariadne to Apollo's wrath? We haven't time to make her another pair of wings. Maybe she will try to sneak aboard Orion's ship. Then I will only have to concern myself with the nameless innocents I leave to Apollo's wrath.

And can we truly escape him? My scream summoned him in the dead of night. Are we just fooling ourselves, thinking we can flee from him across the sea? The sun still shines in Greece.

Would he slaughter Papa and Phoebus when he found us? The sound of Apollo's arrows whizzing still echoes in my head. I certainly know he's capable of such ruthlessness.

The thought of losing Papa draws tears to my eyes once again. Once I start crying, I can never seem to stop.

And what of Phoebus? Has he even survived tonight? At least by the sound of it, the men Apollo killed didn't find him for whatever dark sacrifice they intended me for. Mayhap one good thing about that tragedy is that now Phoebus is safe. Unless there is yet another threat prowling Crete, preying on the vulnerable . . .

I need to push myself up. Make myself return to my tower. I need sleep if I'm to do all that I promised Papa I would. Even if I'm no longer sure I can follow through.

But I cannot make any decisions now, not when I've received only horror without slumber this night.

Instead of rising, though, I curl into myself. My body trembles, and I do not know if it's for fear or for chill. I wasn't cold when Apollo held me. He was warmth and light, and it would have been so easy to lose myself to his embrace. I could have just let him be strong for me forever.

But then I would never be free again.

That terrifies me most of all. If I broke Papa's heart and surrendered myself for the sake of Crete . . . I would lose not only my freedom. I would lose my very identity, along with my desire to be free.

What I said to Apollo is true for the moment. I will never willingly take his Kiss. I will not surrender my heart to him after he's already seized my life.

But what I saw of him tonight . . . There was a gentleness about him, like the warmth of a summer day, that could make me forget the ferocity of his fury. Witnessing his beauty has all but ruined me of the thought of taking on a mortal lover. And his touch . . .

If I sacrificed myself to Apollo, I would fight to protect my humanity and my virtue. But how long would I survive before succumbing to sweet surrender? I have always wanted knowledge and freedom. But if so much of my freedom is already taken from me, would I really cling to the last vestiges of it . . . Or would I sacrifice the reminders of what I'd lost in return for the knowledge of what it is to be ravished by such a being as Apollo?

My will is strong, but is my pride enough to prevent me from becoming a slave to the whims of a man, a male, or whatever Apollo may be referred to? Or will my hubris betray me to passion? Will it force me to surrender pieces of my soul in return for the hope of the continued favor of the one I'm no longer able to live without?

Minos would sacrifice me to keep the sun shining. Would I do the same to keep *Apollo* shining on *me*?

"If you surrender to the Unknown God, you need not surrender to any other."

Still trembling, I slowly push myself up. Lying here with my thoughts circling in my head is doing me no good. Neither is searching for Phoebus or fleeing from Apollo. I will do only what I know I must do, what I said I would.

I glance back at the Caves of the Wind. It is so odd that Apollo took me there when there is a newer temple made of marble with graceful ionic columns on the other edge of the island that seems like it would be more to Apollo's taste. Though, that one focuses more on Dionysus than the rest of those who sit in Olympus and think of how to make mortal lives chaos.

Not that it matters which temple Apollo prefers. What matters now is my next steps, not evaluating *his* decisions.

Trying not to tremble, I slide Phoebus' ring back onto my finger, grateful Apollo didn't ask about it.

That done, I know my next step will be to return home and rest. And then I will wake with the dawn to collect feathers. Decisions can be made beyond that. I will roll the lots and see where they fall. That is all I can do.

That, and keep pretending that I'm still free even now.

Chapter
Twenty-Three

Apollo

"I don't think flowers are going to work."

Artemis quirks a silver eyebrow at me as she parks her chariot next to mine. "You also have a song, don't you?"

After the events of the evening, my melody seems to have become just as frightened of me as Icarus is and fled deeper in my psyche than I can access. I don't even have the heart to tell Artemis that I visited the burial place of our father last night in Anemospilia— or the Cave of Winds as the mortals call it.

Raking my hand through my curls, I pace in front of my own chariot. The sun is already shining down on us since I needed to do something before I went mad.

Every time I close my eyes, I see the rage in Icarus' face as she swears to die just to spite me.

"Artemis, she doesn't just fear me— she hates me!"

My sister stares at me blandly. "What else can she do? You possess greater power than she does, so the only control she has in this forced relationship is how she feels about it and you."

"I don't want to take her control." I claw my hand down my face. "I just want her to be happy."

Artemis shrugs one shoulder as she strides past me. "Then make her happy. Not against her will, but *within* it."

"How?!"

"By finding out what she likes— what she longs for most of all— and then showing her that she can have that *along* with you. That you're not here to prevent her from chasing her dreams or to limit her to your aspirations alone."

I slowly let my hands drop to my sides. "And to do that, I need to—"

Artemis throws her arms into the air. "Talk to her, you big *morosoph*!" She spins on her heels to return to her chariot and untether the moon, muttering something about celibacy being so much simpler.

For a moment, I just stand there, as awkward as if I were in my full mortal form.

She takes pity on me, or else is sick of my presence, because Artemis looks over her shoulder at me, her black eyes sparkling. "Talking to her would be easier to do if you went to the beach, where I spotted a particular maiden pacing the sands."

"How do you know if she's *my* particular maiden? I haven't exactly made introductions."

Artemis snorts as she tosses the moon's tethers aside. "I make it my business to know. Now, I'm off to witness the launch of what promises to be an intriguing hunt from a young Cretan hero— that Orion fellow we watched before."

I wince. I liked him a lot more when he was fighting for his life against a chimera and not catching Icarus' eye.

"Mayhap he'll even survive this quest to kill a manticore. He certainly seems hardy enough, even if he appears to be devoid of all cunning." She steps into her chariot and grasps her reins. "We can't *all* be women, after all."

With that, she's off, swift as the evening breeze. And I glance toward the Minoan shoreline, though it's not visible from Olympus.

"I guess it's off for a hunt of my own." I turn to my chariot and then pause. "Pursuit? Suit? Whatever the mortals call it these days."

I climb into my chariot and follow the same path my sister took.

This time, I decide not to dismount over water.

I jump onto a rock ledge and then climb down.

Just as my sandals touch the beach, Icarus comes around the cliff that forces this alcove on the beach.

Her hair is wound tightly around her head, revealing how wan her face has become. Dark circles highlight her eyes, and her lips are tilted downward. From her expression, one would think each step she takes draws her closer to her execution. But they actually take her closer to me.

"Hello," I whisper.

A basket slips out of her fingers, and several feathers flutter to the sand. "Phoebus!" Icarus charges toward me with new speed, throwing her hands around my neck.

Startled, I wrap my arms around her waist to steady her as her scent of irises and parchments envelops me along with the salty sea breeze.

"I thought you were lost forever," she murmurs against my neck as she holds me tightly, letting her soft body relax against me. "I went searching for you, but—"

She was walking the streets of Crete at night . . . for me?

Ancients curse it all; none of this had to have happened. Once again, I have brought only horror into her life.

As if she can sense my thoughts, Icarus suddenly releases me and steps out of my hold. She narrows her eyes. "Where *were* you last night?"

The distrust in her eyes tells me Phoebes is only a little higher in her esteem than Apollo at the moment. Telling her who I truly am now will only lead to her hating all aspects of me. "I was . . . composing a song."

Her eyebrows climb her temple. "You were . . . composing a song?"

"Er, yes." I have never been more uncomfortable in my long life than I am now. I take my golden lyre from where I've secured it to the belt of my *chiton* and hold it up as an explanation. "For you." Too late I realize she might question how I came into possession of my prized instrument.

But Icarus just gapes at me. "You disappeared last night . . . to compose a song . . . for *me?*"

Once again, it becomes my dearest wish not to draw attention to my hands that seem to be too large for my body. At least so it seems compared to how dainty Icarus' fingers are. "Indeed. Would you like me to play for you?"

She stares at me unblinking for a moment longer before shaking herself out of her daze. "Mayhap later. First, I need to collect those." Icarus gestures up the rocky ledges and the various nests scattered across them.

"Oh." I slide my harp back onto my belt. "I see."

"Don't be so forlorn. I would love to hear it. But I gave my word." I startle. "You bargained?"

Icarus once again glances at me like she suspects me of madness. "No, I didn't agree to do something for something else in return. I merely said I would do something, and that is why I must now do it."

"Or else your life is forfeit?" Horror grips me. I did not think the mortals had anything like the Primordial inability to break a bargain without perishing.

"No." Icarus seems halfway convinced of my madness now as she wrinkles her nose. "It just would be wrong to tell Papa I would do something and then not do it." She turns to where she dropped her basket of feathers, carefully places what she's collected back into it, and then holds it out to me. "Would you mind guarding this while I collect my harvest?"

I take it from her before turning to study the rocky ledge. Then I glance back at her. She's wearing not a *peplos* today, but a *chiton* like mine, skimming her knees. How I did not notice that more of her legs were on display until now, I know not. "How are you going to ascend those ledges? You have not your wings, and they climb almost to the heavens."

Or at least high enough that a fall from them would seriously damage a frail mortal body— if not demolish it.

The vision that keeps haunting me flashes in my mind's eye and the sound of her bones shattering echoes in my ears.

Thankfully, Icarus still stands whole and well before me. She also seems completely unconcerned as she slips off her sandals and walks toward the ledge. "I am perfectly capable of climbing."

I feel uncomfortable warmth on the back of my neck and the palms of my hands. I didn't know that warmth could be uncomfortable, or that it could cause a dampness. But I know enough of the panic lacing through my soul. It's the same sensation I get when I sense the tragedy of a vision will soon unfold in reality.

Icarus was wearing her wings— well, *one* wing— in that vision. But a fall is a fall—

Hurrying toward her, I hand her back her basket. "Here, allow me."

"I can't ask that of you—"

I cup her precious face and let one finger caress her jawline. She is soft and warm, alive and unbroken.

And so she must remain.

"You're not asking," I counter. "*I* am. I won't let you fall."

"I wasn't planning on falling." There is no fight in Icarus' voice though— for once— as she leans into my touch.

"It isn't my plan for you either." I step away from her. Then I slip off my sandals, set my harp next to them, and move toward the ledges. "But let us not test the Fates."

"What about you? If I fell, you might be able to catch me. If you fell, I'm not sure I could catch *you*."

The thought of Icarus' tiny form trying to uphold my bulky mortal frame makes me laugh. I shake my head. "That won't be necessary, my muse. I shall concern myself with catching you, but that works best by preventing you from falling." I grasp the first stone ledge and pull myself up.

"'My muse'?"

Both my feet are now on the cold stone of the ledge that is the opposite of the sand I was just standing on. I grip the next ledge, careful to avoid the bird droppings staining it, and hoist myself onto that one before glancing down at Icarus.

She has her arms crossed and is craning her face toward me. Her lips are pursed like she wants to scold me, but the sparkle in her eyes prohibits her.

I wink at her. "Well, I did compose a song in your honor." The next ledge is the first with a nest, and I have to use both hands and feet to climb to it. How she's made this climb before, I cannot even imagine.

"What if Apollo overheard you, though? Don't you realize how dangerous such an act might be?"

My foot slips, and I almost tumble. But my elbows bite into the next ledge, and I hoist myself up. Then, pretending that didn't just happen, I perch on the edge and smile boldly down at Icarus as I pluck the feathers out of the nest. "I'm not frightened of him."

The sparkle in Icarus' gaze fades completely. "You should be." Her tone is hollow, and I can almost see the memories of last night flash across her face.

Mayhap I should have granted those monsters mercy— for the moment. I could have returned and slaughtered them later. Except, if I had agreed to show mercy for her sake and gone back on it, would that not be going back on my word even if I didn't vow it? That seems to be something else Icarus does not find acceptable.

"You know Apollo has claimed me," Icarus adds. "And he is the god of music as well as the sun. He would take great offense if he knew what you were doing last night."

I know Icarus certainly took offense.

Not sure what else to do with my handful of feathers, I stuff them down the front of my tunic. Hopefully, I tied my belt tightly enough to keep them from fluttering away.

Ignoring the way they irritate my pathetically mortal skin, I climb to the next ledge. "Not to worry, my sweet muse. I would happily enter a musical contest with Apollo to win your hand."

"My hand is not for sale."

"Back," I quickly add. "Win your hand *back*. For you to give to whomever you please."

Though I am at a considerable height now, I still catch Icarus' smile before she ducks her head.

I'm not sure what feels more like soaring— making the sun rise or brightening Icarus' face. I fully intend to do both for the rest of eternity.

I just need to figure out how to claim what the Creator promised to me in a vision.

Chapter Twenty-Four

Icarus

I watch breathlessly as Phoebus continues to stuff his *chiton* with feathers until he reaches the top of the cliff. But I don't dare speak to him until he's safely descended for fear of making him lose concentration.

Once his feet are back on the sand, I hurry to Phoebus' side. "Thank Olympus you didn't fall."

He shrugs confidently. "I wasn't concerned."

"Your constant lack of worry is not a highlight of wisdom."

Phoebus grins. "You just hoped that I would fall so you could catch me as an excuse to hold me in your arms."

My face warms. "Phoebus—"

His grin widens. Then he sneezes violently.

I dive to the side, half startled by the force of it and half relieved he didn't sneeze while climbing.

Phoebus stares at the sand he just sneezed on before glancing up at me. "What under the Firmament was that?"

Confused by his confusion, I stare back at him. "Mayhap you have an allergy to feathers?"

He stares at me blankly for a moment before nodding. "Yes, that must be it." Clearing his throat, Phoebus straightens his back and reapplies his smug grin. "Come now; let me present you the great bounty I have gathered for you."

With that, he slips off one sleeve and then the other. I watch in frozen anticipation as he lowers the top of his *chiton* down to his waist. The feathers remain pillowed inside, the ends of his garment held up enough to protect them from the breeze. I can practically feel the pride beaming off him to be presenting so many feathers to me. There are certainly enough to finish my wings.

But I barely see them as I stare at the uninterrupted glory of his broad chest and well-muscled torso.

"Icarus?"

I stumble backward and drag my gaze to the feathers. I should look up at him, but I can't make myself meet his eyes just now. "I-I'm sorry. That was really hypocritical of me."

"Hypocritical?"

It feels like one of those feathers is lodged in my throat. I try to clear it out. "Nothing."

"It can't possibly be that you were *gawking* at me, could it?" I hear the grin in his voice.

My fingers nearly release their hold on my basket. To distract myself from my fluster, I scoop feathers out of his *chiton* and stuff them in with the others.

For some reason, he doesn't offer any assistance. He just watches me work, silently chuckling. Too late, I realize my fingers and knuckles keep brushing against his bronze skin as I move quickly to complete my task.

At least now there are more feathers in my basket than in his garment, so I try to focus on that rather than my mortification. Unfortunately, my fingers have become extremely stiff and difficult to maneuver since I became so self-aware. They keep brushing against Phoebus' smooth skin as they seek the remaining feathers.

I once again clear my throat. Did I somehow inhale two feathers? "So, what is Elis like? I hear it's quite beautiful." One particularly stubborn feather tries to slide below Phoebus' belt. Desperation to save it from that fate has my hand gliding over his many-tiered abdomen to rescue it. I recoil the moment I can, but the touch of his skin still seems to burn my flesh— in the most distractingly pleasant way possible.

"Oh, we're doing small talk now?" Phoebus' grin widens. "Is that how you resist temptation?"

I scrunch my shoulders up to my ears in an attempt to hide. Then I circle him to claim the feathers on his back.

As I round his side, he leans toward my ear. "Remember, even if I can't see you gawking, it still counts." His warm breath blowing my escaping curls away from my neck somehow makes me shudder.

"It's not even a temptation," I lie through my teeth.

The distracting oaf just grins at the ocean. "If it eases your conscience any, I don't mind." He glances over his shoulder, and I drop my gaze to those last two feathers. "You may gawk at me whenever you please."

"Well, *I* don't please." I claim the feathers. Then, just to be difficult, I draw them up across the sensitive skin of his back before placing them in my nearly overflowing basket.

"Are you ready to hear my song now?" Phoebus turns to face me again in all his half-dressed glory.

"After these are secured." I hold up the basket and avoid glancing at him at all. "The glue needs time to dry before I can test it. And it has to be done today because—"

Because tomorrow is the Summer Solstice.

Now there is dread clogging my throat along with the feathers. "Because Ariadne is seeing off her brother, and then she'll excuse herself for the day to properly wallow in her melancholy. So today is all I have."

Phoebus nods solemnly. "Then let us do this." He turns to walk up the beach.

I stop him by planting a hand on his chest. Then I quickly yank that offending limb back.

He glances down at me with a raised eyebrow.

Why am I behaving like this? I have seen countless men bare-chested, including the beautiful Orion. Why am I behaving any differently around Phoebus?

Maybe because Orion never flirted with me about it. "You should . . . dress yourself first. We don't want to draw any undue attention to ourselves."

"Yes, of course." His mouth spreads in a downright wicked grin. "Wouldn't want that at *all.*" Mercifully, he tugs on his sleeves so that his *chiton* is properly in place. Not so mercifully, he leans toward me, close enough that I can't escape the scent of leather, sea, and air that seems stronger now than when I was alone on this beach. "I'll do my very best not to distract you until *after* your wings are feathered."

I'm not sure if that is a threat or a promise, or which I'd rather it be. So instead of dissecting those husky words, I spin on my heels and hurry back up the beach.

Phoebus is a man of his word, and he does not provide any undue distraction as we meticulously glue and secure the feathers into place.

At least, he doesn't bare his skin or murmur in my ear while we work. He is still distracting just by existing beside me. His warm, firm presence is a little too near because of the shared work. Every time he speaks to ask for instructions, it sends a bolt of awareness through me. And Phoebus' nimble hands help me secure the feathers in half the time.

Once the last feather is secured and Papa's glue is almost spent, I step back and look at our work. I believe this is the finest incarnation these wings have experienced. The white wings reflect the sunlight, and thanks to Phoebus' help, they are fuller than ever before. Full enough to take me all the way to Greece?

I mull this over as I secure the hemp cover over them to protect them from the rain I smell in the sky. The glue is far from waterproof even after drying.

Hopefully, we do not encounter a storm flying. And will Papa's wings be durable enough? He's not here to smooth away my concerns, since King Minos expects him to labor even while half of Crete is at the docks celebrating Orion's departure for his quest. Well, except for Ariadne, who is there lamenting it.

None of Crete will be celebrating soon. Oh, and then there's—

I whirl around to face Phoebus. "We don't have a third pair of wings! And you don't have a ship any longer—"

Phoebus takes both my calloused hands into his, the traces of glue left on them threatening to bind us forever. "I will be well. As will you and your father. There is no need to worry."

"That sounds like something you would say."

"Only because it's true." He grants me a gentle smile, warm as the sun after a cool breeze. Then he tries to tug one hand free. It takes several attempts and elicits more than a few giggles from me, before I have one hand free.

I'm full-out laughing now as I shake out my free limb that feels like it's lost a layer of callouses.

Phoebus chuckles and doesn't look away from me, as if he wants to memorize my features now. As though the moment he can, he's going to create a sculpture or a fresco and name it "Icarus Delighted."

Suddenly self-conscious, I drop my gaze to the hand still captured by his and bound by both glue and desire.

Instead of pulling free, Phoebus tightens his grip. "Now that my vow is fulfilled, where should I play for you?"

"The beach." My words come out breathless, as though I've run down to the dock to give Orion one last farewell and hold Ariadne steady against her sorrow and her rage.

Phoebus nods. Then, using our joined hands, he leads me away from my wings and ever downward.

Where we both nearly tumble into the servant waiting for us, her face one of complete pity. Another woman stands behind, her gaze downcast, but still seething with jealousy. Cubits of the finest blue and gold linen drapes from her arms.

I stop short at this terrible reminder of what my future holds for me if I don't change course.

The seamstress steps forward, the compassion shining in her eyes brighter than the stones hanging from her ears, neck, and wrists. "Chosen of the gods, it is time for your fitting."

Chapter
Twenty-Five

Icarus

I banish my "cousin" to Papa's room and lead the two women into my own chambers. There, I subject myself to the *nymphokomos'* control. As King Minos has decreed, my body is no longer something that belongs to me but exists for her to layer materials over.

Clothes fittings were once something I'd never heard of. They certainly aren't done in Greece. Of course, there, one simply folds a cloth the right way and one is wearing garments. But the Minoans require shape for their ensembles in order to frame the body they love so much. And that requires fittings and *nymphokomos* and needles narrowly missing parts of me I'd like to keep.

A pleated golden skirt is secured around my waist. Then a longer blue skirt is placed over that, this ruffled and bearing a large slit down the front to expose the golden skirt. Over that is placed another blue skirt, longer than the first two and carefully embroidered with gold along the ruffled hem.

I stare straight ahead, pretending to be a statue, not a sacrificial lamb being dressed for the slaughter. The *nymphokomos* is the only one to touch me or even look at me. Her gaze is somehow both focused and distant, like she is also pretending the task she's completing isn't something I've had no choice in. The other servant girl doesn't even look at me. She stares hard at the ground, moving only when asked to offer a layer or a tool to the *nymphokomos*.

Next comes my sleeved corset, the reason I prefer Greek styles. The one time I wore it, I did not like the way it pressed against my chest, augmenting it upward. Nor did I like the way all the ways it *didn't* cover me.

The *nymphokomos* doesn't require me to remove my *perizoma*, so I obey her silent command to loosen my *stróphion*. Then I help her slide the blue corset on.

For being so much smaller than me in every other way, Ariadne's bust is larger. So, this handwoven corset grants me some precarious covering in its looseness even after it is fastened as tightly as possible.

Despite this small mercy, and combined with the lacing, panic threads through me. If I go through with the wedding for the sake of these two women and the rest of Crete, how can I wear this? I know that any notion of Apollo respecting my person is a fantasy. My resisting his advances is likely even more mythological. Yet I still had some desperate hope that I could keep my dignity before mortals, at least.

The thought of Vassilis seeing my chest with none of the layers he's tried to stare through makes me feel ill. Nor should King Minos see any part of me after he has reduced me to a product with which to barter. And the thought of Papa, already heartbroken that I didn't escape with him, seeing me adorned yet humiliated . . .

"The Princess also requested this."

I'm startled to hear the *nymphokomos'* voice after we've spent so much time in silence. But then she holds up a lacy golden breast cloth.

I smile at her consideration. Then I let her fasten the laces around my neck so that the cloth falls over my chest, granting it a bit more coverage.

"Now for your accessories." She takes a golden belt with blue stones sewn onto it from her assistant's hands and secures it around my waist. Then she brings a pair of gold and blue beaded sandals forward. "Not to worry— they fashioned these only for you after the announcement was made."

Thanks to that assurance, I slip my feet comfortably into the sandals and let her lace them up my ankles.

As I admire the colors of the outfit swirling around me, the *nymphokomos* presents me with a small, ornate cedar box. "Your bride gift from King Minos. Jewelry with which to adorn yourself for your bridegroom." Her lips tick downward. "But we do not need to size those. In fact . . ." The *nymphokomos* steps back to admire her handiwork. "I do not think you need any further fittings. That is, if you're comfortable?"

With what this ensemble represents? Never. But the garment itself fits as well as it can for being Minoan cut. And it is something I could feel comfortable in, despite its symbolism.

The *nymphokomos* nods at her servant, who takes that as a signal to depart from my bedroom. Then the *nymphokomos* turns back to me. "Are you *comfortable*, my Lady, Bride of the Sun?"

I look into her eyes for the first time. The pity is still there, along with . . . reverence. "If there is anything I can do to make this . . . transition easier for you. Any ointments or perfumes you would like to accompany you on your journey to the heavens?"

She's not offering me escape like Papa, or deliverance, like Orion. She is offering all that a woman in her station can give a woman in my position. Compassion and respect.

Those feathers are back in my throat, making it hard to swallow. "It's suitable, thank you."

"It's far more than suitable."

At Phoebus' voice, I turn to find him standing in the doorway to my bedroom the *nymphokomos'* servant must have left open with her departure.

He stands there, looking absolutely mesmerized. Phoebus reaches out to grasp the doorpost for support but misses it and nearly topples over before he quickly rights himself.

The *nymphokomos* disregards him and bows toward me. "May you retain the favor of the sun."

With that, she turns and strides out of my chambers, leaving me with these voluminous layers and a dumbstruck Phoebus.

He fidgets, and then I realize that there is something in his hands, a wreathe made of greenery. Not just any leaves, though— laurel leaves.

Phoebus follows my gaze and seems to startle at what he's holding. Then, sheepishly, he steps toward me. "I heard that women like flowers, but you seem to like these especially, even though you always smell like irises."

"You've noticed what I *smell* like?"

Color rushes to Phoebus' face and he pats his cheek, looking confused by his flush. Then he moves closer. "That is, they seem like such a simple adornment compared to your bridal splendor, but mayhap you'll wear it . . . for luck?"

"Olympus knows I need all the luck I can get." Then, since Phoebus still seems rather incapacitated in my presence, I close the remaining distance between us and bow my head.

"My Queen," he announces as he crowns me. It sounds half jested and half like the most solemn thing he's ever spoken.

When I lift my gaze, the wreath tilting awkwardly on my temple, I catch his gaze. There is an intensity burning there hotter than the sun.

"Icarus . . ." He leans toward me.

Is he . . . going to kiss me?

Horror slices through me at the thought. The panic that always comes upon me when I sense a man's intentions turning toward me in that way fills my psyche.

But the tension coiling in my heart has nothing to do with fear, but anticipation. My feet remain planted on the ground rather than fleeing as they have always done before. And I find myself leaning closer . . .

Suddenly, Phoebus jerks backward. "I have given you flowers, but I have yet to give you my song."

I blink several times in surprise. Then I straighten, doing my best to disguise any disappointment on my face. I'm not sure I'm successful as I clear my throat. "If you'll wait outside, I'll join you presently. We still have time to visit the beach before the glue dries."

"Right, yes, of course." Phoebus straightens and steps backward, but still can't seem to tear his gaze away from me. The desire painted plainly on his face dispels any thought that he recoiled from me in revulsion. "I already look forward to seeing you again."

With that, he turns and strides quickly away.

Suddenly feeling much better about this ensemble, I can't stop the smile from spreading across my face as I close my bedroom door. Mayhap it isn't always a terrible thing to have a man's gaze upon me. At least, not when that man is Phoebus . . .

I change as quickly as I can. Phoebus still gazes at me when I rejoin him as though I'm not wearing the *chiton* I reserve for my dirtiest tasks. Despite my garb, I feel like I am a goddess already between the laurel wreath on my head and the warmth in his gaze.

Though glue no longer bonds our hands, they find each other anyway, and then we hurry out of the castle. Thankfully, the few guards here and not celebrating Orion's departure with the rest of Crete are easily skirted. We have no trouble returning to the beach, still as empty as the dock is bustling.

It's an unofficial free day before I truly am free.

Reluctantly releasing Phoebus' hand, I turn to him. "Well? You have a tune for your muse?" I shouldn't be so bold, standing here before the sun. But Apollo is way up here, and it feels like Phoebus and I are the only souls in all the world.

"If she will accept my humble tribute." He removes his lyre from his belt and draws his fingers through the strings. His smile widens to a grin. "And if she is sure is ready for the power of such a song."

I grin back. "I am properly braced for your *humble tribute.*"

Grinning, Phoebus plucks at his lyre. I expect them to be more random notes as he warms up his fingers. I am not expecting the song he weaves. The tune is familiar, but mixed in with the melancholy is a hopeful chord.

Just as I almost place this song, Phoebus opens his mouth, and the most beautiful voice I ever heard weaves lyrics into the tune.

"The dusk deserted us.
The moon sets in the west.
My lover, where are you?
My lover, where are you?"

I shiver at the unbridled art I am witnessing. All of Crete should be here, celebrating the birth of music, for surely it did not exist until just this moment. I have certainly heard no true music until now.

"The Shadows are coming.
The Shades, they are calling.
My lover, where are you?
My lover, where are you?
The darkness has bound me.
But the Sun has found me.
My lover, where are you?
My lover, where are you?"

The melody flows through me, and I can't help but sway with the tune. My body was made to dance as much as it was created to fly, and my feet skip across the sand.

"I tried to be true, but you were not there.
I tried to be true, but you did not care.
The Sun, as my new lover, I choose.
The Sun, as my new lover, I choose.
The glowing orb doth drives away my woes.
The warming, golden rays chase off my foes.
The Sun, as my new lover, I choose
The Sun, as my new lover, I choose."

I've never heard this tune before, but it is an ode worthy of the Bride of the Sun. Of me.

The melancholy of the song is a fitting accompaniment to my life.

And the hope I hear . . . I feel it also, in my soul. Though I certainly know I shouldn't.

"I was fond of his spark.
But his love waned to dark.
My lover, where are you?
My lover, where are you?"

Maybe the hope comes because it's Phoebus who is serenading me. Phoebus, who has shown me that a man's attentions can be something I can appreciate. That there are more than men who are oblivious to me as a woman and men who I can't hide from. Phoebus sees me as a woman, but he doesn't make that something I'm ashamed of, something that makes me want to conceal myself from him.

He doesn't try to control me, and I can challenge him and not be struck down. Not so King Minos, who would toss my life away without my even disobeying. And not so Apollo, who slaughters others in my name yet against my will.

"I tried to be free, but you were not here.

I began to flee, but you were not near.
The Day's new lover he has chosen.
The Day's new lover he has chosen."

The music stops abruptly, and so do my dancing feet. The tone might have been lightened from the original version, but it's still a tragedy. Whether the song refers to Night stealing a lover or Day, it's still theft. It's not truly love.

It's my life, and my life has quickly become the tragedy.

Chapter Twenty-Six

Apollo

As I pluck music from my lyre and Icarus draws grace from the world around her, I feel as though I am in a vision.

If only this *were* a vision. Then I would know that this precious moment would be repeated. Her and me enjoying life in each other's presences.

I usually try to avoid thinking about eternity. There is too much monotony in rising and setting the sun. But if there was just one instance like this every day, with her and me together, I would never grow weary of it.

Icarus' movements are slow, matching the tempo of my music. Her expression is somber as my words wash over her. I wish she felt the same joy I did composing this song for her.

If only she could see how perfect we are together. I can play for her to dance. We can fly together. She would be safe to pursue her dreams and make her inventions come to life. I would make sure of that.

But right now, she thinks she needs to be protected from *me*.

My melody loses hope, and the last notes are all melancholy.

Icarus comes out of the trance I put her in and turns to me. There is so much on her face I cannot describe with words. She seems unable to do so herself, because she doesn't utter a single one of those thoughts. The crown of laurels I placed on her head droops on one side, not quite looking like it did in my vision of her in my bedchambers.

Finally, Icarus blurts, "I'm going in the water!"

I stare at her, completely stupefied, as she rushes to the shoreline, slipping off her sandals and doing just that.

That was not the reaction to my composition I was expecting.

Cautiously, I approach her, not sure what she'll do next. I cast a few wary glances at the water. Since taking this mortal form, this ocean has already done its best to drown me. It even enlisted the assistance of a pond.

Icarus glances back at me, and despite the tension on her face a moment ago, it lights up with amusement. The breeze wildly playing with her curls and the waves dampening the hem of her *chiton* where it rests at her knees. She looks beautiful enough to be a goddess in her own right.

What would she have authority over, though? The ocean belongs to another Primordial. The breeze ought to fall under Artemis and my domain, though all weather refuses to obey. Mayhap it will listen to Icarus if she accepts my Kiss . . .

My heart. That is the domain over which she has complete power. Icarus controlled my destiny from the second night I saw her in a vision and I was consumed with hope to see her a third time.

Meeting her in real life is so other than my visions. She disagrees with me; she loathes who I really am, and she would sooner die than accept immortality on my terms.

But Firmament above, she is *real*. No longer is Icarus a figment for me to dance with. She is a warm body I truly get to hold. She is a beating heart I cannot bear to be stopped. Rather than the beautiful maid who giggled gaily at nothing, she is laughing *at* me.

And she is giggling right now, and I'm missing it.

I blink myself out of my reverie. "What is so amusing?"

"You." Icarus reaches down to splash a wave toward me. It doesn't even reach the rest of the waves that play on the toes of my sandals.

"Me?"

"Yes, you." Icarus shakes her head at me, amusement still pouring out of her, not only in laughter but also in the jubilant gleam in her gaze. "You're frightened of nothing . . . except wading into the ocean."

"I'm not frightened." I cross my arms. "I just remember that the last time I was in the sea, you were dragging me out of it."

"You have finally learned caution— concerning the one thing I have actually proven capable of protecting you from." She splashes toward me again and then gazes deeper into the horizon.

In a moment, whatever caution Icarus has accused me of possessing is tossed like an offering to the wind. I slide out of my sandals and step into the warm water. Then I move toward her, my new horizon, and wrap my arms around her waist.

Icarus startles but doesn't pull away as she glances at me questioningly over her shoulder.

I duck my head toward her ear. "Cautious, am I?"

She inhales sharply.

Emboldened, I use my grip on her waist to spin her to face me. Her calloused hands clamp onto my upper arms for support, and she stares up at me, her wide-eyed gaze for once devoid of suspicion as it darkens.

Similar to the sun above us, as a cloud briefly passes over it.

I smile as the sun's light returns to us. "My dear muse, it appears a siren has lured me to the depths with dark intent."

"Dark intent?" Icarus breathes, her gaze dropping to my lips.

"Indeed. The question is . . ." I duck my head closer to her face so she cannot help but hear. So I cannot avoid her iris scent. And so we can both be granted our hearts' desires to be closer to one another. "Will you deliver me once again from the deep . . . or consume me yourself?"

Another thicker cloud passes over the sun. This one is no fleeting thing, though, and casts a great lingering shade over us.

Something about the newfound privacy of the sun seems to embolden Icarus. Or mayhap she hasn't even noticed the change in our surroundings since she hasn't looked away from me once.

Icarus' hands climb up my arms, wrap around my shoulders, and then clasp behind my neck. "I have already delivered you, so all that remains is to . . . consume you."

With that, she pulls at my neck, until I am pliable clay in her hands, letting her draw my face downward. Her lips lie in wait, claiming mine the moment they are near enough.

Light and heat both seem to flow into me from Icarus' touch, beaming through my entire body and warming my very psyche. If I thought I was overwhelmed by the chaos of physical sensations before, this is so much more. Yet also *not*. It fills my senses more than ever before, but there is order rather than chaos reigning in this moment.

All is as it should be. From Icarus' mouth intricately dancing over mine, to her possessive grip on the back of my neck. Her softness is pressed against me, and my hands have circled her trim waist to keep her close. The water laps at our waists, trying to join us in this moment.

This moment that is over far too soon when Icarus pulls away. She drops her hands from my neck and moves back as far as my hold on her waist will allow her.

The sun returns, reflecting on the golden highlights in Icarus' dark hair that I have never noticed before. Every time I think she can't possibly become more beautiful in my eyes, she does, and without even the ability to morph her form.

"You are beautiful," I whisper with what breath she hasn't stolen from my lungs.

Now I know why Icarus claimed I never kissed before. This mortal tradition is far more than a brush of lips to knuckles. I'm not sure I truly experienced life at all before this true mortal kiss. If this is the gift the Creator gave mortals instead of the Kiss he granted us, I believe He loved them more than the Firstborn of his creation like Father once claimed.

Icarus' gaze shoots up to mine, wide in surprise, before quickly returning to the waters below us. "But?"

"But?" I frown, which seems so unnatural after what Icarus has done to my lips. How can I do anything other than a smile for the rest of eternity? Well, smile *and* taste her lips again . . . "What do you mean? There is no follow-up statement. Your beauty steals my thoughts away, so how can there be?"

She looks back up at me, and confusion etched between her brows.

I run my thumb over those creases, trying to smooth them away for her. "What confounds you, darling?"

"I thought I misread the situation." Icarus purses her lips.

"How so?" I want to resume our kiss so desperately, it's all I can do not to lean forward and just do so. But all my troubles of late have come from rushing into something Icarus did not want or was not ready for, so I restrain myself.

"You didn't kiss me back."

I stare at her, trying to translate her words into something I can understand. Were my lips not also on hers? Yet, while hers had been tender and pressing, mine were . . . stunned and silent.

"Oh, I see, I—" I clear my throat. "My apologies. It would seem there is much I have yet to learn." I take both her hands in mine. "But I am eager to enlist you as my tutor."

A sparkle returns to Icarus' eyes. "I already have a student." Those soft lips of hers tick upward. "But I suppose, since you are in such great need, I can take pity on you."

"The greatest!" I drop to my knees in the sea, pretending to be a beggar pleading for morsels. The water plasters my chiton to my chest as I remain head and shoulders above the waves.

Icarus giggles. "That was your first kiss, wasn't it?"

Now that I know what a mortal kiss can truly be, I'd have to agree with her. "Nonsense. I've kissed . . . before."

Still laughing, she shakes her head. "I am very convinced."

Her words strike me as familiar. She's said them to me before. No, not me— Apollo.

Icarus makes the same realization as I do, because all color drains from her face, and she turns to me with horror pooling in her gaze.

Chapter Twenty-Seven

Icarus

A moment ago, my entire body was warm with Phoebus' touch. Now my blood has gone ice cold. It's just a coincidence that I've had reason to say those same words to both Apollo and Phoebus in such a brief span of time.

Phoebus blinks up at me in confusion, his *chiton* thoroughly drenched by the sea and clinging to the abdomen I had the pleasure of seeing just this morn. He looks so disarmingly innocent as he studies me, yet he gives nothing away in his gaze.

Surely, I did not just willingly kiss the creature that wants to take away all my freedom. I'm just panicking because I've never felt pleasure in a kiss before, and my mind is trying to remove the pleasantness to make it match my expectations.

It has nothing to do with the fact that Phoebus arrived the morn after Apollo's demand. Or the impossibility of having both males' attentions focused on me in such a short time.

"Icarus?" Phoebus slowly stands, a lopsided grin on his face even as concern builds in his brilliant blue gaze. "Is everything well?"

I can't make myself look away from that deep blue I have seen only in the sky and the sea and Apollo's eyes. Mayhap the rest of Apollo differs completely from Phoebus, but it is not unheard of for gods to change forms at will.

Apollo is the god of the sun and music and healing. Phoebus has brightened my life, composed me the most brilliant tune I've ever heard, and healed a part of me I didn't even know was festering.

Fear threads through me, turning all my previous pleasure to ash. I take a step back but stumble against a stone embedded in the sand.

Phoebus lurches forward, wrapping his hands around my waist. I jerk back at his touch, which doesn't halt my descent, and causes his.

We both crash into the waves. I barely have enough time to close my mouth before I'm submerged.

It's shallower here, so I merely need to sit up to breathe again. I swipe my dripping hair out of my face and turn toward Phoebus.

He's also sitting up beside me, his head, torso, and the tops of his knees visible above the water. Spluttering, Phoebus dashes water off his face. "You truly are a siren."

"I think everything is a siren to you," I counter. "You can't blame me for the last two times you almost drowned."

Phoebus narrows his eyes at me. "I wouldn't be so sure about that."

"What do you mean?"

"Never mind." He sighs deeply and leans back, studying me. Mayhap waiting for me to give utterance to what has caused me to react so dramatically.

It's such a mad thing to think, though I'm not sure I can say it aloud. Would he scoff? Be offended? Mayhap be flattered?

Or else reveal that he truly is Apollo— and then what? Gloat over me for acquiring my willing kiss before I even had an obligation to grant it? Punish me for embracing one I thought was another? Snatch me away because he knows of my escape plans?

Sickness washes through me, and I nearly collapse under the waves again. What have I *done*? Papa said not to get distracted. He said not to fly too close to the sun.

And here I am, falling once again for my hubris.

"Icarus, please look at me." Phoebus' tone is gentle. I feel his fingers on my jawline, drawing my face toward him. There's hurt flashing in his eyes, mixing with the wide-open concern.

I close my eyes to escape the intensity, leaning against his hand. I want to lose myself in his touch and forget all my worries and the wedding.

The wedding that I want nothing more than to escape. Yet, from the moment the *nymphokomos* looked me in the eye, knew I never could. Even in Athens, far from all the horrors— maybe— I couldn't escape the guilt. Even if I found my childhood river flowing between laurel shrubs and olive trees, I do not think I could reclaim my girlhood innocence.

Mayhap I was a fool to think I could escape being a man's bartering chip. But at least I can take some pride that I was bartered away for the protection of an entire island. Even if it was my fault for it being endangered in the first place because I flew too close to the sun. . .

Phoebus' thumb grazes over my lips that are still so alive from their time against his. Even if he was stationary, it was still one of the best experiences of my life. At least, since becoming a woman and new expectations were made concerning what I should and should not enjoy.

Though, kissing whom I desire to kiss was never one of those activities. That was granted to men, not women.

Until I stole it in this one short, sweet moment. But, like I realized when Phoebus played me that song, my life is a tragedy. Such sweetness is only meant to be a fleeting sensation. Sacrifice or else hubris must define the rest of my destiny— my downfall.

Tears prick at my eyes, and I don't dare open them. "Phoebus . . ."

"Yes, my darling, my muse?" His other hand reaches around me to tangle in my drenched tresses.

My gaze catches on something floating in the distance. The laurel crown Phoebus gave me, now lost in the waves. Fitting. "I'm going to wed Apollo."

His hands stiffen and his eyes widen. "Wh-what?"

I force my eyes open, feeling the pent-up tears flow down my cheeks. But I don't regret them, because they blur my vision, saving me, in part, from the absolute shock on Phoebus' agape expression.

Then, just in case he's confused, I add, "The god of the sun."

"The Guardian of the Sun," Phoebus corrects.

I blink. "What?"

"Never mind." Phoebus clears his throat. "Do you—" His voice is higher pitched, like when he was singing. Phoebus quickly clears his throat and speaks again, more deeply. "Do you *wish* to wed Apollo?"

Mayhap I'm speaking to the "Guardian of the Sun" himself. Or maybe it's just Phoebus, the closest to a lover I've ever had or wanted. My answer is the same for either.

"No!" I feel my face crumple, and then I rest my head against Phoebus' shoulder. I'm unable to keep it upright when I feel as though the weight of the world is on my shoulders, or at least of Crete. I understand Atlas' pain entirely.

Phoebus wraps his arms around me and then pulls me onto his lap, so I'm a little higher above the waves I'm pouring my tears into.

He says nothing, just holds me as I sob. I weep for my future, which now belongs to another. I cry for the dreams I will need permission to pursue. And I sob because I can't be with Papa and Phoebus in Elios.

In between those laments, I still manage to shed a few tears for the men who were slaughtered by my bridegroom last night. They might have been the greatest *morosophs* of Crete, but in the end, they were mortals begging for mercy. At least one had to have some family that is mourning them now. I wish I didn't have to be sorrowful for them on top of everything else, but it is my duty as the unfortunate witness to their gruesome demise.

I'm marrying a murderer. Except, he's not truly that. Apollo is above mortals and the laws that say we shouldn't harm each other. He is something other. And he wants to make me like him.

"*Never*," I hiss.

"Never?" Phoebus' voice is barely a whisper, like he's not sure he's allowed to speak. "You changed your mind about . . . the marriage?" Whatever he feels about that, he keeps expertly hidden. He waits silently to hear what *I* feel about it.

I shake my head. "I must. I have no choice but to wed him. But what I do have a choice in, he shall never have."

"Such as?"

"My heart. Not unless he carves it out of my chest."

Phoebus recoils in disgust as much as he can with me still on his lap. "He would never!"

I narrow my eyes. "Are you his acolyte now?"

"No. But the gods do not approve of human sacrifices—"

"Except in the form of brides." I grunt.

Phoebus' hand once again finds my face. "What do you want from me, sweet muse? Speak it, and if it is in my power to grant it, to ease your suffering, it will be done."

Grasping the collar of his tunic, I study his features desperately. I want to remember them perfectly, to conjure his face in fond memory when I have nothing else but the whims of a god to fulfill or flee from. I want to remember that once there was an astronomical miracle, where there was a man who wanted me, and whom I wanted in return.

"Icarus?" The gentle timbre of Phoebus' voice is something else I will need to memorize. The lyricism of his words alone can keep me warm when Apollo inevitably discards me as a mortal plaything that he cannot help but grow tired of.

"Phoebus." And if Phoebus turns out to be Apollo, I want to perfectly recall the false face of the one I will hate more than death. That will not warm me so much as set me on fire. Mayhap with enough fire to destroy the very sun so I can break free at last.

"Just tell me what you long for."

Freedom. And if not that, escape. "I want you to kiss me."

Chapter Twenty-Eight

Icarus

For all his bold and noble words earlier, Phoebus stares at me in shock now. "You want me to . . . kiss you?"

I nod slowly, wondering if I have once again misread the situation. The situation being me cradled in his arms and on his lap. "Before Summer Solstice, preferably." I want to taste freedom one last time before it's stolen from me forever.

"When you are to be wed." Phoebus frowns.

My stomach lurches. I know Phoebus fancies me. But surely, he did not grow to care from me too deeply about me— or, Olympus forbid, *love* me— in our brief time together. "I'm sorry. I shouldn't have asked. I won't use you like that."

I begin to stand, but Phoebus' grip on me tightens, and he tugs me back down onto his lap. "You may use me however you wish, sweet muse. That is not my concern. But you have a bridegroom. One you are not fleeing from any longer."

"I am not wed yet."

"But you are betrothed! I thought you did not like to break your word." Phoebus studies me, half in horror and half like his entire future will be governed by my words.

"I am not 'betrothed.' My father assured me he would give me a say before such an arrangement, and they have given me no say. This is, therefore, no betrothal. What I am is *promised*, by lips other than my father's or mine. And I will honor that promise— on the Summer Solstice. Until that day, my kisses are mine to bestow where I may." And mine to avenge when stolen against my will, or would be, if I had any true power.

"And after the Summer Solstice?"

I sigh. "Then at last I will be bound by my own words, my own sacrifice, and I will not give what belongs to Apollo to another."

Phoebus pulls up a sleeve of my *chiton* I did not even realize was slipping down my shoulder, but he does not take his sky-filled eyes away from mine. "And will you give it to Apollo?"

"On the day that the last drop of pride in my body abandons me, I will give myself to him. But I have a lot of pride. And a lot of fight." I clench my teeth.

"Oh, I believe you."

"Mayhap I couldn't last an eternity, but surely a mortal lifetime." If I resist Apollo's Kiss, I can resist all else. Yes, I can survive this sacrifice with my virtue at least intact. Unless Apollo's promises not to touch me against my will were empty lies. "At least willingly, I can resist. Physically, I am no match against him."

Phoebus grips me more tightly. "He won't hurt you!"

I narrow my eyes. "You are quick to come to his defense."

"He won't hurt you because *I* won't let him."

I'm not sure that even with the combined forces of Phoebus, Orion, and my father, any of us can resist Apollo. But I still smile at the notion. It is good to know that not all men are lustful brutes.

Phoebus shifts me in his arms, and then he stands, dragging me out of the water and into the cool breeze rising off the ocean. I cling to him awkwardly as he walks toward the shoreline effortlessly, despite how drenched my hair and garments are.

"What are you doing?" I gasp.

"I thought you would prefer if I honored your request on dry land."

Even though the idea was mine in the first place, the thought of having Phoebus' mouth on mine again sends a jolt of fear through me. Not that I'm frightened of him, but of my own desires. What if I can't follow through with being a sacrificial bride if I taste Phoebus again? Especially since I still have to convince Papa to let me go and—

Papa! "I-I've changed my request."

Phoebus steps onto the dry sand, looks down at me, and blinks. "You no longer desire my kiss?"

"Oh, I do." I drop my gaze. "But Papa is my priority. I do not think he'll want to stay here in Crete after I'm sacrificed. Will you still give him the position as your Master Architect . . . and Master Inventor?"

"I am capable of and willing to grant both requests."

Slowly, I raise my gaze to meet Phoebus'. It is as hot as if twin suns shine from the skies in his eyes. Mutely, I nod. My voice would betray me at this moment if I attempted to use it.

The sun making a halo behind him, Phoebus ducks his head toward me. He's apparently as eager for me as I am desperate for him.

I press a finger to Phoebus' lips, halting him.

He leans back, his soft mouth twisting in confusion.

"Not here, brazenly under the sun." There may be a part of me that suspects Phoebus to be Apollo. That part will be my only saving grace if it turns out to be true, so I can at least tell myself I knew while being duped. But he can also just be Phoebus, and I cannot risk him to Apollo's wrath. Not when I know how merciful my bridegroom can be. "I do not want your blood on my hands."

"You really believe he's a monster, don't you?" He sighs deeply.

"I do not have to believe what my eyes have clearly seen."

Phoebus doesn't disagree with me. He just continues to carry me further up the beach.

"Where are we going?"

He nods toward the mouth of the cave in the cliff. "The sun won't see us in there."

I feel a smile slowly stretching across my lips. "You really want that kiss?"

"Well . . ." Phoebus' gaze slides toward mine. "If it shall be the last one that I ever share with you, I want it to be the subject of legends."

Chapter Twenty-Nine

The Promised Couple

Icarus:

When Phoebus sets me down on the cold stone floor of the cave, I become keenly aware of the fact that my sandals are still on the beach.

However, I have little time to dwell on that or the chill of the cave biting me through my damp garments. The moment I am steady, Phoebus cups my face upward.

His breath fans warmly on my skin. "You'll tell me if I do it wrong?"

"Just . . . move with me."

Phoebus needs no other urging and abruptly claims my mouth with his, sending a wave of heat through me.

I have to grasp Phoebus' forearms for support as he leans me back farther and farther to better kiss me. And kiss me he does. No longer are his lips stationary against mine. Rather, he imitates what I did to him earlier, caressing my lips with constant kisses, covering the distance of my mouth multiple times over.

Remembering that kissing isn't something we have to take turns doing, I return his affection. Every caress is stolen from the destiny laid out for me and made into something all my own. Well, all my own and Phoebus', who is encouraged by my reaction to move more slowly, taking more time enjoying each stolen moment.

My knees tremble as the student outshines the tutor. Without pulling away from our kiss, Phoebus drops one hand from my face to wrap around my waist and hold me steady.

I try to murmur my thanks, but it comes out more against a moan against Phoebus' mouth.

He makes a growling sound and then seems to stumble forward. Mercifully, he catches himself since I'm far from capable of supporting him. Then he staggers us forward until my back is pressed against the cave wall. The hand that was cupping my face reaches to brace against the wall next to my head.

I miss the warmth of his touch, but our hearts have fallen into enough of a rhythm with each other's for me to anticipate his moves and meet them. Our mouths make excellent dance partners.

Earnestly, I cling to Phoebus' arms more tightly. It's not so much for support now as it is for warmth. I'm addicted to his heat soaking into my skin. I arch my body into him as a shiver racks my body despite my blood feeling like it's boiling.

Phoebus cruelly pulls back and frowns down at me. "What's wrong?"

"Nothing." I close the distance between us, more tightly wrapping myself against him and his warmth. "You have been an excellent student."

He smiles, his lips slightly swollen. "I've had the best of tutors."

His words send a rush of heat through me just as much as his touch. Yet, I still shudder, my body not in line with my psyche.

Phoebus frowns. "What's wrong? Why do you keep shaking?"

"Just a little chill."

"A chill?!" His eyes widen like I've just announced I have the plague of lumps.

A moment later, I'm scooped into his arms again. I can hardly complain, since everywhere he touches me feels warm. I just wish he were still kissing me, too.

"Let me see if I can rub some warmth into you." Phoebus settles on the floor of the cave, still cradling me in his lap.

Then he moves so that he has one hand arched behind my back to my arm not nestled against this oven of a body. His other hand finds that arm, too, and he rubs both his hands up and down my limb. He generates so much warmth from that movement that I have hope of not being cold again someday. I sag against him in relief.

"I'll take care of you, Icarus," Phoebus assures, not taking his fingers off my skin. "For as long and as much as you allow me, I'll provide for all your needs."

His promises are vast and foolish, considering I will belong to another tomorrow night. But just now, the exhaustion from last night's panic and lack of sleep is catching up to me, weighing my eyelids down like Sisyphus's burden.

A smile stretches across my face from Phoebus' warmth and continued touch, as well as the memory of his kiss. His chest makes a comfortable pillow.

"You're safe with me, Icarus." His voice washes over me, almost as warm as his touch.

I nestle more firmly against his chest. "I know."

Apollo:

When Artemis began allowing mortal huntresses to join our hunting parties, I was frustrated at first. They slowed us down with their greater needs, requiring sleep every night and far more food than I've ever needed to consume in one sitting. And the slightest inconvenience, whether a tree branch to the face or a friend's accidental arrow to their side, caused them such great pain.

I do not recall many instances before those days of wishing I could have lived as a mortal rather than the son of a Primordial. Of course, there were some weaknesses inherited from being the son of a mortal woman, even an Awoken. But claiming my birthright along with Artemis at our father's passing into the Veil also gave us new power as Guardians of a domain.

Now, though, I'm holding Icarus in my arms. I use my magic to flow warmth into the woman I just thoroughly kissed in the mortal way. And I know I've discovered a great truth. Despite this mortal's body having a proclivity for pain, there is also an increased ability to feel pleasure.

The thrill of the hunt feels like ashes now compared to the nectar of Icarus' lips. Even the song she inspired in my psyche, weaving around my soul, cannot distract me from her presence.

This isn't right. I'm becoming too consumed by her too quickly. She still has a dangerous prophecy hovering over her. And she still hasn't agreed to take my truer Kiss that could protect her from almost every death. Certainly, from a great fall.

Icarus' small hand grasps mine on her arm. I let her carry it to her collarbone, her eyes still lidded. "That arm is plenty warm now. But the rest of me . . ."

Swallowing hard, I obey her request, using one arm to support her against me. The other rubs circles into her delicate flesh as I infuse more magic into her, hoping she won't discover I am the source of the heat rather than my movements.

My fingers move across her collarbone, round her shoulders, and trace her tender neck. I feel the gentle but steady pulse in her throat.

A pulse I am not guaranteed will last forever. The hunt I can always have. For all eternity, it can be Artemis and me and our bows— oh, and her Awoken huntresses. I even have my oracles . . . until time steals them away.

Mortals always die.

Suddenly, I see a flash of an image, a scene beyond this cave. Like a vision . . . but it's not a vision. It's a memory from before Artemis granted her first Kiss.

The sound of wailing drove the stag I was hunting into a trot. Grunting, I turned to follow the source of the noise and demand its silence.

What I found was Artemis kneeling in the forest underbrush, one of her huntresses laid out in her arms, completely still. The other huntresses— all significantly younger and newer to the party than this one— stand solemnly to the side, as if in vigil.

Artemis wailed loudly, a sound I had not heard her make since our father passed into the Veil. He completely vanishing from this world, our mother fading away with him.

Not sure what to do, I stared at the still woman in her arms, Chrysanthe. While the other huntresses had brown or black hair, this woman's was white. Her skin was tanned from her time outdoors and increasingly folding in on itself. She had been the first huntress to fall into my sister's company, the most loyal of all her acolytes.

"What happened to her?!" Artemis demanded, whether of the other huntresses or the Creator, I knew not.

The second huntress stepped forward, and I saw a strand of silver in her dark tresses I had assumed she'd dyed to resemble her mistress. I now wondered if there was a more insidious reason for that new color by the heavy slant of her shoulders and the slightest sagging of her own once pristine skin. "She has passed onto the Underworld, my Lady."

"I know that!" Artemis yelled. "I have seen death before. But Chrysanthe was not shot or stabbed. She merely ran by my side until she toppled over."

Bowing her head in reverence or in grief, the second huntress sighs heavily. "We mortals do not live forever like you, my great Lady. If childbirth or malady does not fell us, time will."

Artemis and I stared at her in bewilderment. Neither of us cared to resume the hunt.

What found that day was not the death of a stag, but the demise of one not meant to live much longer. What I did not find were the words to comfort my sister.

This may be a memory, but in a way, it is also a whisper from the Fates— a dark promise. A prophecy of Icarus' fate, eventually, if she does not accept my Kiss. Time means nothing to us, and everything to the mortals. So the Creator has decreed.

But He also promised me Icarus. Or were those visions just a tease sent to torment me? To make *me* torment to *her*?

Icarus shudders, drawing my attention back to her. Despite all the magic I'm infusing into her skin, her body still feels so chill beneath her damp *chiton*.

Tension stirs in my gut, not only for her state of being, but also my inability to satisfy her needs. Warmth is the most basic of my skills, yet I'm failing. Mayhap the time I was late setting the sun is taking their toll from my magic after all?

It will take all my power to sustain Icarus in her mortality. I will have to be perfectly punctual in our marriage. Especially since I need to be strong enough to grant her my Kiss the moment she requests, so I need not fear her wasting away to nothing and taking my heart with her.

Surely after she kissed me in the mortal custom, she'll accept the traditional Primordial Kiss.

I sat before the bonfire set up outside our home, acting as a witness, along with five other huntresses.

The sixth huntress laid on a dining couch taken from inside our home and set closest to the fire that danced wildly around her. The other five huntresses danced like the fire, forming a circle around us as they chanted.

But I remained still, perched on a tree stump and bracing myself. It had only been a year as mortals calculate time since Artemis bestowed her last Kiss. I was not sure that was long enough for her to have recovered her full strength, though she insisted it was. According to Artemis, she was in no danger, but her mortal huntress was.

I still feared Artemis would give too much of her soul before it had time to replenish. But I also knew the horror that haunted Artemis after she learned death came so early to the mortals.

Artemis stepped forward, the fire casting eerie shadows from her tall profile as she stood over the dining couch.

The huntresses lowered their chant as Artemis raised her voice. "Aster of Athens."

Aster, who had until this moment been completely silent on the couch, inhales sharply.

"You have proven yourself in the hunt this day by felling a manticore. I now grant you the honor of a choice."

If the huntresses are still chanting, I hear it not as I listened to Artemis alone.

"Continue to hunt alongside until the strength departs your body or you choose of your own volition to leave—"

"Never will I forsake you, my Lady!" Aster cries.

"Or else accept my Kiss and become a Sister of the Hunt."

Aster looked ready to shout her agreement, but Artemis lifted her hands and the silence truly fell.

"Your soul will be bound to mine," Artemis announces. "Your life will be extended to match mine, and time will not touch you."

Once again, Aster opened her mouth.

And once again, Artemis silenced her. "But there is a cost. You must remain near to me."

"Happily, my Lady!"

"And you shall no longer desire men, nor the kiss of mortals. Your thrill will be found in the hunt and there you will be satisfied."

Aster inhaled sharply.

Artemis glanced down at Aster just as sharply. "Do you understand?"

"Y-yes, my Lady."

"And do you accept?"

Aster drew one more breath. Then she nodded. "I accept."

"Very well." Then, without a moment of hesitation, Artemis conjured her canine teeth into fangs. Lunging forward, she embedded them into Aster.

Then the Awakening began.

Blinking hard, I force away thoughts of the past and the future that I have yet to secure. I have Icarus to tend to, and she is becoming too cold too quickly.

I scoop her completely into my arms and stand upright. My legs make the strangest prickling sensation and then betray me, sending me lurching forward.

Thunder decides just then to boom, as if mocking me.

Icarus clings to me, fully awake now, judging by her wide open eyes. "Put me down. I think your legs are asleep."

Mortal limbs fall asleep without them? It is the most perplexing of minor pains I've experienced in this mortal form. But the pleasure of holding Icarus close, of kissing her, far outweighs the cost of those minor discomforts. The lot the Creator gave the mortals seems far sweeter than the painless, monotonous life of a Primordial.

Still, I'm not sure why none of my oracles ever complained of this specific ailment, though. I could have searched for a cure. Is it really so trivial that the mortals don't even care to request I make a medicine for it? Or, for that matter, why hasn't anyone mentioned I should find a cure for sneezing?

Thanks to the strange pains, I have to set Icarus against the cave floor. She also staggers before bracing herself on the cave wall. Her *chiton* is no longer dripping, but its dampness clings to her frail form. My natural warmth was enough to dry mine, but not enough to bleed through to hers, it seems.

Icarus shivers again, and I gesture toward the mouth of the cave. "We are no longer kissing, so we might as well endure the sun's watchful eye in return for his warmth."

With that, rain like a waterfall pours out from the Firmament. The droplets hit the sand so hard as to sound like hailstones.

I frown. I *should* be able to control this as easily as I govern the sun. But since Father's death, the weather does not answer us. Only the Creator's mercy prevents the ever-growing storms from wiping out entire mortal civilizations.

That Artemis and I did not inherit this aspect of Father's power strongly points to his death coming from a mortal. One who is now Ascendant. Not only does such a creature need to die for his sins, but also, he poses a danger from the information he could pass on to other mortals.

But Primordial-killing mortals is not my concern right now. Icarus' safety is, and I have only the Creator to plead to for mercy from this storm.

My gaze slides toward Icarus. I'm not sure the Creator will answer my prayers just now to clear this weather away. I cannot tell if He is punishing me for going about this all wrong with Icarus— or if Icarus herself is the punishment.

Icarus, whose hair is frizzing around her beautiful face as she holds herself tightly against another violent shiver. Her arms and shoulders are still rosy with the heat I infused into them. And her lips are swollen from our kiss.

She steps toward me. "I suppose, without the sun, you'll just have to be the one to warm me."

Chapter Thirty

Icarus

For some reason, my words cause Phoebus' face to fall. They must mean something entirely different in Elis.

Clearing my throat, I pluck at the damp chiton that seems to summon every chill breeze in all of Crete to me. Even though every part of me that Phoebus touched feels like it was set on fire by the sun itself, that heat hasn't spread beyond my arms and neck. With how drowsy I feel from all the stress that's been stealing my sleep, I know I need to act now. "Do you mind turning away? I need to get out of this."

The pounding rain drives in more frigid air than what already exists in this cave, and I shudder.

"Of course." Phoebus turns away, which I appreciate.

Even if it's superfluous to ask that of him when he's seen my undergarments before and will see them again before we leave this cave. But the thought of disrobing in front of a man is more than I can bear right now, with all the other emotions coursing through me.

I'm still so surprised that I readily invited and accepted his kiss after . . .

I turn my back to Phoebus' and tug off the wet *chiton*. My skin prickles to be directly exposed to the air, but at least it'll dry faster than if smothered in this damp cloth.

I wonder if I should make Phoebus stand facing away from me a little longer, or else do the wise thing and return to him for body heat, which would work best if he was as disrobed as I am. To save our lives, of course . . .

When I look again at Phoebus, I see that such a request is as superfluous as my last. The muscles of his bare back are exposed to me, with the thick loincloth draping from his waist his only covering. The *chiton* he had been wearing hangs uselessly from his arm, which is reaching back toward me even as he continues to stare deeper into the cave. The lyre he played on the beach rests against the cave wall.

No, the wisest thing would be to avoid the fire that has returned to my core and the desire to kiss not only his mouth, but the bronze flesh before me. I should flee into the storm, no matter how merciless it may be. Because if I am not a maidenly sacrifice, Crete will suffer. And if Phoebus is Apollo, I shall never forgive myself.

And if Phoebus is just Phoebus, then I certainly would understand it if he never forgave me. I've been less than merciful toward the men who look at me with dark intent for the moment, ready to discard me the next. And they never touched me, save for one. It would be unforgiveable for me to grant Phoebus any more than a kiss in this cave. It would be cruel to him, to me— and even Apollo if he counted.

Since I haven't spoken in so long, Phoebus shakes his arm holding the *chiton*. "Mine is dry. You should wear it until yours is likewise."

I blink, startled at the consideration. And then ashamed by the dark path my thoughts took. "Thank you." I slip the garment over myself. It is stretched out, hanging lower and more loosely than it ought, but it covers more skin than before, so it works. Especially since, as Apollo said, it is dry. It also bears a trace of his body heat, and the aroma of his brightness despite the saltwater scent.

"You asked that I make you warm, so warm you shall be."

Smiling at his strange fluctuation between innocence and flirtation, I move to drape my wet *chiton* over a rock so it can dry faster. "I appreciate it. Also, I'm decent now."

When I turn back, he's kneeling in front of me, and I almost fall backward over the rock I set up. "Great bull's horns— I'm not a goddess yet!"

Phoebus glances up at me from under his dark tangles, blue eyes bright despite his ragged appearance and how cold the stone must be against his knees. "To me, you are already." He gestures toward my legs. "May I?"

Not sure what under Olympus he's asking, I merely nod.

He places his hands on my left leg, and I have to reach back to the cave wall for support. Then Phoebus rubs his hands up and down my shin, just like he did for my arms and neck. Warmth from his movement and his touch both fight to dispel the chill of the cave and the outside storm.

"I have a question," he says, dropping his gaze. "If I may be so bold."

"Since I'm wearing your garments, have your hands on my legs, and still taste you on my lips, I'd say you can be bold as you like."

Phoebus' hands slide over my knees, just under the hem of his *chiton*. "It's actually about our kiss. Kissing in general. And *the* Kiss specifically . . ."

It's so strange to see him so awkward with his words even as his hands seem quite confident and capable. I take mercy on him, even as I have to use my other arm to brace myself against the cave wall, lest my knees give out and I topple onto him. "No, that wasn't my first kiss."

He glances up with a jerk even as he drops his hands from my now very warm left leg. "It wasn't?" Phoebus clears his throat and moves to my right leg. "Of course, it wasn't. You have not always been betrothed, after all. And your prowess was unmatched."

I raise an eyebrow because I would hardly count my ability to kiss as "prowess." Except, mayhap, to someone who has nothing he can compare it to.

Phoebus' grip tightens on my calf. "Was it Orion?"

The abject horror with a hint of suffering simmering on his crestfallen expression almost makes me laugh.

Well, a giggle escapes as I shake my head. "Except for his great masculine beauty, you have nothing to be jealous of Orion about."

"Obviously not." Phoebus sniffs like that is the most ridiculous notion and returns to rubbing life in my leg. "It's not his garment you wear, his hands caressing your legs, and it's certainly not him you're dreaming of kissing again the moment he stands."

I raise an eyebrow at such a bold proclamation. "Indeed."

Phoebus traces my knee. "No. Definitely not jealous." His hand climbs. "At all."

Bending forward, I push his hands back down. "It was Vassilis."

"Vassilis?" Wrinkling his nose, Phoebus sits on his hands and leans back to better study my face. "But you seem to despise him."

"I do. I did then, too. But . . ." Sighing deeply, I turn away. I still keep one hand against the cave wall to keep myself upright. Not because the reminders of Phoebus' too-welcome touch still dance across my skin, but because of the memories of the kiss I never wanted. "It was many years ago. Though I had grown into the appearance of a woman much faster than Ariadne, I was still very much a child."

"And you didn't know better?"

I shoot him a glare. "I didn't have a choice! When boys become men, they acquire strength. But when girls become women . . ." I wince and look away. "They *require* strength. Beauty may seem like a gift from the gods or nature or the *Unknown God*— but whatever its source, it is more of a burden than a blessing."

"He hurt you?" Phoebus stands, earnestness engraved on his features and in the depths of his eyes. He takes my hands in his.

Pulling free, I turn away, not from Phoebus, but from men in general. I know deep down that Phoebus would never hurt me. But just now, I cannot bear the sight of any male. "He kissed me. That is all."

But it's a lie. Witnesses would say that a kiss is all that Vassilis stole from me. Yet he seized so much more in that dark moment that seemed never ending as he nearly choked me to death with his suffocating tongue.

In that moment, I lost a part of my girlhood innocence, my belief that the world was brimming with heroes among men. My childhood ended that day, far sooner than I was ready to part with it. And even the excitement of becoming a woman so soon was dashed away.

There was my life before that cruel kiss, and my life after, and they seemed to be lived by entirely different people. I never again played dolls with Ariadne; it no longer seemed like something I ought to be doing. And the fledgling dreams of someday asking Orion to be my first kiss were dashed away. My ability to even find him or any other man desirable was lost until very recently.

"Then I will kill him. That is all."

I steal a glance at Phoebus and find that his earnestness has been replaced by rage. The same rage I felt emanating from Apollo when he slaughtered those men last night.

Suddenly terrified, I step back. "No need. Papa . . . took care of things. He came searching for me before Vassilis grew tired of making me know how he believed one ought to kiss and moved on to darker lessons. I thought Vassilis would die from his injuries that day, but obviously, he survived."

"And he's never touched you again?" Phoebus studies me, like any change of my expression is permission to slaughter King Minos' right hand.

I banish the wretched memories of all the times Vassilis' hand grazed my body as I passed by. "Papa took precautions. Even though, after that dreadful affair, he was given a more strenuous workload than ever before and I often went days without seeing him, Papa ensured I was protected.

Sometimes I thought I heard Vassilis at the door, trying to open it, but Papa's locking mechanism was too good. And even if it wasn't, he wouldn't have survived long enough to touch me again." I clench my fists, remembering all the times I stood back, holding a hammer or an awl, ready to swing it if the locks failed me. "Eventually, he grew tired of the chase." For the most part, anyway.

Phoebus sighs deeply and reaches as if to caress my face.

Instinct has me recoiling.

He quickly drops his hand. "I assure you, Icarus, if Vassilis ever touches you again, it will be the last thing he ever does."

"Because Apollo will smite him?"

"Not even the sun could find his corpse when I am finished with it." A dark smile stretches Phoebus' swollen lips.

Lips *I* made swollen. Because, for the first time in nearly a decade, the thought of kissing a man wasn't repulsive, but desirable.

Phoebus steps back, trying to give me space. As if there can be such a thing with his wide-shouldered form seeming to fill the cave.

Forcing a smile that becomes more real the longer I hold it, I reach a tentative hand toward Phoebus. "Would you like to explore this cave with me?" Nervousness from the affections we shared and the secrets we spilled swallows me. "Or you can stay here, but I honestly should check the tunnels while I'm here, for Ariadne's sake. You don't have to follow me."

"But I will."

When I force my gaze to meet his, there's a teasing smile on his lips.

It grows under my gaze. "Anywhere."

Chapter Thirty-One

Apollo

Artemis really euphonized when she said I was a fool.

Icarus, the woman promised to me from my visions— the wife I long for more than anything— is terrified of men taking advantage of her. And what did I do? Demanded for her to be my bride.

She is my greatest dream. I am her worst nightmare.

"Don't lag too far behind!" Icarus calls as she moves deeper into the shadows of the cave. "I don't want to lose you in the darkness."

Of course, I could illuminate this entire cave. But now doesn't seem like the best time to tell Icarus of my true identity. A few moments ago seemed about right, considering how pleased she was with my touch.

Now, though? She might feel even more threatened to be trapped in this cave with me.

So, I pick up my pace until I'm standing just behind her. "Is this close enough?"

To my great surprise, she reaches behind her to grasp my huge hand in hers. "Perfect."

Hope surges through me once again as I let her take me through the dank darkness. Our steps echo around us, but the sound of rainfall is no longer audible. That could be because it ceased. More likely, though, we are just too deep into the heart of Crete to hear it. It is a cold, black, hollow heart.

I'm not sure I've been this separated from the Firmament before. I don't like it.

"It seemed a lot more terrifying in these tunnels when I was younger," Icarus says gaily, like it isn't terrifying now.

I force a smile in case she can see my face in the shadows. Then I tighten my grip on her hand. "Well, for whatever terror you feel now, know that I am here with you." Don't pull away, whatever you do.

"That's what Orion used to tell Ariadne and me."

And we're back to Orion. *Always* back to him. Hasn't his boat launched yet? He needs to sail right out of her mind.

"Not that he needed to tell Ariadne anything. She's never scared if she's mad enough."

We keep walking, and now there is no light whatsoever, If I weren't clinging to Icarus for dear life, I would think I was alone in the bowels of the earth.

Just touching her isn't enough to ground me, though. My mind is filling with the surrounding void, and I need her voice to dispel it. Even if I have to get her talking about Orion. "And what about you? What makes you less afraid?"

"I don't know. I'm not frightened of much anymore. I've read too many books for that. I'm only scared of—"

I take that as an excuse to step closer to her, so we're standing abreast instead of her leading the way. "What? Being buried alive in utter darkness?"

Icarus laughs like that is an absurd fear or something. "No. But similar, I suppose. I'm terrified of being trapped. Of losing my choice. Of never being able to soar again." Her laughter turns dry. "So, basically all that is happening in my life."

"You *will* soar again. Mayhap Apollo will fly with you?"

"Strange words from someone who was kissing me just moments ago." There's a thread of suspicion in her tone.

I swallow hard. Do I steer her away from this topic, or confess? We are still in this cave. Specifically, where it is too dark and too tight for me to breathe, let alone find my way back when she abandons me in her rage. Of course, then I could always draw on my magic to light my path . . .

Icarus whirls on me, her hand not already joined with mine resting on my naked chest. "Oh!" Now her laughter is stilted, the third brand of her amusement I've heard since coming down here with her. It's beginning to concern me. "I forgot I was wearing your garments."

"You look better in them than I do." I move closer, telling myself it's part of my wooing her. But deep down, I just crave the proximity of her warmth in the crushing depths of this cave.

"You can't even see."

"I have an excellent memory. And an even better imagination."

She smacks my chest now, but I'm ready to capture her hand against my skin. "Let's turn back. We can't see anything for Ariadne like this, and the jagged stones can't be something you want to keep walking on without sandals."

"I forgot you were barefoot, too!" Icarus sighs heavily. "I am so sorry— let's turn back."

Sweet music to my ears. "I'm more disappointed that you can so easily disregard how few garments I'm wearing."

Icarus says nothing, but I imagine she's shaking her head at me. Then she tugs me toward where I can only hope the mouth of the cave is. I don't have the best sense of direction in this patch black closeness.

Precious light appears in the distance, bolstering my hope. It illuminates familiar stalactites, and then we're back in the mouth, Icarus' chiton stilly drying on a large rock. Outside, the rain still falls, but less violently, A puddle of water has appeared in the entrance, invading our domain.

Icarus goes to the entrance and peers out. "I suppose we're stuck in here a little longer, then." She glances at me before ducking her face. "Mayhap we should go back into the darkness where at least I can't see—" She clears her throat.

I cross my arms over my chest and lean back, willing her to look at me. "See what, my muse?"

She stares at her toes. "I'm pretty sure more sculptures resemble you than me, so I'm not sure *I'm* the muse between us."

"That is a travesty that should be corrected forthwith." I dare a step closer to her, studying her body language for any sign that I should give her space again. "If you model for me, I will happily carve stone in your likeness."

This finally gets her to look at me, both her eyebrows raised. "You are a sculptor?"

"With you posing for me, I certainly could endeavor to be one." Especially now, with her curls tangled from my wind, the waves, and me. I'm not sure she's ever looked more lovely than wearing my *chiton* hanging from her frame, even if it was her father's first. The ring on her finger is just from me, though.

A fourth flavor of laughter fills the air, this a much more pleasant giggle. "You're incorrigible."

I take another step toward her. "I'm yours."

Just like that, all the amusement in the room fades away. Her gaze snaps to mine, shock and earnestness entwining with horror and . . . desire?

"You shouldn't say that," she whispers.

Another step. Still, she doesn't back away. "I shouldn't say a lot of things. That wasn't one of them."

"I-I have never had anyone who was mine before." She looks like she wants to look away, but she can't. "Well, I've had Papa, but the law would say *I* belong to *him*. And to King Minos. And to Apollo . . ."

I manage to hold back my wince at the reminder of my folly even as a familiar pressure tugs at my psyche, reminding me of other duties.

But my first responsibility is Icarus.

I step close enough that I can offer my hands to her. "You have too much spirit to belong to any but yourself, Icarus."

"And what of you?"

"You have enough spirit for both of us, Icarus. The Fates have decreed it."

Her fingers move toward mine before hesitating, hovering just over my hands. *"Phoebus."*

Reaching up, I rub the tips of my fingers over the pads of hers. *"Icarus."*

She seizes my hands and pulls me against her. Her arms wrap around me, her fingers exploring the planes of my back.

I don't want to look away from her, with her frizzing curls, long lashes, chapped skin, and lips singing a siren song to me. But I have to. I glance toward the mouth of the cave and see that the rain has abated. It is still dark from the storm, but she is free to go.

She has to be free. It's the only way she can be happy. And maybe she'll even choose me, if I can make her understand how deep my feelings for her and how grand a life I can offer in return for her choosing to stay by my side.

I need to woo her. I need to confess. I need to set her free—

When my gaze returns to her intelligent brown eyes, I forget every thought I ever had. "There's something I need to tell you." What, I cannot recall, but I sense its importance weighing on my soul.

Icarus shakes her head. "No. Don't say anything that will ruin this moment. This last, stolen moment."

The pressure still tugs at my psyche, but I cannot disobey the desire darkening her gaze. "And what would you have me do instead?"

She stands on her tiptoes, trying to draw her face closer to mine. "Kiss me. One. More. Time."

CHAPTER THIRTY-TWO

Icarus

P hoebus doesn't need to be told twice. He cups the back of my head and then meets my waiting mouth with his.

This time, I make sure I kiss him back with the same fervor he gives me. Whether it's my encouragement or because he's simply becoming more confident with this new skill, his kisses are more calculated and possessing. Phoebus teases my bottom lip and then my top.

He does not try to part my lips, though. I wonder if it's because he doesn't know how, or because he remembers the horror on my face when I told him of the death of my childhood. Whichever the reason is, I'm thankful for it. I'm grateful I can lose myself in this moment without worrying about triggering reminders of the monsters outside this cave.

Finally, I have to break away to breathe. Phoebus must be somehow stealing breaths between kisses, though, because he doesn't stop. He slides his mouth to my jawline, tracing the side of my head before finding my neck.

New warmth floods through me, and I wonder how I was cold just earlier today. How could I even know the meaning of the word with Phoebus' searing kisses on my skin?

Suddenly, Phoebus grasps my waist with both hands and lifts me from my feet. I cling to his broad shoulders as he sets me on top of the rock that I had lain my *chiton* on, putting me just a little taller than he is. Then Phoebus continues to kiss me on my neck where he left off.

This new angle makes it harder to trace the muscles in his back, so I draw my hands up to his hair. I tangle my fingers into it, feeling the brine of the sea that makes him smell like the ocean.

"Icarus," Phoebus murmurs as he kisses along my collarbone. More of my skin is available there since I wear his baggy *chiton*. "There's something important that I need to tell you."

My fingers grip his hair unconsciously. "Don't. We don't have time for words. For feelings. We just have *now*."

"Feelings?" Phoebus halts his kisses and gazes up at me, so much hope swimming in his blue eyes.

That was the wrong thing to say. "That is, we don't have time to even *develop* feelings."

He steps closer, his hands bracing me at my hips. "What if we did, though?"

I shake my head, feeling tears prick at my eyes. "Let's not play such games. I already know that I could fall in love with you if things were different. But they aren't. The Fates are cruel, and the gods are crueler, and—" But Papa's Unknown God isn't supposed to be cruel. Yet He's also over all the others. So why is any of this happening?

Why am I allowed to feel myself falling for a man when I am to be wed to a monster? It's such a cruel trick. One that could be crueler . . . No. There is no way that sweet Phoebus can also be vengeful Apollo. Not while there is a semblance of reason in this world.

"But Icarus . . ." Phoebus takes both my hands in his and presses a kiss on each of them. Then he looks up at me imploringly. "I've already fallen for you."

I stare at him but do not see him. Everything is suddenly spinning painfully around, like I am no longer connected properly with the world. "Wh-what do you mean?"

"I love you, Icarus. I fell for you the moment I saw you."

My knees buckle. Then Phoebus' hands are on my waist as he plucks me from the rock and sets me on the ground. I totter into him, enveloped in his warmth and scent. He wraps his arms around me, and part of me wants to melt into his embrace.

But most of me wants to flee. "You can't, though!"

"Of course, I can, obviously. I already do." Finally, my vision clears enough for me to read the concerned confusion as he frowns down at me.

"Why didn't you tell me sooner?" I push away his arms and stumble backward. I shouldn't have kissed him— thrice. I shouldn't have strung him along. But I didn't know, didn't think—

"I tried to, but you kept interrupting me." He cocks his head to one side. "I haven't exactly been shy in my attempts to woo you."

"We can't do this. I'm getting married tomorrow!"

"What if you were marrying *me?*"

I step back, shaking my head as I move toward the mouth of the cave. "Don't do this, Phoebus. You know what's at stake. I already have to sacrifice my freedom. There's no need for me to sacrifice your heart likewise."

"You're right. There isn't." Phoebus doesn't attempt to close the distance between us, but the grin on his face draws him suffocatingly nearer somehow. It's just too big. "I love you, Icarus. Your eyes are brighter than the sun to me, and your smile gives more warmth. Do you. . ." There isn't a hint of hesitation as he reaches his hand toward me. "Do you love me in return?"

For a moment, I stare at him in abject horror. "Apollo would smite you for any of these words."

"I don't care what Apollo would and wouldn't do. What do *you* want?" His fingers flex toward me. "Do you, Icarus— daughter of Daedalus— love me in return?"

I study him, unable to look away. His brown hair I ran my fingers through, the strong arms I clutched, and the brilliant blue eyes like the sky I feel I could soar in forever. Then there is his beautiful bronze body nearly on full display because he covered me instead. Not to mention the mouth that ravished mine . . .

Heat flares through my veins, my lips tingling from his last touch, and my skin burning for his attention again. I feel something toward Phoebus, for sure.

But a day kissing in a cave does not love make. No, love is a choice. A choice I do not have the luxury of making.

Hurt flashes across Phoebus' beautiful face, and he lowers his arm. "Fine, if you cannot confess to loving me, will you at least deny it?"

I open my mouth to do just that, but so many memories tease my mind. Me rescuing him. Him playing his lyre for me. Our fight, our dance, our kisses . . .

There is no denial in me. But I will not be the death of Phoebus by granting affections Apollo has claimed for himself.

So, I do all that I can do. I turn and flee.

CHAPTER THIRTY-THREE

The Promised Couple

Apollo:

I move to the mouth of the cave so I can watch Icarus' retreating form until she dashes around an abutting cliff and out of view. Then my gaze turns to where her sandals are still on the sand next to mine, though the waves draw dangerously near to them.

Those waves witnessed our first glorious kiss.

A smile stretches across my lips, made sacred by Icarus' touch. Then I turn toward where she fled. Because she couldn't deny that she loves Phoebus. Because she's wedding Apollo tomorrow.

Won't she be overjoyed to find out that Phoebus and Apollo are the same . . . tonight?

Enjoying the mere act of smiling because of the way it reminds me of Icarus' touch, I step out of the cave. The world spins strangely around me as I glance up to sense how much longer I have until I can set the sun. Once that is done, I can return to Icarus to soothe her fears for tomorrow.

The moon shines down at me, startling me into action so quickly I nearly topple.

But nothing is as dizzying as seeing the sun begin to set without me.

Icarus:

I don't even remember the journey to my tower. All I know is I'm closing the door and refastening the locking mechanism, more out of habit than anything. Obviously, when Phoebus returns, I'll have to let him in. Hopefully, he'll have come to his senses by then, and will also be wearing more clothing . . .

Glancing down at his *chiton* I'm wearing, I frown. Maybe not.

"There you are, dear girl. And here I was beginning to worry you ran off on us."

At the voice that does not belong in my tower, my haven, I stiffen. Then I slowly turn.

King Minos is reclining on my dining couch as casually as if it were his throne, claiming it with his cloying frankincense stench. Papa stands behind him, his presence alone mitigating the panic welling in my soul. Until I see the stony expression on his face concealing whatever he must think of this encounter.

"M-my King," I say, quickly bowing. "I was simply saying farewell to my favorite beach on your beautiful island."

"Yes, well." Minos shifts, resting his elbow on his knee. "What if I told you it didn't *have* to be farewell?"

I glance between him and Papa in confusion. "Wh-what do you mean? I'm *not* to wed Apollo tomorrow?" I am careful not to look at Papa, who does not know that I was, in fact, planning on doing so.

My only true secret left is the way I nearly lost myself in Phoebus' embrace only moments ago. His words still echo in my head and heart.

"It seems you were keeping a secret from your dear, sweet father."

Horror floods me, banishing every thought of Phoebus as I snap my gaze between Minos and Papa. How can the King possibly have any ability to sense my thoughts?

Papa's face still betrays no emotion but grim stoicism. King Minos, however, slaps his knees and throws back his head with a howl of a laugh.

When he's quite finished, Minos swipes a tear from his eye. "Not to worry, dear girl. You certainly receive no judgement from me. If your bridegroom wishes to play with you a night or two before your wedding rites, that is entirely his prerogative."

As I try to decipher his words, Minos' expression hardens, suddenly losing a trace of amusement. "What I will not allow is my men slaughtered in the streets of my own city."

Realization floods through me, followed by fresh horror. "I begged him not to do it! But Apollo would not be reasoned with—"

"Now, now." King Minos' tone turns deceptively soothing. "Asios told me of the whole gruesome affair. I know you had no hand in it, that the god of the sun did not listen to your pleas for mercy. I'm sure those were not your only pleadings that he ignored last night."

I glance at Papa, wanting to tell him that King Minos is taking that out of context. That for all his sins, Apollo never touched me but to protect me and to heal me. But the heartbreak shining through Papa's stoic mask shatters my ability to speak.

King Minos stands, coming between Papa and me. "Tell me, dear child, do you desire to wed your bridegroom?"

I drop my gaze. "I may have been born in Athens, but I am a daughter of Crete, a servant of the King. My desires are secondary to my duty to you and my obedience to the gods."

Minos' sandals come into my view, and I realize his toes are exceptionally long.

Then a hand clasps my shoulder.

Startled, I look up into Minos' dark gaze, a sly smile spreading across his face. "But what if it became your duty to *disobey* the gods?"

Apollo:

One whistle later, I'm mounting my chariot. I order the swans to fly as quickly as they can while I throw my golden mantle over my shoulders and don my Primordial form.

The dizziness and nausea do not fade away, though, when I discard my mortal form. Because it is not mortal weakness that makes me feel so, but a failure of my duties to the domain I was granted.

Finally, my chariot catches up with Artemis', where it is struggling just slightly under the weight of the sun.

"What are you doing?!" I cry.

Artemis turns to me, and her glare with sharpness and intent. "Where *were* you?!"

"Wooing my bride-to-be. What time is it?"

"Closer to midnight than to what should have been sunset." Artemis purses her lips. "Do you truly not sense what the Firmament is saying?"

For a moment, I still my soul and then reach out.

I find nothing— not even the pressure from before. The Firmament has forsaken me.

"It's punishing you." Artemis ties her reins to the head of her chariot. "Do you even have the strength to Kiss your bride tomorrow?" She moves to the end of her chariot.

I imitate her movements, securing my reins and walking parallel to her. Though my steps are far less graceful, because when I glance down at the world moving by so rapidly beneath us, I nearly topple off my chariot.

The fall from this, or any height, wouldn't kill me. Though with how much the domain is disassociating from me, I'm not sure I would escape the consequences as easily as when I am in full communion with the Firmament. Would I experience the impact as painfully as if I were mortal? Or would I be able to transform into a bird in time?

Forcing my gaze back to Artemis, where she works on untethering the sun from her chariot, I force a smile. "I'm sure I'll have the strength to *kiss* my bride in the mortal way at any time. But as for the Kiss, it won't be necessary tomorrow."

Artemis pauses in her work to put her full strength into a scowl. "Do you want her to die of time like Chrysanthe did?"

"No! Most certainly not." I grip the rim of my chariot for support and draw a deep breath. "But we can afford to wait a short time after our wedding until Icarus is comfortable enough to consent. She is young; she has plenty of time yet to accept my Kiss. Especially since I believe she loves me."

"Really?" The tension between Artemis' silver brows eases somewhat, and she returns to her labor.

"She could not deny it; it was too great a truth for her to twist into deceit." I feel like my very face is competing with the sun in brightness. "I plan to tell her that she has nothing to fear from her bridegroom— the man she loves— this very night."

Artemis holds up the tether.

Clutching my chariot tightly with one hand, I reach for the tether with my other. "Once my duty is fulfilled, of course."

She twists the tether around my hand, and the sun nearly yanks me off my chariot. It takes every last drop of my Primordial blood, and some additional help from Artemis— who grasps the tether again with me— to guide it toward where I can tie it on my own chariot.

"If what you have said is true, and she still has years before time steals her away, then do not grant your bride your Kiss tomorrow. To give her a share of your power when you are so weak might be the last thing you accomplish."

I knot the tether to my chariot three times before daring to look up. "You think expending the last of my strength would kill me?"

"At the very least, it will do her no good, nor you. It could expend the last of your Primordial strength. You need to fulfill your duties to our domain in order to draw on its power. But you need strength from the Firmament in order to accomplish your abilities."

"I would still have my Primordial blood." I'm not very convincing as I stumble toward my reins.

Artemis sighs heavily. "Maybe. Maybe not. I am your heir after all, just as you are mine and the domain could survive with only one of us per the Creator's promise. So just make sure you are not late any longer with your duties, and you'll resume your full strength in time to Kiss your bride soon enough. Oh, and don't forget to actually wed her tomorrow, in case you don't have the strength to carry out your wrath. And if you do not honor your part of the bargain of their failure . . ."

I perish, and there is no hope of anything any longer.

Clearing my throat, I attempt to lighten the mood. "On the bright side—" I flash a grin at my pun.

Artemis rolls her black eyes.

"Tomorrow is the longest day of the year, so I have plenty of time before I have to set the sun."

Time I fully intend to spend with my new bride.

I cling to my reins and grin. With tomorrow comes the dawning of a new era in my life.

CHAPTER THIRTY-FOUR

Icarus

I stare at King Minos in shock, too surprised by his words to know what else I might feel. "D-disobey the gods? What do you mean? How can you speak so?"

"I speak so because I am King." Minos' dark eyes flash dangerously, even though there is yet a smile on his lips. "Why should we be the pawns of gods who are losing their power when we can create new gods in our own images?"

"What?"

"Mainland gods have no place in Crete." Minos leans closer, banishing all sensation of personhood. "A second Minoan god will do us well."

"I-I don't understand."

King Minos steps back, finally releasing his grip on me. "I was willing to sacrifice you for the sake of your ascension. But last night proved you will have no say over the actions of your bridegroom."

I'm still stunned by all that I'm hearing, but there is enough of me returning that I raise my eyebrows. "You mean like I had a say over anything before?"

He doesn't seem to hear my words as he paces away from me. "But I was not willing to sacrifice three of my men to his brutal appetite."

"Those men had a brutal appetite of their own." Why I'm defending Apollo, Olympus only knows.

Minos may as well have donkey ears with how well he listens to me. "I thought we had an easy chance to seize power, my dear child. But I suppose I should know by now that nothing is simple."

I glance between him and Papa, trying to discern what might come next from the King's mouth. Neither betray any hints.

"But the most important rule is that when an opportunity presents itself, simple or otherwise, one must seize it." King Minos folds his hands behind his back and turns to face me again. "One way is for the god to gift it. But even becoming Awoken, you are still subservient to the one who made you so."

"And as you said, Apollo doesn't listen to me ..." I wait for Minos to finish weaving whatever tapestry of a plot he's creating before me.

"So, you do not want to become Awoken, but Ascendant."

"And how does one become Ascendant?"

"By killing a god." Minos glances at Papa like he's in on an inside joke.

Whatever it is, Papa still doesn't look pleased. He hasn't even spoken a word. Though he rarely ever speaks in King Minos' presence—at least not when I am present.

What kind of threats force him to remain silent about his labor in Minos' honor?

Suddenly, the full power of Minos' words comes upon me, and I sag against the door for support. "How does one kill a god?" I glance toward the windows, like Apollo might even now be hovering outside, listening to the conversation. "How does one even *speak* of such a thing?"

"With great cunning."

"I am hardly cunning—"

"You are a woman. You were born so." Minos gestures to accentuate his words.

My mind is churning with the strange and savage turn of events. I wrap my arms around my middle to support myself.

Minos frowns. "I'm sorry— do you *prefer* to let Apollo own your body?"

Papa stiffens, but otherwise doesn't move.

"N-no."

"Then listen closely, my dear." As if he weren't the one to bargain me to Apollo to begin with, he leans conspiratorially toward me. "We mortals may have brief lives compared to the gods, but there is one thing we have that they don't."

"What?"

"The ability to go back on our word."

It's my turn to stiffen. "I would never—"

King Minos holds up a hand. "Not you— *him*. If a god cannot honor their word, then they shall perish. That is a peculiar weakness of theirs. A Primordial cannot *not* make a bargain. And they must honor all bargains and vows they make, or else they face certain death."

Finally, Papa steps forward. "But not immediately. Just as they live long, they can die long. She will be vulnerable to his wrath—"

I stare at Papa in confusion.

Minos just gestures out the window. "Apollo is hardly strong enough for any wrath. Just look how he struggles to set the sun at this late hour."

Not particularly wanting to draw near to Minos, but desperate for some understanding, I move closer to the window.

Outside, the sun is just slipping behind the horizon. "He does not seem to be struggling—"

"It is nearly midnight."

I gasp. *Phoebus.* Is Apollo distracted because he's hunting him down? Or was he delayed because he was the man I was kissing in the cave?

"It would appear the god of the Minoans does not approve of the blood offering Apollo made on Cretan land." Minos clicks his tongue as he shakes his head. He gestures again at the setting sun. "He has evidently made the god of the sun too weak to complete his task. The true god of the Minoans has demanded the god of the sun rather than a mere mortal bride; with the passing of Apollo, not only will you grow more powerful as a new goddess, but so will the reigning god of Crete." Minos mock bows toward me.

"How do you know all this?" I gasp. "I've never heard such things in the temples."

"Kings have a great deal more access to knowledge, my dear. That's how we stay in control."

I glance toward Papa for confirmation, and he just nods.

"So, what will it be, dear girl?" Minos asks, drawing my focus back to him. "Live forever as a pet to a brute, or reign as a goddess in your right?"

At his wording, I almost snort. There is enough so-called cunning in me to know Minos fully intends to make me a puppet he has power over. But I could remove him from my life as a goddess more easily than I would Apollo as his bride.

If I align myself to Minos' plot, I could be rid of both of them. I would be free to wed Phoebus if I so desired and not have to hide him from Apollo's wrath. I could fly as a manifestation of freedom rather than as a desperate flight to it.

I raise my gaze to Minos, not daring a glance at Papa in case I see something in his face that makes me change my mind. "What would you have me do?"

"It's quite simple, really. At the Summer Solstice festival preceding your marriage rites, secure from your bridegroom's lips a vow he will not be able to keep while my bargain with him is already in place."

"And how am I to fool such a powerful being into submitting to my will against his best interests? I doubt even your most ancient wine is capable of that, and we've already clarified he does not listen to *me*."

Minos shakes his head, a small smile on his lips. "You are so naïve. I assure you, there are numerous ways for a fair young maiden like yourself to have your way with any male for at least a short time. But if you need assistance, Ariadne will be along in the morning to help you weave your plot."

I purse my lips together. I feel filthy for even *considering* aligning myself with King Minos. But he's right. I produced a vow from Apollo's lips once before, not even knowing the danger he'd placed himself in . . .

My gaze shifts toward Papa.

Papa shakes his head so subtly that I almost miss it. But I understand his message clearly. He wants us to fly still. He doesn't know that I already changed my plans on that account.

I cannot let Apollo find us and strike him down for trying to protect me. Or smite Phoebus for the crime of wooing me like an actual man should and making me long to wed him instead.

There is only one way I can have them in my life still and not fear their deaths.

Turning from Papa, I meet King Minos' gaze. Then I nod. "It will be done. I shall be Apollo's undoing."

Chapter Thirty-Five

Icarus

"Excellent news." King Minos grins. I'm not sure I've ever seen him smile so much at one time, and I never want to witness so many grins from him again. "Now, I need to ensure you don't run off to do something else that might jeopardize your well-being when you're so important to Crete. I must ask that you don't leave this tower until the festival. I'll have a guard posted outside to encourage you."

With that, he finally departs, taking the suffocating stench of frankincense with him.

The moment King Minos closes the door behind him, Papa is there, sliding every bolt and lock into place.

Then he turns to me, his face flushed and eyes shining. "You don't have to do this."

"Do what? Kill Apollo?" I wince at the words, which is folly. If I can't even speak about my actions, how can I possibly complete them?

Considering I was going to make myself wed him, this seems like the lesser of two evils. The preferred option would just be doing as Papa wants and flying away from it all. But watching Apollo slaughter the two men I care about most in this world is the worst evil of them all.

"You don't have to kill," Papa adds, smoothing back my tangles in desperate need of washing. "I will protect you. I've always protected you." Darkness flashes across his gaze. "Did he take you last night? Before the marriage rites were completed?"

I shake my head. "It wasn't like Minos said. I-I was seeking Phoebus."

Papa drops his hand. "After dark? I told you—"

"I was worried he was lost, that he would be taken." I drop my gaze, catching it on the gleam of Phoebus' golden ring on my finger, a promise of the life he could give me. "Papa, I think I love him. Phoebus, that is."

Silence meets my confession, and I raise my gaze.

Papa's stony expression usually reserved for all but me has returned. "What did I tell you about getting distracted?"

I squeeze my eyes shut so I don't see his disappointment and he can't see my tears. "I'm sorry, Papa. I should have been stronger. I should have known better. I *did* know better—"

"And now you'll try to kill an ancient being on his behalf?" His tone is rising.

He's never yelled at me, and right now, I'm horrified that I've brought him to the verge. "And for you and me! I've seen what Apollo can do. He'll slaughter, and he'll show no mercy when he finds us. No matter how much I beg."

The memories flash through my mind, and I open my eyes in an attempt to escape the *thwacking* noise echoing inside my soul.

Papa wraps his arms around me, and I realize I'm trembling. His tone has softened. "It's not your duty to protect Phoebus— or me."

"And you can't protect me forever!"

His grip on me tightens. "Of course, I can."

I hug him more tightly in return. "We both know that mortals don't live forever. One day, it will just be just me in this world. And it's such a cruel world for women."

"So, you want to be strong enough that no man will ever hurt you again?"

"I want Phoebus by my side," I correct, even though I knew the moment Papa spoke that he uttered the truth.

Because I do want Phoebus, more than I thought it was possible to desire someone or something else when I already have such lofty dreams. But I also want to be free. I want to be able to choose him for love, not necessity, and for companionship, not protection.

I don't want him, Papa, or Apollo destroying my enemies. I want to be capable of destroying them myself.

"Are your wings ready?" Papa asks wearily.

"Yes. I finished them this morning, as I said I would." I turn away.

Papa places a hand on my arm. "I said I would allow you to select your suitor, and I will. If you want to slay Apollo so that you may wed Phoebus, then I will stand by you."

I smile. Then I throw both my arms around his neck. "Thank you, Papa!"

"Don't thank me yet." He clings to me like someone might come and snatch me away from him even now. "I am not sure I can protect you against Apollo's wrath should something go awry. And if it all goes according to plan, I am less sure I can protect you against Minos."

Pulling back enough to see his face, I frown. "You fear King Minos?"

"He is not the fool he presents himself as to the world." Papa's face wrinkles with worry, and a haunted glaze falls over his gaze. "Minos has access to ancient power. Possibly greater power than the Primordials."

"What?" I pull back more. "What are you speaking of?"

Shame flashes across Papa's face before he glances away. "A bridge we can cross when we reach it. Mayhap you should go check your wings . . . just in case."

Biting my lip, I study him warily. Then I nod.

I step into my room and force a brush through my hair, as painful as it is. But the thoughts of leaving those tangles in there a moment longer is more painful.

Then I glance down at my *chiton*. No, not mine— Phoebus'.

Phoebus! Is he still in that cave, wondering why I fled with his clothing? I doubt my *chiton* will fit his frame, but it's not like he couldn't walk around in his loincloth. It's hardly shocking.

I climb out of my window and onto my pulley's plank. Even as it draws me up, I feel a heaviness sinking in my heart. Is he safe? He survived last night, but are two nights alone out there testing the Fates?

And what if he is a traitor, and that's how he spends his nights? After all, Minos has guards outside my tower now.

"But he hasn't confiscated my wings," I mutter to myself as I step onto the tower. "And anyway, Phoebus says he loves me."

That could be a lie. But could he truly have faked brightness in his eyes, the wideness of his smile, and the innocence of his joy around me? I tasted that joy when I kissed him, felt it when I felt him. No man has ever been so open and honest with me as he did during our embraces. Papa certainly has secrets he hides. Phoebus has none.

Feeling a grin growing I cannot stop, I undo the ties holding the hemp covering over my wings. When everything falls away, my wings stand out brilliantly white against the night sky. Only a couple feathers have fallen away, and when I check the others, they don't even threaten to follow suit.

My wings are ready to be used. I ache to pull them on and test them right now, but I know that is not what Papa meant for me to do when he sent me up here.

If I follow through with my plan, will I ever have the chance to fly with them again? Or did I waste the last moments I could have flown kissing Phoebus in a cave before a storm sealed my destiny?

I run a finger over the pads of my lips, which are still tingling with his touch. I wouldn't trade our time in the cave away for anything.

"Good evening, bride."

Startling to have the silence so easily slaughtered, I whirl around to find a new light in the darkness, competing with the moon. Rays like sunshine gleam from golden curls and bronze skin on display from under the scantest layer of clothes— a golden mantle and a loincloth. An open grin broadcasts brilliant white.

But it is Apollo's ethereal blue eyes that my gaze locks on and makes me shiver.

It takes me longer than it should to see that he's standing on a chariot carved out of gold and pulled by four great swans.

I stagger backward in shock, first at seeing him, then in fear as the memories of our last encounter flow through me. Finally, horror nearly knocks me to the ground as I remember what I am yet to do to him.

It never occurred to me that I would need to kill someone one day. I know enough of it that I will never be the same afterward. Rather like if I were to lose my maidenhead, I assume. It would seem that one way or another, I am doomed to lose my innocence to Apollo.

"Come now, bride," Apollo coos, driving his chariot around my tower to approach me. He offers a hand toward me, as if expecting me to take it. "You have nothing to be afeared of from me.

I step back, the center of the tower evidently being the safest place for me. "When King Minos agreed to give you to me at Summer Solstice, he meant after the festivals, not at the first brush of midnight." Fear like I've never known grips me. Will all our last-ditch plots be in vain and leave me snatched away without even getting to say farewell to my father?

"Our rites will commence after the festivals begin. But I wanted to see you one more time before you adorned yourself in your bridal splendor." His gaze goes over me like I'm already gowned and not wearing a man's garments.

Crossing my arms across my chest, I glare at him. Mayhap he'll smote me for my insolence and save me the coming pain of either the touch of his kiss or the sight of his corpse. "A lifetime with me isn't enough for you?"

"No." His expression is soft and his gaze warm. I did not realize that a being so much more powerful than I could also be so tender. "Would you fly with me?"

I stagger back a step in surprise this time. "Whatever for?"

"Because I want you to know that you can do all that you love to do now as my bride." He gestures to his chariot. "I can fly you anywhere you desire to go."

Despite myself, I glance toward my wings. "I can already fly myself anywhere I long to go." Not quite correct, but true enough in this conversation.

"Put them on and join me. That way, you're free to fly away whenever you desire."

I ease closer to my wings, but now I keep my gaze locked on the mysterious entity that is hovering just outside my tower. "What are you trying to do?"

"Woo you, obviously."

The way he says the words makes me tremble. It is so much like Phoebus . . . But no, that can't be. I've already dismissed that possibility, haven't I . . .?

Their eyes, though, are the same. "If you wanted to woo me, you shouldn't have forced me into this." If a man truly wants to make me fall for him, he should respect my boundaries like Phoebus.

Unless Phoebus and Apollo are the same . . .

Apollo flexes his hand. "I want to show you that you can be happy with me. *Free* even."

My fingers glide over the feathers. "And if I can't be happy with you? Will you let me go? Will you truly free me?"

Hurt flashes across Apollo's face, which is a dizzying thing to see on such a perfect visage. "I think you will be happy, though. If you just come with me, you can see."

"*A Primordial ... must honor all bargains and vows they make, or else they face certain death.*"

I turn away from him for a moment, even though not facing him makes goosebumps break out on my neck. But I need to think. To plot. To conspire.

Cunning does not come to me nearly as naturally as King Minos predicted.

Apollo comes around the tower again so that he's hovering behind my wing stand. "Icarus?"

"I will go with you." I strap my wings onto my back. "I return for something from you."

He stiffens. "Like a bargain?"

"Just like a bargain." My fingers are clumsy with my straps despite all the focus I've directed toward them.

Then larger fingers are on the straps, properly tightening them around me and sealing the weight of my wings to my shoulders.

I lift my gaze to meet Apollo's where he stands on the tower just before me, his warmth invading my person.

"What do you require of me, my bride?" he whispers.

To stand somewhere far away from me where I can forget about the way your proximity makes me want to fall against you and be warmed to my core.

"A-a vow." I drop my gaze to his chest, covered in only a golden mantle. It does not help with my focus.

"Besides the marriage rites?"

"Those were your request, not mine."

Suddenly, Apollo is on one knee before me so that we're eye level again. From this proximity, I still cannot find any difference between his blue orbs and Phoebus'. Especially when they are filled with the same warmth and wonder directed toward me. "What do you wish me to vow, my sun?"

I stagger backward, and I foolishly hope he blames it on the awkwardness of my wings rather than what it was— a pathetic escape attempt. "I-I don't know yet. I'll tell you at the festival. So it can be a public vow, in the witness of many."

And so that I can decide if I can truly follow through on killing him. Mayhap I should just turn and flee. Apollo is too bright, too beautiful to be snuffed out.

Snuffed out like those men he slaughtered in my name. Like he'd do the same to Papa and Phoebus . . . If he isn't Phoebus.

I clench my fists and lift my chin. "Do you agree to the terms of my bargain?"

Apollo gazes down at me in confusion. "You know it doesn't need to be a public vow for me to adhere to it. I am bound to whatever I promise you." He steps closer, his warmth once again encompassing me. This time, I haven't the will to escape it.

Especially as he leans down to whisper in my ear. "All I need is you and me. No one else. Nothing else. And the vow is made."

I shiver despite how warm I am. Then I clear my throat twice before I can trust it with words. "I said what I said."

He sighs. "Then so it shall be." A moment later, the smile returns to his face. Then he takes a merciful step toward his chariot, granting me the ability to breathe again.

Until he pauses and looks back. Then, a smile blooming on his face, he offers me his hand. "Come, my bride, and fly with me. I will show you the stars like you've never seen them before."

Chapter Thirty-Six

Apollo

For a long moment, I stand in place, the smile frozen on my face as I wait for Icarus to determine whether my promise of a vow is enough for her now. I flex my fingers, desperate to touch her again.

But she doesn't know that I'm the same man she tutored in the mortal custom of kissing. She will soon, though.

When that time comes, will she want to kiss me again . . . or push me off the chariot?

Mayhap this wasn't the best setting for the reveal; this is a terrible plan.

Suddenly, Icarus' small, calloused fingers are touching my skin. I feel her essence like a heatwave moving up my arm even though she holds only my hand.

Never mind— this is the most perfect of all plans.

Her very kissable lips thin together. "Let's be off, then."

"As you wish, my bride." I step onto my chariot that I cleared of my lyre, bow, and quiver earlier. The last thing I need is Icarus recognizing my instrument before I have a chance to explain, or panicking when she sees the weapon that I slew her enemies with.

I regrettably release Icarus so that I can place both hands on her waist. I hoist her into the chariot behind me.

Icarus makes a little squeak, and then totters into me, both her hands splaying on my chest.

Memories of earlier today flood through me, and it takes all my willpower not to return to what we began. "Good evening to you as well, sunshine."

She tenses. Then Icarus jumps back.

I grasp her wrists before she can topple out the back of the chariot.

"I know you're wearing your wings," I add, moving us both farther into my chariot. "But let us not test the Fates, shall we?"

Icarus snorts like her plummeting to her death isn't the subject of my every nightmare.

Her wearing her wings does not appease me, either. That she wears her wings in the vision I'm haunted by of her falling to her death has me half-tempted to make them unusable. But knowing Icarus, she would insist on using them anyway, even with a wing missing. I cannot risk making the prophecy self-fulfilling.

I loosen my grip on her and take the reins. "You may want to hold onto me."

"I don't think that's what I want to do at all." Icarus crosses her arms and scowls at me. Like her lips aren't still swollen from my kiss.

Glancing heavenward, I wonder if the Firmament is on her side or mine. Considering it's still not speaking to me, I would wager hers. "I'll try to keep the swans at a slower pace, but if you want to reach the Spire and back again in time for you to slumber . . ."

"The Spire?" Icarus moves a little closer, her curiosity winning over her rage.

I'll have to remember to play on her curiosity when we are wed. "It seems like a suitable distance to traverse, and the view of it is really quite remarkable . . ."

"Fine." She lightly places her hands on my hips, as though the awkwardness of the touch which spans the skin at my sides and hem of my loincloth, will make it somehow less sensual.

I glance back at her. "Try not to accidentally strip me back there."

Icarus blinks, then her eyes widen in panic. "What?"

With a wink, I swat my reins. My swans, tired of hovering in place, soar into action immediately.

The speed has my bride-to-be wrapping her arms tighter around me. Her fingers dig into my abdomen, and I feel the side of her face pressed against my back.

I grin as I guide us away from Crete and over the waves.

After a few moments, Icarus' tense form softens. Then, slowly, she draws away from me.

Holding the reins steady, I glance back at her. Icarus doesn't seem to notice as she grasps the side of the chariot before releasing me. I miss her touch immediately, but this gives me a better view of her profile as she smiles down at the dark waters we're flying over.

There is something about admiring her beauty while she admires beauty in return . . . I don't think she'd ever tire of the sunrises and sunsets the Creator paints through my chariot. And I will certainly never tire of *her*. Honestly, I can barely comprehend how I lived so many eons with my visions only starting last year to give me hope for this moment.

The stars reflect in her wide eyes as her hair flows with the breeze. The garment that was once against my skin whips around her legs. Her wings remain folded against her back, but they make her profile seem even more ethereal. And is that the hint of a smile teasing her lips, prophesying a future where she might be happy in this chariot with me?

She senses my gaze and turns toward me. Rather than repulsion, Icarus just studies me, no emotion on her face. It isn't the same desire from earlier, but it is better than she has ever looked at me as Apollo before.

Icarus' gaze slides past me, and then her eyes widen. "The Spire!"

Turning, I see we are indeed quickly approaching our destination. Suddenly, I wished I said something farther, like the mainland. But she is still only a mortal and will need her rest. Tomorrow is, after all, the longest day of the year.

If my sense of the future has taught me anything, it's that it will also be the longest day of my life.

Especially since I have moments left before I tell her who I am to calm all her fears. The thought of uttering those necessary words to her makes *me* know fear as I have never known it before, though.

Icarus moves closer to me to get a better view of the spire. But I can't help feeling pleased she'd step toward me even as Apollo. I guide the swans into a winding path so that we circle the Spire and give her the full view of the tiny walled island.

After a few twists, I turn Kyknos back toward Crete.

My bride-to-be stands behind me, watching the Spire fade into the distance. Then, suddenly, her warmth is just behind me. Not touching me, but *there*.

"Why are you doing this?" she asks, her voice so low it's almost stolen by the breeze.

I would fight the wind for the right to hear her sweet voice. Just because the rebellious element won't submit to my sister and me doesn't give it a right to steal from me.

"Doing what?" I ask casually, like I don't want to sweep her in my arms and embrace her again. It's already been far too long since I kissed her. But I am not the hourglass who measures the time between our touches; she is.

"Wooing me? Like you have not already secured my hand in marriage."

Even though it's foolhardy to free my own hands, I secure the reigns to the bridle of my chariot. Then I turn to face her, clutching the chariot walls on either side of me to keep from cupping her face. "I want far more than your hand."

She ducks her face. "So why not take me by force like you took my freedom?"

I sigh. "I did not mean to do even that."

Confused, she glances back up at me, her intelligent brown gaze threatening to find out more secrets than I even knew I had. "You do not wish to wed me?"

"No, sunshine, I do. More than anything. But when I demanded you for a bride, I saw you as a damsel locked in a tower by a cruel tyrant. You were mine to rescue. Now I know the truth."

"And what is that?"

"That you were always only yours, and you were only biding your time before you rescued yourself."

Icarus says nothing.

"Did I get that wrong as well?"

She shakes her head, suddenly looking everywhere but at me.

Mayhap I should have put more clothing on to set her at ease.

"When should I expect you at the festival?" she finally asks, her tone cool, with the slightest wavering in her voice.

She's already ready to flee, and I haven't even told her who I am. Will learning that I am Phoebus convince her to stay, or drive her to fly away all the faster?

I'm not sure I'm courageous enough to know for sure. But mayhap . . . "I will come to you for the first dance, though you will not see me in this form."

Icarus' gaze snaps back to mine, and her emotions are completely honest before me, not concealing what they are.

And they are horror.

Contagious horror, sinking claws into my chest and injecting fear into me. She is ready to despise me in every form.

But surely, after the way she embraced Phoebus, she's ready to forgive his shortcomings. Like that he's me?

I will find out tomorrow. I am not courageous enough to face the truth today. "And for the final dance— that I will come to you as your bridegroom."

"And take me as your sacrifice." She turns away from me, her wings, even closed, are a wall between us as she moves toward the edge of the chariot.

"Don't think of it like that." I step toward her but restrain from reaching for her. "All those people who you hurt you, who contained you— you will be as a goddess to them."

"But as a slave to you." She glances at me over her shoulder. Tears shine in her eyes despite the fiery rage burning in her gaze. Water and fire together.

"Don't think of our marriage like that." I drop to one knee before her. "You will be my equal— the Queen of my domain, which is the Firmament itself!"

"But I didn't want the Firmament. I just wanted to fly." Icarus closes her eyes, but not before a tear escapes the cage of her long lashes.

"And you will fly forever!"

"At what cost!" She spins to face me, throwing out her arms so that the wings secured against them flare out behind her.

"Nothing that you aren't willing to pay." I drop to my other knee. I'm not sure if there was ever a time a Primordial begged a mortal, let alone kneeled before one.

But Icarus is no mere mortal, and I will be anything she wants me to be just to have her nearby.

Her gaze is now both fire and ice as she stares down at my humble position before her.

I have nothing to lose but her. "Remember, I want more than just your hand. But it must come from you and you alone. And I will give every piece of my heart, every part of my soul, in exchange for the chance to show you that I can be the guardian of your affections as well as the sun."

"And if I give you nothing?"

"Then I will still give you everything, as will be your right as my wife." She has to see that she wants to choose me. After all, the Creator chose her for me.

Or . . . did He? My first vision promised me a dance, which I received. The second vision gave her to both me and to death. And it didn't start haunting me until I tried to seize the perceived promise of the first prophecy to myself.

What have I *done?*

Icarus stiffens. "I will see you at the festival tomorrow."

With that, she dives backward.

I hurry to the edge of my chariot just as she soars back upward. Icarus elegantly twists in the air as she changes course to catch the same breeze my swans are soaring on.

She sails far above me, her expression fierce and determined, but there is no avoiding the pleasure gleaming in her gaze as she soars. Every flap of her wings is strength, and every glide she allows between is cunning. Her every movement is grace.

"My bride," I whisper, unable to look away, "and my muse."

Chapter Thirty-Seven

Icarus

Normally, I feel a slight burning in my muscles as I fly, especially when I haven't soared for several days. But there is too much fire in my soul to notice any physical ailment. Even though I don't glance back, I am all-too aware that Apollo is following me.

Or should I say, *Phoebus?*

I want to scream, to turn back and shout in his face. To demand power over the Firmament now so I can make it rain down fire upon him.

"My bride and my muse."

Whether he meant for me to overhear his words or the breeze betrayed him by drawing it to my ears, I know not. I only know I was right but ignored my gut. I pretended to know nothing just long enough to be fooled by the very charade I saw through.

I let him kiss me— and not just once, or twice.

If I weren't flying, I would kick something hard. I'm not sure which of us is a greater fool. Me, for ignoring my intuition and telling myself there would be no consequences for my folly. Or him, for thinking I will ever willingly kiss him again.

Him. Most definitely him. I don't believe there is an official god of fools yet. Apollo can surely fulfill that role.

And a fool isn't all he is. The wind howling around my ears as sounds so much like the screams of the men Apollo slaughtered. That *Phoebus* slew. Sweet, thoughtful Phoebus, who had never been kissed before. *Coincidently*, neither had Apollo.

I land on the top of my tower with no memory of my return journey but blind rage. Of course, after taking my freedom, Apollo also robbed me of my joy in flight.

And the Spire. That was my sacred goal to push myself to my limits to achieve. Now that Apollo has flown me to it, it has become a hollow victory. Our burgeoning romance seems equally hollow.

Disengaging my wings, I turn back to him, daring him to approach me while I'm in this state.

However, Apollo seems perfectly content to see that I am once again in my father's house before turning his chariot and flying off. Mayhap because he's seen the look on my face.

I bite back the urge to hurl insults at him and focus on propping my wings carefully on their display. *They* don't deserve my rage. Besides, I may have need of them yet.

Except, he knows about them— about my plan. Olympus above, Apollo *helped* me glue the feathers in place!

Staggering backward in horror, I stare at the place where we stood so close together. I thought we were just two mortals rebelling against one who would make himself god over me. But all along he was playing me. Playing *with* me like a toy. Why? For what purpose? To ensure I didn't fly away?

Papa says the Unknown God gave us all willpower, the ability to choose. But men only seem to choose to control me. And I keep flying too close to the sun, making decisions from hubris that threaten to destroy everything.

Will Apollo come to destroy my precious wings the moment I step downstairs?

I'd like to see him try. I'm certain I could get a few scratches in before he threw me off the tower or what other method he'd prefer to discard me when he sees that his suit will never be accepted.

Because I don't care how much Apollo thinks he loves me. I won't be his fool for a second time.

I close my eyes, not sure if I'm trembling from fear, sorrow, or rage. Even science has betrayed me, making men so much stronger than women and Primordials so much mightier than mortals.

Clutching my hand, I feel the gold signet ring from Phoebus—no *Apollo*. I tear it off my finger and consider throwing it. But, no, it's worth too much. What was a token of what Phoebus could give me can be how I buy a life of my own.

"Icarus?"

Forcing my eyes open, I find Papa stepping over the last stair to join me on the tower, concern etched in the lines of his face.

My rage melts away just a fraction, allowing grief and humiliation to swirl within me. I want to hide from Papa, but I also need him more than ever.

I run to him and wrap my arms around my neck. "Oh, Papa."

His muscular arms immediately encircle me. "Are you considering flight, after all?"

Shaking my head, I hold him more tightly to keep from falling any further than I already have. "No, Papa. Apollo must die."

"Because of Phoebus?"

"Yes." I clench my jaw. "Entirely because of Phoebus. He dies with Apollo."

Danger. Threats. Violence. Tall shadows all around me, closing in. They want my blood to flow.

Terror flows through me. I remember screaming once but cannot remember how to do it again.

But then there is light, taller than all the shadows combined. Safety. Assurances. More violence. The shadows have all shed blood, coating me everywhere but my hands. Horror intermixes with my fear.

And then comes the rage.

I turn to the light, and it becomes gradually smaller while I grow taller. Embraces. Secrets. Then the greatest violence at all.

Now the blood is on my hands, and I cannot get it off, no matter how many times I wipe them on my peplos. *It sinks into my psyche. I think I'm going to drown in it.*

Finally, I remember how to scream.

"Icarus, wake up! Icarus, it's just a nightmare!"

My eyes slide open, and I find Papa looming over me, shaking my shoulders.

"It's just a dream, little bird," he whispers soothingly.

I shake my head back and forth. "No, Papa, it wasn't. It was far worse than a dream. It was a *prophecy.*"

Papa stills. Then he pulls away.

My hand comes down on his, capturing it, though it is too dark to see his face. "Papa, why do you believe in the Unknown God?"

He does not seem to expect my question, but he does not leave me with it. "Because when I look around, I see order in the world that allows me to discover and create within it. Chaos may come from so many creatures using their gift of choice to make wrong decisions, but the order remains nonetheless."

"The gods, those you call Primordials, also make many wrong decisions and cause chaos."

"Indeed. Which is why I know there must be a higher power beyond them, a final moral authority. It is the only explanation for the deeper order in the chaos and the higher call of morality in my soul."

My nightmare and what it foretells flitters through my psyche. I pull my hand away from Papa, almost feeling the stickiness of Apollo's blood on it now. "That moral authority . . ."

"Will judge us all, mortal and Primordial, for the decisions we made with the will He gave us and for the chaos we introduced to His order." Papa sighs deeply.

"Am I being judged for flying too close to the sun?" I whisper.

Papa sighs. Then he gently brushes my sweat-drenched hair off my temple. "I fear His wrath, but not for your sins. It is I who fled too far from the light of day. Sometimes I fear that Apollo demanding the sacrifice of my only child is an extension of the Unknown God's judgement for all I've done."

I tense. "And if it is?" It is already a nigh-impossible task rebelling against the Primordials so many call gods. Can we also succeed against the one being Papa identifies as God?

Sighing again, Papa bows his head. "I can only hope He will forgive for all I have done in Minos' name."

I rub my hand up and down my sheets as I stare into the darkness. "May He forgive all we shall *both* do in Minos' name."

Papa sets a platter of fried eggs with *staka* before me. Even though I normally adore the rare treat of buttercream on my favored meal with which to break my fast, I stare at it mutely.

Today, though, I doubt I'll have any more luck consuming it than I did sleeping last night.

"You need your strength," Papa says, his deep voice gentle as he sits across from me. "Eat even if you do not taste."

Feeling like a puppet, I cut a bite and stuff it into my mouth. I might as well be consuming ashes, but I choke it down. I cannot be weak when I take my vengeance.

Papa smiles sadly. "That's my girl."

I force a few more bites down my throat, and then a pounding on the door distracts me from the blandness.

Gesturing for me to stay, Papa stands and goes to the door. After checking through the peephole, he sighs. Then he glances back at me. "Are you sure you do not want to fly?"

In response, I stuff another bite of eggs into my mouth.

Papa sighs and then undoes the locks.

Ariadne bursts in, the seamstress and her attendant just behind her. When Ariadne's gaze falls on me, she smiles, though it doesn't reach her eyes. In her hands is the long *loutrophoros* vase containing the sacred waters for the first of my wedding rites, the pre-nuptial bath. "Good morning, future goddess of the day."

Standing before the copper mirror, I take in my reflection wearing Ariadne's blue and gold ensemble. She stands beside me, garbed in fewer skirts and dyed cerulean blue. It is clear which of us is the bride and future goddess.

Yet I no longer wear the ring gifted to me from my bridegroom. Instead, I wear gold jewelry with blue stones around my neck and wrists and one anklet composed of animal bones. There is nothing familiar about me when I stare into my reflection.

Not even my face, for a strange mask made of gold and carved to look like the sun covers it. There are holes for my eyes, nose, and mouth. But even those are covered by the golden gossamer material flowing from the veil both before and behind, covering my hair despite the attention given to winding it into so many ornaments. Garbed so, it is clear that I am a woman, but there are no other distinguishing factors of my personhood. It is as though I exist only as a sacrifice.

I awkwardly smooth down my breast cloth so that it is not *too* apparent that I'm a woman. Then I force my gaze from the macabrely impersonal reflection that barely even looks human to Ariadne.

She wears neither a mask nor a veil, but she is almost unrecognizable from the vacancy in her normally sparkling gaze and the pallor to her skin. And I didn't realize it before— lost as I am in the sea of my own suffering— but Ariadne hasn't spoken a word since her greeting when entering my tower.

Nor did she remove her sandals to put on her more decorative pair. Every movement she's made has been stiff, and she hasn't looked me in the eye once.

I did not think I could feel anything beyond the rage, dread, and regret already racing through me. But now worry worms through my psyche as well.

Gesturing to our attendants to leave us, I turn her to face me. She moves in compliance with my direction. Something she's certainly never done while I was tutoring her.

"Ari, are you well?" I ask. I know I'm not, but just for now, I can pretend the bath I took in Ariadne's bathing room came from the aqueduct. Pretend it was not with water from the *loutrophoros* vase. Surely, I have not already finished the first rite of marriage with the being I am to slay, my now partial-husband . . .

"Today tastes of tragedy," she answers without a trace of passion, either rage or sorrow.

"Because of my wedding or because of something else?" I can barely think beyond the fact that I go to kill the one man whose kiss I welcomed, but I must ask her for the sake of our friendship.

"Your wedding is part of the tragedy." Ariadne closes her eyes and gulps a deep breath. "*Most* of the tragedy."

"What else has come to pass?"

Her eyes slide open and meet mine. For a moment I see undiluted shock, fear, shame, and horror swimming in her dulled gaze. Then she looks away.

"Just . . . be careful what you wish for," Ariadne whispers. "Because when the Fates give it to you, you may just regret ever being born."

"Ari?"

She dodges me when I reach for her. "We need to focus on your ceremony and all the rites that accompany it." When Ariadne's gaze locks on mine again, there is a sheen of tears in her eyes, but they do not conceal her fierce determination. "You may be Crete's only hope for salvation."

Chapter
Thirty-Eight

The Promised Couple

Icarus:

"**Y**ou may be Crete's only hope for salvation."

Ariadne's words echo in my head, the sheer magnitude of meaning making them impossible to dismiss. The words should increase the weight on my shoulders, but instead, they release the pressure I feel in my soul.

No longer is slaying Phoebus— *Apollo*— about vengeance, which would be a relief for a moment before haunting me for the rest of my eternal days. This is about the same reason I was going to wed him, even though it was against my inclination to deliver Crete. Only now, instead of me being the sacrificial lamb, *he* is.

Flanked by guards, attendants, and Papa, we draw near the dancing hall. Then King Minos is between us, as if summoned by a dark ritual. Ariadne stiffens and refuses to look at him.

King Minos doesn't seem to notice as he smiles at us in a way that makes me feel as though I need another bath. "Ah, the two loveliest faces in all of Crete."

Now that Orion is absent, I suppose that's true.

Since I'm already set to slay the man that I thought I was falling for, taking Minos' hand seems an insignificant evil. Ariadne ignores his gesture toward her, though.

So, Minos just ignores her as we walk together toward the dancing hall.

We pass two servants whispering together in a corner.

"Why did the sun take so long to set last night?" asks one of Ariadne's newer handmaidens.

A kitchen boy shrugs. "Maybe he wanted to make us think it was Summer Solstice already so he could seize his bride sooner." His gaze falls on me, and he immediately clams up.

The attendant still hasn't seen me. "Or maybe he changed his mind and decided he no longer wanted the girl and wanted to delay as long as possible."

As the kitchen boy furtively gestures for her to be silent, Minos leads us out of earshot. He guides us into the dancing hall he had designed for Ariadne to celebrate her love of dance.

Now it will be a threshold of sacrifice.

King Minos lifts his hands in the air, and I notice a glimmer of gold on his wrist. It is the exact shade of Apollo's hair, and looks to be the same texture, braided into a bracelet. A boon from my bridegroom?

Of course, Minos would have no issue taking a gift from the being he intends to slaughter. He looks far too gleeful as looks upon his people with double-minded intent. "All hail your future goddess!"

The room, which had been bustling with at least a hundred souls in bright silks, their bodies already shining with sweat, stills. The sounds of conversation and music that had guided us here fall silent. So begins the pre-nuptial festivities— the *proaulia*— and the second wedding rite between myself and my victim.

Almost as one, the room bows toward us.

A fresh wave of panic strikes through me like one of Zeus's lightning bolts— yet it seems to sever my feelings from this situation.

This surely cannot be me they are bowing to, nor is it my face hidden behind a mask and veils. It certainly won't be *my* hands stained with blood.

I glance back at Papa. He nods once, the confidence in his gaze anchoring me back to my body and this dancing hall. I can do this; I am capable.

Apollo will perish this day— if not in the name of my vengeance then for the sake of Crete's deliverance.

Straightening my shoulders, I turn back to the crowd bowing before me.

Except, there is one man who does not bow.

Wearing a golden *chiton* I know he didn't receive from my father, a grin that should not be directed toward me, and the mortal form I kissed, Phoebus-Apollo strides toward me. His brown hair is perfectly combed rather than being the golden curls that should be framing his shining blue eyes. But there is a confidence in his gait as he strides toward me that I should have known from the beginning didn't belong to a mere mortal.

Phoebus halts before me and bows at his waist. Then he seizes my left hand and draws it up to his lips. He kisses it tenderly as his gaze locks with mine through my ridiculously cumbersome mask.

I choke on my breath. Even disguised as a mortal, he is too beautiful, too bright for this world. And even brushing his mouth to my hand, I can feel him again, kissing me everywhere he did before.

"Bride of the Sun," Phoebus murmurs, "may I have this dance?"

Apollo:
It is a lucky thing that I already saw Icarus in her bridal splendor already, or else seeing her fully arrayed now might have paralyzed me.

And then I wouldn't be holding her close as I lead her in the same dance maneuvers I saw in the vision.

Except, unlike the vision, I have her hand in mine and her warmth soaking into me. Her scent of irises and sweet spices engulfs me.

The only downside is I cannot see her beautiful face, and I cannot even read her eyes to see what she thinks. Surely, she must suspect the truth by now. Does it please her to know she is wedding not a stranger but the man she taught to kiss in a cave?

Icarus did not resist when I took her to dance, her hand in mine and her waist beneath my touch as I've danced with her both dreaming and waking hundreds of times before. Unlike all previous dances, though, her movements are too compliant for me to be confident that she is feeling herself. There isn't a trace of joy or any sign that she's enjoying herself as much as she normally does dancing. Of course, it's hard to read her with her face covered.

But I need to know. If she doesn't choose me, I'd be a monster to take her, anyway. And the Creator has already shown me how he would punish me for going about everything so very wrong.

"Are you allowed to remove the mask?" I ask.

"I do not think I am." She gives no further explanation or even comment on whether or not she approves of the mask.

This does not bode well. I force my smile to beam brighter as I twirl her away and then draw her back, just a little closer than before. "Am *I* allowed to remove the mask?"

"My bridegroom may remove the mask and veils at the appropriate time." She speaks with no emotion in her voice, neither joy nor fear, merely resignation.

Pursing my lips, I drop her hand and then fully encircle her slim waist with my grip. I lift her off the ground, above me, and spin her in the sky to cheer her up.

When I set Icarus back down, I ignore the whispers of the surrounding couples, watching us more than dancing with each other.

Not that I can blame them. I do not want to look away from Icarus either.

I lean toward her, so that my next words are for her ears only. "And will your bridegroom also be allowed to remove your gown?" My gaze drops to the strange covering over her chest, and then I quickly revert my eyes to her garish mask.

"Every law proclaims it legal." She turns away from me, as if to spin herself with no help from me.

Before she can escape, I grasp her hand and draw her back to me, her back against my chest. I tighten my grip on her hand while my other wraps around her stomach and rests there, sealing her to me. I continue to guide us to the rhythm of the music.

Once again, I lean toward her. "What I meant was not whether the law allowed it, but if *you* would allow it."

"What I would or would not like to allow means nothing in the face of what I *must* or must *not* permit. I am a woman, and it was foolish of me to dream otherwise."

I lean my face closer to her, my lips nearly grazing the patch of skin between her veil and neck cloth. "You did not seem foolish when you spoke to me of your dreams and aspirations."

"That I spoke them to you was the greatest folly of all." She breaks partly away from me and swirls out like she meant to before. We are joined only by the clasp of one of our hands as she stands across from me. Even with her mask and veil, I can tell she's glaring at me. I fear she might even be crying.

None of this was what was supposed to happen when she discovered the truth. Mayhap I can pretend to just be Phoebus after all. If she agrees to run away and wed me today instead of going through with the sacrifice to Apollo, the bargain would still be appeased; she would still be mine.

But what was meant to help her see the truth of my love for her would just be a lie to bind her to me falsely.

I feel fear as I never did before. Is it because I'm wearing a mortal form, or would it still exist as long as Icarus is on the verge of rejecting me? A cowardly part of my heart longs to summon my swans to me. They bear the chariot where I replaced my harp— the weapon of choice for wooing Icarus— and my bow and quiver— the weapon of choice for any enemies that may arise.

Instead, I tug Icarus back to face me. To my surprise, it's her who reaches behind me, her hand splaying possessively on the back of my head. Her nails bite into my scalp, snagging at strands of hair. She says nothing, just breathes so heavily that her chest brushes against mine with our new proximity.

"I take all your words as seriously as you meant them," I murmur, clutching her back. "And I certainly meant *all* of mine."

"Which ones? It must be so tiring to keep everything straight between your facades." She lifts one leg partly around my waist, her skirt flaring around us and the sunlight reflecting off the sheen of the material.

"Every word I spoke to you, no matter which mouth spoke them, was uttered from the same heart." I dip forward, lowering her before me. "I will not take from you what you do not wish to give. No touch you receive from me will be unwelcome."

"*Everything* about you is unwelcome."

I have no time to wince. We are in the final moments. If I cannot turn this around, *I* am in my final moments. "You can still pursue your dreams to invent and dance and soar. Just under my protection."

"You mean in your cage?" She laughs dryly, no mirth in her tone. "It would seem I am no longer a flower whose beauty has been plucked, but a bird captured to be a novelty— a *pet.*"

"You are none of that." I feel my throat closing with emotion even though her voice remains devoid of anything but coolness. "And yet . . ." I draw her upright, my hands dropping to her hips. "Yet you are *everything.*"

Icarus plants both feet on the ground. Then she slowly raises her hands above her head as she continues to sway in my grip. "Because you *love* me?"

"As I have said before and will say again with a vow."

She spins in place, and I wonder if she's even listening. But I *need* her to listen. Not because her future happiness is on the line.

But because my life is.

I will not be one of the monsters that Artemis' huntresses flee from. And I cannot live without Icarus. I have woven a web for myself, created from my own hubris, and Icarus alone can save me.

I tighten my grip on her, halting her mid-twirl. "You can't pretend to feel nothing for me. I'm not the only one who was smiling in the cave."

Icarus' Hades-kissed mask just stares blankly at me. Her words are just as empty. "Love is a choice. A choice I do not have the luxury of making."

Horror floods me. "But it is a choice we *both* can make." Before I realize what I'm doing, I drop to one knee before her. Memories of how she flew away from me when I begged her to consider my love last night flash through my mind. My mortal body breaks out into a cold sweat.

But what has begun cannot be undone.

Suddenly, Icarus is tapping at my elbows, trying to tug me up. "Not yet. *Please,* not yet."

"I'll give you your private vow first and then the public vow I promised."

"This is hardly private."

I glance past her and realize everyone has halted dancing and is now studying us. The quiet wasn't just because I was enraptured in Icarus, but because the crowd was trying to eavesdrop. Only Ariadne doesn't appear to be listening. Though I know she is likely paying the closest attention of all. She just disguises it well it as she dances with a tall man with a strong nose and a silver wreathe on his head.

Standing, I allow her to lead me out into the gardens. A few people are milling around out here, and she picks up her speed, tugging me past the swan pond and back into the castle. This appears to be an antechamber used for storage, as we are finally alone except for an assortment of what appears to be gardening supplies.

Icarus drops her hold on me. Then she grasps her mask and tugs it off, casting it to the ground. When she turns to me, her bangs are damp across her scalp, her skin is flushed, and her eyes are wide with a storm of emotions waging within.

"What can you possibly vow to me that can make up for what I'm losing?!" she demands, her voice breaking. "And don't say your love. Love doesn't force someone's hand."

I stare at her, the life I built for us in my mind crumbling before me. Everything I did was in vain because of one false step at the beginning.

"I-I'm sorry," I whisper. "I'm sorry that my dream is your nightmare."

She says nothing, just studies me warily, tottering back and forth, as though on the heels of her feet.

I want to reach for her, to steady her or to ground me, I know not. But I clench my fists to my side and take a step back. "I had a prophecy. *You* were my vision. And I thought . . . I thought that made you mine, that the Creator had promised you to me somehow." But the brightest of blessings can so easily become the darkest of curses when misused.

"You thought you owned me already?"

"I forgot that the Creator never forces Himself on anyone, no matter how much better His path is for those He loves. And I am so much less than He is." I shake my head.

When I look up again, Icarus has her arms wrapped around her chest. She's no longer tottering back and forth, but completely shivering, like my words are too great for her frail mortal form.

I want to look away from the weakness she's choosing for herself and me, but I can't. I need to look her in the eyes as I sentence myself to a severing of my immortality. "I love you, Icarus. And because I love you, I release you from our betrothal."

Chapter Thirty-Nine

Icarus

I stare at Phoebus— *Apollo*— in shock. The rage coursing in my veins cools at his words, turning to stone and then crumbling to dust.

"Y-you're setting me free?" I whisper.

"Yes. I will make a public vow of it, since it was technically King Minos that I made the bargain with, with Crete as the stake." Phoebus awkwardly rakes a hand through his hair, looking as lost and mortal as I feel.

For a moment, we just stare at each other. Then Phoebus nods at me. "I'll go resume my other form and make my announcement, then." He moves to walk past me.

My mind is still trying to process all that has been said. But my hand snakes out and grasps his elbow.

Phoebus pauses and glances back at me. And the moment my gaze lock with the twin skies that are his eyes, all my feminine fury and righteous rage ebbs like a receding tide. I feel naked and vulnerable without it.

"If you retract your bargain without our honoring it . . ." I lick my lips, and Phoebus' gaze immediately drops to my mouth. "Isn't that a death sentence for Primordials? That is what you are, isn't it?"

"Yes, I'm a Primordial." He studies me, obviously weighing his next words. "And yes, breaking a bargain is not something a Primordial survives. But that is hardly your problem. I am the one who arranged this, and on me alone shall the consequences fall."

"But I don't want you to die." My words are barely a whisper but no less true for their low volume. They are certainly no less startling to me after I've spent the night intending to kill him myself. But now he's giving himself into my hand and . . .

Phoebus gives me a small smile with the lips I wish I could stop thinking about— especially now. "I was the fool to enter a bargain and make the stakes of failing as grave as smiting an entire island. I will not put that on either of our consciences. I must put their minds at ease and make them know they do not need to punish you for not wedding me, because they will suffer no consequences for it."

Once again, he tries to walk away. But my grip tightens on his elbow.

"Are those the only two options? You smite Crete or you perish?"

Phoebus opens his mouth, closes it, opens and closes it again, and then just smiles sadly.

"Right," I breathe, understanding him perfectly. "If I wed you today, per the terms of the bargain you struck with King Minos, you would not need to relent your wrath and die for showing mercy."

"But I set you free—"

"I could still choose you."

Phoebus goes rigid under my touch. Hope rises in his gaze like the sun in the east.

I quickly turn away. "I'm not saying that I will. I just need . . . a moment to consider everything."

"Of course." He finally escapes my grip. "I will wait for you in the dancing hall. When you see me there, I will once again be in my true form, so that none can mistake who speaks the declaration I shall make. Crete shall be safe one way or another."

With that, he turns to stride away.

I watch him until I cannot see him any longer as the scent of frankincense wafts into my nostrils. I tear my gaze from the garden to find King Minos leaning in the back entrance, a smug smile on his face. Ariadne stands behind him, her expression devoid of her spirit and filled only with suffering. Just behind her is Vassilis, whose gaze lingers too low beneath mine to read his expression, not that it is difficult to determine his thoughts.

"Well done, my dear." King Minos strides past me to close the door Phoebus left open. "Our little sun god appears to have played right into your hand. Or was that your *cousin?* It's so hard to keep track of your suitors these days."

Scowling at him, I hurry to Ariadne and take her hands in mine. I want her to look at me, to show some sign that she's still in her shell of a body, somehow, but she just looks through me.

I glare at Minos. "What did you do to her?!"

"I simply reminded her who has the power on Crete. All authority is mine to give or take away." He spins toward me, that offensive smile still marring his face.

Unable to look away from the predatory gleam in his eyes, I try to rub some warmth into Ariadne's icy hands.

Minos meanders back toward us. "Speaking of authority, tell me, why didn't you extract the vow I commanded of you when dearest Apollo was begging to give it to you?" He cocks his head to one side. "Are you truly so dramatic that it must be done publicly?" Minos clucks his tongue. "Women can be so cruel sometimes. Isn't that right, Ariadne?"

"What did you do to her?" I hiss.

"The same as I'll do to you if you do not go out into that dancing hall and extract the necessary vow from your *cousin.*"

Icy rage flows through me as I see what he's done to Ariadne and as I sense what he's trying to do to me. Whatever it takes to control us both and kill Apollo in the process.

Phoebus may not even be mortal, but he's a hundred times the man Minos will ever be.

I whirl toward the king, placing myself between father and daughter. "No."

Minos frowns at me in confusion more than anything. "'No'?"

Hoping my trembling isn't noticeable, I lift my chin high. "No, I will not obey. No, I will not let you have power over me any longer. No, I will not comply because you have decided to have authority over me."

For a long moment, Minos is silent. Then, "So, you do not wish to be a goddess in your own right, then?"

"Consort to the Sun will be enough of a title for me."

"Trying to shuffle off one man's power to submit to another's. How disappointing. You should have chosen me." Minos flicks his wrist. "Ariadne, you have further use to me, after all. Put on the gown made for you, dearest daughter."

Ariadne pulls her icy hands from mine and grips my sleeves instead.

I shrug away from her. "What are you doing?"

"I'm so sorry." Her voice is hollow.

"We can fight together," I whisper.

"Maybe as a goddess. But no mortal woman can defy him." She slips off her sandal, revealing a stump where there used to be a pinky toe.

Gasping, I stumble backward. My blood cools from rage to horror, slowing my movements, slowing even my ability to process.

"Do hurry, my dears," Minos calls, stooping to pluck up my discarded mask, his back toward us in his nonchalance. "Or Vassilis and I will be forced to assist."

I glance toward the doorway and find Vassilis still leering at me. I slam the door closed in his face.

"I'm so sorry," Ariadne whispers, grasping my sleeves again. "But today, at least, there is no escape."

239

Then she yanks off my dress.

Chapter Forty

The Unpromised Couple

Apollo:

My first entrance into the dancing hall went unnoticed until I began dancing with the bride of honor. Now everyone looks at me as I stride into the room. If there were whispered speculations of my identity before, now no one is unsure, and all fall to their knees.

I remain in my same attire as before but feel more myself with my golden curls and mantle. Though, I do miss the somehow grounding feeling of being mortal. Not so much the discomfort and awkwardness that came with it, though.

If Icarus rejects my suit once and for all there will be no form that I can take to escape the pain. Or the certain death that shall come upon me one way or another when I do not take her as my bride this day.

I glance toward the windows, taking in the sun beaming in the sky. My constant companion has become the hourglass counting down toward my fate.

There is another wave of shushing noises, and I turn toward the crowd, lowered enough before me to reveal the woman stepping into the dancing hall. Icarus has once again put on that garish mask, and I briefly play at the thought of removing it for her, since she does not appear fond of it. But, no, I will not shame her so in front of these witnesses.

And I certainly will make no rash action while I do not yet know her decision.

For a moment, I stand frozen across the dancing hall from her, nothing between us but space as all of Crete shows deference to us. But all I long for is a word from her lips.

Instead, all Icarus does is study me, still as a statue and uncannily resembling one as well with her mask. My entire life, long as it has been, flashes through my mind's eye while I wait for my sentencing from the woman in the blue and golden gown.

Icarus:

Wearing Ariadne's cerulean blue gown, I scan the hallways for Papa as Vassilis drags me toward our tower. King Minos has departed, no doubt to witness his plot unfold. And Ariadne is with him as the one through which it unfolds.

I tug my arm, but Vassilis just tightens his grip, his nails piercing my skin. "Come now, little morsel. You can still be *my* goddess."

"Unhand me at once!" I hiss, trying to let my rage overwhelm my fear. Where's Papa? He needs to rescue me so I can rescue Phoebus— Apollo.

If I am not given to him as a bride this day, he will have to execute his wrath. Which he cannot do if he vows not to do it— to Ariadne.

I don't want him to destroy Crete. But I don't want him to be tricked into sealing his own demise, either.

Vassilis scoffs and tugs me toward himself. "I only obey Minos' orders, wench." His disgusting lips trail along my shoulders as he whispers, "And he doesn't need you to be a maidenly sacrifice any longer."

Horror washes over me, and I jerk backward, nearly toppling over the side of the winding staircase to escape. Only his continued grip on me keeps me from falling over.

"Come now, little one, am I truly *that* repulsive?" He loosens his grip on me, and chasm below seems to tug at me. "You would truly choose death over my kiss?"

I glance between Vassilis and the drop. It seems so far because I've known these stairs since I was a child. But I've since fallen from greater heights than between here and the stairs just below me. I may be sore, but if I position myself correctly, I'll be uninjured. I'll be fully capable of running.

Vassilis loosens his grip just a little more as he steps closer to me, drawing the threat of either his embrace or a fall closer to fruition. "Don't pretend like you didn't enjoy my kiss when you were younger."

My gaze snaps to him. "I was a child!"

He sneers. "I'm sure Apollo appreciated the lesson I gave you. I could teach you so much more, little morsel. I don't believe you've grown up on me as much as you think."

I choke down the gag of utter revulsion threatening to escape. Then I paste on a smile. "You're right, Vassilis."

My childhood nightmare bares his teeth in what might be considered a smile to some, but just seems like a threat to me. "Of course. I knew you still wanted me."

"That's not the part you were right about."

Then I wrench my hand out of his grip and fall.

Apollo:

I'm going to fall.

My feet are both on the marble floor, but my soul hangs over a great abyss. The Fates are prepared to cut the string keeping me from plummeting beyond the Veil.

A word from Icarus can save me, though. Or snap the string sooner.

Icarus gives me no word. However, she finally shifts, giving me the barest of nods.

Joy blooms within me like the sun rising in my heart. "I have a vow to make unto you, my bride, as a token of my love that shall be as undying as you will be, my wife." I beam at her, more certain than I have been of anything in my entire life, even the continuity of the sun under my father's reign.

I will not fail Icarus. Not after she saved me from death.

Icarus:

I do not fall to my death. For a horrifying moment, I don't think I'll get my body oriented in time. But then I land on the steps below in a staggered crouch. I slip down a couple of stairs but stop the descent.

Then, even though my knees feel like they've been smashed in, I jump to my feet.

Above me, Vassilis hurls insults and curses. I don't wait for him to come after me with more than words.

"If you surrender to the Unknown God, you need not surrender to any other."

Ignoring the pain in favor of my fear and desperation, I rush down the last of the stairs. Then I hurry toward the dancing hall.

I may have only moments left to keep that lovesick fool from falling into Minos' trap. And there's nothing to do but fly to his side as swiftly as possible.

Apollo:

I take another step toward Icarus. Then another. She doesn't move to close the distance between us, but neither does she flee from me.

I can see that even if I had the strength to give her my Kiss today, she would not take it. But if I could convince her to wed me in the span of three sunrises, I can surely woo her to immortality, eventually.

The tugging in my blood reminds me of the vow I made her that I can no longer ignore. The time has come to give her my second vow.

I reach my hands to the Firmament that I govern. "In the sun's witness, I decree that no harm shall fall upon Crete by my hand as a testament of my affections."

The crowd claps uncertainly before moving to a thunderous applause when they see it doesn't displease me. How can I be displeased? I'm smiling at the woman I love.

Except, something is wrong. She's just standing there, saying nothing. And then there's movement behind her, drawing my gaze.

Another woman slides into the room, her frizzy curls falling over her rosy face. She's wearing the wrong gown, but it's obviously Icarus staring at me with her horrified gaze.

But if that's her—

I turn back to the woman I've confessed my love to, believing she accepted my suit and my survival.

Was it a lie? Was it *all* a lie?

Slowly, the woman in the blue gown lifts her mask from her head. Princess Ariadne stares blearily at me.

The vow I made her entwines with my soul, binding me against the bargain I already made in an impossible trap. I feel as though the strength is being pulled from my psyche, a preparation for the Fates to end me.

Confused, I turn back to Icarus, hoping for some kind of explanation. She knows I would have sacrificed myself for both her and Crete willingly. So why did she feel the need to play such a cruel joke on me?

However, Icarus is no longer standing at the entrance, or anywhere else in the dancing hall. She's gone, my sun set behind the horizon. It's just as well, she doesn't need to see the way my knees buckle as it becomes clear to my Primordial blood that I am coming to an end of my immorality.

Ariadne watches me with no expression, a silent witness as I hit the ground, kneeling before those who were just prostrate before me.

Guards— apparently ready for this moment— surround and bind me with rope. As if I shouldn't have the strength to tear through these and throw the men away from me.

Or I would have the strength, even dying, if I hadn't let Icarus distract me from my duties. Mayhap it was all a trap from the beginning. Of course, Icarus couldn't control my visions.

But in the past, they have always foretold tragedy. All this time, I feared Icarus falling, but it was me. I fell for *her*.

Now I am the tragedy.

Chapter Forty-One

Icarus

I feel as though the world is shattering around me as Apollo's words ring out through the crowd.

"In the sun's witness, I decree that no harm shall fall upon Crete by my hand as a testament of my affections."

My mouth is open to call him off, but it's too late. After everything, it's too late.

Crete is saved, and Apollo—

Apollo needs my hand in marriage, or he won't survive.

I try to rush at him, to demand the marriage rites here and now—as though any priest will go against King Minos' wishes.

But then arms wrap around my waist and tug me backward, lifting me off my feet.

"Let me go!" I cry, my words lost in the roar of applause as the Minoans celebrate their liberation from fear.

The man holding me ignores me as he yanks me out of the dancing hall and halfway down the hall.

Finally, I wrest free of his grip and turn, ready to strike Vassilis. I find Papa's worry-lined face instead.

"Papa!" Emotions crash over me like waves, and I throw my arms around him.

"We have no time." Half picking me up again, he takes me toward the stairs.

"What are you doing?!"

"Yes, what *are* you doing?"

Turning, I find King Minos standing in the hall just outside the dancing hall. He studies us with a wry grin while he shines his fingernails on his purple linen.

"My daughter is having a fit of emotions," Papa answers. "You know how it is with young girls. I'm just taking her to her room where she won't be a bother to anyone."

I turn my glare to Papa. A "*fit*"? After I was used, betrayed, almost assaulted, and now fear for the life of the man I almost love and the wellbeing of my dearest friend . . . My horror is confined to a "fit"?

Papa gives me a warning glare before turning a pleasant smile to Minos, the least deserving of all men.

Minos shrugs. "See that she is kept out of the way. I would hate to see something happen to the apple of your eye." With that, he turns back and strides into the room where Apollo is being restrained like a wild animal.

Rage flows through me anew, and I try to return to his side. But Papa's grip on me tightens and tugs me toward the stairs.

"What are you doing?!" I cry.

"The man had no mercy on his own daughter," Papa hisses. "Do you think he'll have mercy on mine?"

The sheer fear etched across Papa's visage has me following him up the stairs. Thankfully, Vassilis no longer stands outside our tower, and we make it inside safely. Papa falls upon the locks with more earnestness than I've ever seen from him.

"Phoebus is going to perish," I gasp, my thoughts catching up with me. "Apollo will die!"

"That was what you wanted." Papa fastens the last bolt and then rushes to his room.

I follow him. "I-I changed my mind. I couldn't do it."

Papa throws the hemp covering off his own wings. "Then you can take comfort that the betrayal didn't come from your hand."

"But I don't want him to die *at all*."

"Death is all that awaits any of us in Crete." Papa grabs a pre-packed satchel and tosses it at me. Then he slings the other over his shoulder. "Minos is mad. Now that he'll have the power of Apollo under his thumb, there will be no limit to his horrors."

I finger the strap of my satchel. "Then we have to stop him."

"He is too mighty for such things."

"But you are cunning!"

Papa turns to me, a brokenness in his expression. "I have given everything to Minos— all the contents of my mind sacrificed to his delusions. The moment he learns I have nothing left I'm willing to give, he will take all I have left." He reaches to touch my face before pulling back. Then Papa grabs his wings and strides past me. "I promised to protect you, and this is the only way I can honor that vow. We fly today."

"You also promised me I could wed whom I wish."

He freezes halfway to the stairway to the top of our tower. "Icarus . . ."

"I thought I hated him," I whisper. "It was easier to face that than the fact that he'd won. And that the prize was my heart of all the foolish things to gamble . . ."

Papa hunches his shoulders. "Icarus, what are you saying?"

"I think I'm falling for him! And . . . I need to save him. Or at least try to." I bury my face behind my hands, the flight before me losing all joy. The thought of flying ever again causing only sorrow.

It will only ever remind me of him, the man who flew with me, only to fall. And he fell by what he thought was my hand . . .

Despite Papa's promise, I knew deep down love wasn't a choice I would be able to make. I thought Minos would control it, and he did. But it seems my heart had a bigger part in sentencing me to whom I was to care about despite all reason.

But I can still make it my choice. I can still accept it despite my hubris. I can still determine my destiny . . . "I can still rescue him. If I give myself to him in marriage on the Summer Solstice per the terms of the original bargain, he does not die when he is unable to carry out his wrath."

"Apollo will be heavily guarded while Minos waits for the last of his life to leave him and his power to enter Ariadne. He's likely not even on Crete any longer—"

Papa stops himself, but too late. I hurry forward and place my hand on his shoulder. "But you know where he's taking him, don't you? You are one of Minos' chief advisors—"

With a sigh, Papa sets his wings on the floor and turns to me. "He's going to be on a heavily armed ship. We have no chance to extract him from there—"

"But we might be able to reach him where they're taking him? At least long enough to complete the marriage rites and restore his life— his power? Then he can deliver us from there."

"Icarus, please think about this. Just last night, you were ready to slay him with your own hands. Now you would entwine your life to his forever?"

I close my eyes. Breathe deeply and then exhale. Try to sort out my current emotions and consider my future wellbeing. Which course would give me a possibility of future happiness, or else spare me from great sorrow?

"I-I don't know. But I know I don't want this."

"That's not a good enough reason to risk our lives."

Opening my eyes, I look into Papa's brown gaze I inherited. "I do want to marry him on my own terms, and if these are the terms, then so be it. We can work out life together, if he's alive for me to work it out with."

It's Papa's turn to slide his eyes closed, his expression pained. "We can never return to Crete, at least not as long as Minos is in power."

"But Ariadne—"

"We can send word to Orion, but not even Apollo can raise his hand against Crete— or its king— should we rescue him. And Minos has more than one way to fell a Primordial and consume its power."

I glance around my tower, suddenly realizing this is the last I'll ever see it. What seemed like a prison all this time suddenly reminds me that it's the home I've abided in for so long.

"Grab whatever you can't leave behind." Papa gestures to my satchel. "With or without Apollo, we flee today."

"With Apollo." I hurry to my room and grab the golden signet ring he gifted me. I slide it on over my thumb. "He is what I refuse to flee without."

Papa sighs. "Then I shall honor my vow to let you select your bridegroom and hope to Olympus I do not fail on my promise to protect you in the process." He turns to ascend the stairs.

I climb onto my pulley system one last time. "Do you know where Minos has taken Apollo?"

He sighs again. "Yes. The Spire."

Chapter Forty-Two

The Unpromised Couple

Apollo:

I t is laughable the amount of security Minos has placed around me on this small barge. I am kept in the brig, bound with ropes and chains alike. Two mortals— large for their kind but still smaller than my default physique— sit within the brig with me. Two more stand guard outside. Occasionally, Vassilis comes to gloat at me on the other side of the bars of my brig.

"Still right where I left you." Vassilis grins, his teeth yellowed from too much wine. "Well, I better go check on the Princess. Mayhap she will have absorbed all your power by the time I return." With that, he mercifully spares me from his presence again.

I snort as I glance from the bars and the guards. Even though I left my bow behind when I came to the ball, it would still be a simple thing to slay them all. Except, the Firmament is not ready to give me a portion of its power, not until I re-earn its trust. Something I cannot do at the moment.

Not that I would slay Ariadne and Icarus. Mayhap they tricked me into this, but I was the fool who stumbled into this trap. Vassilis deserves my wrath for something far darker than this betrayal, though. I would happily slay him. I can only hope that when Artemis seeks vengeance, he will be her prey.

Artemis . . . She won't even know that something is amiss since the sun is not due to set yet. Of course, when it does, so sets my last chance to save my life.

Even if Artemis did know, there is nothing she can do. Even if I was given false hope when I made my vow, I still entered the bargain willingly, and then the vow. There is nothing she can do to interfere with another Primordial's bargain. And now, it will fall on her to rise and set the sun.

The Fates will likely take their time finding the end of the string that represents my life. I may live in Minos' captivity for a considerable length of time before I finally fade away. I could, theoretically, summon my Primordial power from my blood rather than my domain, and transform into a snake that can twist out of these chains and escape. I could live my last days free.

But the memory of what a fool I have played would follow me, and that is the greatest torment of all. If Icarus had merely broken my heart, I could have dealt with it. But that she broke my trust as well . . .

I close my eyes, but then I see her as I saw her for a year. Happily dancing, free and jubilant.

And, now that I see it— alone. All she ever needed to be joyful was freedom. Not me or my love.

No, my love only ever earned me misery.

I lean back against the hard wooden bench chained to the wall. Soon, I'll have to consider using what strength I have left to escape, if only to give Artemis my last goodbye. For now, though, I will conserve my energy.

And try not to remember the other repeating vision I have of Icarus, the one where I appear to be present.

In that one, she plummets to her death.

At least, with me not in her life, she can be free and safe. Mayhap also cold and cruel, but such is the way with mortals.

Icarus:

Papa and I stand on the on the opposite sides of the tower as we stretch out our wings.

He tests his with a few flaps before coming to inspect my straps like I haven't flown without his inspection dozens of times before. "After we rescue him, you are certain your bridegroom will be able to protect you?"

His words are so final, like he's already writing himself out of my life. I want to assure him that Phoebus said he could be his Master Architect.

But we aren't rescuing Phoebus— we're liberating Apollo, and he is so jealous of my attentions.

Licking my suddenly dry lips, I remember the blood Apollo has spilled for me already. "He can protect me." I want to ask if Papa will be able to take care of himself without me, but of course, he can.

Papa tightens the strap on my left elbow. "And you'll be happy?"

"As happy as a woman can ever be." I gasp as he tightens the harness over my shoulders.

"It's not too late to change your mind." Papa tightens the belt on my right elbow now. "The mainland is a greater distance, but we can make it in a day if we go straight there. If we go to the spire, we will need either your bridegroom's assistance, or a night's rest in Minos' territory before departing for it."

Suddenly, I remember Phoebus— Apollo— falling into the swan pond in his desperation to retrieve a feather for me. The light in his eyes, the ease of his smile, and the eagerness of his touch . . .

How could I have ever feared a man filled with such goodness? Mayhap he slaughtered Minos' servants. But look at what his servants are doing to him now. It is no sin to slay the wicked, is it?

Above all, though, I know he's trapped. Minos has him as caged like the King once contained me— only I at least could fly. And when I thought I was losing that, Apollo taught me how to soar on his chariot and on his lips.

It's time I returned the favor.

I nod, more confident than I was even downstairs. "I throw my lot in with Apollo."

Papa tightens the belt at my waist a little too tightly. As he hurries to adjust it, a woman's voice invades our conversation.

"Well, that is a relief to hear."

I turn my head and startle to find a woman standing just beyond the tower, perched on a silver chariot drawn by five golden-horned deer. The wind blows equally silver tresses around the woman's face, and black eyes meet mine.

My jaw drops, and Papa stiffens. I turn awkwardly toward her, and because of my still outstretched arms, Papa has to move with me.

"I had come to bargain for my brother's life, but it appears I need to offer a boon instead." The ethereal woman smiles, her teeth flashing.

"A-Artemis?!" I gasp. I attempt to bow, but my wings and Papa both hinder me.

The goddess waves my sorry attempts at deference away, then her smile deepens. "What a pleasure to finally meet you, future sister of mine."

Apollo:
Maybe I shouldn't tell my sister.

I consider this alternative as I'm prodded up the winding staircase of the Spire that I took Icarus to just last night.

If I told Artemis, she might do something foolhardy, like refuse to raise the moon and set the sun. But she can't afford to weaken now that she'll have twice the responsibilities. We have already lost control of the weather. If we fail the mortals with the lights of the Firmament, chaos will descend— along with every evil the Creator instructed us to prevent.

"Welcome to your new temple!" jeers one of Minos' men, and then I'm pushed through an open doorway.

I turn just in time to see Asios shaking his head at a scoffing man.

Vassilis walks past them, his dark eyes twinkling with glee. "Well, now, if it isn't the god who thought he could rob me of my Icarus. Look how the mighty have fallen."

Something rises above the brokenness spreading throughout my body from my heart. Something hot with rage. Because even if it was Icarus who wronged me, this monster hurt her first. "She is no more yours than she is mine."

"Oh, she will be mine soon enough. Minos has promised her to me at last. And he knows I'm far more of a threat to him than you ever were."

I clench my fists in my binds. "You will not touch her."

"I will not obey a dead god." Vassilis turns away from me to stride back toward the entrance. Then he glances over his shoulder. "But *she* will obey my every whim as if I were the complete pantheon."

Growling, I lunge at him.

Suddenly, Vassilis is on the other side of the entrance just as the door slams in my face. I throw myself against it repeatedly, trying to burst through my hands are bound. Bolts slide into place on the other side, and though the door shudders, it does not open.

Then all my strength is gone, and I can only slump against it as I turn to take in my new surroundings.

My new "temple" is like Icarus' tower in its rounded shape. However, it has no other rooms or furniture— or anything other than splinters and patches in the wood that weren't meant to be windows.

One such patch is large enough for me to fit through if I reverted to my mortal form. I could escape through there if I so desire. Avenge myself on Vassilis at the very least.

I call upon my magical blood to turn me into a bird of prey so I can soar for a few moments.

Nothing happens.

Frowning, I glance down at myself. I'm still in my natural form with no sign of morphing.

Neglecting my Firmament caused more weakness than even I expected. Or mayhap it's the broken heart. My heart's never been so shattered before. Its symptoms are all new to me. Even music has abandoned me now.

Kyknos and the other swans are tethered to my chariot. They will hear my order from anywhere and come to me.

They will also obey Artemis' order when she has to call them home.

I slide down the wall and slump against the floor. Mayhap Icarus was a trap from the beginning, but I am still sick at the thought of failing her. I cannot even bear the thought of failing Artemis. I've failed the Firmament and myself, fool as I've been.

At least Icarus must be soaring free by now. Vassilis will never touch her because she was always meant to be free. Just as I was always meant to fall for her.

"So, Creator," I mutter, since soon I will see the One Whom I've failed the most, "this is why you did not create us to feel pleasure. Because the accompanying pain is simply too great a sacrifice."

Chapter Forty-Three

Icarus

One would think I would be used to coming face to face with Primordials after thoroughly kissing one in the cave.

But seeing Artemis in her splendor has my knees knocking. I bow awkwardly despite my wings. "My Lady of the Hunt!"

Artemis gestures at me from her chariot. "Please, rise. I came for your alliance, not your servitude."

"We are indeed going to rescue your brother." I gesture at Papa, so she knows not to smite him even though he didn't bow.

"Good. I could not force your hand, same as I cannot punish Minos for his treachery." Artemis' beautiful face scrunches in a strangely human way. "I cannot interfere with another Primordial's bargain, even if he's my foolhardy brother."

"We go all the same, my Lady." I glance toward the sun, making sure it's still high enough in the sky to give me hope I can make it to the Spire in time.

"And for that, I grant you my boon." She hands me a bracelet that is woven of silver cords that shimmer in such a way to imply it must be made of strands of her gorgeous hair.

"But *I* am supposed to give *you* an offering on my wedding day," I say.

Artemis shakes her head and gestures toward the bracelet. "This is the Cuff of the Hunt. It will guide you toward the prey you most desire. In this case, my brother."

I feel my skin warm. "I would hardly call your brother prey."

"Yet he is in another's trap." Artemis slides the bracelet over my wrist, her touch as cool as Apollo's is warm. Then she reclaims her reins. "Because of the bargain, I cannot actively assist you in your flight. But I shall wait by my brother's prison to officiate the marriage rites."

"If you know where he is," Papa mutters, "can you not rescue him yourself?"

My eyes widen, and I glance between Papa and Artemis warily.

"Not from certain death." Artemis displays no trace of being offended in her perfect face. "Please make it to his side before I have no choice but to set the sun."

With that, she swats her reins, and the breeze whisks her away far more swiftly than it promises to carry us.

I glance at Papa. He glances back at me. Then he holds up something I didn't see before. A gossamer veil secured to a golden wreathe. "If you are to wed, we must honor the rites."

"Y-yes." I'm startled by the beauty of the garment. "Where did this come from?"

"As I told Minos, I can provide your wedding trousseau." He gently places the golden wreath on my head, pinning it to my hair. The veil falls gracefully over my face. I can see through it, but I'm still relieved when he pushes it up over my head.

Papa steps back, studying me. There is moisture in his eyes. "Are you quite certain this is the path—"

I nod once. Then, because that's not enough to convince either of us, I rush forward, jump off the tower, spreading out my wings.

Thanks to the after current Artemis left behind, my wings are carried on the breeze, and I elevate.

A moment later, Papa takes to the skies behind me, then we're both flying toward where the Spire and its walls are just barely visible in the distance. The bracelet on my wrist tugs me forward. But not as surely as my heart does.

I know the moment I cross as far as I've ever flown before. That moment should fill me with jubilee, but instead exhaustion like never before fills every cavity of my body.

The Spire is clearly visible, and more than half of the journey is behind us. But Papa was certainly correct to say that we would need to rest before making a return journey or escaping to Athens. I can barely imagine flapping my arms one more time, let alone—

My movements slow, and I drop several cubits.

"Icarus!" Papa yells above me.

I have to crane my head to see him. While his face is flushed and sweat shines through his *chiton* and drips from his beard, he keeps his pace steady.

If a man twice my age can do this, so can I. Especially since *I'm* the one with love for Apollo in my heart.

Closing my eyes, I remember the way he froze under my kiss in the sea. The way he eagerly returned my caresses in the cave. The hope in his gaze as he proposed to me—

"Icarus, keep the same pace to conserve your strength!"

I open my eyes and find myself sailing several cubits above Papa now.

Gritting my teeth, I slow my flaps until I'm just above Papa, enough out of the way that our flapping wings won't intersect.

"Unknown God, save us!"

At Papa's sudden proclamation, I look away from focusing on keeping a safe distance between us and turn forward.

Clouds so dark they are almost black, an affront to the Summer Solstice, swirls around the Spire. The wind becomes a little faster and a little chillier.

I glance at Papa, and though he doesn't turn away from the storm brewing before us, I know he fears the same thing I do. If it rains, we won't have long before our waxy glue dissolves and the feathers are torn off.

But it's too late to turn back. We would be fighting the breeze, and I barely have the strength to make it to the Spire, let alone anywhere else. And it's still too far to swim to the Spire, especially with how choppy the waves are becoming. And I would surely drown trying to swim back to Crete.

Forward is the only option.

I scan the sky desperately for some sign of Artemis. Does she who control the moon not also have control of the weather? But there is no sign of her.

Except— is that the moon rising over the sun? What an eerie picture the sky paints. The sun and moon hang together. The light of the Summer Solstice above the ever-darkening clouds. Apollo's time is running out at the same time our window for reaching him safely is shrinking.

And then a bolt of lightning flashes.

Chapter Forty-Four

The Unpromised Couple

Apollo:

Apparently, my visions are the last of my gifts to leave me. For being so honored by physicians, I cannot heal myself. Artemis, who I think glanced in at me before soaring off is apparently unable to look upon my condition when she cannot heal me either. Even if this weren't a result of my broken bargain, her healing abilities are limited to childbirth, anyway.

But the visions . . . they plague me every time I close my eyes.

The sky is darkening outside, even with Artemis stubbornly milking the Summer Solstice for all its worth. But I see the glare of the sun in my mind's eye. And though thunder is all I am supposed to hear over the sound of the crashing waves, I also detect the voice of evil itself.

There is no escaping the vision and its harsh shades of blood red and regal purple.

"Enjoy your new bride, Apollo!"

Though this isn't real and can never be real, I dive toward the source of the voice, relying on instinct and memories of past visions.

"Or maybe Hades will enjoy her instead."

I crash into a man just as a terrifying scream rips through the air.

Without a glance at the man that I've collided with, I dive again over the ledge, after the woman I know was thrown off or jumped.

My vision returns to me despite the sudden change in direction, and I see her, the woman of my dreams, trapped in my nightmares.

Icarus is falling like always, her hair haloing her wide-eyed face. Her skirts are wrapped around her legs, and her arms are spread out. The one remaining wing hangs awkwardly.

I utter incessant prayers in my heart while I draw on every power available to me that might be able to make me move faster.

Her gaze collides with mine. "I love you."

The shocking words send me stumbling out of the vision. I'm actually on my feet again, even though I gave up hope that I'd ever stand again an hour ago.

Since I'm on my feet now, I stumble toward the largest "window" so I can gaze out at the sun one last time. There are blessings in this.

I was part of the vision of Icarus' fall. Now that I'm not in it, mayhap it will never come to pass.

Also, Artemis is truly immortal now until she produces an heir. All the promises the Creator gave rest solely on her shoulders.

But there are also some issues.

Artemis is also going to be alone for the first time in all the eons we've lived together. She will have greater responsibilities to fulfill if she wants to keep her power and prevent mortal suffering.

If Vassilis has the opportunity, he will torment Icarus. My condolence is that Icarus and her father must be halfway across the sea by now.

I blow a golden curl out of my face and lean heavily against the hole.

The sun shines brightly above, or at least tries to, despite the dark clouds coming over it. And the moon is rising as well. I suppose I don't have much longer, even on the longest day of the year.

To think, last night I thought today was the dawn of a new era in my life. It seems to be the only false prophecy I ever made. Or mayhap it is still true. It will be the beginning of my life beyond the Veil.

At least I shall see Father and Mother again.

My gaze lowers to study the ever-growing storm. Lightning flashes briefly illuminate the sky, reminding me of Father. Why this portion of his power did not come to us, I know not. The thunder answers with loud nonsense that alleviates no mystery. A waterspout is generating near to the shore of this tiny island. Wouldn't it be ironic if it was what the Fates used to slay me, the son of Zeus?

Grunting, I watch its path and then startle.

Are those two people flying into this storm?

I jolt upright. "Icarus!"

Icarus:

The waterspout could be a problem.

If the wind doesn't whip us off course, if the rain doesn't disintegrate glue holding our wings together, and if the lightning doesn't set us on fire, the waterspout could drag us down to the crashing waves to drown.

If I didn't know better, I would say Zeus was punishing me.

The silver bracelet Artemis gave me tugs me forward, and despite the rapid loss of light, I can make out a figure peering out of the top of the spire. A flash of lightning illuminates golden curls.

"Apollo!" I scream, but my word is lost to the roll of thunder surrounding us.

Then I pass into the storm.

The winds were wild outside the clouds, but now I feel them yanking at my limbs. If it weren't for the brace I'm wearing, my arms would be bent forward. Several feathers go swirling into the sky. And the pounding rain soaking my hair to my scalp and beating down on my body threatens to loosen more. If the rains themselves don't successfully push me down into the violent waves.

Though I can barely see, the Cuff of the Hunt draws me forward. But Apollo isn't the only one I am concerned about losing track of in this storm.

I turn my head toward Papa to gauge his condition. He's keeping pace, but I see on his face he knows we don't have much more time before the elements consume us.

"Your veil!" he yells, as if that's the most important thing right now.

Above us, another bolt of lightning, this one passing through the clouds just above us, illuminates the seriousness on his face and makes my hair stand on end.

I suppose the procession to the groom is part of the marriage rites. If the wings are my chariot then the lightning bolts are my torches. And a bride must be veiled.

Bowing my head, I let the veil fall over my face. It immediately sticks to my face from the amount of precipitation it's already absorbed. I gasp at the drowning sensation.

I blow it off my face enough to move my mouth. "Apollo, I come to honor the bargain between you and Crete."

More thunder booms, and I can only hope Primordials have special hearing, or else this is all for naught.

"Apollo!" I scream with all the fury in my throat. "I sacrifice myself to you as your bride!"

Suddenly, another bolt of lightning flashes, illuminating the figure in the tower. For a horrifying moment, I think Apollo has just been killed by his own father. But then I realize the light didn't come from above— it's *him* who's glowing.

Hope fills me to see the sun at the other end of this storm.

"I, Daedalus," Papa calls beside me, stealing my attention even as the winds try to steal me, "give my daughter to Apollo!"

Are we really doing this right now? Commencing the wedding rites while still in the sky?

Another flash of light— this one actually a bolt of lightning— slices between Papa and me. I feel the heat of it on my skin, and it strikes Papa's left wing. The feathers instantly catch fire despite the pouring rain around us.

"Papa!" I scream, trying to flap toward him, even as several more of my own feathers blow away from me. The wind is greedy, though, and tugs at my entire person, trying to draw me toward the waterspout.

Unbalanced against the merciless downpour and violent winds, Papa plummets.

I scream.

Then a hole is punched through the clouds above us, allowing both moonlight and sunlight to stream in. Along with those glorious beams, five deer rush straight downward, drawing a silver chariot after my papa.

Before I can see if Artemis makes it to him, the wind preys on my diversion and new angle. It yanks me backward, and then I'm following a spiraling path pulling me into the waterspout.

I'm disoriented, with flashes of light around me, making it harder to pull free of the pull. One light seems to draw nearer to me.

And then instead of breathing air diluted with water, I'm immersed in a wall of water and a void I cannot inhale. Instead of spiraling in an ever-decreasing circle, I'm trapped— spinning in a tiny one that traps me. Yet, it threatens to spew me out at the same time.

If it did, would I be able to orient myself in time? I think it's pulling me higher rather than lower, and I've never crashed from this height. Even with water below me, it might still kill me.

I cannot tell up from down. But my arm bearing the Cuff of the Hunt still stretches out in faith.

Suddenly, light pierces through the wall, trapping me in the void. Not just light— a hand.

I take it, and it tugs me out, gasping and choking, but free. Instead of falling, powerful arms hold me against a firm body.

"Icarus, I accept your sacrifice," Apollo says as his chariot carries us away from the waterspout. "And in return, I give myself to you as your husband."

For all the extremes beating down on my body, it is the tenderness in his voice as he grants a vow not required of him that makes tears pool in my eyes.

Then I remember Papa and tear my gaze away from Apollo to see Artemis flying toward us in her chariot. Papa stands behind her, one wing outstretched and the other only a wing charred frame with only a few feathers hanging from it.

I sigh in relief. Then I gasp as Apollo tightens his grip on me and directs the chariot upward. We break through the cloud bank and into the clear sky. The sun and moon both shine down on us and the chariot steadies, the witnesses to our rites.

"Now that I have taken you into my domain, our marriage is legalized." Apollo glances down at me, a smile spreading across his magnificent jawline even as unease shines from his blue gaze. "Is that . . . all right?"

My hands loosen their grip on the front of his *chiton* I didn't realize I was grasping, and slide around his neck. I draw closer to him. "I have fled the bad. I have found the better."

If I had thought Apollo was shining before, he rivals the sun now. Then one hand leaves my waist to grasp the edge of the veil. We have come to the final component of the rites, the ritualistic unveiling.

Apollo takes far too long, slowly lifting the veil. When it's off my nose, I gasp in the clear air. This encourages him to tug it the rest of the way off and let what remains of it flutter to the chariot floor.

I must look a wreck after my long flight and the heavy storm, but Apollo gazes at me like I'm a goddess already. He gently cups my chin, his fingers caressing my lips.

His eyes water, looking like rain in a sunny sky. "I am yours forever, Bride of the Sun."

Chapter Forty-Five

The Newlywed Couple

Apollo:

A moment ago, I was collapsed in a prison, wondering how the Fates would end me. Now I'm soaring through the Firmament, holding my wife. *My wife!*

The horror of the Summer Solstice festival and the storm below us melt away as I fill my senses with only her. Her dark hair drips onto the damp cerulean dress that hugs her athletic figure. Icarus' deep brown eyes find mine, distracting me from continuing my perusal. My hands still do, though, with one finger running over her petal-soft face, searching for cuts. The other hand runs up and down her back, and arms, seeking any signs of broken bones I need to heal.

And though Icarus smells like spices, sweat, and the storm itself, the scent of irises remains. Music blares so loudly in my psyche, I'm certain she can hear it, too, in the rhythm of my heartbeat.

"Oh, Icarus," I murmur. "I thought you'd banished me from your side forever. And here you are! I thought you loathed me. That you wanted me dead—"

"None of those are true," she whispers, her voice hoarse from screaming. "They have never been true." Icarus pauses and bites her lower lip. "Well, mayhap the last one was for a *moment...*"

I blink.

"But none of that matters now." Icarus smiles at me, the sun behind her painting her silhouette warmly. "I chose you. Take me to your home." Suddenly, horror and then sorrow flashes across her expression. "Papa!"

She scans the area for him just as Artemis bursts out of the clouds, Daedalus on the chariot behind her.

"Papa!" Icarus yells again, waving franticly.

He smiles at her and waves back. "My little bird."

Icarus turns back to me. "Will you let me see him safely to Athens before you whisk me away?"

"You don't want him to come live with us?"

Her eyes widen. "You would allow that?"

"I said I would from the beginning." I tuck a wisp of hair behind her ear. "He will be my Master Architect and you my Master Inventor. *And* my wife, but I couldn't add that part yet."

She hugs me more tightly, pressing her soft body against me. "Thank you so much!" Icarus presses a light kiss to my jawline.

My body, cooler from my diminishing power, roars with heat. "May I . . . may I kiss you also?"

Icarus pulls back slightly, her brows furrowed. "I-I'm not ready for the Kiss—"

"Not *the* Kiss. *A* kiss." I draw one of her hands up to my mouth to demonstrate.

"Oh." The lines in her face soften, and then a smile plays at her sweet lips as some of her spark returns to her gaze. "Yes. You may kiss your bride."

I grin. Then I hook one arm around her waist as I turn to use the other to tug on the reins tied to the end of my chariot.

My swans obey, speeding toward the horizon rather than gently flying in circles.

"Oh!" Icarus cries, half-laughing as she tightens her hold on me.

Releasing my grip on the reins, I trust the swans to fly us around the storm so I can place my hand on Icarus' face. I trace my finger down her temple, sliding another curl behind her ear, before drawing my hand up her jawline to tip her face toward mine.

"Our kiss can begin whenever you're ready," I whisper, my tone low and husky.

"For *this*, my love, I'm ready."

My eyes widen. "Your 'love'?!"

Giggling, she closes the distance between our lips.

Icarus:

I didn't mean to blurt out that title— that confession. But it hardly seems right to take back the truth, even if it's the first time either of us are realizing that I love Apollo. Mayhap it's more special this way, with us discovering it together. Our first joint act as a couple.

And this kiss makes an excellent second act.

Similar to the first time we embraced so, Apollo's mouth is frozen with shock beneath mine. I tease his lips with promises of passion, showing affection to one and then the other and then both—

Apollo eventually remembers what I tutored him in the cave, because he kisses me back, taking control. One hand tightens at my waist, as if he's afraid someone will take me from him, while his other hand snags in my tangles. It is a dizzying effect, even without the chariot dancing us through the heavens.

I fall against him, but he holds me steady. Liberated by this, I reach up to trace my fingers over the face I was sure I would never long to touch. I miss the minor flaws I familiarized myself with on Phoebus. But I can accustom myself even to the divine beauty of Apollo with time, I'm sure. That will be something I have plenty of, after all.

And his eyes are the same. His soul. I did not wed a stranger.

My fingers find his golden curls, and I smile as Apollo's kisses progress from gentleness to earnestness. Yes, I think I can learn to enjoy learning more about my new husband and align Phoebus and Apollo in my mind. With time.

Time that Apollo does not seem to think we have, as his kisses become nearly desperate and his lips stray from mine. He traces my jawline with pecks, moving down to my neck.

I take the opportunity to breathe, which Apollo does not seem concerned with at the moment. I gasp as he presses a longer, lingering kiss on my pulse. Then I glance around at our surroundings as Apollo continues to kiss my skin.

The storm appears to be drifting away from the island. A lone figure stands on the tall wall facing it, watching it go. *Ariadne.*

I place my hands on Apollo's chest and lightly push him away.

He moans, giving me one more kiss on the shoulder before pulling back. "What is it, sunshine?"

"I want to speak to Ariadne." I nod toward where the wind whips at her hair and skirts, still the same ones she took off me.

Apollo purses his lips. "Is that safe?"

I scan the wall, finding no trace of Minos or Vassilis between the stretch of bricks between the two guard towers. Then I nod.

He sighs and presses one more kiss to the top of my head. "Very well. Whatever my bride requires on her wedding day. I'll find my sister and inform her and your father of our next destination being Elis. And then I really need to finish setting the sun."

Nodding again, I'm not sure what to say as he glides the chariot down to the wall and then helps me off it.

Ariadne turns toward us, but says nothing as Apollo glides away from us, though his gaze remains on me. Only after he disappears near the storm clouds does she break the silence between us.

"So, it would seem that you are the one who becomes a goddess today."

CHAPTER FORTY-SIX

The Newlywed Couple

Icarus:

The emotionless void of Ariadne's words gives me no context if what has happened pleases or displeases her.

Then she turns to me, and I see tearstains on her face. "Will he make you happy?"

The memory of Apollo's kisses make me flush. "I think we'll be happy together, yes."

The shadow of a smile crosses over her face. "Then go with him. Get away from here and never look back."

I step forward and hold out my hands. "Come with us. I can give you a home away from Minos."

Ariadne studies me for a moment, and I see hope in her gaze, but then she looks away. "I cannot."

"You can!" I take her hands in mine. "We can continue your studies, send word to Orion to join us, and make a life for ourselves far away from Crete."

Shaking her head, she pulls away. "I am the Princess of Crete. I cannot flee while my people suffer."

"Ari—"

"My mind is made up, and none can change it." Her expression softens. "I will miss you dearly, though."

My heart aches, and I pull her into a hug. "My home will always be open to you."

"As will mine, once my father is overthrown."

I feel my jaw drop and pull out of her tightening embrace.

There is a defiant glint in Ariadne's eyes that was so dead just earlier this morn. A wry smile stretches across her face. "Do you doubt me?"

"Not a whit." My gaze slides to the boon Artemis gave me. I quickly slide it off my wrist and hand it to her. "But this may prove useful."

Frowning in confusion, she takes it. "What is this?"

"Artemis' hair. It is the Cuff of the Hunt. It will lead you to what your heart most desires."

"This is a great boon." Ariadne slides it on and glances up at me, tears welling in her eyes. "Thank you."

"It's the least I could do after stealing your chance at becoming the new goddess of the sun."

"Queen of Crete shall be quite enough for me." Ariadne leans forward and kisses me on each cheek. "Until our paths cross again, friend."

"I hope so too, Ari. May the Unknown God grant us such favor."

Nodding, Ariadne reluctantly pulls away. "I should prepare for my return trip. I want to ensure I don't get left here when I would so dearly love to see Father's wrath when Vassilis returns to give him the news."

With that, she makes her way to the leftmost guard tower.

I stare after her for a long while, even after she moves inside and vanishes from view. Then I turn toward the storm, merely a backdrop. The thunder is barely audible now, though I still smell the storm itself.

Even though it's blowing away, I still sense incoming danger. Unless there is something other than the storm troubling me—

Bony hands close over my wrist. "I was just thinking of you, little morsel."

Apollo:

Leaving Artemis to explain our living arrangements in Elis on Mount Olympus, I ride toward the sun. After nearly breaking a bargain and then entering the violent storm, my energy is almost depleted. But my strength will be renewed once I finish setting the sun. Then I can carry my bride far away from this cruel land.

My bride. I have a bride. And she's *Icarus*.

She came for me. She *chose* me. And she enjoyed my kiss. Someday, Creator willing, she'll accept my *Kiss*. Then we can live together forever, my dark vision behind us now that I've rescued her from being hurled out of the sky . . .

As I ascend, though, the sun shines in my eyes. It gleams just like it does in my visions.

In my visions, it just wasn't about her falling from the sky. It was about *someone* hurling her down.

I yank my swans around, and we hurry back toward I left Icarus in the cruel land I mean to take her away from.

"I can't wait to enjoy Apollo's new bride."

The words so like my nightmare strike me like an arrow to my heart. Except, this isn't a vision any longer.

Jealously, the sun shines over the landscape, trying to blur my vision after so much time spent in a storm. But my back is to it, and I know where I left Icarus.

If I can change how the sun affects my sight like it did in the vision, mayhap I can change the ending of this prophecy. Though I've never seen a vision alter its ending before, mayhap this will be the exception. Perhaps all those times it haunted my nightmarish visions were to give me the fodder to find a new way. I *must* find a new way. Eternity is far too long to live without my wife.

I find Icarus standing on the same wall I left her on. But Ariadne is no longer in sight; rather it is Vassilis standing beside Icarus now.

Ignoring my threat, Vassilis has a hold of Icarus. He's trying to drag her closer to him, but she's pulling away so hard, and at such an angle, I think she's already pulled her arm out of socket.

My swans are angled toward them like so many arrows in my quiver. My quiver!

I snatch up my bow from the bottom of my chariot.

Icarus twists so that her wings knock into Vassilis. He growls and grabs hold of them.

"Very well, little morsel," he growls. "You said you chose death over my kiss, a fall to my embrace. So be it." With that, Vassilis rends Icarus' wings apart, feathers fluttering and wood splintering. One wing falls from the wall.

Just like my vision.

I draw an arrow. "Unhand her, Vassilis, and I may yet show you mercy."

He glances up. Instead of obeying, he grabs Icarus' other arm and places her directly in front of him, a human shield.

"Enjoy your new bride, Apollo!"

I notch my arrow. I have full faith in my archery skills to shoot his face. But I'm far enough that he'll have time to react to my arrow. To push Icarus up in its path.

As if reading my thoughts, a sickening smile stretches across Vassilis' face. "Or maybe Hades will enjoy her instead."

Then I see as I've seen several times before in my vision. And then I see it over and over again, as though time got stuck in this one moment and I'm cursed to watch it happen continuously.

Vassilis pushes Icarus off the wall. Her scream slices like a dagger, seeming to hew time in half. There was before she fell, and there is now.

The tormenting visions have prepared me for this moment. That is the purpose of them, to help me avert a tragedy. I have to believe it to be so.

Instead of throwing myself onto Vassilis, I twist my chariot just as I come upon the wall. My back wheel knocks into him and sends him flying. I don't watch to see where he lands, though. I'm already moving straight downward, flying toward where Icarus is falling.

"Icarus!" I yell, pushing my swans to fly faster than they've ever flown before. Faster than I can fall. Surely, faster than Icarus can fall.

Icarus . . . her hair haloes her wide-eyed face just as in my vision. Her skirts wrap around her legs, and her arms are spread out. But they are as useless to halt her fall as her one wing.

We both seem trapped in an hourglass, sand slowly filtering to the lower level. And once we reach it, time is out.

Please, Creator, make me move faster. Let me reach her in time. She's my bride— my wife! The one I was certain You promised me. The one who willingly gave herself to me.

Icarus' gaze collides with mine. "I love you."

"Then let me save you!" *Let me save her!*

She smiles. "Yes."

Then she hits the ground.

Chapter Forty-Seven

Apollo

"**N**o!" I scream, trying to drown out the sound of Icarus' mortal body cracking.

My swans tilt upward before they can also collide with the ground. The wheel of my chariot slides across the sand for a moment before lifting off again.

I jump off, letting my swans fly to where they will. There is only one destination for me— by Icarus' side.

"No!" I yell again, as though it is time that is under my command and not the Firmament. As though I can make it unwind and give me the chance to pluck my wife away from her destiny.

But my vision is fulfilled just as they always are, with scarlet staining her blue gown.

Dropping to my knees beside Icarus, I take her hand in mind. "Look at me, my love—, my sun. Can you hear me?"

Above me, I hear a lament matching the one in my soul. Daedalus? I'm not sure; I cannot look up. Cannot look away from her. "Icarus, don't leave me."

Her eyes flutter open, though not all the way. Icarus' brown gaze is glazed with pain, but it focuses on me even though her face does not move.

"You yet live!" Relief floods me before turning to ice from the icy dread already within me. Mortals are always courting Hades, ready to run away with him at a moment's notice.

I have only a moment to secure her to my side, a last desperate chance before she's lost to me forever.

"You told me to save you, and I will." I summon fangs to my mouth like I have practiced before, when Artemis and I inherited the ability to make mortals Awoken. Though I've never actually given my Kiss, I let instinct take over now.

Carefully, so I don't move Icarus' body and cause more pain, I place my Primordial fangs against her throat that I kissed only moments ago. Her pulse was so strong then, but I can barely detect it now.

Then I pierce her flesh.

Power moves out of me, and I lose almost all my strength at once. I nearly collapse on top of her, but I brace myself with arms.

Sweat beads on my temples. A normal sensation while I wear my mortal form. But this is the first I've ever experienced as a Primordial. I wasn't supposed to give her my Kiss until my strength renewed. Time ran out, though.

Could giving her my Kiss drain me utterly? I don't care if I perish. But if I tie her soul to mine, I take her with me. Like Father did Mother.

My fangs retract without my telling them to, and then arms are yanking me off her.

"You're not strong enough!" Artemis yells.

I try to fight her, but I barely have the strength to remain upright, let alone pull away. "I have to be! She's dying!"

Across from me, Daedalus discards his tattered wings, falls on his knees, and takes Icarus' limp hand in his. Tears are streaming down his ruddy face, and he appears to be trying to speak, but is unable to. His entire body is trembling. I have never seen a stronger man brought lower.

Then I see it. Flashes of golden light streaming from where I bit her. My power trying to course through her, though far more slowly than I've seen it move for any of Artemis' transformations.

Artemis' transformations.

I whirl on my sister. "You can save her!"

Artemis stiffens. "She has to accept my Kiss—"

"She told me to save her!" I finally yank away, nearly toppling onto Icarus. But my shaking arm again braces me as I point to where my magic has stunted its flow. "So, I'm telling you to save her in my name."

Daedalus lifts his tear-stained face. "*Please.*"

Artemis glances between Icarus and me. "You know the blessing my Kiss carries. I don't know if what you've given her of your soul will be enough to counteract that."

"I don't care! Just save her." I stare down at Icarus, her chest barely moving and blood beginning to dribble from the side of her mouth. "Nothing else matters, except that she is alive and free."

"*Save her!*" Daedalus yells.

"Very well." Artemis moves around me and summons her fangs.

Daedalus stares at them warily, but he does not move from his place at Icarus' side.

Then Artemis plunges her teeth into the opposite side of Icarus' neck from where I Kissed her.

In the distance, I hear Vassilis' obnoxious laughter. Without turning away from Icarus, I notch an arrow on my bow and shoot. I hear it make impact, Vassilis cry out and then— several moments later— the sound of his body crashing into the ground like Icarus.

Icarus, who is responding to Artemis' Kiss. More light flows from where Artemis is infusing her power, moving far faster than mine did. It wraps like tendrils across her skin.

Too terrified to hope, too weak not to, I take Icarus' hand. "Come back to me, Icarus. Return to me and live free."

CHAPTER FORTY-EIGHT

Icarus

I missed the smell of this forest.

 It's so strange; I don't recall where I was beyond these woods, but I am pleased to have returned. Olive and pomegranate trees wave in the wind, releasing a delicious aroma. Laurel shrubs grow nearly as tall as the trees. They were always my favorite plant; I'm not sure why.

 Mayhap it's how close these grow to the sweetly flowing river. The bubbling of the creek draws me toward it as if it were a siren's song.

 I loved the ocean once because I loved this river first.

 Eagerly seeking the river, my bare feet happily slide through the soft grass as my white peplos *flowing freely around me. Somewhere, beyond the bright blue skies above, I sense pain trying to invade my sanctuary. But surely it can't find me here, in this haven. The trees will protect me— and the sky.*

 The sky that is so very, very blue. It reminds me of something . . .

 "Icarus."

 Startling to hear something other than birdsong and breeze and bubbling creek, I whirl around.

An awe-inspiring man stands before me. No— more than a man. His beauty is too great, too symmetrical. The sun itself seems to reflect from his golden curls. And his eyes ...

I gasp. "Who are you?"

Pain flashes in those beautiful eyes. Hurt that is supposed to be banished from this haven. Who is he to think he can commit such sacrilege by bringing it here? "I'm your husband."

Gasping again, I stumble backward. My feet splash into the refreshing creek. I would do anything to lie down in it and let its cold fingers wrap around my body and swallow my soul. "That cannot be!"

He moves closer. "And why not?"

"Because I am a maiden."

"So you are." He takes another encroaching step. His strides are much larger than mine. If I were to flee, he could overtake me quickly.

Men always take what they want over your will.

"Please don't hurt me," I whisper.

"I'm not going to hurt you." His hard, beautiful features soften. "I just want to take you home with me." He points up at the sky.

"But I don't want to go home. I want to remain here." I gesture at the creek that has risen to my waist now that I'm halfway across it.

The man who claims to be my husband shakes his head. "I cannot let you remain here, in mortality. It is time that you Awoke."

"But I don't want to—"

He lunges at me.

Turning, I flee. But the cold water slows me down. And his strides are already so great—

Still, I make it to the other side of the creek.

"Icarus!" the male calls, and then I hear him stomping through the water. "Return to me!"

"No!" I scream, running as swiftly as I can. But I know it's not fast enough. I'm never fast enough to escape.

I wasn't supposed to have to escape. This forest was supposed to protect me— keep all the evil out.

"Forest!" I cry. "Deliver me!"

No sooner do those words leave my mouth than my back snaps into place.

I cry out at the shock of it, and my whole body goes rigid.

When I glance down, I see what seems to be bark spreading across my skin. My lovely white *chiton* becomes green leaves.

Once again, I try to flee, but my feet are rooted in place. I stretch out an arm and watch as it becomes a branch with five smaller branches. I'm becoming a tree?

The man who claims to be my husband cries out, and then his arms encircle my torso, but I no longer feel him.

I no longer feel anything but the forest.

Chapter Forty-Nine

The Tragic Couple

Apollo:

I'm alternating between begging the Creator to give Icarus back and pleading with her to awaken just in case she's too stubborn to listen to Him.

"Icarus," I gasp, "return to me."

Artemis pulls back, looking drained from the amount of power she banished from her soul to flow through Icarus' body. Silver streams of light flow visibly through Icarus except where my gold magic already dwells, making my wife look like a moonbeam.

Daedalus hasn't moved from Icarus' side. I'm not sure he intends to move from it, whether she lives or dies. He just holds her hand, weeping and murmuring his own prayers under his breath.

I glance back at Artemis, who has slumped wearily. Then I return my gaze to Icarus. She is no longer bleeding, but she also still hasn't reopened her eyes. "Icarus, my love?"

She gasps and her eyes fly open. Then Icarus sits bolt upright, glancing around franticly as she takes desperate breaths.

Daedalus wraps his arms around her torso before she can fall backward. "My bird! You've flown back to me!"

"Where am I?" she gasps, her gaze hazy like she's not seeing what we see. "*What* am I?"

"You're Icarus," I answer rather dumbly.

Her breathing slows, and she sags into her father's arms. "I'm Icarus . . . just Icarus."

She's not *just* Icarus. She's my radiant bride. But this hardly seems like the time to mention that.

I move toward her, but then Artemis places a hand on my shoulder to push herself upright. "We need to depart. Now."

At the warning in her voice, I glance around. The wall is lined by a small army of men watching us.

Daedalus stands, Icarus in his arms. Her wing is on the ground with his.

Artemis gestures to her chariot. "I will take you to Elis."

I jump up, taking Artemis with me. "I can take her in my chariot—"

"No." Artemis steps away. "You need to set the sun before you lose what's left of your power."

She's right, but I clench my jaw as I whistle for Kyknos to return. It's far too soon to be parted from Icarus. But it's because I didn't perform my duties in the first place that I wasn't able to fully save her.

Daedalus, Icarus, and Artemis climb into the silver chariot as my golden chariot lands. I try to catch Icarus' gaze, but she refuses to look in my direction.

My heart aches, but I'll calculate the cost of the sacrifices made later. For now, I need to see to the sun.

Artemis flies off, and then I climb into my chariot.

The garrison on the wall watches us, but no arrow flies. It would be folly to engage whom they consider the god and goddess of archery in such a matter, after all.

I watch as Artemis flies Icarus and Daedalus northward, toward our home. Then I soar directly up to set the sun on the day of my wedding. And, I fear, my marriage itself.

Icarus:

My body feels as though it has been pulled inside out. Every *daktylos* of my body seems to be on fire, but it's a cleansing burn.

I lean against Papa as he holds me in place on the chariot. There seems to be strength mounting inside me, building to be greater than anything I've ever experienced before. But for now, I need my father's support. Especially since being airborne with Artemis driving is making me quite queasy.

Papa gently rubs my back. "What do you remember, my child?"

Pushing away the strange dream that is trying to convince me it's reality, I purse my lips. "I remember speaking to Ariadne and then Vassilis throwing me off. Apollo was reaching for me as I fell, and—"

I stiffen, and Papa rubs my back faster.

"I'm married, aren't I?" Of course, I am; I'm not sure why I'm asking. I remember my flight, our vows in the storm, the kiss in the chariot . . .

But that kiss feels like such a dry memory now. Like I plucked what appeared to be a fresh laurel, but it withered away to nothing as I set it on my head. I think I enjoyed Apollo's touch at the time, but the sensations seem so removed from me now. And the thought of repeating such an action seems like a disuse of my time and body.

"You are wed," Papa finally answers. "I gave you to Apollo as you requested."

I scrunch up my nose. Why would I ever wish for such a thing?

"There's something you should know." Artemis doesn't glance back as she speaks, but I hear her clearly, nonetheless. "It was my Kiss that Awoke you."

"Oh." I glance down at myself and see spirals of what appear to be silver coursing through my body. My mind isn't ready to process that yet, and I quickly turn back to Artemis, whose ethereal beauty seem more natural. "Thank you?"

"For reasons I know not, the Creator blessed my Kiss with an added boon besides making mortals Awoken. It also grants them the gift of celibacy."

I blink. "What?"

"There is no need to concern yourself." Finally, Artemis glances back. In the ever-darkening sky, her silver hair reflects the moonlight, and her black eyes shine even against the night. "My brother is aware of the circumstances. He will not force this marriage on you." Under her breath, she adds, "Again."

With that, she falls silent. Papa doesn't seem to have much to say on the subject himself, and I hardly know what to think. So, I just look over Papa's shoulder to see the last splashes of violet as the sun sets on the horizon.

"This will be your new home."

Artemis lands the chariot on top of a cliff on a mountain. The ledge is occupied by an open wood and thatch home.

Two women dressed in leather armor, their dark hair pulled away from their lovely but ferocious-looking faces, hurry out of it. They bow toward Artemis, glance at Papa and me curiously, and then hurry to attend to the deer.

I study the two-story building with a thatch roof that they lead the deer to. It is not what I expected, but it will be livable. "Thank you for your generosity."

Artemis glances back at me and then frowns at the direction of my gaze. "No, not there— those are the stables." She points toward the left. "There."

Following her gesture, I would tumble out of the chariot if it weren't for Papa's grip on me.

Before us rises a great, elegant marble construct similar to the Temple of Dionysus. However, the center of this building, with its open view inside thanks to the walls consisting of only columns, is twice as long and twice as wide as the temple in Crete. I see a sumptuous banquet table in the center and several more women in leather armor milling about it.

That is not all there is to the building, though. Abutting the temple-like structure on both the right and left sides are nearly identical domed towers. They are connected to this great hall, each one half the hall's size and twice its height. The tower on the right is encased in silver rather than marble, while the one on the left is plated in gold.

My jaw drops, but I'm still not done gazing at this property. The Doric pillared walls of the hall connecting the two towers reveal an expansive training yard brimming with archery ranges and wooden obstacle courses. There is a great pond in the center, perfectly curved and crystal blue. Several more leather-clad women move freely around it, throwing javelins and spears with ease.

Beyond even that is a great forest stretching over the hill we are on further than my eye can see. It calls to me like the forest in my dream.

"This is beautiful." Tears sting my eyes.

"Thank you." Artemis gestures at the silver tower. "My quarters are there, where my huntresses stay. I would offer you a place there, but Apollo's tower has far more available rooms." She gestures toward the golden tower. "He leaves his closest acolytes among their fellow mortals as oracles."

A cold horror threads through me at the thought of being kept close to Apollo, but I remain silent as I follow Artemis up the marble steps and into the great hall.

The women we pass wave at Artemis, only a couple showing deference with a bow. Artemis doesn't seem to mind, though, sharing inside jokes with them as she goes.

Then we come to an arched gateway that leads to a golden tunnel. I follow Artemis through, and it opens into a dome with several golden doors leading out from that dome. Light shines down at us from the glass ceilings above, revealing the sun hovering over us, but not in the sky. I'm not sure how the ceilings are glass from here and gold from outside, but mayhap that isn't the final ceiling above us, and the sun is stored in a greater dome above?

I shake my head. No, that's madness. And certainly not scientific . . .

But I'm the one wed to the being who rises and sets the sun, so what is science at this point?

"That is Apollo's bedchamber," Artemis says, gesturing to the door opposite of the one we came through. It is larger than the others.

I swallow hard.

"To the left is his music room, and to the right he practices with medicines. All the other rooms are yours to choose from. Help yourself to one each."

With that, Artemis turns and strides away.

"This room will do," Papa says, leading me to the room just off the hallway. "Let's get you settled in so you can rest."

I don't feel tired. But my body is also losing its basic functions, so mayhap I am. Either way, I don't fight him as he leads me into a room shaped like a triangle. Its narrowest point leads from the doorway and broadens into two greater angles.

A bed is against the wall between those two sharp corners, with a large chest at the foot of the bed. Shelves are built into the walls on either side sporting books, astronomer equipment, quills, and scrolls. It is a simple room, but beautiful. In here, gold is merely the accent, with the walls painted in a fresco of a sunset of dark colors creeping over the bright.

Papa guides me to the bed and helps me sit on it before moving toward the chest. I hear his joints complaining loudly that he put them through more labor than his age should permit in a day.

He opens the chest at the foot of the bed. "There are several fine garments in here, should you wish to change."

I lay down on the bed in my filthy dress without consciously doing so, answering that question for both of us. There's barely enough strength in me to tug off the golden wreathe that once held my veil in place free and toss it aside.

I'm asleep before Papa even leaves the room.

CHAPTER FIFTY

Icarus

I wake from too much light invading my eyelids.

Opening my eyes, I find Apollo looming over me. With a startle, I nearly topple off my bed.

Apollo doesn't move closer, though. He just studies me with a forlorn expression. "Are you feeling recovered?"

The left side of my neck burns in his presence. No, not burns—pleasantly warms. I notice that on my side of the bedroom door is a mirror and sit up in my bed to better inspect myself. Silver rivers still glimmer across my visible skin, except for the right side of my neck, where gold flows, ducking under my bodice.

"It won't be visible forever," Apollo assures. "It will fade away from visibility once you are Awoken to the deepest layers of your psyche and the transformation is complete."

"Oh." I trail my fingers alongside my neck and then awkwardly drop my hand. That's when I notice the gold signet ring on my finger.

"You're beautiful," Apollo blurts.

I glance up at him before quickly dropping my gaze, my skin warming with no connection to the magic coursing through me, altering my very being. My heart, though, feels cold. It aches with remembrance of a time it should have swelled at such an admission. Even if it came from a poet like Apollo who is capable of being more eloquent. But it seems so much more sincere this way.

"But if the transformation makes you uncomfortable, you can use the private bathing room that is two doors to the right of my bedchambers. Unless you prefer the larger bathhouse Artemis supplied her huntresses. I'll obviously offer your father access to mine as well . . ."

For being the god of music, Apollo's words flow too quickly to be harmonious.

I can't help but smile. "Your bathing room will do. That is . . .?"

"Of course; it shall be private to you when you utilize it."

"Thank you." I duck my gaze again. "I think I will be happy here."

"That is my dearest hope."

Pursing my lips together, I tug off my golden ring. My finger feels immediately naked without it, but I place it in Apollo's palm, anyway.

When I force my gaze up to his, he is crestfallen.

I blink in surprise. "You told me to return this when you had honored your promise to give me a home. And you have."

"So, I have." Apollo closes his hand over the ring and stands. "So, I have."

In silence, I watch as he moves toward the door.

Then Apollo pauses and glances back. "I will leave you to rest, then. Unless there is something I can heal for you. In which case, just let me know."

"Thank you."

He ducks his head. "Of course, my w—" He clears his throat. "My Master Inventor."

With that, he's gone.

The bathing room is far superior to even Ariadne's private bathing room she shared with me. This room is also triangular with a fresco of a clear day, the sun shining brightly in a blue sky. There are tiles surrounding the pool, but most of the room is the bath itself. The water is perfectly warm and varies in depth, going deeper as it flows further away from the door, which is also a mirror.

The mirror reveals that silver flows through all of me but where the gold gleams. I sink into the water to my neck and let it wash away the tension of all that has come to pass in just a day.

My flight, my marriage, my death, and my ascension. It is more than my mind can process, so I don't even bother to think. It is a while before I force myself to move even to rub the available ointments into my hair and skin.

Irises and laurels float in the water with me. Because Apollo likes them, or because he realized they are my favorite plants?

The laurel wreath identical to the one sitting in the corner that he made me seems to suggest as much.

I push the thought of Apollo far from my mind.

It's only after the silver lines of Primordial power in me wrinkle that I force myself to emerge. I pull on a golden *peplos* that flows so lightly over my skin, I'm half afraid that I'm wearing only sunbeams.

I let my damp hair flow freely around me since it does not appear to be frizzing up. Mayhap being an Awoken has removed that mortal annoyance from my life, at least.

Then I slide on a pair of leather sandals and search for Papa, Apollo, or even Artemis. I find all of them seated at the grand table in the center chambers, along with half a dozen women wearing leather. Artemis' huntresses?

Now I can see why Phoebus— *Apollo*— thought nothing of having me dine at the same time as he. It seems to be simply how things are done here on . . . Olympus?

I glance around, like I might catch sight of another god or goddess— or "Guardian," as they seem to prefer to be called. And Papa calls them "Primordials" . . . I sigh. I'm merely stalling at this point.

When I shuffle out to join them, Apollo's gaze finds me immediately. He doesn't say anything, just studies me as though I am more brilliant than the sun.

Then one of the leather-clad women notices me and stands. "All hail the Bride of the Sun!"

The other women turn to me and applaud. Not sure what to do, I shuffle back a step.

Artemis notices my discomfort and gestures for the women to be silent. "No need for fanfare. Icarus is practically a huntress herself."

This seems to placate the women, who all send me smiles, which is preferable to praise. I dare to move closer to the table even as my psyche spins at the realization that my childhood dream has come true at last.

Just when I no longer desired it. And now I desire nothing at all.

Apollo and Papa both stand. Then Papa notices Apollo and sits back down, while Apollo goes to pull out the dining couch next to his own.

Giving him a thankful smile, I sit, turning away from him immediately. But not before I see the glint of his golden ring gracing his finger as it was meant to.

Papa sits across from me, so the person sitting on my other side is one of the huntresses. This one has light brown hair and gentle features that make her look more like a princess than a huntress, even in her leathers.

She smiles at me as Apollo fills my chalice with an amber liquid. "Salutations, Icarus."

"Salutations. And what's your name?"

"Aster. I originally hailed from Athens. "

"So did I." Smiling, I bring the *kylix* to my lips, and the sweetest substance I've ever tasted comes to my tongue. It is thick, like honey, but with an airier taste. I accidentally moan.

Apollo grins. "Like the ambrosia, do you?"

Too ashamed to speak, I only mutter an affirmation. But I'm not ashamed enough to resist draining the chalice dry.

My husband is ready with a refill, and I wonder if there are no servants here.

Aster leans toward me. "Tell me, did you appreciate the flowers?"

I blink. "Flowers?"

"Didn't Apollo give you flowers?"

The wreath I left in the corner of the bathing room flits through my psyche, but I say nothing.

The woman sitting directly across from Aster— just as beautiful though in a different way, with sharp cheekbones and raven black hair— grunts. "Look at her, Aster. She obviously is a woman of sport rather than finery. What she'll prefer is to practice with us."

Since I'm not sure what else there is for me to do, I nod. "Yes, I would like that."

The woman across from me smiles with one side of her mouth, which I think is considerable for her.

"That's Tyche," Aster said. "She hails from Thebes."

Tyche grunts.

I smile at them both as I bring that sweet nectar back to my lips.

"Just don't overexert yourself."

I roll my eyes at Papa as I take his offered *kylix* of the clearest water I've ever seen. "I'm not even tired."

"Yes, well, it was just last night your back was broken." Horror flashes across his face, and he leans to the side to check my spine.

"Fine, I'll take a break from running and try archery."

Papa doesn't look convinced, but he nods and turns back to the scrolls of temple designs he was given to study in the shade of a gazebo. Then he hesitates and glances back at me. "Also, Icarus, I know you often wonder why I serve an Unknown God."

I nod my farewell to Aster as she leads the pack of huntresses that I was running with away from me. Then I turn back to Papa. "I have wondered that, yes."

Papa gestures to the beautiful forest around us and the mountains beyond. "This is why— because He has made Himself known."

Slowly, I turn to take in the beauty, almost achingly lovely with the greenery of the forest and the majesty of the mountains. "I see." The grounds belonging to the twins are truly massive. What I first saw is just the beginning, a hill overhanging still more flatland for training and a couple of smaller buildings. And beyond that is a breathtaking forest that seems to beckon to the silver flowing in me like a siren's call.

"Good." Smiling, Papa returns to his work.

I smile also as I stroll toward the archery range. The only other huntress here is Tyche, shooting arrows into a straw bullseye.

I inspect a rack of bows. "Is it all right if I use one of these?"

She grunts and nearly hits the center of her bullseye. I take that as an affirmative. Grabbing the bow, I help myself to a quiver of practice arrows as well and then stand across from the bullseye next to hers. For a moment, I wait to see if she'll offer any instruction, but she doesn't even glance my way.

Oh, well, I'm sure a bow is far simpler to figure out than a pair of wings.

Pulling the string back, I remember there's supposed to be an arrow involved, too. I notch it awkwardly and watch it sway away from my bow.

"Here, let me show you."

I startle and my arrow knocks Tyche's arrow off course, sending them both into the grass.

With a harrumph, Tyche storms off, muttering something about serenades being *too* effective.

Then I turn to where Apollo is standing near me, a small smile on his face. "I can teach you how to shoot . . . if you'd like."

He really is quite beautiful, my husband, with the sun gleaming off his hair and such depth in the blue of his eyes. His one-sleeved *chiton* reveals quite a bit of his broad chest that I once found attractive. That I *should* still like to see. But it's just . . . different.

I swallow hard. "Yes. Please."

Apollo's smile broadens, and then he steps close to me, enveloping me with the scent of sky and sea and invading me with his not unwelcome warmth.

"Just hold it right here." Apollo mimics my words as he takes my arrow and notches it from the other side, so it is resting against the wood rather than moving away.

"Oh." I flush at such a silly error. "I suppose you're the tutor now, and I'm the student."

"Your lessons were far more interesting than mine." Apollo glances at me just long enough for me to see the heat in his expression before he turns away.

I clear my throat.

Apollo continues in a steady, teaching tone. "Now that the arrow's posture is correct, let's perfect yours." He places a hand on my lower back, a touch that seems to burn right through my *peplos*. The pressure on his fingers forces me to arch back. Then Apollo wraps his arms around me, one hand resting on the crook of my elbow, holding my bow, and the other consuming the hand holding my arrow.

"Then?" I gasp. Mayhap Artemis' celibacy is wearing off. It certainly feels like a possibility now that Apollo is all around me.

"Concentrate on what you desire." Apollo's voice is low as he leans toward my ear.

And his gaze is on me.

"Then?" I fight to keep my rigid posture and not melt against him.

"Relax your fingers." He caresses my hand. "Inhale. Then exhale."

Just as I breathe out, my arrow flies free. It whizzes through the air and hits the circle just outside the center.

I grin. "That's a pretty decent shot for my first time, isn't it?"

"Yes." Apollo glances at it for a moment before turning his undivided attention back to me. "You were brilliant."

My smile grows as I turn to him. His face is just before mine and his lips are a mere breath away from mine. If I leaned in, I could discover the wonder of kissing him again.

Or feel nothing but a reminder of how much I've changed and what I've lost.

I pull away and pretend I don't see the surprise or disappointment flashing across Apollo's face. "I think I should quit while I'm ahead." I walk past him to hang up my bow and quiver.

Apollo clears his throat. "That's just as well, because there's something I want to show you."

When I turn back to him, his smile has returned, and we can both pretend I didn't rebuff him.

"It's back in my quarters." His grin grows. "I think it's something you'll really wish to see."

Chapter Fifty-One

Icarus

I follow Apollo back to his quarters. There is an undertone of anxiety in my heart, but most of me trusts him. And there is a part of me, flowing into my heart, that anticipates whatever this might be.

"In here." Apollo opens the door next to mine. Then he moves aside, revealing a room with a fresco featuring the dark colors of a solar eclipse.

There are barrels of supplies lining the walls and a shelf of carpenter tools. In the center, there is a familiar frame, the stand I built my wings on.

I gasp and hurry to inspect it. It contains all the same scuff marks that make it mine. My fingers run over it, and then I turn to Apollo, unable to hide my grin. "You went back for it?"

Apollo shuffles one foot awkwardly, which might have suited his mortal form but is so out of place now. "Anything for my Master Inventor. I filled the buckets with the supplies you used the first time, gathered by a few of my sister's huntresses. Since you're practically one of them, after all."

Smiling, I duck my head. Then I dare a glance up. "Does it bother you?"

"Does what bother me?" He blinks a little too innocently.

I giggle nervously. "Nothing." My hand returns to the frame, trailing over it possessively.

Apollo follows my movements, longing in his gaze.

"Would you like to help me?"

He snaps his gaze to mine. "Help you . . .?"

"Rebuild my wings." I gesture toward the frame before remembering this isn't Phoebus, who had nothing better to do than haunt my days. This is Apollo, the Primordial Guardian of the Sun.

And I'm already failing to be what he asked of me, yet here I am asking for more.

Apollo steps into the room that suddenly seems ten times smaller with his presence. "I would like nothing better."

It's suddenly impossible to breathe. Yet, I would have it no other way. "Do one of these barrels include plywood?"

"I think we are becoming quite adept at this," I say, stepping back to inspect the fully functioning frame we've built.

"We certainly make a good team." Apollo grins at me. Then he glances at the door. "But unfortunately, I must go set the sun."

"I certainly don't want to keep you from that!" But I also don't want him to leave. Not yet. Not when so many memories of our short but beautiful romance are fresh in my mind from every brush and lean. It doesn't feel the same now, but I'm remembering what it was like.

Just being in his presence is joy. "May I . . . may I join you?"

Apollo's entire face lights up. "Of course." He offers me his hand. I take it, and then he leads me toward the stables.

His golden chariot is already out, with the three swans tethered. The sun he summons, though I cannot say how.

Stepping closer, I try to wrap my mind around what I am seeing. But the sun seems to shrink and grow at intervals, fitting whatever I'm capable of believing at the moment.

"Are you ready?" Apollo steps into his chariot and holds his hand out to me once again.

"I'm not sure," I confess, concerning so many things. "But I will follow you anywhere."

He smiles, takes my hand, and helps me up. Then I surprise him by wrapping my arms around his waist.

Apollo startles and glances back at me.

"I didn't really enjoy this the last time I tried it," I whisper. "Actually, I did, and I hated myself for it. But now . . . I thought I would do it again, just this once for the woman I used to be. If you don't mind?"

"Not at all." His tone is undecipherable, and his face unreadable as he turns to grasp the reins.

Then he flies us literally into the sunset.

The flight made me feel weightless, like no troubles could find me up here.

But now that we're landing, all my problems reveal that they've been lying in wait. Like what Apollo might expect from me now.

I don't say a word as he takes hold of my waist and lifts me off the chariot. But then he releases me and gestures toward what appears to be a fire on the training grounds.

"What's going on?" New fear grips me. Did Minos somehow find us here? Has he slain Papa?

"Artemis is preparing to lead her acolytes on a hunt after she sets the moon tomorrow. They are celebrating in preparation. Would you like to join them?"

"The festival or the hunt?"

He shrugs one shoulder. "Both?"

"Are you going to the hunt?"

Apollo shakes his head sadly. "Not this time. I'm still restoring my strength."

Because of me. "Then I'll stay as well."

He blinks. "Really?"

"I'd like my first hunt to be with you, my husband. It's the least I can do after everything." I move toward the festival.

Apollo grasps my elbow. "You don't owe me anything. You know that, right?"

"You and Artemis saved my life—"

"Only after you risked it to save mine . . . " Apollo smiles sadly. "I just want you to be happy, Icarus."

We both know that's not true; that he desires more concerning me. But it's sweet of him to say.

"Let's just enjoy this festival," I whisper.

He nods and we move toward the bonfire.

In the haze, I see half a dozen huntresses either chatting, laughing, and sharpening their weapons. Papa sits awkwardly amongst them. When he sees me, he gestures quickly toward a stump next to him. I think it has more to do with me being someone he knows than making sure I have a seat.

As I make my way to the designated stump, I glance over at the crowd again. "Where's Artemis?"

"Raising the moon. The festival will begin once she arrives. In the meantime . . ."

There is no stump next to the one Papa saved for me, but Apollo doesn't seem to mind as he remains standing. Then he pulls out his golden lyre. "Which tune should I play?"

He glances at everyone, but then his gaze falls on me and remains there.

"'The Ninth Part of my Soul'," I blurt without thinking.

"Very well." He strums at the harp. Then the most melodious tune comes from it, before his deep, sweet voice follows.

"I dance with you under the moon
Yet, my soul, you're spinning away."

Why was this the song I suggested? Why is he capable of holding my gaze as he plays when I want nothing more than to duck behind Papa to hide all the sensations I seem to feel and yet *not* feel at the same time?

"I thought you were waiting for me to start the festival." Artemis' voice rings out through the night as she strides forward, even more beautiful in the moonlight.

"I haven't even gotten to your favorite song yet," Apollo assures.

Artemis smiles, and even her teeth gleam. "Ah, yes, the altered version you created of 'Why Can't I Break Free?' for all my huntresses who did."

The women cheer, and Apollo begins a much more upbeat song, the last notes of the tune he played for me lost to the night. Yet, they remain trapped in my mind, echoing repeatedly as they demand to be finished.

Apollo doesn't play it to relieve my tension. Not that I request again. Nor even that he glances my way.

When Papa excuses himself, I remain a little longer in case Apollo is lured to the empty stump beside me. Instead, I get Aster.

I lean toward her, hoping she can hear me over the jubilee. "Do other Primordials reside here on Mount Olympus?"

Aster smiles as she continues clapping with the beat, and I'm not sure she heard me. But then she says, "This ledge is Artemis and Apollo's home. But Mount Olympus has several more cliffs below us bearing magnificent temple-homes of the other Guardians. Though there aren't as many as our fellow mortals believe, though."

"Oh." There is much to research still. The inquisitive part of my psyche delights in that.

But not as much of the rest of me as Apollo twirls, still strumming his lyre and singing. There is such innocent joy on his face.

Suddenly, Aster leans toward me, her voice just loud enough for me to make it out over the music. "If ever one of us would break free of Artemis' blessing," she whispers loudly over the joyful chaos around us, "it would be for him." Then she winks at me.

I smile back but say nothing. Then I excuse myself before the next tune starts and lures me to dance despite myself.

No, I can't dance yet. Not until I've flown.

Once I'm nestled into my heavenly bed, I hear Apollo's confident stride as he walks into his chambers. I freeze, terrified and exhilarated all at once.

Those footfalls move right past my room, and then I hear his own bedroom door open and close.

I exhale. There is nothing on this earth that could have truly prepared me for all that I was to experience as the Bride of the Sun.

CHAPTER FIFTY-TWO

Icarus

W hen I awaken, it takes me a moment to decide whether I truly want to rise. My entire body is sore, but it's also restless.

I sit up and blearily stare at my reflection in the mirror of my door. It takes me a moment to register what I'm seeing. When I do, I tumble out of bed. Then I jump up and rush to the mirror.

It reveals up close the same as it showed from afar. No longer is it merely threads of silver on my face. Silver still flows on the right side of my face, brushing over the corner of my lips and coiling around my eye. But now gold does the same on my left side.

Glancing down, I see that my left arm has also become gold instead of silver.

I slide my *peplos* off and see that the same is true across my entire body. I am half silver and half gold.

Not sure what else to do, I decide to do what I was planning on doing already when I awoke— return to Apollo's private bath.

Since I'm already undressed, I wrap a sheet of linen around my body and grab a golden *chiton* to change into.

I carefully glance out my door to ensure neither Papa nor Apollo are around. Then I hurry to the bathing room door and swing it open.

And nearly topple over. I thought my reflection would be the most shocking thing I beheld this morn at least. But nothing could prepare me for the sight of Apollo in the bath.

A yelp escapes my throat, and he startles. Then I hear a sudden sound from across the hall, like someone is jumping out of bed.

To protect Papa from the sight of either Apollo or me less than clad, I hurry into the bathing room and close the door behind me. Too late, I realize that is the last thing I should have done. I am obviously still far too close to being asleep to be thinking correctly.

Apollo stares at me in surprise. I turn away from him to resist the temptation— or the lack of temptation— to do the same to him. Still, I feel his gaze climb up and down my person.

Just as I can't escape the lingering sensation of his gaze, I can't deny the smirk in his voice as he says, "Come to join me? You know firsthand my need for protection in all bodies of water . . ."

"No. I, er—"

A sudden pounding on the door has me almost jumping into the bath with Apollo despite my words.

"Icarus!" Papa bellows from the other side. "Are you well?"

Apollo falls silent.

I clear my throat and raise my voice. "Yes, I'm well. The water was just . . . warmer than expected."

Papa sighs loud enough for me to hear him through the glass and the gold. "Thank the Unknown God. I can't take any more frights."

"Sorry, Papa." I wince.

He doesn't respond, and I hear his footsteps move away from the bath.

I release a loud sigh of my own until I glance down, and all relief is gone.

Apollo has moved closer to me and is now leaning against the edge of the pool. He's resting his chin on his elbows as he stares innocently up at me. "The water *is* warm, but comfortably so. I recommend you try it before dismissing it out of hand."

"I am well aware of the perfect temperature of the water, *siren*."
Apollo grins.

"What I do not understand is this." I carefully extend my left ankle toward him so he can see the gold spirals.

He doesn't seem to know what he's supposed to be looking at but accepts the challenge with great enthusiasm. Apollo takes my foot in hand, making it seem dainty compared to him.

I grip the fresco with one hand while the other more tightly clutches my linen sheet. My clean *chiton* flutters to the tiles.

Suddenly, Apollo gasps. "It's gold!"

It took him that long to realize that? "Yes. What does that mean? Yesterday, all that was gold was my neck. But it seems to have spread."

Eyes wide, Apollo steps back and glances over me anew. "Indeed."

"What does it mean?"

"I'll have to see the full extent of the spread."

I narrow my eyes.

Apollo blinks with faux innocence once again. "I am just trying to assist in this unprecedented situation."

"If it's unprecedented, then how can you help?"

"By accumulating as much knowledge as possible." Apollo nods solemnly before a boyish smile spreads across his face. "I must say, Master Inventor, that you certainly have been an interesting first Kiss."

My skin warms, and I glance away. "I think this conversation would be better said if you put some clothing on."

"And I think it would be better if you—"

I glare at him, and he tosses both hands in the air as if to stop the force of it.

"This is serious . . ." I purse my lips. "I think?"

"The Primordial magic is still bonding with your soul." Finally, Apollo speaks with a serious tone rather than his dangerous flirtations. "It spreads through your body as your life force is entwined with ours. Of course, I've never seen someone with Kisses from two different Primordials. I think . . . I think your soul is deciding which of us it prefers to be bonded with."

Ducking my head, I wiggle my toes. "And you think my soul is choosing you?"

"So it would seem. Of course, I would know for sure if—"

I glare at him again and he laughs. Then he turns away from me to move toward where a towel is waiting for him on the other side of the pool.

Averting my gaze, I remember too late that there is a mirror on the door. I have to quickly glance away again.

"The bath is all yours, my muse."

When I dare to turn toward Apollo again, he is mostly decent, wearing another one-shouldered *chiton*. He strides toward me without a care in the world and comes to stand just in front of me.

I don't speak, don't breathe, don't even *blink* as Apollo reaches toward me. He hesitates for a moment and then runs a finger down a golden vein on my face.

My eyes flutter shut as the left side of my body warms. And the right side turns icy.

"If that is what is happening," Apollo whispers, his voice husky. "I do sincerely hope that you choose me."

With that, he drops his hand and then steps outside of the bathroom, closing the door firmly between us.

The bathing room should seem bigger now, but I still sense him like a ghost. His touch is still somehow tracing my face.

Sagging against the wall, I draw a shaky finger up to trace the path left behind by my husband's touch.

I know what Apollo hopes will come to pass, and I know what the Icarus of less than a fortnight would choose.

But is that still what the Icarus that I am now desires? What the Icarus of the future will be content with?

I've always wanted to hunt with Artemis. Yet, it's not her that wed. Nor is it her that I wish had stayed in this room with me.

"I have to be sure," I whisper to myself. "If the Unknown God has heard my prayers and finally given me a chance to direct my destiny . . . If this is finally something over which I have a choice in my life, I need to be certain. I will have an eternity to reap the consequences."

But how can I choose when my own emotions have abandoned me? Even logic seems reversed here on Mount Olympus, where my husband flies the sun into the sky. There needs to be another guiding counsel for me to submit to before my fate is sealed without my blessing . . .

"If you surrender to the Unknown God, you need not surrender to any other."

But what choice is His will, and which is once again my hubris?

Can it be possible that I am finally meant to fly too close to the sun?

Chapter Fifty-Three

Icarus

F or only needing to feed three people today, the dining table is well laden with both the fruit of the hunt and the fruit of the field. However, it is lonely to be the only person eating from it.

I'm not sure where Apollo has vanished, and half of me wishes he could sit beside me as we drink the ambrosia. The other part of me— likely the part with Artemis' magic flowing through it— hopes to never see him again. Because if I do, I might imagine him standing in that bath—

I push away from my dining couch and stand. Where's Papa? He at least should dine with me.

A moment later, I'm knocking on his bedroom door. It's not that door that he opens, though.

"Icarus, do you want to see the workshop of the Master Architect of Apollo?" Papa grins proudly and steps aside so that I can see another triangular room.

This one has the fresco of the sun shining through a downpour, a rainbow painted brightly on the wall. It has shelves piled high with scrolls, quills, inkpots, and wooden measuring tools. A table in the center of the room is laden with both an existing design and a scroll where the plans of another are being slowly inked out.

"I'm in charge of preparing a temple for Apollo's next oracle." Papa grins, and I'm not sure I've seen him this happy since before we came into Minos' household.

I smile to see his joy again. "Are you coming to break your fast?"

Papa glances longingly back toward his burgeoning design. "Eventually. But don't wait for me."

"Of course." I force a smile that becomes real with his, and then go to dine alone.

I spend the rest of the morning alone likewise, carefully gluing feathers onto my wings. I miss having an extra set of hands assisting me, someone to converse with, and a friend I can pretend not to enjoy brushing against.

But Apollo does not join me, so it is only I that glues the feathers in place. So that is what I do, not allowing myself to leave until the deed is done.

My body aches, but my psyche soars with accomplishment completed. Then I step away from my work to take an afternoon snack. I don't make it to the dining hall, though, because my bed becomes a siren I cannot ignore.

When I awaken from my nap, the first thing I do is check my status as an Awoken. A little more gold has stretched around my neck, but otherwise, nothing has changed.

But it will change and soon, and I need to determine how I even wish it to change. To do that, I need to go to the place that helps me think best. The sky.

My wings are dry enough, so I carry them out of the building. From the sound of it, Papa is still hard at work in his own workshop. I hope he finally ate something.

Apollo is still nowhere to be seen, but that is just as well. I do not need a distraction as I face my decision.

I strap on my wings and check the wind. Then I take off running on the hill before jumping.

The breeze grasps me instantly, and I glide within the safety of its grip.

I take a moment to accustom myself to the currents of the wind up here, but once I do, I'm rising and dipping easily. Freedom blows my hair back and bats the skirt against my legs.

Up here, I can finally breathe again. Soon I'll be able to think, to consider the dilemma before me. But for now, I'm safe to just exist.

"My love, I'll play for you.
With a song I'll bargain you free."

The deep, melodious tone of Apollo's voice envelops me like an embrace. I almost forget to tilt my wings to glide on the next breeze.

I glance around for him, but do not see him. He must be hidden in the tree line where he cannot see that I am near. At this moment, Apollo sings only for himself.

Twisting and flapping, I do my best to remain in hearing distance so it is no longer true that he sings just for him.

He makes his tone higher and sweeter as he sings what must be the female part of this hauntingly tragic tune.

"Your sweet song made Death cry.
For his tears, a trade will be.
Take heed, for Death is sly.
I live and choose to do so free."

He's singing about me and my desire to be free. Yet, how free am I truly when either decision I choose is affected by one outside influence or another? Both the sun and the moon course through my veins.

The rest of my very long lifespan will be affected, along with others' happiness. *His* happiness.

"My lover, where are you?
Please don't fly from me again."

I bite my tongue to keep from crying out that I'm just above him. Because that's not entirely true. The Icarus he loved faded away when Phoebus did. And then she died again with my mortality. I am a new woman now— one on the brink of a decision of two destinies.

"I'm coming up behind.
Don't look back. Don't force bargain.
Trust who sought you to find.
Lest you force me to ascend."

I will never be free of every external and internal influence. I wasn't as a mortal, and I am not now as a Primordial. I simply need to choose despite that. Because of that?

"My lover, why leave me?
I saw the sun and looked back.
But the moon's you chose to be.
What does she have that I lacked?"

Nothing! I want to yell it. To explain that it has nothing to do with him, just me,

But as the breeze carries me away from the sweet tune he weaves, I know that's not true. Just as all I decide is affected by others, so all I decide affects them. We are none of us true individuals. What affects Papa affects me. And what affects me affects Apollo.

I merely have to decide, once and for all, where the lots will fall.

As the last chords of Apollo's voice rattles through my mind, I think I finally know what I want. Now I just need the courage to see it through.

Chapter Fifty-Four

Apollo

It may be early in eternity to think this, but I am not sure I will ever tire of walking into my chambers and finding Icarus there.

Granted, it's not quite as exciting finding her in her workshop as it was seeing her in my bathing room this morning. But observing her hard at work on something she delights in doing warms me to my soul.

Her back is to me as she rearranges her wings on the stand, smoothing out feathers. She is angled so that I only see the side of her that bears my magic.

I lean against the doorway and clear my throat.

Icarus startles and turns to face me, though not completely. I still see only her golden-lined profile. "Oh, hello."

"Hello." I smile, keeping any trace of sorrow away from my face. I will recover from the consequences I brought upon myself with my hubris soon enough. Time dilutes all pain to a certain extent. Soon I will simply enjoy Icarus' presence with no regrets.

Surely my missteps in my suit of her were not so great that the Creator pins this level of pain to my soul forever. Then again, I was a Primordial who sought joy beyond what was allotted to me. Now pain is the necessary price for the few moments of pleasure I stole on Icarus' lips.

Icarus continues to gaze at me, and I realize with a start that she's waiting for me to say something else.

"I was going to set the sun. I wanted to know if perhaps you would like to join me?" Feeling her trusting arms around me can satisfy me for an eternity, I'm sure.

"It's that time already?" Icarus jumps to her feet before shaking her head, sitting down again, and composing herself, all without turning to face me completely. "Not this evening."

It takes me a moment to realize she's turned down my invitation. With that realization comes an arrow to my heart that already feels so vulnerable. I drew from so much of its pain to finally manifest the tune she gave me into life.

With it came a vision of another tragic couple doomed many years into the future. I think this tune, spawned by my sight of Icarus, is for them. And one day, I will correct the words to match the tale I saw. But right now, my pain is too blinding for me to see past the tragedy that is Icarus and me.

For a few moments, this song will be ours. Especially since that melody would not exist in the beauty that it is without my pain taking my abilities to new heights. It is like Icarus' pulley, for while my gift ascends, my heart sinks to new depths— drowning in the ocean of sorrow it mistakenly thought Icarus could save it from.

I keep my pain away from my expression; it will be useful to me in my compositions but allowed nowhere else. "Of course. It can be tedious, I suppose. But duty is duty." With a nod that I hope doesn't look as awkward as it feels, I turn and stride away.

"I'm sorry," I whisper as I fly for home with the sun in tow.

Artemis soars past me, eager to rise to the moon and return to her hunt. We probably won't share any words today, which suits me just fine.

It's not her I need to speak to. Nor even the Firmament, which is finally forgiving me. The sense of pleasure is a dull hum compared to the roar of approval I'm used to, but it is warming up to me. Soon, I shall have reclaimed its trust and my full range of abilities again.

But the Firmament is not the only broken bond I need to repair. "I apologized to Icarus for my hubris for pursuing her like I owned her. But I owe her Creator the same apology, when He's the only one Who truly owns her.

The visions may have been promises, but I should have trusted in them rather than seeking to seize them by force.

Another vision yet to be fulfilled tickles at my mind of Icarus, glowing gold and standing in my bedchambers by night.

A vision I wish with all my being would come true. But I decimated the course that could take us to the fulfillment of that prophecy when I neglected my duties and couldn't fully bind Icarus to myself. Not to mention when I repulsed her so much by my overbearing nature that she cannot even bear to share my chariot— let alone my bed.

"Apollo, don't let me fall."

The vision teases at me again, wisps of blue and gold, and I push it away. Mayhap it was a promise once, but it is certainly not something I am meant to seize. Such things are given willingly or become grave curses.

I land my chariot and release the swans into the stables. With all the huntresses away, it's up to me to feed them and ensure they are ready for flight tomorrow. And the sun is always my duty to put in its dome until dawn.

Already, after a full day of doing everything on time, I feel strong again. The Creator has been more merciful than I deserve to restore me to what I once was.

There is a deep silence over all as I step into my home. Usually, I miss the huntresses' banter and Artemis' teasing, but today I am glad for the solitude. It fits my present mood.

Daedalus and Icarus must have both already turned in for the night, because there is the same silence in my quarters.

Resisting the urge to check if Icarus is yet awake and willing to speak about . . . anything, really, as long as I get to hear her voice, I make my way into my own room, closing the door partway behind me. I haven't the strength to finish the job, so instead I move across the triangular hall that leads to my larger room. It's unhindered by the physical confines of the mortal realm. It is a large half-circle with a staircase in the center that leads up to where I keep the sun.

There are plenty of torches I could call to life in this room if I wanted to illuminate the fresco of a sunrise painted around my walls. But I have no desire to see the bright colors in my dark mood.

It is bad enough that I can make out the mattress far larger than I need against one wall. Extensions of my two work rooms are opposite it. I make my way to the balcony that extends over the edge of Olympus, revealing civilizations of mortals below— those I serve by guarding the sun.

This is the purpose the Creator gave me, and the destiny He has not revoked. Every morning and evening, it is how I will live in gratitude that I have not lost this as well.

"Apollo."

I sigh. I should have known that watching the rising moon from my balcony would trigger anew the vision I've been doing my best to forget.

But since it is part of the prophecy, and perhaps the only way I will come close to seeing Icarus pleased with me, I turn to face it head-on.

As I anticipated, Icarus stands on my marble floor, the doors I left open closed behind her.

But Icarus, for looking so small and fragile in the largeness of my bedroom, somehow fills every corner with her presence. Her scent drifts over to me, her iris scent combating the aroma of nature outside.

"Apollo," she whispers again, and my heart thrills to hear her say my real name so sweetly, even though I know it's not real. That it can never be real.

Icarus moves closer, and stray moonbeams reflect off her gleaming curls that tumble from beneath the laurel crown I gave her and over her shoulders. One of those shoulders is bare, while the other is draped with the blue linen of a *peplos* that flows down her slim figure, skimming her thighs.

I want to gaze upon her forever, but I know the part I must play in this vision, so I straighten and then bow. "My bride."

Icarus does not respond, just steps ever closer. She seems to give off her own light, a gentle gold repelling the silver of the moon, no trace of Artemis within her at all. There is a determination in Icarus' gaze that nearly conceals a heat that can warm me for an eon to come.

She comes to a halt before me. I want to close the distance between us, but I don't dare frighten her away. Now that the vision has pulled me in so deep, I do not want to awaken.

I let her reach out and place a hand on my chest. It is warm. How do I feel her when this is just a fantasy? Why does she feel like my own soul?

"Apollo," she murmurs, "I'm ready. Don't—" Her strong, sweet voice cracks for just a moment before returning in confidence. "Don't let me fall."

My hand closes over hers, and it's as real as I am. I nearly choke. "Never."

Smiling, Icarus moves closer, stretching beyond the limits of the vision I truly saw only once. She slides her hand not on my chest around my shoulders to play with the ends of my golden curls.

And I cannot deny that every sensation coursing through me has only ever come from her actual presence. "This is real?"

"Believe me, Apollo, I'm *not* a dream." She laughs her self-deprecating chuckle.

Yet I gaze down at her, nearly dumbstruck by her beauty. "You are *my* dream."

Her laugher turns to a nervous giggle, and she glances away from me.

I bring my free hand up to her face and gently caress her soft skin that no longer bears different veins of magic. Rather than any sign of mortality or Artemis, she bears only the shimmer of the sun. I've never seen anyone else glow gold like I do, but Icarus wears it more magnificently than I ever did.

I want to give her everything that is mine just so she can make it better with her touch. "How is this possible? You're fully Awoken. But you're not . . ."

"Not bound to the moon?" Icarus somehow moves closer to me, so that only her hand on my chest keeps her from pressing completely against me. She lifts one leg to wrap around my waist like when we were dancing.

"Are you cold?" I whisper, even though her heat is invading my body.

"You'll just have to be the one to warm me."

My hand not caressing her face hurries to grasp her thigh, exposed to my touch as her short skirt moves with her. I only meant to give her support, to keep her from falling like I promised, but now I feel as though I've lost all sense of balance. *I'm* the one falling now.

And I don't care what the consequences of impact will be as long as it is Icarus who caused the fall.

"Though I suppose your magic has already done that." Icarus cocks her head to one side.

"I gave you so little," I choke out, rapidly losing control of my ability to speak as her touch overwhelms me. "Artemis saved your life. This shouldn't be possible—"

Icarus brushes her lips over my jawline, a featherlight touch that might as well be a lightning bolt to me. Her iris scent is something I do not think I will ever be able to escape now. "But I chose *you*."

I stare down at her in complete and utter shock. "Why?"

She purses her lips, considering, and I curse myself for giving her mouth something to do other than kissing me. "I suppose because you chose me first and yet gave me the choice of whether to choose you in return."

I stare down at her, trying to make myself understand her words. But they are almost too beautiful, too perfect, even for a Primordial mind.

"I have fled the bad. I have found the better." Icarus smiles at the recital of her wedding vows before the smile slowly drops off her face. "Do you . . . do you have anything to say to that?" She glances away again.

My hand on her face drops to her chin, and I tilt her back to face me. "May I kiss you?"

A smile spreads across her lips that are sweeter than ambrosia. "You may."

Grinning, I press my lips to hers. All the pain of the last few days melts in the presence of her passion as she kisses me back.

Barely knowing what I'm doing, I grip Icarus' other leg and help her wind it around me. Then, still exchanging desperate kisses with my bride, I spin us both around the room. It is perhaps the most ungraceful dance ever attempted, but it is the most beautiful one I think either of us has ever experienced.

Her laurel crown falls away in our dance, but I don't think either of us mind.

Icarus' giggles are the sweet music to our choreography until she has to pull away from our kiss to gasp breaths between her laughter. Her eyes are shining like two suns when they meet mine. "Can we stay up until it's time to rise the sun?"

"Doing what?"

"Just . . . move with me."

Unable to resist, I press a kiss to the corner of her mouth. Pleasure so great it is almost pain fills my chest, and I hold her more tightly. "I think, my muse, my sunshine, my *Icarus*— that can be arranged."

She bats her eyelashes at me, the one sleeve of her *peplos* beginning to droop over her shoulder. "As a favor to your Master Inventor?"

"Yes." I kiss her nose. "And to my dearest wife." My lips find her newly exposed shoulder next. "The other half of my soul."

"And you are both my Phoebus and my Apollo."

I spin us around again to the tune of her laughter, and then lean down so that our lips once again touch. "I am indeed yours, only Queen of the Sun."

Epilogue

Ariadne

I am the only Princess of Crete.

Which is fortunate for everyone else. I wouldn't wish this role upon any other woman. There are no privileges, only responsibilities.

The chief of which is keeping my father from feeding my people to the unnatural monster he has locked away in an underground labyrinth. The second greatest responsibility is to convince my father that I fear him and this beast. But simultaneously, I need to fool *myself* into thinking that I don't.

Convincing *him* is not difficult at all as I kneel before him in the blue and golden garments that were originally intended for my *gamos*. Instead, they were the chains used to sacrifice my dearest friend to a god, only to make it the bait to lure that god to his death.

Now that the plot has gone awry, I can only hope that it will not become the shroud I wear when sacrificed to the monster that has already had a taste of me.

Father sits upon his marble throne carved with the heads of bulls in the arms. The creatures never struck fear into my soul until last night. His expression is the pleasant, unconcerned visage he has constructed for himself like a master sculptor. But I can see by the way his hands clench the bull horns so tightly that his knuckles whiten, that he is not pleased with the news he has been given.

Wrath is about to come upon us all. I could hide behind the gypsum benches or inside the lustral basin, but it would still find me.

Thankfully, Father's gaze is on Asios alone. I have never been more thankful to be so easily dismissed by my sire.

The stench of frankincense is shared by all, though, a reminder of how easily Father can mask the stench of death.

"You're telling me," Father begins slowly, "that we had a dying god in our custody. And not only did he escape, but he did so with the *one* woman who could ensure his survival?!"

Asios is already on his knees, but now he puts his face on the ground. "Many pardons, my King. We were not prepared for the goddess of the moon—"

"You should have been!" Now Father's façade falls from his face as he launches to his feet. "Opportunities like that do not just rain from the heavens! We need to seize every single one of them or else always live under the tyranny of the gods."

Just as suddenly as he exploded, Father resumes his cool mask of indifference. His gaze is still dangerous, though, threatening lightning from a clear sky.

And it is now directed only at me. "Ariadne, my dearest daughter, what part did you play in this?"

"None, Father." I bow low, keeping my gaze downcast as he prefers it. "I was merely waiting for the full transfer of Apollo's abilities to flow into me when I felt the connection snap. I wanted to be a goddess as much as you desired me to be one." I keep all traces of a threat out of my voice. I could have stopped him as a goddess.

My father is not the only one who has learned to disguise his emotions.

"Yet, you are not a goddess and there is a no-doubt vengeful god free to hunt us."

I highly doubt that Apollo will return. Not after the desperate escape I witnessed. Watching from the windows, I thought Icarus had died, only for the heavens and earth to be moved with my desperate prayer to bring her back. I doubt either she or her new husband are in any haste to return to the place where they both nearly perished.

Artemis, though, could pose a real problem for my father. Too bad for him.

"I am sorry, Papa," I whisper, using the rare pet name and adding a slight tremble to my words, even though my heart is too cold to express genuine contrition. And any possibility of showing honest affection is gone, fed to his monster along with my flesh. "But I was not aware it was my duty to keep the prisoner detained."

Asios flinches.

"You're right." Father's gaze slides back toward the new highest-ranking member of his military. "Where is Supreme Commander Vassilis? He will know the cost of failing me."

The right hand of my father's right hand whimpers. I take pity on him and answer in his place. "Oh, Vassilis? He's dead."

All the blood drains from Father's face, and he whirls on me. "How?"

"Apollo."

All sense of calm wilts away from the King's face, and he roars with rage, so that even those outside this chamber must hear it. I fear even the beast below senses it, its appetite whetted for whomever Father will feed him in his rage.

It won't be me.

At my summoning, tears rain down my face. "It has been a very taxing day. I-I can barely grasp all that has come to pass myself. All my friends gone in a single swoop . . ." I lost only one friend today, but she is enough to drive me to true sorrow.

Father glances my way, and my tears seem to make him forget the absolute coldness in my tone when I announced Vassilis' demise.

His tone does not soften, but it becomes less than a roar. "Yes, yes, I know how upsetting such things must be to your delicate feminine sensibilities. You may retire."

"Thank you, Papa." I bow low again. Then, with a sweep of my skirts, I turn to leave Asios to endure Father's wrath alone.

By the desperate pleas following me out, it is a far greater sentence than Vassilis would have ever seen.

But I cannot think of him. It is first my duty to deliver my innocent people from the maws of the monster and the greed of Minos. Those who would feed their own to the bull-man like Asios are my lowest priority.

I storm toward my chambers, ignoring the whispers of the curious servants who are still trying to piece together the events of the day. They do not know that it is night alone that they must fear.

Because my father has somehow come into possession of a power more ancient, I fear, than the gods. And something that may just be more powerful. But the gods are our only desperate hope of stopping it.

The doors to my quarters swing open without my speaking. But I raise my voice when I see my handmaiden standing silently by. "Leave me!"

The woman doesn't question me as she hurries out of my quarters. I do not even have to glance back to ensure she's obeyed my order as I step deeper into my room.

My mind mulls over the problem before me as my fingers yank off skirt after skirt, leaving a trail as I move into the deepest room of my chambers. My corset and every other cloth follow until I am stripped to the loincloth I put on after the trials of that fateful night. Rather than the tightly clinging *perizoma*, this is the short, skirt-like garment that falls to my upper thigh with more coverage than a normal breechcloth. It is the garment worn by the brave bull-jumpers.

In a matter of speaking, I must jump a bull to save my people.

I release my hair from its confines and draw the thick strands over both my shoulders as a covering of sorts. Then I move toward the skin of old wine set on my smallest table per my directions. One of the kitchen boys is quite taken with me and will obey my every command with no thought of social mores or my father's rage.

Of course, I will never reveal to the monster who controls the beast who brought me his oldest skin of wine. Just making the request put the poor boy's life in danger. But it is a necessary sacrifice for the summoning of the last hope for Crete.

I move toward the altar set up in the corner of my bedchambers. One by one, I light each of the candles set on the different shelf-like levels of the stone piece.

At this altar, I've prayed for favor from every god known to be just, yet no justice has come. I've called upon each one known for their mercy, yet no mercy has been shown.

After the way Apollo almost perished at my father's hand because he fell in love with Icarus, I understand now. Minos is an evil beyond even the chaos of the pantheon. He will seek any good that exists in his adversary and use it as either a weakness or a chance to corrupt.

So, it is not a good god I will summon, nor one who is just and merciful. Selfishness is the only way to combat selfishness,. If I can make the most self-absorbed of the gods see that it is in his best interest to defeat Minos— or if I can give him a prize worthy enough for the endeavor— only then will we be evenly matched.

Only then will I be capable of delivering my people.

Kneeling before the altar, I hesitate for a moment. If I do this, there will be no going back.

"My mind is made up, and none can change it," I whisper.

I take the wineskin and chant the words the priestess at the temple gave me. Then I take the skin, rip off the top, and pour it over my head.

I chant the words again as I rise, then I spin once, twice, three times before kneeling again before the altar.

Finally comes the last words of the ritual: "Bacchus, I summon thee."

Suddenly, every light is snuffed out from the candles at once. A deep chill flows into the room like an unwelcome presence. Then I sense that another presence has truly invaded my chambers.

Fear grips me like I faced last night when the unknown became something that I could not escape. I want to turn to look upon the being I summoned. But I do not dare be so bold with him. Not yet, when I need to sway him to my side.

When I need him to accept the sacrifice of my hand in return for delivering my people out of my father's.

Dripping with sweet and sticky wine, I stare straight ahead. Mayhap I should have prayed to Icarus' so-called higher deity— her Unknown God— instead.

Finally, the silence is broken by something other than the pounding of my heart.

A voice thick as honey and tone that is sinfully low reaches through the shadows. It seems to wrap invisible hands around my unfortunately exposed skin.

"Well, well, well. And what do we have here?"

ABOUT THE AUTHOR

Jes Drew is the author of the Cursed Fae of Orphydice Manor Series, the Sunset at Dawn trilogy, Love of Legends, The Samurai's Student saga, the Ninja and Hunter trilogy, the Howling Twenties trilogy, the Kristian Clark saga/The Man on the Run series, the Castaways trilogy, The Dystopian Takeover trilogy, Summers of Yesteryear series, The Clockwork Faerie Tale Novellas, the Legends of the Master Spy series, The New ESE Files series, *Tales from Parallel Worlds, Genie and Serena, Accidentally on the Run, This Side of Heaven, The Death of a Hero, Bound by Death, An Enduring Hope,* and *Trapped by Vengeance.*

She has three degrees, including a Master of Arts in Behavioral Counseling. Also, she has about five million houseplants (and counting— the plants and not the degrees . . . unless she relapses).

She is still debating if having a Fae husband is worth the hassle. Contact her at author.jes.drew@gmail.com.

Note from the Author

I wrote this book during the most tumultuous August I think I've ever lived through. It began with a tragedy and ended with a tornado. And in between, I stopped believing in love— romantic love, not love in general. This story was a safe haven for me in the midst of the grief and chaos, but Icarus inherited my loss of faith in love.

There were moments when I thought the story would be like the three tragedies it was based on (Icarus, Apollo and Daphne, and Swan Lake) and not get a HEA. But I wanted this to be a series of standalone romances and you can't do that without happily ever after, so I fought for the dream. I fought for Icarus and I fought *against* Icarus and I fought against my own heartbreak.

And I think I won. Maybe not in real love— Artemis' kiss and all that— but in this book I did. I ensured Icarus's happiness after grieving for Daedalus' pain when I was a child so many years ago. And I secured my own dream for a series of standalone romances based off Greek myth retellings.

So fight for your happily ever for now. Take every victory, no matter how partial or painful. You can't control the tone of the chapter in your life, but you can be the one who decides your own story will not be a tragedy, but a triumph.

Acknowledgements

This book is the outpouring of my heart and has been shaped into beauty by the support of those around me.

Katy Maureman is once again the editing brains behind this operation. The cover that inspired this book to begin was created by the talented artists at GetPremades. And Maddy Moore and Paige Coffer have once again brought my characters to life.

My Royal Spies street team and author friends like Anastasis Blythe and Abigail Manning helped launch this book. And my readers, first those who started this journey in Kindle Vella and now all of you now, thank you for giving this story a chance.

Finally, I could not write like I do if I did not have my family—every single one of them. Especially Nicki Chapelway, my sister, bestie, and fellow Greek myth enthusiast.

Finally, all gratitude to Jesus Christ, Who has carried me safely through every chapter of my life, no matter how high or how low.

ALSO BY JES DREW
Thankfully

Cursed Fae of Orphydice Manor Book 0.5: *Entreaty of Shadows*
Cursed Fae of Orphydice Manor Book One: *Embrace of Shadows*
Cursed Fae of Orphydice Manor Book 1.5: *Blood of Destruction*
Cursed Fae of Orphydice Manor Book Two: *Bond of Destruction*
Cursed Fae of Orphydice Manor Book 2.5: *King of Unraveling*
Cursed Fae of Orphydice Manor Book Three: *Kiss of Unraveling*
Cursed Fae of Orphydice Manor Book 3.5: *Desert of Death* (Currently releasing as a serial)
Cursed Fae of Orphydice Manor, Book Four: *Duet of Death*

Starry Kingdoms of the Fae: *Bound by Death*

Love of Legends, Book One: *Bride of the Sun*
Love of Legends, Book Two: *Princess of the Maze* (currently releasing as a serial)

Sunset at Dawn, Prequel: *Courtships & Court Intrigue*
Sunset at Dawn, Book One: *Betrayal & Banditry*
Sunset at Dawn, Book Two: *Treason & Thievery*

Hope Ever After: *An Enduring Hope* (a Wild Swans retelling)(all profit goes to O.U.R.)

The Samurai's Student, Season One: *Year of the Tiger* (Fully released as a serial)
The Samurai's Student, Season Two: *Night of the Ninja* (Currently releasing as a serial)

The Ninja and Hunter Trilogy, Book One: *The Time I Saved the Day*
The Ninja and Hunter Trilogy, Book Two: *The Time I Saved a Damsel in Distress*
The Ninja and Hunter Trilogy, Book Three: *The Time I Saved the World*

The Castaways Trilogy, Book One: *Castaways*
The Castaways Trilogy, Book Two: *Fugitives*
The Castaways Trilogy, Book Three: *Targets*

The Dystopian Takeover Trilogy, Book One: *Mind of Darkness*
The Dystopian Takeover Trilogy, Book Two: *Fists of Injustice*
The Dystopian Takeover Trilogy, Book Three: *Heart of Steel*

The Summers of Yesteryear Series, Book One: *At Summer's End*
The Summers of Yesteryear Series, Book Two: *Echoes of Summer*
The Summers of Yesteryear Series, Book Three: *Summer Again*

The Death of a Hero (And other Peacemaker short stories) (All profit goes to Exodus Road)

The Howling Twenties Trilogy, Book One: *Wolf Claw*
The Howling Twenties Trilogy, Book Two: *Wolf Curse*
The Howling Twenties Trilogy, Book Three: *Wolf Cure*
The Howling Twenties Omnibus

Tales of Parallel Worlds (An anthology of short stories and poems from The Howling Twenties Trilogy and beyond) (All profit goes to Polaris)
Genie and Serena, PI (All profit goes to Polaris)

The Clockwork Faerie Tale Novellas, Book One: *Red as Blood* (A Snow White and the Seven Dwarves/Snow White and Rose Red retelling)
The Clockwork Faerie Tale Novellas, Book Two: *Sleep Like Poison* (A Sleeping Beauty retelling)
The Clockwork Faerie Tale Novellas, Book Three: *Wisps at Night* (An Aladdin and the Magic Lamp retelling)
The Clockwork Faerie Tale Novellas, Book Four: *Ship to Nowhere* (A Sindbad and the Seven Seas retelling)

Kristian Clark and the Agency Trap, Book One: *The Bachelor Missions*
Kristian Clark and the Agency Trap, Book Two: *In the Rogue*
Kristian Clark and the Agency Trap, Book 2.5: *Ruptured Reality* (And other short stories) (All profit goes to Human Coalition)
Marina Ivanov, PI (A Kristian Clark short story) (All profit goes to Human Coalition)
Codename: Christmas Carol (A Kristian Clark short story)

Kristian Clark and the American Agenda, Book One: *Agents Adam and Eve*
Kristian Clark and the American Agenda, Book Two: *Operation Paradise Lost*
Kristian Clark and the American Agenda, Book 2.5: *Eden In-Between* (And other short stories) (All profit goes to Human Coalition)
Eitan Cohren, MIA (A Kristian Clark short story) (All profit goes to Human Coalition)

The Man on the Run Season One, Episode One: *Kristian Clark and the Holy Heist* (A Kristian Clark re-release)
The Man on the Run, Season One, Episode Two: *Kristian Clark and the Kidnapped Code* (A Kristian Clark re-release)

Legends of the Master Spy, Book One: *My Wife, the President*
Legends of the Master Spy, Book Two: *The First First Gentleman*

The New ESE Files, Book One: *The Ghost of You*
The New ESE Files, Book Two: *New Teacher in Town*

The Accidental Superheroes series, book one: *Accidentally on the Run*

This Side of Heaven (A Poetry Collection)(All profit goes to Birthright)

COMING SOON

Lord willing

Love of Legends, Book Two: *Princess of the Maze* (in ebook and print)

Of Seas and Tides: *Trapped by Vengeance*

Cursed Fae of Orphydice Manor, Book 3.5: *Desert of Death* (in ebook and print)
Cursed Fae of Orphydice Manor, Book 4.5: *Marriage of Fall and Frost* (a Zahra and Lateef epilogue)

A Bound by Death companion novel: *Bound by Life* (The Prince Regent of Day's story)

Sunset at Dawn, Book Three: *Romance & Robbery* (first as a serial)

The Samurai's Student, Season One: *Year of the Tiger* (in ebook and print)

The Clockwork Faerie Novellas, Book Five: *Rose with Thorns* (A Beauty and the Beast retelling)

The Man on the Run, Season One, Episode Three: *Kristian Clark and the* Roman Revenge(A Kristian Clark re-release)

Legends of the Master Spy, Book Three: *We the Elite*

The New ESE Files, Book Three: *The Assassin Next Door*

Jesse's Angels, Book One: *College Royale*

The Faith Trilogy, Book One: *Invisible Faith*

BY NICKI CHAPELWAY

Harbinger of the End: A Tale of Loki and Sigyn

And They all Bow Down: A Viking Arranged Marriage

Starry Kingdoms of the Fae, Book Eight: *Bound by Knighthood*

Of Seas and Tides: *Trapped by Magic*

An Apprentice of Death:
Book One: *An Apprentice of Death*
Book Two: *A House of Blood*

My Time in Amar:
Book One: *A Week of Werewolves, Faeries, and Fancy Dresses*
Book Two: *A Time of Tribulation, Pirates, and Lost Princesses*
Book Three: *A Season of Subterfuge, Courtiers, and War Councils*

Return to Amar:
Book One: *A Certain Sort of Madness*
Book Two: *A Matter of Curiosity*

Winter Cursed:
Winter Cursed
A Winter Grim and Lonely

A Winter Dark and Deadly

Of Dreams and Nightmares:
Book One: *Of Gold and Iron*
Book Two: *Of Stars and Shadows*
Book Three: *Of Dawn and Fire*

Rage like the gods:
Prequel: *Between gods and Demigods*
Book One: *Rage like the gods*

What the gods Did:
Book One: *The gods Created Monsters*

A Legend of Ruskhazar: *A Tale of gods and Glory*

Listen to the songs
Apollo composed

Made in the USA
Columbia, SC
18 June 2024